Lost In Between

Finding *Me* Duet #1

K.L. KREIG

Lost In Between

Published by K. L. Kreig
ISBN-13: 978-1-943443-23-9
ISBN-10: 1-943443-23-8

Cover Art by Kellie Dennis of Book Cover By Design
Interior Formatting by Author E.M.S.
Editing by Nikki Busch Editing

Published in the United States of America.

Lost.
Sometimes getting lost is how we find ourselves.

~ Robert Tew

Willow

Prologue • 4 years ago

I GLANCE AT THE DEAR John letter crumpled slightly in my hand, my messy handwriting scrawled across the plain white paper.

My words are simple but ruthless. Said with purpose. They are intended to wound. Cut ties.

It's wrong, what I'm doing, but grief is an all-consuming net of self-destruction, and I am twisted up so tight in its unforgiving, barbed rope it's cutting off my circulation.

And it's not fair to him to have to deal with that anymore.

It's my fault, really. I let this go too far. I let him think he could have parts of me that were unavailable. Hell, I fooled myself into thinking the same thing. I knew it would catch up with us at some point, and apparently, tonight is that night.

I don't know who I am anymore. Maybe I never did.

I grab the duffel I'd stuffed in the corner of the closet earlier and take one last look around the dark room. I swallow the hard lump of emotion sticking in my throat when my eyes land on my fiancé, asleep and completely unaware of what's about to hit him. But when he wakes and finds me gone, somehow I don't think he'll be too surprised either.

I replay his harsh words from our argument earlier, the

ones I can't forget. *"People can't love you if you don't let them, Willow."*

Yeah. He's right. They can't hurt me, either.

I lay my good-bye out on the dresser and smooth the wrinkles with my hands. I twist the band of promises and forever from my left ring finger and gently set it beside the note.

With one last glance at my callous, heartless words...

I don't love you anymore.
I'm sorry.

...I walk through his house and out the front door. Outside I drag in a mouthful of cool night air, feeling strangely lighter with each lungful. A moment ago, the weight of the world was pressing me down until I thought I would suffocate. Now I just feel weightless.

Empty.

Alone.

And so damn lost I'm not sure it's possible for anyone to find me, including me.

Willow

Chapter One • Present Day

MY GOWN SELLS FALSE TRUTHS. Makeup covers the lies. Fake smiles and soft words divert and deceive. Three carats on my left hand blind all, except me.

I know the truth.

I take myself in, from the perfectly coifed hair to the French manicured toes peeking out from my sling-back shoes. I stare at myself in the full-length mirror, not recognizing the superficial woman staring back.

A frown turns down the corner of her mouth. Condemnation clouds her unusual green eyes. Sorrow plays in the thin lines on her face and in the slight slump of her bare shoulders.

She's judging me.

She should.

I'm a horrible, awful person.

In less than ten minutes, I will let my father walk me down an aisle lined with fresh flowers and silk bows tacked onto the corners of every other pew.

I will reach the end, let Daddy kiss my cheek with tears blurring his vision, and give me away to another man.

I will take my fiancé's hand in mine, gaze into his puppy dog eyes overflowing with joy, and betroth myself for life to someone who is noble and loyal and kind.

I will promise to love, honor, and cherish him all the days of my life.

I will exchange in-sickness-and-in-health-forever vows in front of God, our family, and friends to a great man out of spite and revenge. A ploy. As a giant fuck-you to the man I really love but can't have.

I will marry a man I genuinely respect the hell out of and love...but just as my very best friend.

Who does that?

A destructive, selfish bitch. That's who.

I let my gaze fall down the length—

"Hey, babe!" my roommate, Sierra, yells as she walks down the hall. The sound penetrates the room I've closed myself in. I shake my head in disgust, my recording ruined. No matter how many times I ask her to be quiet when she comes home, it doesn't sink in.

I need a bigger place with privacy and a separate, soundproofed space where I can work in peace and quiet. Not this makeshift area I've constructed in the corner of my bedroom.

Sadly, my bank account disagrees.

"Dammit, Sierra. I have asked you repeatedly not to yell when you come in. Now I have to start over," I whine when she throws open my door.

"Oh, my bad. Were you in the middle of a recording?"

A withering look is my only reply.

"I'm sorry." Her tone is contrite. I know she means it. That won't keep her from doing it again. And again. And again.

"It's just an audition. It's fine." I tear off my headphones and switch off my mic, glancing one more time at the prologue of the romance I was just narrating. This one starts out more dramatic than others, no doubt to draw readers in, but it will end the way they all do. With a happily ever after.

I try to avoid these types of reads. The poignant stories of hope and love and second chances. Two soul mates finding each other against all odds, living happily ever after. But with the popularity of audiobooks on the rise, and the fact my Master of Fine Arts degree doesn't pay my mountain of bills, I put my acting skills to use in a way that would.

I prefer mysteries or historical pieces myself. Hell, give me a good manual to narrate any day. Unfortunately, I've had to expand my knowledge to all genres, including romance. A necessary evil, but I've found that my sultry voice is in quite the demand, and that fits within the erotica and romance arena better than science fiction or children's stories.

"Do you work tonight?" Sierra asks as I swipe my empty Pepsi bottle from my desk and head past her, making my way down the stairs to the kitchen.

"Yeah. I wasn't supposed to, but Holly caught a bad case of the flu, so I'm filling in." I don't mind, though. I can always use the extra cash.

A quick glance at the clock above the stove shows it's only 4:00 p.m. I still have four hours before I have to leave. Plenty of time for a workout, a quick bite, another take, and a shower. In that order.

While I love my day job and it's starting to gain momentum, I'm still relatively new in this industry, and I work for a smaller publisher. Pay is commensurate with experience and size, and since I'm on the smaller end of both, so are the biweekly deposits into my bank account. It's not remotely sufficient to pay the monthly expenses that keep my stomach in a constant ball of knots.

"This one under fifty?"

"Ser," I chastise, pulling out my insulated water bottle from the cupboard.

Her dainty eyebrows rise along with one corner of her mouth. "Well?"

I sigh, unscrewing the top so I can fill it with ice. I'm not ashamed of my part-time job. I have nothing to be ashamed of. Would I do it out of choice? Absolutely not. But it's a necessity, plain and simple.

"I don't know," I hedge.

Actually, I'm lying through my teeth. Paul Graber is a fifty-five-year-old hotelier from Boston with three bloodthirsty ex-wives, four grown children, and five grandchildren. He owns over thirty high-end boutique hotels and three full-service resorts. He's in town for a political fundraiser, to which I understand he's a generous donor.

Or so I've been told by Randi, my boss. Randi can be a hard-ass, but she watches our backs and gives us everything we need to know to do our jobs and do them well.

"Liar." She calls me out. Plucking a red grape from the fruit bowl, she pops it in her mouth, asking between chews, "Been with this guy before?"

Sierra is one of only two people who know what I do on the side. She doesn't judge, but she worries on my behalf. She needn't. The men I'm with are vetted thoroughly and completely, and if they are out of line, they are banned.

"No, but he told Randi he'd be in town several times over the next few months, so if tonight goes well, he could become a regular."

I hate to say it, but the only thing I think of when I look at men like Paul Graber, who will pay his hard-earned money for a night with me, is *cash cow*.

That may sound cold and calloused, but I'm a realist. I've learned life is hard, unforgiving. No one takes care of you but you. So, if men like Paul Graber want to use me for their own selfish reasons, why shouldn't I do the same? Besides, I know exactly where I stand with my clients, and deep down, that's an oddly comforting feeling.

Okay. Subject change.

"So, how's Raul?" I ask while filling my bottle with water from the tap.

"A cheating rat, dick-sucking bastard," she replies tersely. I hear the slight wobble in her voice and suddenly feel like a heel. Had I been paying attention when she flung open my bedroom door, I probably would have noticed her red-rimmed eyes before five minutes into our conversation.

"Oh, Ser, no. What happened?" I reach across the kitchen island and grab her hand. She's not the touchy-feely type, so the fact that she doesn't pull away tells me an awful lot.

She's hurting.

Bad.

I love my best friend, Sierra, more than anyone in the world, but her taste in men sucks rocks. At five eleven, she's striking in a goth sort of way. She's the rare type who has natural, enviable curves—34-28-32—can eat anything she wants, anytime she wants, and hasn't worked out a day in her life. She walks among the 1 percent of women the other 99 percent hate on principle alone.

She's brash and unapologetic. She also has the biggest heart of anyone I know. But the bigger the heart, the bigger the bull's-eye, my mother always used to say. And the easier it is to hit.

"My postcoital glow was pissed out when he got a phone call from a chick named Barbi. Fucking Barbi, Lowenbrau." I smile at her childhood nickname for me, her grandfather's favorite beer. "Who names their fucking kid Barbi?"

"Someone with a fairy-tale complex?" I shrug my shoulder.

Her voice drops when she continues. "He was in the shower when his phone lit up. I told myself not to look, but it was the fifth time in an hour."

"Did you answer?"

"When I saw a pair of pierced double Ds as the caller ID, bet your ass I did."

And this is why I'm not out searching for my Prince Charming, a fictional character made up by Walt Disney.

"Ouch." I actually wince.

"Yeah. Ouch." Her eyes fall, but not before I see a wayward tear trickling down her face. "I think he wanted me to find out. Otherwise he would have taken the phone with him in the bathroom, right?"

My head is already absently nodding in agreement. It's been

so long since I've had a real relationship, or a real date for that matter, that I'm severely short on good advice. I give her hand a big squeeze, saying the only thing I can. "He's undeserving of you."

"Why does this always happen to me? I'm sweet enough, aren't I?"

My eyebrows kiss my hairline.

"Maybe that's my problem. Maybe I need to change."

I grab both hands in mine, making her look at me. "Don't you dare. Be who you are, Sierra, not who someone wants you to be." Now this I know something about. It's exhausting being what others want instead of being yourself. At least I can use that to my benefit now.

"So, said a better way: go fuck yourself, Raul, right?"

"Right. Let white-trash Barbi have his cheating ass."

"I bet she has a mullet."

"And her broken-down single-wide's not even pink." I laugh.

"She probably ran Walgreen's out of blue eye shadow," she says, looking more upbeat with each catty dig.

"Yeah. With two brats attached to her hips and a Kool menthol dangling from her bony hot-pink fingernails."

We laugh at the image we're conjuring of Miss Pierced Double Ds until water runs freely down Sierra's face. Then she stops, sniffles, and discreetly wipes her tears.

This is it. The end of our conversation. I won't mention the tears—she'll just excuse them away anyway—and she won't ever mention her philandering ex again. But that's what we do. We both hold a lot of toxicity inside. Sometimes I think the EPA should slap a warning label on both of us.

"Want an omelet?"

"You and your 'breakfast for dinner' shit. It's really weird in case I haven't already mentioned that a hundred times before."

She loves it. It grew on her the second time I made her my mouthwatering fluffy eggs stuffed to the brim with veggies and crispy pancetta.

"I'm unconventional, what can I say?" And it reminds me of my family. The way things used to be back when I was happy and life had limitless potential. "We're out of eggs, so I'll stop by the store and pick some up on my way back from the gym. Wanna come?" I ask, knowing full well what the answer will be, but hoping she'll say yes just this once anyway.

"Please. The only time I work up a sweat is in the bedroom, girl. You know that."

"There's a kickboxing class in half an hour. Could be a good stress reliever," I add excitedly, hoping to entice her. It would be nice to have a buddy at the gym, but it would be far more entertaining to watch her uncoordinated and poorly timed kicks and punches.

"That's what Melvin is for, chicky." She stands and grabs the *People* magazine from the countertop before heading out of the room.

"New man in your life you haven't told me about yet?" I tease, knowing full well who Melvin is. Or *what* he is, I should say.

"Yep. He came yesterday." She spins back around. "The best qualities about Melvin are he's one hundred percent faithful and he's supposed to get me off in under thirty seconds. Impossible qualities in real dick. Oh, pick up some double-A batteries at the store, will you? Get the super pack. Call me when dinner's ready."

I nod and watch sad Sierra disappear down the hall. When I hear her bedroom door close softly and Chris Cornell's "Nearly Forgot My Broken Heart" drifting through the thin walls, I know she'll get a little high and cry in private, but once she steps foot back out of that space, her fuck-the-world mask will slip back into place until the next asshole cracks it apart again and the cycle repeats.

We are so alike, she and I. Always have been. We show the world what they want to see and keep the brokenness inside, marinating in our own secluded well of sadness and bitter tears. I think that's why we gravitated toward each other in the third grade when Sierra's family moved to Seattle.

Sierra's been by my side for every pain, every wound, every bruise, every mistake, every horrific event that's plagued my life as I have for hers. We've held each other's hair out of the toilet when our sorrows ran too deep, we've twined our fingers in heartbreak, and with arms around the other, we've literally held each other's pieces together in mourning. There's no better person put on the face of planet Earth than Sierra Wiseman.

A fit last name, I always thought. She's taught me more about life than nearly anyone else. I only wish she could teach me how to actually live it.

Shaw

Chapter Two

"THE FAMOUS SHAW MERCER. PLEASURE to see you again." Jack Hancock's handshake is firm, confident, like the man himself.

"It's been too long, Jack." I grip his hand just as confidently.

"Yes, it has. Noah." Jack takes turns acknowledging Noah, my managing partner and best friend since the day we were born, shaking his hand before leaning in close to us. "We should plan a little *night out* soon, if you know what I mean." He tacks on the last part in a hushed voice.

I clasp him on the shoulder. A quick glance at Noah shows he's effectively holding in a smirk. "Sure. I think we can manage that. Just let me know when you're free."

"I'll have Peggy get with your assistant to work out calendars?"

"Sounds good. Now," I wave to a group of suited, important men seated at the long conference room table only a few feet away. "Shall we?"

He starts forward but hesitates.

"Something wrong, Jack?"

"Today's a big day," he says. His eyes catch mine. Shadows eclipse his excitement. "CJ should be here."

"He'd be proud," I tell him, knowing exactly what's running through his mind. The tragic death of a brilliant man nearly hamstrung Aurora Pharmaceuticals, but with our help, they pushed through.

He nods, taking a seat at the center of the table. I sit at the head, Noah to my right, Aamir Vaishnavi, the practice leader of our pharmaceutical and medical products consulting division to my left.

Noah Wilder and I are equal partners-owners in Wildemer & Company, one of the fastest revenue-growing global management consulting firms in the world. We'd been groomed for these roles since the day we were born, only three weeks apart. We were educated at the most exclusive private schools, attended Cambridge for our undergrads, and completed our MBAs at the prestigious Wharton School of Business. We've been joined at the hip since the date of conception.

Our great grandfathers, Walter Wilder and Artie Mercer, started this family business in 1926. Less than thirty years later, they had a dozen offices in the United States and serviced over twenty Asian and European countries.

Noah and I have taken what our forefathers built and elevated it to brand-new heights. When we took the reins only eight short years ago from our fathers, we'd already had a solid strategy for growing this successful business, focusing our expansion efforts on industries, rather than on global domination. We created four new specialty divisions, the fastest-growing one being our pharmaceutical and medical products group.

This is all I've ever wanted to do. Since I was four years old and the smell of leather and success in my father's home office lingered in my nostrils, I knew I had to be part of the family legacy. Be part of something important. Life changing. I was always expected to, but at the age when boys were playing with Matchbox cars and video games and starting to grasp what the pleasures from touching their dicks actually meant, I knew I *wanted* to. Big difference. Expectation versus desire.

What we do, what we're part of, could help so many people and their families, and the fact that my firm could be part of this is an incredible sense of accomplishment. This is why I live and breathe this company. I like money just as much as the next guy, but this...*this* is why I come to work every day.

Only today, the reason we're sitting here *is* money.

It's time for Aurora Pharmaceuticals to go from a privately held company to a publicly traded one. Another specialty of ours.

"Jack, I wanted to start by thanking you again for your partnership and the trust you've placed in Wildemer." I look around at the twenty sets of eyes hanging on my every word. "You'll see from the agenda in front of you, we're here today to review the final prospectus for the IPO launch. As you're all very well aware, our analysis demonstrates the first-to-market advantage gains you six percentage points greater market share over a period of at least ten years. Time to strike while the iron's hot. You ready to take your company public, Jack?"

One of our first and biggest pharma clients, Aurora Pharmaceuticals is a mid-cap specialty pharmaceutical company that's sitting on a breakthrough biotech drug. Using our sophisticated analytical tools, we managed to push it through all three phases of clinical trials about twelve months earlier than they would have on their own.

With their brainpower and our analytics, last year they were able to file a new drug application with the FDA for a revolutionary biologic that will change the face of a disease that cripples families and taxes the health care system.

Because of that, they also stand to make a fuckload of money when their initial public offering goes live.

He grins. "I won't rest until it's blue chip."

"That's what I like to hear."

He laughs, and smiling, I nod to Aamir. "As you know, you're in very capable hands with Aamir here. He will lead us through the discussion today. Aamir?"

"Thank you, Mr. Mercer. On page one of the prospectus, we've indicated sixty-nine million shares will be available for sale with AP offering fifty-one million, and the remaining eighteen million split between two investment firms..." With both legal teams around the table, I settle in as Aamir starts reviewing the details of the hundred-plus-page document.

Six long but very fruitful hours later, Noah and I enter our chauffeured Lincoln MKC. "Back to the office, gentlemen?" Mark calls through the open partition.

"Yes," we chime in unison.

"I bet that guy got all kinds of shit in high school with a name like that. Jack Hancock."

Noah laughs while taking out his e-cig. He's been smoke-free for the last six weeks, the longest he's gone without breaking. He's tried so many times before I've lost count, but since his father was diagnosed with throat cancer at the young age of fifty-nine, and he's watched him slowly waste away, he's bound and determined not to follow him to an early grave.

I'm proud of him. I can't imagine needing anything that bad that it consumes your every waking and sleeping thought. I've never had that type of addiction in my life. To anything. To anyone. Don't plan to either. God knows I've had to watch the ones I love suffer enough with shit like that.

"Maybe, but who's laughing now? Pretty soon he'll be running the most lucrative pharma company in the world and richer than a Saudi oil sheik."

"Touché." He takes another drag and moans in nicotine-induced bliss.

I pull my cell from my pocket, quickly scanning my missed calls.

Two from my mother, one from my sister, Gemma, and one from Lianna. I sigh at that one, and when I open my text messages to see three from Lianna, I scowl. Jesus Christ. She's harder to get rid of than a tick, sucking the life force right out of me.

Call me.
I need to talk to you.
Please, Shaw. Please.

"You owe me for the fundraiser tonight," Noah reminds me. The one I called in a favor to get him to attend.

"You're full of shit. Working a roomful of hot women? You should actually owe me the favor, not the other way around."

He laughs while I scroll through the rest of my messages. When I see one from Annabelle, my baby sister—*Still on for a little family bonding?*—I quickly respond.

Me: *Promise to show?*

She replies immediately.

AB: *Promises only break.*
Me: *I thought I was special.*
AB: *You're full of yourself.*
Me: *See you later?*

Silence. Damn her.

"She bailing?"

"Who?"

"Bluebelle. Who else?"

Taking a deep breath, I throw my phone on the leather seat beside me and look out the window, watching the city pass as we head back to our offices.

"I have no fucking idea. That girl is as elusive as Nessie."

He chuckles. "You're comparing your baby sister to the Loch Ness Monster?"

"Sometimes she is a monster."

"Isn't this little par-tay for her anyway? Her big 2-1?"

At thirty-six, I am the eldest of four. Gemma is two years younger than me, and Lincoln is two years younger than her, but almost sixteen years separate my youngest sibling, Annabelle, and myself. She was an "oops," and she not only has classic "baby" syndrome, for some reason she also never fails to throw the fact that she wasn't wanted into my parents' faces every opportunity she gets. It's a conundrum I just can't work out because my parents have never treated her any differently than the rest of us. In fact, they try to overcompensate for her bad attitude, and she practically gets away with murder.

All of that notwithstanding, or maybe because of it, Annabelle and I are the closest of all my siblings, but it doesn't mean she doesn't piss me off something fierce. She does. Constantly.

"Yep. Doesn't mean she'll show. You know she's notorious for hanging my parents out to dry. I'm sure my mom spent all day cooking up her favorite meal, and she'll either be three hours late or won't come at all. I don't know what to do about her."

"You can't control people, Merc. I know that's hard for you to accept sometimes."

He's not being condescending; he's trying to be a friend—not telling me anything I don't already know. I can control a lot of things in my life, most things in fact, but trying to control Annabelle is akin to controlling a raging river overflowing its banks. I can line the entire fucking thing with sandbags and she'll still find a damn hole somewhere to slink through.

"How is she doing?" he asks tentatively, voicing the one question that's been plaguing my own mind for weeks now. What he really means is: *Is she using again?*

Noah is intimately familiar with the problems my baby sister gets herself into. In fact, he's had to help me bail her out of one too many of them over the years. Annabelle's been through inpatient rehab for drug addiction twice already in her short lifetime. The first time was four years ago, and this last time she's managed to make it more than nine months sober.

Just when we think she's on the straight and narrow, though, she drifts again. She fights a lot of demons she refuses to discuss. That's a big part of the problem. We're battling an unknown. I wish I knew what the hell was going on inside her head so I could help her fix it. I love her, but sometimes I want to lock her in her bedroom for the next twenty years.

"I wish I knew. She doesn't seem to be as erratic as she usually is, but she's also not been around much, which is a classic red flag."

"Could be school's just kicking her ass."

I grunt, suspicious.

"Well, if she doesn't show tonight then maybe you should pay her a little visit. I can go with you if you want."

"Yeah. Thanks," I mumble. I don't want to know what I'll walk into when I knock unannounced on her apartment door, but burying my head like my parents do isn't an option either.

The sound of my phone buzzing draws our attention. Lianna's face pops up. Noah starts laughing.

"Man, she still stalking you?"

"Stalking. Good adjective," I reply as I push the reject button, sending her to voice mail. I'll later delete it without listening.

"We could give her another go. I'm game."

"Nah. You can have her, Wildman. I'm done. I'm pretty sure she and her mother were about a week shy of sending out wedding invitations to five hundred of their closest friends." I think it's true. I stumbled across a prototype on Lianna's kitchen counter when I went to get a glass of water in the middle of the night a few months back.

His mouth curls. "Too bad. That was one hell of a good time. I've never heard a woman howl like a banshee before. Didn't really think it was humanly possible."

"She was loud, wasn't she?" I laugh, remembering that night. It was undoubtedly hot, but there won't be a repeat. At least not with her.

I casually dated Lianna for almost six months. Apparently, it was about five months and three weeks too long, because unbeknownst to me, both of our mothers were already designing our nursery. Seriously. I had no choice but to break it off, which was too bad. I liked Lianna. She was intelligent and a good lay. I liked spending the little free time I had with her, but that's all it was. I was never going to marry her. Never intended to carry on the family name. Never thought of a future with her. I thought we were just having a good time. When everyone started planning more, including Lianna, it had to end.

I'm not being heartless, just honest when I say a woman will never be a priority for me. My company, my family, those are where my focus lies.

Mark stops in front of our building. My watch tells me I have about three hours before my ass needs to be sitting in my mother's dining room chair, cloth napkin in my lap. If it's one thing my mother loathes, it's tardiness. Even at my age, I am not immune to her wrath if I'm not sitting in my spot at seven on the dot.

The moment I reach for the door handle, Noah asks, "Say, you don't think your mother would...you know."

My forehead scrunches. "Would what?"

"Sabotage you by asking Lianna over tonight? She knows you'd just sit there and take it like the little obedient son you are. She was crushed when you broke it off."

I exit the car, yelling behind me, "Fuck off. I'm the furthest fucking thing from a lap dog." Except he's right. When it comes to my parents, even as a grown-ass man, I have a hard time saying no to either of them, especially my father. I've had to politely suffer through more "blind dates" over the last five years than I care to count, and since I broke up with Lianna, they've only escalated.

Fucking great. I'm sure I'll have a nice surprise waiting for me later.

"Maybe I'll join you at that fundraiser after all. Bluebelle probably won't even come to her own damn party," I tell Noah when he catches up.

"Except you won't. You won't disappoint Adelle or Preston Mercer like that. Besides, I'm quite sure the son of the mayor wouldn't be welcome at his competitor's fundraiser. Don't worry, though. I'll scope out all the pretty girls for you tonight. Find you the perfect Stepford wife while you suffer through your little family drama."

We walk through the glass front doors of Wildemer's headquarters in downtown Seattle's central business district, nodding at the security guards before making our way toward the elevators. When we enter, I punch the button for the thirty-ninth floor.

"I have a better idea," I say, turning to him. "Why don't you find me a good fuck instead. I could really use one of those."

"Don't you mean *we*?"

One shoulder rises. "Semantics."

"You're on. I'm pretty sure there will be plenty of loose legs at tonight's event. I'll let you know if I hit pay dirt, but you'll owe me if I save your ass from whoever's sitting to your right for sea scallops tonight."

"That's one debt I'll gladly pay."

We exit, heading our separate ways. I feel a little lighter. Maybe tonight won't end so badly after all.

"Good luck," Noah hollers.

"You too," I retort, hoping like hell I get a text later.

Willow

Chapter Three

STILL A SWEATY MESS FROM kickboxing, I drop two bags of groceries onto the back seat of my Fiat when my cell rings. My initial tendency is not to answer, but on the off chance it might be Randi or Millie, I dig it out of my purse.

Millie. My heart races.

"What's wrong, Millie?" I ask anxiously as I slide into the driver's side and shut the door, closing out the noise of a screaming baby in the car next to me. It's a typical July day in Seattle. Cloudy with some slight drizzle. I start my car. The wipers kick in as I hear a familiar voice through the speaker.

"Willow, I'm sorry to bother you, dear, but your mother is insistent she talk to you right now." She sounds frustrated, probably having tried to talk my mom down for the last half hour.

"It's fine, Millie. No problem at all. How is she doing today?"

"Agitated. Very confused. Not good."

"I'm so sorry." My mother is impossible to deal with when she gets like this. "Put her on. I'll talk to her."

I hear rustling in the background as the phone changes

hands. Then my momma's shaky voice comes on the line.

"Young lady, I need you to call your father right now. Tell him he needs to come get me out of this prison this very instant."

A pang of debilitating sadness knocks my breath away. *I wish I could.* It takes a few seconds to get it back so I can talk. "Momma, you're not in prison. You're home."

"This is not my home, Willow August. We live at 8250 Lane Drive in a two-story Victorian. This...this is a shoddy colonial." I almost laugh at the way she spits out colonial as if it were a cuss word, but I don't. None of this is funny. Especially since the address she's remembering is the first house she and my father shared together after they were married. They've lived in my childhood home now for twenty-six years, since the day I was born. "How do you expect me to stay here? And since when did Charles hire a maid? I don't think she's a maid at all. I think she's his whore." She says the last part in a loud whisper.

I breathe out long and slow, bringing my fist up to rub the soft ache behind my breastbone that never seems to ebb. *I'm sorry,* I want to scream. *I'm sorry I didn't know. I'm sorry I couldn't save him. Please forgive me.*

"Momma, that's not true. You are home, and Millie takes care of you now. Daddy's gone. Remember?" We have this conversation all the time. She doesn't remember. I'm lucky when she remembers me. Sometimes, it's not just death that thieves our loved ones from us but something far crueler.

"Of...of course I remember," she says with attitude, but marginally calmer than seconds ago.

A glance at the digital clock tells me I don't have time for this, but if it means making my mother happy and easier for Millie to handle, I'll be late tonight. Paul Graber will simply have to deal. "Why don't you tell me about your day?"

That settles her. For the next half hour, I sit in the grocery store parking lot watching people come and go with both my engine and tears running, listening to my mother tell me about a day I know she clearly remembers but happened sixteen years ago. I clearly remember it too because shortly after that everything changed.

The human mind is a complex thing. A three-pound gelatinous piece of gray matter filled with thousands of fragile, twisted nerves, veins, and arteries, each unique quadrant responsible for its own distinct functions. I've spent countless hours reading up on the human brain and how it works. Only with everything I've learned, I know nothing at all. I still don't know how to help the person I love who is stuck inside herself and can't find her way out.

"I was going to make some apple pie tonight for the girls when they get back from the store with Charles, but now I can't because...because...I can't...what was I saying?" she trails off.

I easily envision the confusion on her aging face. It crushes me.

"Momma, Millie's going to give you some medicine. You need to take it. Okay?"

"But I don't trust her. She's trying to poison me. Get rid of me so she can have your father."

I choke on a sob.

"She's not poisoning you. Trust me. Would I let her hurt you?"

"No, Violet. You would never let anyone hurt your momma."

Pain, barbed and quick, cleaves my heart. God, this disease is insanely hateful. Not only to the patient but to their families.

"Then do as Millie asks. Please, Momma. For me. I love you." My voice is soft, coaxing, almost destroyed.

"For you, Vi Bear. I love you, too."

Sometimes it's hard to breathe.

The chime of the doorbell in the middle of the night.

Muted voices followed by my mother's piercing screams.

The sick, knowing feeling that came over me when I stepped out of my bedroom and saw Violet's door open, comforter unwrinkled, still tucked in neatly at the edges.

"Thank you," I croak brokenly, blinking away the moisture gathering in my eyes. Most of the time I don't let these conversations get to me because I understand my mother can't help it, but damn. Today it's hitting me square in the solar plexus for some reason.

More clanking, then Millie is back on the line. "Thanks, Willow," she says softly. We're both silent for a few heartbeats. I count mine beating out of my chest. "I'm sorry."

"Yeah. So am I."

"Umm..."

My stomach sinks. "What is it, Millie? You can tell me."

"I'm sorry, but the water heater is acting up again."

"Christ," I mutter angrily. That's another few hundred dollars I'll have to come up with. Guess I know where tonight's paycheck is going. "I'll call the repairman. Weren't they just out a few months ago?"

"It's hard to find good help sometimes."

It is, which is why I'm so grateful for Millie.

"I'm glad I have you. I'm glad Momma has you, Millie. I'm sorry if I don't tell you that enough. I don't know what I'd do without you."

"No thanks necessary, Willow. You know how much I love you and your mother like my own." Thank God for that.

"I'll see you Sunday?" I whisper.

"Sure thing, sweetie. Have a good night."

"Thanks." I push end, drop the phone into my lap, and sit stock-still, trying not to let the guilt that weighs a metric ton sink me. It doesn't matter how many times I tell myself it's not my fault—I have a hard time believing it. I should have known. Why didn't I know? I could have done something, couldn't I? I should have done something. I missed the signs. How could I miss the signs?

A quick ping breaks the silence, saving me from a slew of

pointless questions I'll never have answers to. I pick up my phone and laugh a watery laugh.

Ser: *I'm starving.*

My fingers fly over the keyboard.

Me: *Oh, so now eggs for supper sounds good?*

Three bubbles pop up, followed by a quick reply.

Ser: *Bitch, hurry up.*

My friend is uncanny. It's almost like she knew I'd slipped back in time and she needed to save me from the guilt I let ride me like a merciless bitch if I'm not careful.

I should have known. I could have done something. How could I miss the signs? They're irrational, these thoughts. As an adult, I understand this. I do. Yet my fingers have fossilized around an illogical ideal that I could have somehow prevented the destruction of our entire family.

Taking a few deep breaths, I mentally box up all the shit of the last half hour. Shit that's futile to dwell on. My mother needs me. I'm all she has left. I can't let her down. She's my focus now.

Remembering that and the fact I'm running late, I dry my eyes the best I can and shove my car in reverse. Easing from the parking lot, I turn on the radio and hum mindlessly to a new country tune that I don't even care for, trying to get my mind right for tonight.

I'm stopped at a red light just blocks from home when a force from behind slams me forward, causing my seatbelt to lock and my head to knock violently against the headrest.

"What the hell?" I gasp. It takes a few blurry seconds to register what happened.

Son of a bitch. I was just rear-ended.

Could this day possibly get worse?

A glance in my rearview mirror shows a man sitting in a sleek black SUV, unmoving. Throwing the gear into park, I open my door, step out, and walk around to the back of my little car to see what kind of damage this asshole just did. I look over to see he's still sitting in his vehicle looking down at something, trying to act like nothing just happened, when pieces of my yellow plastic fender litter the ground.

My mouth falls open while my temper flares.

I walk over to his tinted window and pound on it hard, hoping it cracks. "Hey, asshole!" I yell. I do not have time for this. Or the patience. Or the money.

When the window finally rolls down, slowly, I'm about ready to let a string of expletives fly when they instantly stick in the back of my throat.

Staring at me, with dark aviators covering his eyes, is the most gorgeous man I have ever seen.

Drop-dead-on-the-spot beautiful.

I would buy anything he's selling.

Air. I would buy air.

I feel his eyes piercing into me as I take in his strong, square jaw, which is covered in what looks to be a five-o'clock shadow but I know is a carefully shaved masterpiece instead. His lips are plump, the bottom one a bit fuller. Shit, what I'd give to pinch that flesh between my teeth. Blacker-than-midnight hair is closely cropped on the sides but a bit longer on top, with that little flip thing in the front that I want to run my fingers through as he grazes between my legs. Rounding out the devilish package is what has to be a custom-tailored suit. The gray jacket molds perfectly to his broad, toned form. I just know the bright blue tie knotted around his neck would set off his eyes if I could see them.

Breathtaking. Breath stealing.

Why am I here again?

I know my mouth is hanging open when he says, "Can I help you?"

Holy hell. His commanding baritone voice matches his sinful looks. It feels like melted chocolate if you ran it through your fingers. Soft, silky, and oh so dirty.

Pull yourself together, Willow. Your car is lying in pieces.

"Can you help me?" I spit, my fury rising again. "Can you *help* me? Are you kidding? Yes, you can help me. You just hit my car!" My finger stabs the misty air in the direction where my parked Fiat now sits idle while traffic slowly weaves around us.

The phone he's holding in his hand chimes, and he looks down.

He.

Looks.

Down.

"I hit you? I could have sworn that you hit me," he says absently as his lithe, perfectly manicured fingertips caress the keypad like a lover.

I'm dumbfounded. Struck mute. I look around to see if maybe there are hidden cameras around and I'm being punked. Sierra is infamous for shit like this. Deciding that I'm not and he's just a pompous bastard, albeit a stunning one, I take matters into my own hands.

"Are you on drugs?" I go to reach for his glasses to check for dilated pupils when his hand comes up lightning fast, latching onto my wrist.

I audibly gasp at the feeling of tiny electric pulses shooting through me from the place he touches my bare skin. I feel him everywhere, like thousands of fingers ghosting over me, in me. It's the most strangely erotic thing I've ever experienced and very disconcerting that this stranger has the ability to awaken things in me I thought long dead.

If he feels a tenth of what I do, he doesn't let on. Yet he must not, because his face is still glued to the screen in his other hand. Yanking my wrist from his grip, the unwelcome feeling dissipates. My brain function restarts.

"I want your insurance card," I bite.

"Are you still here?"

I suck in an angry breath. "You have some nerve, you know that? You rear-end an innocent person sitting at a red light and try to blame it on them? I don't know who the hell you think you are, but I'm not leaving until I get your insurance information. You damaged my car, and you're going to pay for it. I could be injured you know."

I grab my neck, rolling it around on my shoulders for effect. I'm not, but everyone knows the strain of whiplash happens days later.

Now he looks up through the front windshield, still ignoring the fact that I'm standing here. He lounges nonchalantly in his car as if it's such an everyday occurrence for him to smash into someone else that he doesn't even react anymore.

"How do I know it wasn't like that before you backed into me?"

"Whaaaat?" I choke in utter disbelief. "*I* backed into *you*? What the hell do you think I did? Threw her into reverse when I saw you pull up?"

He shrugs, finally turning my way. I'm disgusted with myself for the way I'm enthralled with his lips even as they spill patronizing words. "People do strange shit all the time when they see a nice car, sweetheart. Wouldn't be the first time someone's tried to take advantage of me like that."

I blink. I blink again. I keep blinking, not sure how I'm supposed to respond to this unfounded accusation. *Do people really do that?*

"Yes, my naive little Goldilocks, people *do* really do that."

I huff, furious that not only did I use my outside voice, but that the name he called me, which was laced with ridicule, went straight to the apex of my thighs, making my sex clench. It's now throbbing with unwanted desire for this despicable person.

I'm disgusted with not only him but *my* reaction to him.

Heading to the front of his car, I pick up several pieces of broken parts from the concrete, walk back, and, sticking my hand inside his open window, dump them unceremoniously into his Armani-clad lap. If I'm lucky, one will tear a hole in his eight-hundred-dollar slacks.

I turn my palm up, saying evenly, "Your insurance card. Now."

His phone chimes again, but this time he doesn't drop his gaze. It remains on me. At least I think it does, because I can't see a damn thing behind the reflective glass shrouding his mysterious eyes. I watch myself watch him and for the first time realize how I look.

I'm horrified.

My face is red and splotchy, both from working out and from my mental breakdown only minutes ago. Mascara is not only caked underneath my bloodshot eyes, it's streaked down the right side of my cheek. My golden, sweaty hair is pasted to my forehead, and what's not flattened to my scalp is sticking straight out of my ponytail like my finger was just pulled from a socket in the nick of time.

But what's most horrifying is that my dark nipples are poking straight through my tiny light yellow and very *wet* sports bra. They're so big you could probably see them from outer space.

No wonder he thinks I'm a freaking loon trying to con him. I look the part.

When his pink tongue darts out and moistens his supple lips, my thighs quiver as I wonder what his wetness would feel like mingled with mine.

My God in heaven, I need to get the hell out of here before I do something stupid, like crawl through his window and rub myself all over his lap like a dog in heat. How is it possible to be so attracted to someone and hate him even more?

Shaking my hand back and forth, I arch a brow and remain silent. He chuckles lightly before reaching for his wallet, sitting in the middle console. I try to remain unaffected by that dark tone of his feathering down my spine. Removing a business card, he sets it in my upturned hand, careful not to touch me, which I'm secretly grateful for. Or not.

"I'm not looking for a date. I'm looking for payment."

A smirk tilts the corner of his lush mouth. Although I can't see his eyes, I know it reaches them. He's enjoying this now. Smug looks impossibly sexy on him. Oy!

He nods to the crisp white stock with scarlet lettering now weighing heavy in my palm. "Call that number. It will be taken care of."

"This had better be real," I warn, drawing my hand back just enough to rest it on the doorjamb. I don't let my eyes drop to the card even though they want to. Even though I'm dying to learn what name was gifted to such an exquisitely assholish creature.

When he leans toward me, I swear I can't breathe. The oxygen in the force field now surrounding us is replaced with thick longing. Just mine, I'm sure. Bushy, manly brows rise above his glasses when he speaks. "I may not like it, but I always own up to my mistakes."

"Yeah, well you'll forgive me if I don't trust you after you tried blaming your 'mistakes' on me." I use air quotes to mock his word selection, hoping it distracts him from how breathless I sound.

Shaking my head, I walk away, but not before his laughter reaches my ears, making my nipples tingle. When I open my door, instead of getting in, I reach for my cell phone and walk back to where our cars are almost joined. Throwing a fake smile in his direction I open up my camera and snap a few pictures, both of my car and his, which hardly has any damage. But I'm not doing it for that purpose. I want his license plate in case this card turns out to be for one Cherry Pitt at the local strip joint instead.

Without a look back, I hop into my now wrecked Fiat and put it in drive. Luckily for me the light is green, so I hit the gas, trying my hardest not to look back.

I get all the way through the intersection before I give in to my urge to burn this handsome man's features into my memory one last time. A reflexive grin breaks out when I look back to see him, sans glasses, smiling. He's watching me with a full-blown, genuine smile that bathes his entire car in golden rays.

Sweet baby Jesus in a manger.

Suddenly I'm glad he had those glasses on earlier. I'm quite sure I would have fallen into him and gotten lost. Just before I peel my stare away, I swear our eyes connect. But then he fades from my vision when he turns left while I continue straight.

Taking a deep, full breath for the first time in fifteen minutes, I replay every second of what just happened for the next three blocks. It's not until I pull into my parking spot that I peek at the now crumpled card still in my hand.

DANE KNOWLES
WILDEMER & COMPANY
206-555-3298

Huh. That's it? I expected even his name to run tiny shivers of throbbing need through me. It doesn't. He doesn't look like a Dane. And isn't it typical to add a fancy title to a business card to impress everyone you hand it to?

I test his name on my tongue.

Dane.

Nope. Nothing. Nada. No zing. No shivers. No mad desire to have his head between my legs.

In fact, now that I'm away from Dane's intoxicating presence, I'm convinced I made up my entire reaction to him as an escape from real life, if only momentarily. There is no way someone I've just met can cause that type of visceral reaction in me.

I look at the dash and realize it's almost seven. I will most certainly be late and Sierra won't get fed. Refocusing on the evening ahead, I begin to get my game face on, stepping into a different persona. Put my Master of Fine Arts degree to work. I block Dane Knowles from my mind, compartmentalizing him like I do everything else. The only thing I'll be getting out of that egotistical jackass is a brand-new bumper, nothing more.

Just as well. A guy who goes around hitting other people and tries to weasel his way out of it is not the kind I need in my life.

Shaw

Chapter Four

WHEN I PULLED INTO THE driveway, I fully expected to see Lianna's white Lexus waiting for me, signaling that my mother had, in fact, sabotaged me again. But it wasn't. I breathed a small sigh of relief that I wouldn't have to make small talk with a woman whose heart I know I crushed in order to please my mother.

Despite my intent to delete her voice mails from earlier, I had listened to them on the drive here and promptly texted Noah that he'd better not fail me tonight. Lianna is an independent, proud, well-cultured woman who comes from a good family, which is why I think my parents gravitated toward her. They wanted us to breed mini Liannas, move back to my family's homestead, preferably next door, and live the life *they* want for me.

That's not what *I* want, though. Now or ever. And I may not want to date Lianna anymore but I also never wanted to hurt her. The cultured, usually strong woman whose sobs echoed off the interior of my Range Rover sounded devastated. Broken. I feel guilty I didn't break things off earlier so she didn't have time to get so attached.

"You're late," my mother scolds when I step into the foyer.

"Unavoidable. My apologies." I kiss her cheek and hope she drops it. I don't feel like discussing the strange little mishap on the way here. Or why I'm still thinking of the demanding, disheveled little sprite that stood outside my SUV with nipples that could cut glass. Or why her fierce attitude caused a rock-hard erection that didn't abate until halfway across Lake Washington.

She was a fucking hot mess, but strangely, she was a hot mess I wanted to dive into headfirst, asking questions later. Much, much later, after I'd fucked her completely boneless. I haven't had that kind of intense, primitive reaction to a woman in a very, very long time.

Head in the game, Shaw.

Telling my dick to deflate before my mother notices my semi, I ask, "Birthday girl?" while striding through the entryway into the spacious kitchen lined with windows that afford the most exquisite view of Lake Washington I've yet to find. Yanking open the fridge, I pull out a beer before turning back to my mother.

She doesn't have to say a word. I can tell by the crestfallen look on her face that Annabelle is not only *not* here, she hasn't called either. It's now seven twenty. Damn her to hell.

"Where's everyone else?" I cross the kitchen and tug her into my arms. She wraps her thin limbs around me, and I whisper, "She may still show."

I hear my five-year-old niece's high musical laugh echoing from somewhere outside, although it's dark. God, I love her. She could get me to do anything she wants with a simple bat of the most incredible lashes I've ever seen on a human being.

"Cora wanted to catch some crappie, so Grandpa let her drop a line off the dock."

Cora is obsessed with fish, just like I used to be at her age.

"Ah. Nicholas with them?"

"And let his baby sister show him up?" She steps out of my hold before adding, "Gemma is out with your father, and Evan is watching *Bear in the Big Blue House* with Eli. He's got a bit of a cold and is cranky."

My antisocial brother-in-law, Evan, will use any excuse to get away from family time. Now if there happened to be a beautiful woman wrapped around my waist it would be a different story. I have no idea what my sister sees in that cheating loser, but I think her patience is wearing a little thin. Finally.

My gaze falls to the lake just feet away from my parents' incredible state-of-the-art home. I see several shadows against the darkening horizon at the end of the dock. My father is kneeling, talking to Cora, and Gemma looks to be helping Nicholas reel in his line.

I grew up here, in this house, on the water. Mercer Island. This haven in the middle of Lake Washington was named after my descendants, who founded it. I love it. I love everything about it. The tranquility, the view, the smell, the memories. It feels right every time I'm here.

"And Linc? Where's he?" When I spoke with my younger brother the other day, he said he would be here "with bells on." I wouldn't doubt it was literal.

"One of his sous chefs called in sick, and they have three events scheduled tonight, so he had to pinch hit." She sounds as disappointed as I am.

My brother is the executive director and chef at Seattle's premier cooking school. Like me, he's married to his career, and because our schedules rarely mesh, we don't get to spend a lot of time together.

"Have you tried calling her?"

"You know all that does is upset her. She'll think I'm checking up on her, accuse me of all sorts of things that aren't true."

"Then I'll call her." I whip out my phone to give Annabelle a fucking earful when my mother places a firm hand on my arm.

"Don't. It's fine."

"No. No, it's not fine." My voice elevates with each word I speak. "She's an inconsiderate, spoiled brat."

I look around the kitchen and realize that my mother not only made homemade cannoli, she also made her famous spaghetti sauce with veal meatballs, a timeless recipe passed down from generation to generation. It takes all day for the spices to blend just right. Whenever my mother makes this dish, she starts early in the morning and watches it like a newborn infant, tweaking this or that until she's satisfied it's just right.

"Shaw, please. I don't want to upset her."

"Upset *her*?" I yell. "What about you? I knew you would do this. I knew you would slave all day and just brush it aside when she doesn't show. Why do you let her get away with this shit, Mom?"

"What's going on in here?" my father's deep voice booms. He's insanely protective of my mother, which is another thing I don't understand. He'll jump my ass for raising my voice to my mother yet not say a word to Annabelle for upsetting her and being a no-show at her own goddamn party. It's infuriating. It's been the source of many arguments between us.

My mother's hands find my father's. "Nothing, Preston. Let's just sit down for dinner, okay?"

Preston Mercer lets his gaze fall between me and the love of his life, no doubt deciding if he should push the issue or not, but it's all decided when a little voice screams, "Unca Shaw!"

Looking in the direction of the earsplitting noise, I see Cora slide to a halt in front of me with a dark, writhing thing clutched tightly between her two tiny hands.

"I caught a fish!"

Beaming from ear to ear, she holds her prize proudly above her head. I squat down to take a closer look.

"Wow, Coraboo. You're probably going to be the most famous fisherwoman who ever lived, you know that?"

"You think?" she asks with the kind of excitement only five-year-olds have.

"I know."

"Look at his pretty eyes. They look like yours," she says with awe.

She's comparing me to an aquatic animal? When she shoves her catch in my face for me to inspect, I stumble backward, falling on my ass, and she loses her hold on the creature desperately trying to wriggle back into its life-saving habitat.

The whole room erupts into laughter and chaos as Cora and her seven-year-old brother try unsuccessfully to wrangle the fish, which is flopping all over the stone floor, closer to taking its last breath with every second that passes. Finally, my father reaches down and easily scoops it up.

"How about we put this one back in the lake, boo?" he asks Cora.

"Why?" she whines, bottom lip now quivering. "I wanna keep him. He's my pet."

"We are keeping him, boo. You want your pet to be safe, right?"

"Yes."

"Then he has to go back in the water. We'll keep him here in my special lake so we can see him again next time you come."

"Oh." She thinks hard on that. "Okay. But can I name him?"

"Sure, sweetie." They head back out to the water, Nicholas on their heels. They immediately begin arguing about what to call a fish they'll never see again.

"It amazes me every time," my sister Gemma says with a little chuckle when she extends her hand to help me up. I refuse it, jumping easily to my feet.

"What does?" I look down, frowning at the dark wet spot now on my thigh, probably from the fish. This suit is headed to the cleaners.

"That you can fall so head over heels for a little girl, but no woman can catch your eye."

"Fuck, don't start on me already, Gem," I grumble before tipping my bottle and swallowing the last of my now warm beer. I unpocket my cell to be sure I haven't missed a text from

Noah, which is ridiculous because I know the fundraiser hasn't started yet.

Jesus, it could be a very long night.

"Gemma, why don't you grab some glasses and, Shaw, please uncork the two bottles of wine chilling in the fridge," my mother suggests, seemingly rescuing me. It's not my first rodeo, though. I know it's only a brief reprieve before she has me captive at the dinner table and can start in on me herself.

On the sly, I send Annabelle a quick text asking her where the fuck she is but receive no reply.

Fifteen minutes later, everyone is in their respective spots. Grace has been said, an absolute requirement at the Mercer household, and the meal is being passed when we hear a loud commotion at the front door.

Gem and I exchange looks, both of us wondering which Annabelle is about to walk into the room. Erratic and combative or good-natured and appreciative. She plays both hands very well.

Just before I see her, I hear voices—*voices*, plural. My gaze floats first to my mother, then to the one empty place setting.

"Did you know she was bringing someone?"

She shrugs and rises from the table just as my little sister rounds the corner.

It's only been a few weeks since I've seen Annabelle, but her razor-straight hair has been colored again, this time to jet black. It looks like the dead of night and contrasts sharply with her fair, pale skin and brilliant blue eyes. She's also changed her style, adding severe bangs and a few layers in her long locks. Painted-on black, high-waisted jeans and a black cut-off sleeveless tee that says "If Monday Had A Face I Would Punch It" hug her slim frame. Simple black Chucks round out her outfit.

She has enough money through her partial trust fund to shop Gucci, Burberry, and Oscar de la Renta, but she looks like she just came from a cheap department store instead.

As inappropriate as her outfit is for a family dinner,

especially a Mercer family dinner, what's worse is the uninvited tiny female she's practically dragging behind her. This little girl is the epitome of clueless.

Short, stark blond hair. Wary hazel eyes. A slight blush on her tanned cheeks.

But it's what she's wearing that's put a hush on the entire room. If she coughs, her generous breasts will shoot out of the deep purple corset cinched around her trim waist, more appropriate for the bedroom than the dining room. A two-inch long skirt showcases her toned legs but barely covers her butt cheeks. High-heeled short boots elevate her short frame by several inches.

She looks like a slutted-up version of Miley Cyrus. Oh, wait…bad comparison.

I hear Gemma, who is sitting next to me, pretend to cough as she covers up a laugh. My eyes flit across the table to Evan, her husband, only to find his tongue practically wagging and his wide eyes bugging out of his head like a cartoon character. When my gaze lands on my father, his face is beet red. His jaw is ticking furiously. He. Is. Fuming.

"Sorry we're late. Pile up on the 90." *Bullshit.* I just drove the 90. She kisses my mom and turns with a flourish to the room. "Everyone this is Trixie." *Trixie? Really? Reeeeally?* "Trix," she continues, going around the table pointing at each person as she ticks them off until she gets to me. "And this is my very single, very successful, and smokin' hot brother, Shaw."

Huh? She used no descriptors for anyone else. A bad feeling swarms me.

Annabelle hops over to give me a hug, or that's what it seems like until she tugs my dress shirt from my pants and up my torso.

"What the hell?" I slap her hands away and haphazardly tuck it back in. "What are you doing, Bluebelle?" I try to catch her eyes to see if they're bloodshot or dilated. She's acting like a fucking lunatic.

"What? I just wanted to show Trix your cool 3-D tattoo. Trix was thinking of getting a tattoo, and I was explaining it to her. She wanted to see it."

"Annabelle Marie," my father warns on a low growl.

"Sorry, Daddy," she replies contritely. Another move she has down pat. "Hey Gemamma, would you mind moving so Trix can sit next to Shaw?"

Christ.

Help me.

This time Gemma doesn't hold it in. She laughs loudly as she scoots her chair back and picks up her plate, all the while shaking her head.

"Oh no, that's okay—" Trixie tries to protest but Annabelle cuts her off. This poor girl has no idea what she's gotten herself into.

"It's fine. She doesn't mind. Besides, it's my day, so I get what I want."

"Terror," I mumble underneath my breath.

"What, Shaw?" Annabelle asks sweetly. She knows exactly what I said.

"Nothing, Bluebelle," I reply just as sugary, but my glare says it all. When I get two seconds alone with her I'm going to rip her a new one, and she knows it.

A couple minutes later, an extra chair is brought in, and I'm seated next to a girl who can't be more than twelve but is trying to act twenty-five.

"I'll get a place setting for you dear," my mother tells *Trixie,* who is watching this whole thing unfold like an unexpected circus act. She's uncomfortable. At least there's that.

"Oh no, Mother. I'll get it." Annabelle jumps up. "Trixie's a vegetarian." Her eyes drop to the veal meatballs. "So, I'll just get her something she can eat, if you don't mind."

I'm going to fucking kill her.

"I'll help," I announce, throwing my napkin on my plate.

I exchange a look with my father, who silently begs me to get this train wreck under control. I seem to be the only one who has any influence on Annabelle whatsoever. My silent response is that I'll do my best. It just never seems to be enough where she's concerned.

"Just what the fuck do you think you're doing, Bluebelle?" I hiss lowly once I get into the kitchen, trying not to be overheard.

She opens several cupboards, pulling together an extra place setting for her uninvited guest. My mom would never turn a soul away. Hell, she nurses injured, bug-infested birds back to health, but had my younger sister pulled this shit at my house, both she and her "friend" would be thrown out on their asses. I love my little sister to pieces, but she's the most disrespectful little brat I've ever come across.

"I have no idea what you're talking about, Shawshank."

I shake my head at the ridiculous nickname my baby sister tagged me with. From the age of thirteen to sixteen, Annabelle obsessively watched *The Shawshank Redemption* like she was plotting a future prison break or something and needed a blueprint. It's not really stretching the truth because sixteen is when all hell cut loose with her, and she *has* spent a night—or several—in jail.

"You're practically undressing me in front of your jailbait pixie fairy for fuck's sake. What is she? Sixteen?"

Annabelle yanks open the refrigerator and fills her arms with hummus, cheese, and already-diced vegetables. God forbid her "guest" would eat what my mother worked all day slaving over.

"No, dumbass. And her name is *Trixie*." She emphasizes her preposterous name again. As if anyone could forget. Gemma walks in right at the moment Annabelle announces in a tone that implies Trix and I are perfect goddamn soul mates. "She's nineteen, and she's your perfect match."

"Nineteen?" Both Gemma and I cry in unison. Christ, I could practically be her father. The thought makes me shudder.

"Oh my God, Shaw. Do you always have to be so melodramatic? She's beautiful, has a big rack, and I heard she was your type. It's a gift, really. You should be thanking me with like a new car or a European vacation or something, not bitching me out. Jesus, you ungrateful snob."

I pinch the bridge of my nose, trying to rein in my temper before I take her over my knee and beat her bratty ass until it blisters. A good spanking would do her wonders. Maybe if my parents had laid a hand on her when she was little, she wouldn't be such an obnoxious snot today.

"And what *type* would that be exactly?" I ask on an exaggerated exhale. I cannot wait to hear this.

"She's into threesomes."

My jaw drops open in silent horror at the same time Gemma gasps and covers her mouth with the back of her hand to either suppress a smile or a curse; it could go either way. "For the love of Mary, Bluebelle, we're supposed to be finding him a wife, not a whore. God knows he doesn't need any more of those."

"Hey," I protest, visually hurling blades at Gemma while Sister Christian over there shrugs nonchalantly like Gemma didn't just insult her friend. "I thought you were on my side here?"

"I *am* on your side. You need a wife, not another plaything to break."

"I don't want a goddamn wife!" I shout, incensed at both references. And I don't break women unless that's what they're into. "How many times and how many ways do I have to say the same damn thing before you get it through your thick skull? And you"—I turn my ire toward my free-spirited little sister—"butt out of my sex life. If I so much as catch a whiff of perfume I don't recognize or hear a high-pitched, unfamiliar laugh when I step foot in this house again, I'm banning every single female family member from my life for a year."

"You don't mean that," I hear my mother say softly behind me.

"And that goes for you, too!" I whip around and pin her with my angry glare. My mother may not have had a hand in this little charade tonight, but she's been the instigator many times before, and I've pleasantly, respectfully kept my mouth shut.

Well, I'm done.

Enough is fucking enough.

"Don't talk to your mother like that," my father says in a low voice.

My hands slap against my thighs after I throw them unceremoniously in the air. "Dad, with all due respect, this isn't any of your business."

"How you speak to your mother is absolutely my business, Shaw. I don't care how many years out of diapers you get or how many zeros you have in your bank account, you will treat your mother with the respect she's earned. Understand me?"

I clench my jaw and breathe deep before pulling my mom in for a hug and whispering an apology in her ear. She hugs me tightly so I know I'm forgiven.

When I release her and look around, I see my entire family, minus the kids, standing in the kitchen. "Say, if everyone is in here, who's with Pixie in there?" Gemma's two-timing husband, that's who. He probably already has the kids in front of the tube and his dick out waiting to be sucked. Gemma's face turns stony right before she hurries out of the kitchen. It's as if she's read my mind.

"Come on, let's eat."

"Just a minute, Adelle. I need a moment with Shaw. Go ahead and start. We'll catch up." He kisses her lightly before they exchange a knowing glance, one that says I'm going to get hit with something I won't like. And my mother is in on it.

Apology rescinded.

Everyone files out, leaving my father and me alone. My gut churns at the serious look on his face.

"I need your help, son."

Then he asks something of me I can't deny him. Something he knows I won't say no to, because while I have no compunction telling other people to fuck off, I am loyal to my family. I'd do anything for them, especially my father. I'd do *anything* to help him achieve his dreams.

Running Wildemer & Company was always *my* dream, but it was never my father's. While he ran the family business for over thirty years and did a hell of a job, it was never his passion. He did it to please *his* father, not himself. He did it to fulfill his familial obligation, all the while forgoing what he wanted to accomplish. It wasn't until he retired a few years ago that he started truly living *his* dream. And his dream is in jeopardy.

This is my curse, I think. My weakness. I'd like to think it's the only one I have.

I'm a ruthless businessman. I make multimillion-dollar decisions every single day. I co-own a company worth over a billion dollars and growing. I'm responsible for thousands of lives, thousands of families. I'm steadfast in my convictions, my beliefs, my rules.

But I am devoted to my family. Every flawed one of them.

I have no problem telling anyone else no. Anyone except the ones I love, that is.

Willow

Chapter Five

I ARRIVE AT THE FOUR Seasons a full thirty minutes late. I'd called Randi so she could give Mr. Graber a heads-up as we always work through her or her liaison instead of contacting the client directly. To say she was less than happy is an understatement, but at least she was sympathetic.

"Your performance reflects directly on me and my ability to effectively manage my business. Good, bad, or indifferent. You're late, I lose money. You're sick, I have to scramble. You act like a cunt, I'll cut your fucking head off before you know what's happened. Clients don't like to pay top dollar for mediocre, Summer. They come to me because I'm the best. I employ only the elite, the cream of the crop. My business depends solely on you, and your livelihood depends on me. Like it or not, we need each other, but make no mistake—you fuck up, you're out. I have a hundred girls waiting to take your place."

I don't how many times over the past two years I've heard those words in one form or another. She rules the baby she created from nothing with an iron fist and ruthless bravado, making no apology for it. But for whatever reason, Randi does have a soft spot for me, so while I still have to meet all of her impossible standards and endure a lecture every time I screw up, I also get leeway others don't.

Pushing everything about this day away—my mother, the accident, and the gorgeous, arrogant bastard still dancing behind my vision—I take a calming breath and slip into Summer, the only name any of my clients know me by.

Tonight, I'll play a sophisticated and slightly haughty socialite accompanying my very rich older "friend" Paul Graber to Seattle's next Democratic mayoral hopeful's big fundraiser. If all goes well, this will turn into a regular occurrence. Dinners. More fundraisers. Anywhere a man like Paul Graber wants to be seen with a beautiful woman on his arm. I'll even travel if that's what he requires, as long as it doesn't interfere with my day job.

My hope is this client can turn into a regular. While I've never been fortunate enough to have a regular before, there are definite pros and cons. Of course, the only pro I care about is a steady income.

But the cons? There are many, the biggest of which is attachment. I've seen one too many of Randi's employees either fall hopelessly in love with their client or vice versa, and this is no movie. There is no red ball gown, million-dollar jewels to return, or raunchy sex on pianos in darkened ballrooms at three in the morning.

For some in this lifestyle, that's what they're looking for. The golden goose. Maybe even love. I don't know. For me this is a way to make ends meet until I can build my own business successfully enough that I don't need the extra money. I am not looking for a boyfriend, husband, or sugar daddy. I don't want expensive jewels or to be set up in a penthouse apartment with a black Amex on the nightstand. I want to do a job, period. Professionally, without messy emotions attached.

Besides, I don't believe there can be a happily ever after riding on the coattails of clandestine negotiations and false fronts. But hey, that's just me.

"We're here," Abraam announces as he slows the vehicle to

a subtle stop. Pasting a smile on my face when my driver opens the door, I exit the limo.

Randi has two simple rules when it comes to her men and women.

One: Never use your real name.

Two: Never let your client pick you up at home. We either drive ourselves, or she pulls out a chauffeur-driven car or limo for bigger, high profile events like this to ensure her investments shine.

"Have a nice evening, ma'am. I'll be here when you're ready."

"Thanks, Abraam." I give him a fleeting smile and turn my attention to scan the area for Mr. Paul Graber, whose picture I studied again on the way here. It doesn't take me long to spot him waiting with another handsome gentleman by the roped-off entrance.

As I approach him, I understand why he's been married three times already. His pictures don't do him justice. For an older man, he is good-looking in a George Clooney sort of way.

His thick hair is graying around the temples. His face is clean, free of whiskers. If the way his sharp black suit fits his lean frame is any indication, he's still very active. He exudes confidence, control. And the smile he gives me should put me at ease, but there's something else there. Something that feels a little...*off.*

He takes my hand and runs his lips lightly over my knuckles. It gives me the shivers, though not in a sexual way. More like an *I'm headed into a cemetery at the witching hour* way. "Well, Randi wasn't exaggerating when she said you were stunning," he says genteelly, that hair-raising smile back on his face.

Since I had about thirty minutes to shower and dress, Sierra fixed my hair while I quickly applied my makeup. She complained the entire time about being hungry, but she did a knockout job with the quick and simple updo she threw together.

I have tendrils of blond locks cascading around my face and down my back, which complement my smoky, sultry makeup perfectly. My black, floor-length, fitted dress is simple, yet elegant. And knowing Paul Graber stood at only five feet eight inches, I opted for one-inch, open-toed heels on my five-five frame.

"Thank you. My apologies for my tardiness."

He takes a step back, allowing his eyes to deliberately rake over me.

This is part of the job, being scrutinized, and I'd be lying if I said I didn't hate it. I knew what this job entailed—and what it *didn't*—when I took it, but that doesn't mean I enjoy being treated like a commodity. I feel slimy residue left behind everywhere his gaze touches. It makes me feel dirty, used.

His heated eyes finally find mine again, and I swallow, hoping to restart my saliva glands, which seem to have dried up from this awkwardness. A quick glance at the man standing behind Paul shows that he's hungrily taking me in as well. I'm already starting to feel like chum in the water on *Shark Week*.

I take long, deep breaths, working to relax my jaw.

"I'm a stickler for punctuality, but I have to say you were certainly worth the wait. You are lovely," Paul says softly. His compliment slithers down my back like a poisonous snake ready to strike. "Shall we?"

He crooks his arm and holds it out for me to take. I slip my hand underneath, setting my palm lightly on the top of his elbow, and he leads me inside, the unknown guard dog following behind.

At first touch, I get the completely opposite feeling of the one my Drive By invoked. Where he was fire underneath his cool façade, this man is ice shrouded in refinement. Where he was cloaked in mystery, this man is easier to read than the alphabet. Where my thoughts had run rampant with uncorked desire, this man makes me want to put on a chastity belt and throw away the key.

The question that's weighing on my mind the most, though,

is why, oh why do I wish I were standing here with that smug bastard who wouldn't give me the time of day instead of the man currently looking at me like he'd just as soon take me in the back room and fuck me instead of mingling with a bunch of rich, pompous snobs?

I don't know, but I know I don't like it.

We mingled. We ate dinner. I suffered through a blowhard politician giving the same regurgitated speech I think all politicians are spoon-fed about tax reform, public education funding, and bringing back the middle class. We mingled some more. I smiled. I fawned. I made appropriate small talk. I made Paul Graber feel like a god, which is my job and it's a job I do well.

I excused myself from him a while ago when I needed a break from the mind-numbing discussion of zoning permits and tax incentives to hit the restroom and get myself another gin and tonic.

I allow myself two cocktails when with a client.

This is my third.

I may even have a fourth.

Paul Graber and his "associate," Ian, have turned out to be handsier and harder to handle than an eight-legged sea monster. My hopes of having him turn into a regular have effectively been flushed down the toilet. Turns out either they don't understand the rules, or they weren't quite truthful about the type of service they were looking for. When I check in at the end of the evening, I'll have to give Randi a heads-up.

Randi has varying types of escorts for varying client tastes. Some are exactly what you'd think an escort is. He or she will do absolutely anything—*anything*—a client desires…for the right amount of cash.

But I'm not one of them.

Turns out there are a lot of people who want nothing

more than to hire eye candy for an evening. No sex. No goodnight kiss. No expectations after the car door closes. It's a niche market that Randi has capitalized on and a side of her business that's more than doubled in the past twenty-four months.

I'm what Randi has dubbed a "party favor." We look pretty, we adorn our clients, we dote, we mingle, we act the part we're given, and we go home at the end of the "date" a few hundred or thousand dollars richer, with our legs shut and our pride intact. I could make three times the amount I do if I sold more than my time, but I won't. I may be desperate for extra income, but I'd never sell my body or my conscience to do it, not that I judge those who do. It's just not right for me.

Most of the time, this job is okay. Sometimes even enjoyable. I meet interesting people. I dine at the finest restaurants. Drink the most expensive wines. If I wanted to make a living doing nothing but this, which many of Randi's employees do, I could. At three hundred fifty dollars an hour, it would be a very lucrative one.

But hanging like a pretty bauble off the arm of some rich man isn't the life I want even if that affords me the financial freedom I crave. I'm not sure what that life is anymore, and I think that's part of my problem. I'm floundering. If I'm honest, I have been for a long time.

I fell into acting because it seemed like I'd done it my entire life. I was good at it. I had to be the strong one. I had to pretend as though I was holding everything together on the outside while I silently fell apart on the inside. I foolishly thought I could make a living out of it. Then everything changed again, and I had to grow up fast.

So here I stand, leaning against the beautiful golden art deco wall of the awe-inspiring Four Seasons ballroom, drowning the sorrows of my shitty day and my financial woes in a tumbler of liquor, disappointed this night is not turning out as I'd hoped.

Needing just a couple more minutes to myself before rejoining my "date," I'm sipping my cocktail and watching impeccably dressed power-hungry men and women with superiority complexes expertly work the room, kiss asses, and vie for the upper hand when someone sidles up next to me.

"Now what's a sweet pretty thing like yourself doing unprotected in a room full of ruthless predators?" a throaty male rumbles close to my ear. It's the sort of deliciously deep voice that instantly wets a woman's panties regardless of what his face looks like, and without so much as looking at this man, I already know he plays in the big leagues.

Even though I would bet this guy has the sexy looks to match his even sexier timbre, I don't give into temptation to verify it. For two more minutes I just want to be me instead of this false front I'm forced to wear. I put my glass to my lips and tip it, eyes forward.

I fully expect him to leave when his question is greeted with silence. He doesn't. He stays right beside me, and we stand quietly for a few beats together.

Then I start to feel bad. Maybe he needed a break as much as I did, and I'm just being a bitch for no reason. Maybe he's just trying to be nice. What a novel concept. Maybe I should return the favor.

I notice a beautiful, statuesque brunette gazing our way, and if I'm not mistaken, she has a little venom in her eyes.

"She yours?"

"Who?"

I nod to the woman who's discreetly trying to watch our little interaction out of the corner of her eye. "The brunette with voodoo eyes."

He laughs loudly, drawing a few eyes our way, including hers. "Voodoo eyes?"

"Yeah. I think maybe if she had one of those little dolls in that tiny purse, she'd be hexing it and stabbing needles through the eye about now, hoping she'd blind me."

He takes a few seconds to respond before he mumbles, "I

think maybe you're right." But he doesn't elaborate, making me wonder if she's one of the many women he's left heartbroken. More than likely.

"Your first time at one of these?"

"Yes," I find myself answering truthfully.

"It can be a little overwhelming."

I hum noncommittally, staring straight ahead.

"You from around here?"

"Montlake." While I live in a two-bedroom condo with Sierra in Beacon Hill now, I did grow up in Montlake, so it's not really a lie.

"Fancy. You here with someone?"

Aaaand it begins. I force myself to hold in an exhale of disappointment.

"I'm Noah, by the way." When I don't respond, he prods, "And you would be..."

"Unavailable," I retort with just enough heat to make sure he gets the point. I keep my eyes fixed on the way the moonlight shines off the dark waters of Puget Sound, still not looking at the man behind the silky voice.

Dark and deadly chuckles deeply. I fight the smile tugging my mouth.

"I don't need your marital status, dollface. I can see by your empty left hand—you're single."

"Looks can be deceiving."

"Yes. They can." Did I make that up, or did his voice just drop an octave from husky to huskier? "For example, you looked a little lost over here, and I thought you needed to be rescued, but I think perhaps I was mistaken."

"So, you don't think I'm lost anymore?" I ask sarcastically, finishing my cocktail.

"No. You're lost, all right. I just don't think you want to be found."

My breath catches at his perceptivity. My head snaps in his direction, and...

I was right. His face does match his sinful voice. He's

undoubtedly gorgeous and intense. No wonder Voodoo Eyes is jealous. I would be too if this guy had crushed me.

His lean form, covered in shiny charcoal material, towers above me. Dark eyes penetrate mine, searching for secrets he thinks he can find but won't. I feel an immediate attraction to him, but it's different from the one I felt earlier today toward the guy who rammed into me. That one was visceral. It came from someplace deep inside me that this guy could never reach. But I feel a sort of strange kinship with him, as if he could be a really good friend if I let him get that close.

"What's your name, beautiful?" he asks again in a low, coaxing voice. Ninety-nine percent of women would give in, let their name flow like hot lava hoping to burn a path into this man's heart.

I'm not one of them.

Pushing back from the wall I was leaning against, I hand my empty glass to a passing waiter and turn my full attention to the smooth-talking Adonis holding it up with me. "All right, take off your shirt."

"Excuse me?" One of his brows quirks up in amusement.

I let my eyes drift down his solid, masculine form, hoping like hell this doesn't backfire on me. "Your shirt. Take. It. Off. If I'm forced to make a decision now on whether to fuck you, I need to look at the goods first."

His gaze floats briefly around the room, and for the first time I gather I've made this confident man a little uncomfortable. I bite my lip to suppress a smile.

"Who said I wanted to fuck you?"

"Don't you?" I challenge. *What in God's name are you doing, Willow?*

"I—" He chuckles, shaking his head slightly.

I take a step closer, looking up his six-foot-plus height and lower my voice. "Well? What are you waiting for?"

An entertained smile stretches his face, making the skin around his eyes crinkle slightly. "Who the hell are you?"

"There you are, Summer. I've been looking everywhere for

you," a male voice slurs. The fumes from the bourbon Paul's been drowning in all night almost make me dizzy when they drift over my shoulder.

Noah's brows lift at the mention of my name—my fake name. I cringe a little. I hadn't been Summer at all while I was bantering with Noah. I'd been Willow, and I'd actually enjoyed myself for the first time in a long time.

"I'm sorry I was delayed, Paul. I was just heading back from the ladies'. This gracious gentleman saved me from a rather nasty fall when my heel caught on the carpet."

My eyes slide to Noah. I almost laugh at the confused look he has about my sudden change in demeanor. His gaze drags from mine to meet that of the man standing by my side, whose hand now rests possessively at the small of my back.

Yeah, I didn't miss that. Neither did Noah.

"Well, I'll be damned. Noah Wilder," Paul says. "Surprised to see you here." He sticks out his free hand, which Noah takes in a firm shake.

"Keeping my options open." He winks. "How's business, Paul?"

"Running into a little snag in the expansion, but I'm working it out. You?"

"Couldn't be better."

"This guy's gonna give Preston a run for his money." Paul nods in the direction of the mayoral candidate.

"Putting all your chips into a new basket, eh?"

Paul shrugs nonchalantly. "The other basket seems to have sprung a leak."

"Or maybe it's just overflowing," Noah responds coolly. I have no idea what this cryptic discussion means, and I don't know this man at all, but I do sense he's covering a slow, simmering anger. "How's Velma?" Noah's darkened eyes flit back to mine briefly before sticking to Paul again.

"I wouldn't know. We've parted ways." He sounds sad and regretful, except in bad form, he was dissing his "not *quite*" third ex's prowess in bed when he didn't think I was listening. Prick.

Pasting me to his side like I'm a prize Noah will thief away, he asks, "So, you settle down yet?"

"Too slippery for that." They laugh. I roll my eyes—mentally, because I've slipped back into the doting Summer. "Aren't you going to introduce me to this beauty?" Noah turns his attention back to me with a gleam in his eye that I can't decipher.

"Not on your life. I wouldn't put it past you to try stealing her out from under me." He leans toward Noah and drops his voice. "And I kinda like this one. Maybe she'll be number four."

I start coughing, choking on saliva that's made its way down my windpipe when I inhaled sharply at his insinuation.

"Are you okay?" they both ask in unison.

I hold up a finger while the other hand covers my mouth. "Fine," I rasp. I point in the direction of the restroom before I take off, leaving the two of them behind.

When I return a few minutes later, I'm slightly disappointed to spot the smooth-talking Noah across the room, now in deep discussion with an older couple. His eyes find mine, silently asking if I'm all right. When I nod, he smiles and politely returns it before turning his attention back to the man with the salt-and-pepper hair.

Wishing I could leave, but knowing I can't, I reluctantly wind my way through the thick crowd back to my date for the evening. I keep tabs on Noah for a while, even see him talking to Ian for a bit before he disappears.

Standing by Paul's side, I make small talk for the next hour and a half before he's ready to call it a night. I quickly text Abraam as the three of us walk outside together. Ian trails behind us while Paul leans on me heavily in his drunkenness.

This is the part of the night that generally goes without incident. After all, the client knows what they've purchased. They know the rules. They sign off on them. Randi is very meticulous about policies, procedures, and documentation.

But Paul and Ian apparently have other ideas.

Paul purrs drunkenly in my ear, "I would very much like it if you would accompany me back to my hotel tonight."

I glance back at Ian to catch him openly ogling my ass. I'm quite sure even if I wanted to agree—although thinking about it makes me want to throw up in my mouth a little—they'd both end up with a nasty case of whiskey dick, and I'd be left to pleasure myself.

"I appreciate the offer, Paul, but we both know this evening ends here." I am polite and cordial and pray hard that Abraam arrives from the parking garage any second.

"Oh, come now, *Summer*." Beefy fingers bite into my biceps when he yanks me into him. "We both know what you do for a living."

I grit my teeth trying to keep calm, but nerves cause my stomach to churn. The crowd has thinned considerably, and the area he's led us to is pretty dark. These two men could easily force me into their car before anyone realizes what's happened.

"You need to let me go," I grit.

I try to squirm free but feel body heat at my back. I flinch when unwelcomed hands ghost my waist. "It'll be worth your while, cupcake," Ian disgustingly hums against my neck. My earlier thoughts about whiskey dick die when I feel his erection prodding my lower back. "Maybe we'll even leave you a nice fat tip in the morning if we're thoroughly satisfied."

Oh shit. Shit. Shit. I could be in some very serious trouble here.

I'm trying to figure out how to play along yet stall until Abraam arrives when a dark, sexy, saving voice drawls, "There a problem here?"

Noah.

Relief hits me so fast my knees almost give. Paul's grip loosens, and Ian takes a step back. Seizing the opportunity, I shake Paul's hold and step to the side, no longer sandwiched between these two repulsive men. I breathe a sigh of relief when Abraam pulls around the corner.

"Fine, fine, Noah." Paul staggers a little when he loses my body as leverage.

Incredibly embarrassed, I don't want to so much as look at Noah, but when I finally brave a glance at him, I don't recognize the easygoing man teasing and flirting with me earlier. The man I see before me now is fierce, protective. Livid as hell.

Abraam parks and is rounding the car when Noah sets his hand on my lower back, ushering me forward. "You okay? You look shook up," he says lowly, his cheek close to mine.

"I…I'm fine." But my voice wobbles, giving me away. My adrenaline was pumping earlier, but now that the altercation is over, I shake uncontrollably.

"Everything okay, ma'am?" Abraam asks when he opens the door. His gaze volleys between the three men. Abraam is big and bulky, former military. He could easily take down any one of them if necessary. He wouldn't hesitate if he thought they were a danger to me.

"Yes," I whisper on a thin smile. "A little too much to drink, I think."

"Make sure the lady gets home safely," Noah commands, helping me into the interior. He leans inside and looks at me pointedly. "You really should be more careful with the company you keep, doll."

"Life doesn't always grant us choices," I blurt before I know what's coming out of my mouth.

His mouth turns down slightly. "All the same, choose more carefully next time." His concern is genuine. I nod, and he surprises me by cupping my cheek, kissing me lightly on the forehead.

"Noah," I call before the door closes. When he pokes his head back in, I add quietly, "Thank you."

He nods sharply, his lips tightly pressed together. The overhead light extinguishes, and we pull away from the curb as I watch a heated exchange between two drunken men and my savior.

For the first time since I started working for Randi, I

question what the hell I'm doing and if there's another way. But I know there's not, or I would have figured it out already.

I don't break often. It's self-indulgent and doesn't change your circumstances. All you get from your brief pity party is a stuffy nose and throbbing temples.

But for the second time that day, I fall apart and let the tears freely flow.

I miss my family.

Shaw

Chapter Six

"SO, LET ME GET THIS straight," Noah starts after throwing back the last of his drink, pounding the now dry glass on the table. "You're going to start dating Lianna again because...*why*?"

Confusion draws his features down, and it would be funny if this situation weren't fucked six ways from yesterday. The mere thought of calling Lianna and asking her to do this favor for me—more importantly, for my father—makes my skin crawl. But I don't know what else to do. There's not a woman in my past I can call on for this type of thing, and I can't very well just pick one off the corner of Third and Cherry Street.

"Another one, handsome?" our scantily covered waitress, Gina, nods to Noah's empty. She has a dozen tables she's responsible for, yet she's been hovering over ours like we're her VIPs for the evening.

"Sure thing, darling." Noah winks flirtatiously, reeling her in with his suave looks and dual dimples. We are a well-oiled machine, Noah and me. He's better being the relaxed, carefree flirt; I excel at dominating and controlling. It works for us when we're down for a night of pure gluttonous indulgence.

Tonight, the way Noah's running his hand lightly up the

back of Gina's bare thigh makes it clear his head is in the den of depravity. The way her eyes are glazing over, it's apparent she is amenable.

Gina leans over, exaggerating her reach for the glass. The move pushes her D-cup plumped-up tits even farther. I see a hint of her dark brown areolas, and my dick stirs. If that little gesture wasn't her unspoken invitation, then the message is loud and clear when she bites her lip and looks to *both* of us, rasping, "I get off at eleven."

She is beautiful, and it's obvious she's only looking for a single night of debauchery, not promises of tomorrow. Just the kind of woman I need right now. I imagine my dick sinking between her fleshy lips as Noah pounds into her from behind, making her cry around me. Making me squirt down her long, supple throat.

Days ago, I would have been all over her blatant invitation, but now...now I've made a promise I need to somehow keep that does not involve getting her back to Hotel 1000 and onto my cock.

I sigh heavily, watching dessert walk away, slim hips enticingly swaying. It's been far too long since I've been laid. I'm getting both antsy and less picky. I need release that doesn't involve some lube, my own hand, and thoughts of a disheveled blond nymph whose bare spanked ass I'd like to see bent high in the air over the hood of my Rover.

"So...Lianna?"

Fuck. Unnamed sparkling blue eyes that blaze with fire transform into Lianna's desolate mocha ones.

"Yeah, Lianna."

"You're going to date her again because your father *asked* you to?" he asks incredulously. "And you're considering it?"

"It's not that simple, Noah."

"The fuck it's not. It's pretty damn simple to me. To help get your father reelected for his second term as Seattle's mayor, you're going to shackle yourself to a woman who will get her claws so far into you they'll petrify. Jesus Christ,

Merc, if he *asked* you to marry her, too, would you?"

My father wasn't actually elected into his current mayoral position. When the existing mayor can no longer meet his or her duties, due to say death, the city council president is next in line. So, this election will be my father's first official election by the people into a role he was clearly born for. Politics was always my father's passion, not business. While Preston Mercer is a great businessman, he's an even better politician. I want to help him live his dream any way I can, just as he helped me live mine.

"This isn't about Lianna, Noah. He didn't ask me to start dating *her* again specifically. He asked me to settle down for a while with one woman and..."

"And what?"

I eye Noah. I have no issues with what we do. Every encounter we have together with a woman is pleasurable and consensual. I love fucking a woman solo, but if she wants, I also enjoy helping her achieve her fantasy of being dominated by two men at once.

It's not something we set out to do intentionally. We stumbled into it quite by accident one drunken night at a college frat party when I walked in on Noah fucking Katrina, a girl we'd both been interested in. When I turned to leave, she asked me to stay. Asked me if she could suck my cock while Noah continued pounding into her. Noah shrugged like he didn't care, and come on, let's be honest...what red-blooded nineteen-year-old male is going to turn down that little request? Not fucking one.

"He's heard rumors about us. What we do. And so apparently has Wicklow Harrington the fucking third." My father's rival for the mayoral seat.

"Your sex life is not on the ballot, my friend. Your dad's reelection should not involve you. You're a grown man who can fuck who he wants, when he wants, how he wants."

"You're right. It shouldn't. But we both know it will. Harrington has some pretty powerful and questionable backing, and he's also got the union in his hip pocket. He wants to win, and he's starting to dig deep. Dad told me he already found out about Bluebelle's latest rehab stay, though that's supposed to be buried. It's only a matter of time before his cronies find out some of the other shit."

"Fuck." Noah runs a hand through his hair.

"Yeah. And then there's Gemma's cheating asshole of a husband, and of course, let's not forget about Lincoln and the way he uses fashion to express his gender identity. My father may have the most favorable rating of any mayor in the past fifty years, but all that means is Harrington will bring bigger guns."

"So, this race is going to turn personal against your family? All the skeletons unearthed?"

"According to my father, yes. Harrington is an unscrupulous low-life prick. He'll do anything to win, and I'll do anything to save my family from being dragged through political mudslinging."

Even date Lianna again. *Christ help me.*

"Look, Merc," he says, leaning forward. "I understand you want to protect your family. I understand you don't want Bluebelle's juvie or criminal records exposed or Linc's...*predilections* aired for all to judge, but I don't understand how you settling down with a girl is supposed to stop all that. Won't that make them just dig harder, turn more rocks?"

My shoulder lifts. I'd said the same thing to my father when he suggested it. "My father's new campaign manager thinks that focusing the limelight away from them and on myself and my love life will divert media attention from the more unsavory parts of Preston Mercer's children's lives."

"And because you're Seattle's unattached golden boy, well, one of them"—he smirks—"it will be a media frenzy if he's supposedly settling down with someone serious. Drawing away from any negativity, right?"

I nod slowly. "Something like that, yes."

"Well...shit. He may have a point there."

"My sentiments exactly." I take another sip of my drink, savoring the slow burn.

After a few beats of silence, Noah asks, "Have you already called Lianna?"

"Not yet. I can't make myself dial her number."

"What if I had an alternative to Lianna?"

"What do you mean 'an alternative to Lianna'?" I reply with hesitation.

"Just what I said. I need to follow up on a couple of things, but what if I found you someone who is more than happy to play your girlfriend for a few months. Wouldn't be free, of course, but it also wouldn't land you back into Cruella Deville's hands. Then shortly after the election, but not too soon so it looks staged, you two can have a very public breakup. Then you're home free. No ties, no theknot.com, no forevers. You go back to your life, she goes back to hers. The end."

"Theknot.com? The fuck is that?"

"I don't know, some wedding shit that brides use. I caught Maris on it all the time when she was planning her wedding last year. Anyway, forget about that. What I'm proposing is a viable alternative to your problem. You help your dad, but you don't sell yourself back to bridezilla in the process."

I sit back and study Noah for a minute, trying to process what he's saying. "Are you suggesting I hire a whore?" I ask, my mind spinning.

"Not...*exactly*." The grin that splits his lips is mischievous.

"Christ, Noah, I can't hire a whore. What if that fell into Harrington's hands? That would be far worse for my father than if it leaked that I enjoyed the occasional kink."

"Nothing would lead back to you, I promise. I would handle it all. Besides, she is not a whore." If I wasn't mistaken he sounded a little protective.

"Then what is she? A do-gooder who just happens to need a little extra cash?"

"I think maybe," he answers thoughtfully. When I scowl, he adds, "Trust me, Merc. I wouldn't do anything that would hurt you or Preston's chances of reelection."

"How is it you know a woman like that anyway?" Like me, I

know Noah beds a lot of women, but I've never known him to need to pay for one.

Before he can answer, Gina returns to our secluded corner with two fresh cocktails, one for each of us, although I didn't order another one.

"On me, babe." She licks her lips then brushes them against the shell of my ear, placing her hand dangerously high on my thigh. "And by on me, I mean that literally. I've heard that Macallan tastes best when it's licked straight from my pussy."

Jesus Christ. I'm not sure I've ever come across a woman so brash and bold and willing. While it should be a total turn-on, strangely it's not. I like mine to leave something to the imagination. I even like to work for it a little.

The corner of the club we're in is relatively dark. Hell, we could probably take her right here without anyone being the wiser, but I can't break my promise to my father, especially just seventy-two hours later.

Can I?

"Sorry, sweetheart. Appreciate the offer, but it's not happening tonight."

I gently remove the hand that's now stroking my denim-covered cock. The moment I do, her lips stop their trek across my jaw.

"Shit," I hear Noah murmur. He's sorely disappointed.

Gina's face falls, and she straightens, looking angry. "But I thought—"

"Hey," Noah grabs her wrist and pulls her between his spread legs before settling his hands on her hips. "I'm still game if you are, doll."

"Yeah?" she asks tentatively, bobbing her eyes back and forth between us. I can see she's still hoping I'll change my mind.

Noah reaches up and tilts her face back to meet his. "Yeah, but just a little one-on-one action, okay?"

I watch him slide his hands leisurely over her curves until he reaches the hem of her skirt. His fingers disappear underneath as they crawl back up. Her breathing picks up when he tugs her closer and begins massaging what I imagine is her tight, bare ass. I know he's sunk two fingers deep inside her undoubtedly soaked channel when her breath catches, her eyes flutter closed, and her mouth falls silently open.

"Okay?" he prods again gruffly. His bicep flexes lightly with each slight pump of his hand. I adjust my rapidly hardening dick.

She nods before gripping Noah's shoulders when her legs start shaking.

"Do you want to come, sugar?" he drawls. He picks up the pace, fingering her in earnest now. Leaning forward, he runs his tongue along the exposed patch of tanned skin just below her belly button ring.

"God, yes," she whispers hoarsely.

"You want to show my friend here what he's going to be missing?" Noah taunts, throwing a devious smirk in my direction.

Her lids pop open, and dilated, glazed eyes fix on me. I keep my face neutral, taking a casual sip of my Scotch as I watch Noah expertly work her closer to the edge, but deliberately not letting her fall.

"Watch him," Noah commands thickly.

My jaw tightens, but I don't stop him. I should, because it's careless. If anyone snaps a picture of this, it would be hard to explain to my father. A quick sweep of the club, however, shows there are no patrons in the immediate vicinity. I hear voices, but don't see a soul.

Taking my silence as approval, with a fluid move, he spins her so her back faces his front. He scoots over so they're in the corner. Placing her hands on the table, he bends her slightly forward so I have a perfect view down her generous cleavage.

When Noah reaches around and yanks down both her uniform top along with the cups of that lacy number she's sporting, he gives me an even better look. Her tits pop out, squished together by the material still cupping them. He tweaks her already-hard nipples none too gently, bringing them to red, pointed peaks that now scrape the table with each rough jab of his fingers between her thighs.

"Don't look away from him," Noah says gruffly. Jesus, I can hear how wet she is from across the table. "Fuck yes. I can't wait to eat this juicy cunt later."

Holy hell, she is beyond desirable, and I toy with the idea of joining in. Of biting down on that delectable bud while Noah eats her right here until her chest is flush and she pants her way through one orgasm after the next. The thought of being caught any other time would be a complete turn-on, and I'd already have my cock in hand, but tonight it's the *only* thought that holds me back.

Noah brazenly lifts one side of her skirt and sinks his teeth into her backside. She opens her mouth, but no sound comes out.

As I watch Noah send this girl into space, I try to remain unaffected. I try not to let my cock throb, thinking of the relief I would find within her. But mostly I try not to think of the blue-eyed imp with mascara streaked down her face and wet golden hair plastered to her head. I try not to imagine what *her* moans of ecstasy would sound like or how her beautiful face would contort when I pushed her to places that made her uncomfortable but gave her pleasure she'd never known before.

Me, not Noah. While I've not had one issue sharing a woman with my best friend all these years, the thought of him feeling her tight pussy clench around his cock as she unravels or of her watching him with the same look of raw desire Gina is giving me, stirs a pot of something in my gut that's pretty damn close to jealousy.

Before I know it, I'm ripped from my little sprite fantasy by Gina softly crying out. She reaches out and briefly fists my shirt, her eyes screwed shut in ecstasy, her entire body shaking as Noah's grip tightens to keep her from falling.

There's nothing I love more than to watch a woman come,

and Gina is spectacular. Before I know what I'm doing, the backs of my knuckles stroke over one dark, distended nip. Her eyes blink open, and she slams them shut when I can't resist rolling the rock-hard bud between my fingers. I grip her chin and bring her mouth to mine for a brief chaste kiss then force my back to meet the booth once more. It's all I can do not to push her to her knees to suck me.

Spent, she sags onto Noah's lap. He gently holds her for a few moments until she comes all the way down. A couple minutes later, he sends her on her way with a pat to her ass and promises of more to come later.

"What the fuck was that?" I grit angrily after Gina wobbles away on legs that look like rubber. I'm not really mad at Noah, I'm mad at myself for having thoughts about a woman I've never had before. A woman I wouldn't mind playing my girlfriend for a few months so I could experience every delectable inch of that fantastic tight little body she put on display for everyone to see. A woman I apparently need to excise from my every fucking thought.

Noah's grin is shit-ass. "Just wanted to give you a taste of what you'll be giving up for the next few months. It's July. Election's not till November." He tips his drink to me before downing the rest. "So…about my offer. Want me to look into it?"

I don't answer for several minutes, trying to meticulously think through all my options. As much as I hate to admit it, though it isn't the best alternative, it's certainly better than being glued to Lianna again, possibly for life. "Don't you do a thing without running the details by me first."

He grins victoriously and nods.

"I mean it, Noah. I need to approve every last aspect."

"Got it. Give me a few days. Do not—and I repeat—do not call fucking Lianna no matter how much pressure your father puts on you."

"No worries there."

"You sure you don't want one last night of sin and debauchery before your balls are in a sling for a while?"

I laugh. "Want? Yes. Have? No. I think I'll let you take the fair Gina tonight."

His shoulder rises and drops. "Your loss." Though Gina does, I don't think he really cares if I'm there or not.

"No doubt," I agree quietly, thinking of our eager waitress.

Fifteen minutes later, after I leave my friend behind and wait for the valet to bring my car around, I find myself secretly hoping that whoever Noah comes up with as my fake girlfriend for the next few months will look an awful lot like my golden angel.

I make a mental note to check with Dane again in the morning to see if she's called. Hell, if I thought I could convince *her* to attend a few functions, stop for a few photo ops, and spread herself out naked in my bed for a few short weeks, I'd do it in a hot second.

Unfortunately, because I was nothing short of a bastard, I would have a better shot at winning the next mayor's seat myself than convincing her to let me do anything but cut her a nice fat check for a new Matchbox bumper for that death trap of a car.

And doesn't that just figure. The one woman I wouldn't mind having for a while likely doesn't want anything to do with me.

Willow

Chapter Seven

I PULL UP OUTSIDE RANDI'S secluded $2.7 million home in Windermere. Parking beside a fancy silver sports car, I shut off my inferior Fiat and sit for a moment or two. I have had the week from hell and am not in the mood for another lecture from Randi, but she's one person you don't say no to. She summons, you answer.

After four days, we finally found a repairman to check the water heater in my momma's house and got the bad news it needs to be replaced. After I've already spent three hundred dollars on repairs, now I have to shell out another seven hundred for a new one. Plus, Momma's had a particularly bad week and came down with a cold earlier, which we're always worried will turn into pneumonia. She seems to be better, but I always wonder what will take her from me. Alzheimer's doesn't kill. You can live years and years in a perfectly healthy body while your mind wastes away, rendering you completely helpless and infantile.

Knowing I've taken too much time already, I step from my car and make my way over the cobblestones and up three matching stairs. As if she was waiting for me, Randi's housekeeper, Graciella, immediately opens the glass French doors and ushers me inside.

Looking back to be sure I rolled up my window in case of a sudden downpour, I frown at my crumpled bumper. With everything else going on, I haven't had a chance to call "Dane" and start the process of getting that taken care of, not that I'll the have time to get it fixed anyway. Damn that aviator asshole for making my life harder.

"This way, ma'am." Graciella gestures.

Following her in silence, I take in the massive, resort-like palace. The entire open space is decorated in whites and light grays, and there are more windows and skylights than I can possibly count. The lines are sharp, sleek, and modern as one room flows seamlessly into the next. We walk through the entryway and pass three large bay windows to my right, where a lap pool spans the length of the house.

I've only been to Randi's home once, when my friend Jo tricked me into an interview. I met Jo in my freshman year of college, and we became fast friends though we couldn't be more opposite. She's black to my white in every sense of the word. Skin, hair, eyes, heart. But somehow, we clicked.

It wasn't until my life fell apart financially a few years ago that I learned of Jo's employment with Randi. And it wasn't until Randi expanded her business plan to offer "party favors" that I considered working for her. I am her first and probably most successful experiment, though she'll never admit the last part.

By the time we reach Randi's office, I'm a ball of nerves.

I was too shaken up to talk to her the night of the fundraiser last week, sending a quick text that I'd update her the next day. When I did call her, I was too embarrassed to let her know I'd gotten myself into a bad situation.

I should have been smarter. I shouldn't have had that last cocktail. I should have made sure Abraam was waiting for me when we exited. I shouldn't have let them lead me to a secluded area. I should have done a lot of things differently, and I didn't want her to know how massively I'd screwed up, so I sugarcoated the truth.

She was unusually silent before she told me how disappointed she was, which meant she'd talked to the client. Who knows what lies he filled her mind with. For the past few days, I've had absolutely no idea where I stand with her. Am I going to be fired? Is that why she wanted to see me privately?

I think about my mother, her house, the care she needs, and the weighty financial crap hanging over my head. Although I've done nothing but waffle between quitting or staying all week, knowing I may not have the income from this job to help care for my only living relative makes me weak with worry. I could always give up my place with Sierra and move back home, saving a few bucks on rent, but I've been holding that as a last resort. As much as I love my mother, I need my independence. Besides, it's hard to work when she's around, and that's just another river of guilt I wade through daily.

Graciella stops and knocks on a closed door. Randi's husky voice tersely responds, "What is it?"

Well then...guess that answers that.

Fuck it, I think. Maybe this is my next sign. If she wants to fire me, she can fire me. I'll just find another way to make ends meet. I have no idea what it will be, but I'll figure it out. What I won't do is beg.

Graciella enters and announces, "Your guest has arrived, ma'am."

"Thank you, Graciella. Be sure we're not disturbed, and close the door on your way out."

"Of course, ma'am." Graciella nods politely to me before silently leaving us alone.

Always dressed to the nines, today is no different. A stark white dress that hugs every one of Randi's curves leaves little to the imagination. Not only is Randi a hard-nosed businesswoman, she is also beautiful and perfectly proportioned. Barely over the five-foot mark, the four-inch spikes she has on her feet raise her to my height.

"Have a seat, Willow."

Oh shit. This is bad. Randi never calls me anything but my stage name. It causes less confusion that way and ensures no one slips up, accidentally using one of her employees' real names in front of a client.

"I'm fired, aren't I?" I ask after I slide into a plush crème chair.

Don't beg, Willow. Do. Not. Beg.

Perfectly plucked brows pinch together. "Why would you think that?"

"Because you...because you used my real name."

"Ah." Randi crosses her lean legs, gets comfortable in her high-backed chair, and assesses me for so long I begin to sweat.

"Look, Randi—"

She waves her hand, cutting me off. "Are you still interested in a regular?"

"What?" I immediately think of Paul Graber and shudder. "Look, I'm not sure what Paul Graber told you, but—"

"Forget about him. I have."

"But I thought you were disappointed?"

A brow lifts, pulling up one corner of her lip like the two are connected. "Let's just say I've been enlightened."

She knows. Of course she knows. "Okay." I'm confused about how she found out. There's no way it was from Graber himself, and Abraam didn't see anything that I'm aware of. But I won't press her further. She wouldn't tell me anyway.

"So, are you? Interested?"

I've been contemplating resigning, and now it appears she plans to give me my cash cow, filleted and cooked to a perfect medium rare. But do I still want that?

"I suppose that depends," I hedge.

Her eyes widen in surprise. "On?"

"What the requirements are."

The room falls silent as she studies me. Finally, clasping her hands, she leans forward and places her elbows on her desk. Softening her voice, she turns motherly, which she frequently does with me. I've often wondered how old Randi is. I have a feeling she's far older than her youthful face lets on. "He asked for you, specifically. Was adamant about it, in fact."

"Me? Who? And how does he know me?"

She doesn't answer my questions, instead saying, "This is a good opportunity for you, Willow, but it's your decision, of course."

Before the incident at the Four Seasons, I would have jumped at this. Wanted it desperately, even. But now I'm hesitant. Scared, if I'm truthful. I've often thought if I had a regular for a while, I could save enough to take a hiatus from this job, concentrating on my narration business, growing my clientele. Hell, if I was paid enough, maybe I'd never have to come back.

But a regular could turn out like Paul Graber, too. Wanting things that aren't on the menu. Expecting them.

"Is it a previous client of mine?"

"No."

"What if he turns out like Paul?"

"Then I'll cut his balls off myself," she retorts hotly. Yeah. She knows.

I roll the options around in my head. I know I don't have to commit, so it won't hurt to at least consider it. After a few deep breaths, I ask, "Do you have a dossier I can review?"

She smiles lightly. "I'll do you one better."

Punching a button on her office phone, she looks at me, eyes twinkling as Graciella's voice floats through the speaker. "Yes, ma'am."

"Show our other guest in now."

"Right away, ma'am."

Randi stands and makes her way toward a door opposite the one I entered. "I'll give you two some privacy. You can show yourself out when you're finished. Oh, and Willow...I hope you make the right decision. We both know this life is not for you."

I'm confused. Is she telling me to run or stay?

Then she's gone, and I'm left staring vacantly at the empty room. This is the first time in two years she's alluded to the fact I don't really belong here, and while she's right, that stings just a little. We've never discussed my circumstances. Why I'm here, why I need the money. Everyone has a story, I suppose. Young girls don't grow up thinking they'll sell themselves in any fashion to make a living.

But this whole thing is beyond bizarre. Meeting a client in private? At Randi's personal home? Who the hell is this guy that he has that much clout? And why would he ask for me specifically if we haven't met before? I begin to pace, wondering just what the *fuck* is going on and why I'm sticking around to find out.

I'm not left wondering for long. When the door opens and my mysterious suitor is revealed, I'm so stunned all I can breathe is...

"You?"

Shaw

Chapter Eight

AS LONG AS NOAH AND I have known one another and as close as we are, he's far from an open book. He holds some of life's secrets so close to the vest, he'll likely take them to his grave. So how he knows Ms. Randi Deveraux of La Dolce Vita is still a mystery he won't divulge.

When he told me his plan and showed me the picture of the woman who'd play my love interest for the next several months, I was immediately drawn to her, but it took me a few seconds to realize why.

It was *her*.

My spicy little Goldilocks.

The one I haven't heard from.

The one I haven't been able to get out of my fucking head for the past eight days.

The one my cock involuntarily gets hard for in the dark of night.

The glossy-colored print I stared at for long minutes was a complete contradiction to the fiery woman I'd met.

On paper, her exterior was flawless. Not one sculpted eyebrow out of place. Striking blue eyes rimmed with the right amount of shadow, liner, and mascara that made them alluring but not slutty. Pouty lips painted a deep shade of maroon, lined impeccably so the stain didn't seep, then glossed enough in the middle to draw your attention to their fullness. Hair curled into loose ribbons that fell over her shoulders and down her slim back.

But while the outside was practiced perfection, the inside screamed dead. Not damaged, not broken or bruised, but lifeless. This beautiful creature went through the motions. She moved through life without living. I don't know how I saw it, or why, but I know it wasn't a product of my overactive imagination. This woman's pain was rooted deep, but she put on an award-winning façade that told the outside world otherwise.

I saw the same thing when I stared into her fierce eyes under the cover of my sunglasses days ago, but I also saw something else. Smoking embers buried under piles of ash. God help me, but for some reason I want to be the man who stokes those smoldering cinders until they spark into a burning inferno, bringing her roaring back to life.

Standing before her now, I've no doubt I'm the igniter, the single match needed to wake her from the living dead.

"Summer, is it?" I close the door behind me and move to the couch, gesturing for her to sit.

She doesn't. She just blinks rapidly like she's seeing a ghost. That makes me smile for some reason.

I know the name she's using is fake. I hate it. Not the name, per se, but the fact that I don't know her real one. I told Ms. Deveraux my circumstances and my concern around using a fake name. The press will eventually find out, and it's best if we're up front in the beginning rather than them thinking we're hiding something once they start to dig. That would be disastrous. She agreed but told me the decision was up to Summer. If she agreed to my terms, I could plead my case. If not, then her anonymity was still protected.

"You don't look like a Summer," I say casually as I take a seat and cross my legs.

Although in a way she does. She's hot and sultry, and I've no doubt she's nice and moist in the place I'm dying to drive my cock. Jesus, she is absolutely mouthwatering. And she has the sexiest fucking voice I have ever heard. It's no wonder I can't stop thinking about her.

She crosses her arms and cocks a hip in irritation. "Is that so? What do I look like then?"

Mine.

Why that disturbing word pops into my head, I haven't a clue. *She is yours temporarily, though. If* she agrees.

"How is your neck by the way?"

That seems to catch her off guard because her cocky bravado falters. "Uh…fine. It's fine." She unconsciously reaches up to palm it. My fingers itch, wishing they were on her skin instead. I still remember the electricity that ran down my arm when I touched her before. It set my cock on fire, and it hasn't stopped burning since. "You're lucky, you know. I could be wearing a neck brace right now and be lawyered up."

"And you'd still be just as beautiful." I ignore the lawyer comment. I know it's just a dig. When she blushes and looks away, my grin gets wider, and I allow myself a few seconds to absorb her, head to toe. I find myself zeroing in on that tiny diamond stud in her nose, now catching the light. I first noticed it when she pounded on the window of my Rover calling me names. I generally find them childish, yet on her, I find myself incredibly turned on by it.

"Why don't you take a seat?" *On my lap would be preferable.*

Defiant eyes snap back to mine. "Hit and run anyone else lately?"

"Hit and run?" I chuckle. "I didn't hit and run you. I took accountability."

"Yeah. After I dumped car parts into your lap, it was pretty hard to deny it any longer."

Hell. This woman is full of restrained passion. She just needs someone to help her unleash it in a very controlled manner.

"Why haven't you called about your car? Change your mind on whose fault it was?" I'm goading her, but *Hot. Damn.* The sparks firing from her are overly addictive.

"Oh, it was your fault, all right," she snaps. "And I've been...busy."

"Yes, I can imagine you have a very full schedule." I sound more sarcastic than I intend, but the thought of her with other men makes me feel exactly the way I felt when I thought of Noah with her.

Her lips thin. She's madder than a hornet. I'm harder than a two by four.

"Why are you here, Drive By?"

Drive By? I laugh at her feisty spirit. God, I want to kiss her. Feel her tongue sparring eagerly with mine. See if she tastes of rage and raw energy.

"I was under the impression you were agreeable to meeting with me."

When Noah set this up, I insisted on three things.

One: it take place in Ms. Deveraux's private home with her alone. There's no way in hell I will be caught on film coming and going from her "business."

Two: I meet with Ms. Deveraux in advance and work through the contractual details to my satisfaction. Let's just say I now feel comfortable we have a mutual interest in keeping this arrangement buried deep.

And three: I be allowed to personally meet with "Summer" before she signs the contract. Surprisingly, that was the toughest piece to negotiate. Seems Ms. Deveraux is very protective of her, or maybe she's that way with all of her employees.

Everything I have done to secure her has deviated from Ms. Deveraux's normal course of business, but this situation is far from normal. It's reckless at worst. Precarious at best.

"How did you find me?"

Sheer, dumb luck.

"I'm very resourceful."

Her forehead creases. "This is a mistake."

She turns to leave, and I panic. True blistering panic sears through me at the thought she's about to walk through that door and I may never see her again. I don't know her real name. I don't know how to contact her, and if this meeting goes south, I know I won't get anything further about her from Randi Deveraux. If she walks out on me now, I highly doubt she'll give me the time of day when she finally does call Dane about her car.

I don't know why I care so damn much that I spend the next few months with her and only her. I just do.

"Wait," I plead.

She stops but doesn't turn. I have no idea what possesses me, but I close the distance between us until I'm a whisper away. Our body heat plays off each other, growing hotter by the second.

"You haven't even listened to my proposal," I say against her ear.

Her breath kicks up. Good. She's not unaffected by me, and that will play into my hand nicely.

"You can get someone else." Her reply is soft and lacks conviction.

Drawing her long hair off her shoulder, I let my finger feather across her bare flesh. It's soft and silky. She shivers. I suppress a moan. Fuck, I want her so much. It makes no sense.

"I don't want anyone else," I tell her truthfully, keeping my voice low.

"Why?"

I don't know why. I have no idea what it is about her that draws me in. I wish I did. I need to stop it. I should end this right now—look at a dozen other pictures and pick a woman whose very presence doesn't twist me into knots and make me have thoughts I've never had before. Thoughts that make me uncomfortable. It's unnerving.

But, fuck me. I can't. There is just something different about this woman, and I won't rest until I find out what it is.

"Have a seat. Just hear me out. Please," I tack on sincerely.

She stands motionless, and I wonder what her next move will be. My hands curl into fists as I restrain myself from throwing her over my shoulder and hauling her to my house. I think she could benefit greatly from a hard hand and a red ass. I have a feeling she might even enjoy it.

When she floats effortlessly to one of the velvet-covered chairs, I release a veiled breath. Picking up the contract from the edge of Ms. Deveraux's desk, I make myself comfortable across from her and place the paperwork on the table separating us. Her eyes drop to it, but she makes no move to pick it up.

"So, what's your proposal, Mr. Knowles?"

"Mr. Knowles?"

"That's your name, right? Dane Knowles. Wildemer & Company?"

Amused, I rest my elbows on my knees and grin at her. "No. Dane is my assistant. I told you to call him and he'd take care of the damage to your death box."

"Death box?" She sounds offended.

"Do you know what the safety rating is on that little tin can you drive?" When she opens her mouth to respond, I talk over her. "Five point seven out of ten. You're basically driving around in your own steel coffin."

I expect a hot retort or for her to leave in a huff. What I don't expect is a genuine, breathtaking smile that lights up her face like summer and makes my cock knock uncomfortably on my zipper in a futile attempt to reach her. My God, she's trying to kill me already.

"Are you a walking Kelly Blue Book of safety ratings, Mr....?"

"I have a vast array of useless Trivial Pursuit knowledge up here," I retort with a smirk, finger pointing to my temple. I'll never admit that I looked it up after our little accident. She could be seriously hurt in that ridiculous miniature box on wheels that somehow passes for a fucking car. Hell, had I hit her any harder, she would be in the hospital. "And I'm Shaw. Shaw Mercer."

"Shaw Mercer," she repeats slowly like she's tasting my name for the first time. Savoring every consonant and every vowel. Fuck. I sit back and cross one leg over the other to hide my rock-hard erection.

"Any relation to Preston Mercer?"

I nod, impressed that she tied me back to my father instead of referring to me as one of Seattle's most eligible bachelors. She's intelligent and up on politics. I like that. Immensely. If you ask three-fourths of the residents of Seattle, they wouldn't be able to tell you how many branches of government there are, something that's taught in middle school, let alone who the mayor of Seattle is.

"So why is the mayor's son…*here*?"

Her eyes are locked on mine, waiting on an answer.

When she swallows, I follow the delicate line of her neck down to the swell of her breasts that peek out from the light pink strapless flowing dress she's wearing like a fucking Greek goddess. One flick of my finger and I could find out the color of her areolas and the size of her nipples before I draw one into my mouth for a sample. My mouth waters at the thought.

The conversation that Ms. Deveraux and I had earlier about expectations sits hard in the pit of my stomach. On one hand, I was relieved to get confirmation she doesn't sell herself, only her "time," but now that I'm sitting here in front of her, I won't rest until she lets me explore every square inch of not only her perfect body, but her complex mind. I want to know her like no one else has.

When our gazes connect again I'm sure mine is full of unmistakable heat. Hers definitely is.

She clears her throat. The flush spreading across her collarbone is adorable. "I think you have the wrong idea about what it is I do."

"I don't," I state plainly.

"I don't sleep with my clients, Mr. Mercer."

Oh, but you will. We both know our ingredients are explosive.

"Women would pay to have sex with me, not the other way around."

She huffs a laugh as a wry look crosses her face. "Then what is it you need if not a good fuck?"

I chuckle, and when I lean forward, she straightens her spine. I love that even the simplest of movements I make in her direction affect her, just like she does to me. "Is that what I'll be missing with you? A good fuck?" I won't be missing a damn thing. She will be mine in every conceivable way. I know it and so does she.

"Not just good. Life altering," she banters smoothly.

Now it's my turn to smile slowly. What I wouldn't give to throw her up against the wall and show her just what a life-altering fuck really is. For what seems like forever we stare at each other in some sort of weird silent challenge where we're waiting to see what move the other will make.

Shaking myself out of her spell, I pick up the papers and hand them to her.

"What's this?"

"Your employment contract."

"All the paperwork is handled through Randi."

"I want a little extra insurance."

She quickly flips through the five-page document before lifting her eyes. "Nondisclosure agreement? This is sounding very fifty shades-ish. And just so you know, if I find any mention of hard limits or safe words, that's a deal breaker."

I can't help but laugh loudly.

"I'm not kidding," she says, her voice stern.

"Trust me, Goldilocks, if I could have gotten that past your warrior she-devil, I would have."

Her eyes narrow, but I see a little twitch at the corner of her mouth, so I forge ahead, making a mental note to invest in handcuffs and a flogger. Or six.

"The duration is for approximately the next four months. Ten hours a week, maybe more, maybe less, depending on my schedule. You may be required to travel, and you will be available at all times when I need you, day or night. You will attend social events, fundraisers, business dinners, and family functions. You will be photographed, and it's only fair to warn you, you will likely be hounded by the press, but I'll try to shield you as much as possible."

She regards me quietly. I wish I could tell what's spinning around in that pretty little head of hers. A corner of my mouth tips when she says, "Reelection is just around the corner."

Not a question, and I don't answer, but score another point for her.

For not the first time I wonder if this little plan of Noah's will backfire, taking us all down in a curl of hot flames. She figured out what I was doing within two minutes. Lianna would be a far safer, more believable choice. But there's also an undeniable, powerfully charged connection between us that will be hard for people to refute.

"And what is my role, specifically?"

Deciding I don't care if this entire thing blows up in my face because that means I won't get what I want—which is her—I stand and step around the table, holding out my hand.

When she tentatively sets hers in mine, I help her up and wrap one arm around her waist.

Pulling her close, I bask in the hitch of her breath. Cupping her cheek, I savor the baby-fine skin under the pad of my thumb. I take a deep breath, drinking in her delicately floral scent. She's intoxicating, and my head is already spinning.

"What are you doing?" she whispers, her small hands going to my chest.

Dipping my head, I trail my nose along her jaw, stopping so my lips brush her ear. "Making sure we have chemistry."

She mutters a curse under her breath I know I'm not meant to hear before stuttering, "Wh…why?"

Fuck, if she only knew the dirty things running through my head right now.

"Because, my wide-eyed little pretty, you're going to play my new love interest. My girlfriend. My *serious* girlfriend." I emphasize the word so she understands what she's getting herself into. I won't pay her to be in my bed, but that doesn't mean she won't end up there anyway.

"I...I haven't agreed to anything yet." Her breathlessness is testing me, and she's only about half an inch away from finding out exactly how much.

Walking into this meeting, I had already agreed to what I thought was a generous offer with her boss, madam, keeper, whatever she's called. But after the last fifteen minutes, I've decided I will pay whatever it takes to have her. To own her. I think I would give away my own soul.

Framing her face with both hands now, I lean in until my mouth is a hairsbreadth from hers. Her eyes fall to my lips. I feel her wariness, but I also feel her hunger. She parts her lips, and I watch with a deep ache in my groin as her tongue darts out to moisten them in anticipation of my kiss.

I restrain from slamming my mouth to hers, taking what I want. What she wants me to take, regardless of how she's trying to refute me.

"But you will. Everyone has a price, *Summer*. What's yours?"

Willow

Chapter Nine

"YOU DID WHAT?"

"I think I just sold myself for two hundred and fifty thousand dollars."

I stare at the dark TV in our dimly lit apartment, eyes drying out because my lids are stuck in the up position. Trying to figure out what the hell just happened and how I let it. One minute I was on my way out the door, the next I was sampling his name and signing a binding contract without so much as a superficial legal review.

Not that it could be put in front of any judge and hold up in a court of law, mind you. Randi's business isn't exactly aboveboard. The nondisclosure agreement could, I suppose, and that means I should keep my mouth firmly shut. Yet here I am, babbling like a running brook.

My gorgeous friend, Jo, sits regally in the chair to my right. Her long, leather-clad legs are crossed, one over the other. "This is good news," she announces.

"Yeah," I murmur in agreement. Good news. Then why do I feel I've woken a hibernating bear?

Sierra drops down beside me with a Blow Pop pinched

between her teeth. When she pulls it out, it makes a slurping noise that would generally send shivers up my spine, but right now I can't even care.

"I thought this was what you wanted? To find a regular so you could save up some money, focus on your *real* job, and get the hell out of what was supposed to be a temporary gap?"

"I did. I do. I just..."

"How long is the gig?" Jo asks.

"Four months, give or take, I guess."

"Does he have a deformity?" It's Sierra's turn to chime in.

"No."

Sierra holds her sucker out to me. I take it, sticking it in my mouth. It's cherry, my favorite. Then she rapid-fires question after question.

"Is he a dwarf?"

"No." I huff a laugh.

"Is he bald? I mean, that's kinda hot on the right guy, but I know it's not your cup of tea."

"No." He has the most beautiful inky locks. I want to weave my fingers through them as he takes my mouth like he has a right to.

"Is he married?" she asks tentatively.

When she waves her fingers, I return the sucker. "No. Definitely not." I don't know a lot about Shaw Mercer, but parading a girlfriend around when he's married during his father's reelection campaign is something I know he wouldn't do. No...he's using me for a specific purpose and he wouldn't admit it, but I know it has everything to do with that first Tuesday in November and the candidate that could "give Preston a run for his money."

"Is he hot coffee?"

My laughter echoes off the walls. Hot coffee is our code word for a smoking hot stranger you would fuck in the back room without so much as exchanging names.

Sierra sits up and leans my way. "Oh my God. I knew it! He's a steaming cup of hot fucking coffee, isn't he? That's the problem. You *like* him."

She doesn't know how close to the truth she is. He's arrogant, overconfident, even a little condescending, and it should turn me off, but, God…it so *doesn't.*

"Does your hot coffee have a small dick?"

"Jesus, Sierra. How would I know?"

Lies.

I have a pretty damn good idea that the bulge I felt pressing hard into my lower belly when I stared into the world's most enthralling ocean-blue pools I have ever seen is more than enough to keep me—I mean, a *woman*—satisfied.

"Girl, you're holding back on us now. He's hot, he's rich, and he's got a big dick." Relaxing against the cushions, she throws her feet up on the coffee table and pops the sucker back in her mouth, mumbling around the candy, "Sounds like the perfect trifecta to me."

I give Sierra a look, but I can't deny he is. Seemingly perfect.

"He's…" I trail off, not knowing exactly how to explain Shaw Mercer.

He's what?

Gorgeous? Check.

Commanding? Check.

Larger than life? Double check.

Possesses mind-altering sex appeal? God, if I could fit a dozen checks in this box, I would.

But none of these things are what I'm truly worried about.

I've never met a man who seems to see into the real me. All the way into the blackest of the black. It's impossible. I'm too shrouded. Impenetrable. A steel fortress. Not even the man I was engaged to could pierce that dark place, and he tried for three years. But I also can't deny that's what I felt when I gazed up his six-two frame into eyes that dove right into my very center. I've been home for hours, yet I still feel him lodged there, like an irritating splinter.

"He's what? Dreamy?" She singsongs as her face turns wistful. Clasping her hands together, she sets her chin on them and rocks back and forth.

"Shut it."

She pushes me when I smack her arm, and we giggle when our hands turn into a flurry of slaps until my skin smarts.

After I catch my breath, I ease back and softly confess, "He's…" *Dangerous*. "Drive By."

That sucker comes out again with a pop. "The bastard who rammed into you last week?" she asks with a high-pitched voice.

I chuckle, still not believing it myself. How can this be a coincidence? "One and the same."

She turns her head my way at the same time I turn mine toward her. "So, letting hot coffee scald your insides once or twice is off the table then, huh?"

"Oh my God," I screech. I give her a good shove on the shoulder. "I don't sleep with my clients. You know that."

She laughs, falling against the arm of the couch. "You know what they say about rules."

I don't have sex with clients. It's my one hard-and-fast rule. Not only is mixing business with pleasure a bad idea, but men who need to pay for the company of a woman in any fashion are not the type of guys I want to end the night in bed with.

Except Shaw. For the first time ever, I am truly tempted to break my own self-imposed policy.

I dare a glance at Jo, who is unusually quiet. She seems indifferent to our conversation. I know otherwise. She sees *it*. The lies I'm trying to tell myself already. And like a true friend, she calls me out on them.

"Men like him use this service for a reason." Jo's raised, painted-on eyebrows punctuate what I already know to be true.

"I know that."

"And it's not to find their next wife."

I know that, too. And that's not what I want from Shaw

Mercer, anyway. Why, then, does that reminder feel like a blow that will sting for a while?

"Got it," I croak.

One Jimmy Choo-covered foot swings back and forth as her French-tipped nails start tapping in a rhythmic pattern against the leather of her chair. "Do you, Low?"

I blink a couple of times so I can stall. I need to steady my voice so I sound believable. "Of course I do. This is a job. Another act. Nothing more."

She regards me for so long, I know I'm busted. "There aren't many women who can do what I do day in and day out without getting attached. You're not one of them."

Jo is not a party favor. She's the real deal. Commanding over a grand an hour, she is the most highly sought-after escort at La Dolce Vita. She's worldly, cultured, and no nonsense. She also has a deeper, thicker, blacker hole than even I do. And while sometimes I wish I could crack myself open, displaying my scarred insides to the right person, Jo has managed to shut that side of herself off completely.

"I know that, Jo."

"Then you keep it business like you always do. Get in, get out, get a nice fat bank account, and quit this fucking job," Sierra offers. Peeking at Jo she adds, "No offense."

"None taken." She means it. She doesn't give a rip what people think about how she's chosen to make a living.

Sierra clasps my hand in hers and squeezes. "Just business, right?"

Yeah. Just business.

Except when Shaw's lips brushed against mine as he held my face between his smooth hands, it didn't feel like *just business.* My entire body jolted. He's sex incarnate. Irresistible. Cockily, he knows it. Had he stripped me and taken me right in Randi's office, I would have let him. I almost fucking *asked* him to but managed to swallow the words.

I want the enigmatic Shaw Mercer in a way I've not wanted another man, and that scares the ever-living shit out of me.

This uncomfortable chemistry between us will take me down. I see my demise, my heartbreak before it even starts. The end before the beginning.

I don't let people close for a very good reason, and he has managed to bore his way under my skin faster in thirty minutes than anyone has before.

God, I should never have agreed to this. If I'd given myself twenty-four hours to think about it, instead of signing on the spot when he agreed to pay an additional hundred thousand dollar bonus if he left with an executed contract, I would have come to that conclusion.

If I were smart, I would call Randi now. Tell her I changed my mind. She may not like it but she'd go to bat for me. She'd recommend someone else, and I'd never have to speak to him again.

One phone call and this is all over.

I eye the cell on the end table next to me but don't reach for it, because let's face it—money talks and I need the money. Two hundred fifty thousand dollars is a ridiculous sum for pretending to be someone else. For doing what I do best. I haven't netted a quarter of that in the entire two years I've been doing this, and I would be a fool to turn it down when that's the entire reason I took this job in the first place.

Four months of my life is a small price to pay to get out from under this financial stress plaguing me. If Shaw wants to pay me a stupid amount of money to play his girlfriend, I will take it and walk away with a clean conscience when our contract ends.

But Jo is right. I can't lie to myself either because *that* will get me in over my head faster than the rising tide. I may be attracted to him, but no doubt Shaw Mercer is the kind of man who puts his wants and needs above everyone else's, and I have lived my whole life being an afterthought, starring in a supporting role.

I may do that for my job, but that's intentional. I won't be willingly put in that position ever again.

I can do this. On my terms. My way. Without handing over anything of me in the process. I know I can. *It's just another job.*

I lock eyes with Jo and say out loud, for me more than her, "I can do this," at the same I try ignoring how that splinter he left behind is already burning like a mother.

Willow

Chapter Ten

AFTER BEING BUZZED THROUGH THE security gate, I drive slowly until Shaw's house comes into view. I park, shut off my car, and stare at the monstrosity of a home in front of me: a quiet, secluded, three-story beauty overlooking Yarrow Bay. It's majestic, commanding, larger than life.

Just like the man inside.

Before I left Randi's, I agreed to meet Shaw at his home so we could talk through the details of our arrangement. He thought it best to spend some time together privately before our first public outing so we can get our stories straight as to where we met and how long we've known each other. All things that normal couples would know off the top of their heads when quizzed. While I was nervous about spending any time alone with him, I had to agree it makes sense.

Last night I lay awake for hours thinking this whole situation through, acknowledging these feelings he's stirred inside me. I need to face them and deal with them instead of pretending they don't exist.

Spending ten hours or more a week for months on end without ending up in his bed will be no easy feat. But Shaw is paying me to be his girlfriend, which says a lot about him, actually. He can't—or won't—commit, and apparently, he has no one in his past willing to help him out.

This arrangement is only temporary, and I'd do well to remember that. If I fall into bed with Shaw, I can easily see myself falling for more than just his sexy body. I can't allow that to happen.

Think of the endgame, Willow. Think of the endgame.

"You can do this. Think of your mother," I mumble to myself.

Taking a fortifying breath, I exit my car and make my way up the walk to Shaw's front door. I ring the doorbell and wait. The butterflies in my belly stir when I hear feet padding across the floor. Then they all lodge in my throat when he opens the door and I'm left staring into his captivating blue eyes.

Holy mother of all saints, he is so beautiful.

I am in trouble.

Big-ass trouble.

"I thought maybe you were going to change your mind." His low voice rumbles through my blood, shaking every cell awake. Traitors. All of them.

Cocking my head, I try to act like I'm not a mass of trembling nerves. "Why would you think that?"

"Because you've been sitting in your car for the last ten minutes." He cocks a brow. His smugness digs under my skin.

"Well, I had something to take care of first."

A smile curls a corner of his mouth. He knows I'm lying.

You'd better pull on your big girl panties and stop acting like a bumbling idiot.

"You going to let me come in, Drive By, or are we going to have this conversation on the front step? I can do either."

Much better.

He grins and steps aside, gallantly waving me inside. "By all means, come in."

"Thank you," I mutter as I pass him, trying to ignore the

way my body flares to life being in such close proximity to his, or the way the air tingles with the electric currents arcing between us. I also try not to notice how damn sensual his bare feet are. They're feet. Just feet. *Sexy* feet.

Shit.

I slip off my shoes, and he quietly leads us through the entryway, each step quiet against the stunning red oak flooring. It must be a bitch to keep clean, but it looks spotless, as does everything else.

Most times a house this big and excessive is cold and hollow. Lonely. An outer façade unhappy people use to ineffectively fill a hole deep in their soul. Typical houses like this scream wealth and gluttony and pretension, generally making me want to roll my eyes. But Shaw's house is different.

Dressed in deep reds and various hues of browns, it feels warm and homey and safe. It's perfection, really. Like him. Like an idiot, I gaze around in complete awe.

The floor plan is open but surprisingly inviting. The main living area runs effortlessly into the dining room, which flows into a clearly gourmet kitchen. Ebony cabinets appear to be custom made. Appliances are top of the line. A twelve-foot island takes up the center space, covered in rich mocha- and sand-swirled granite. The south side of the house is made of solid glass with a stunning view of the bay.

When my attention falls to the biggest, thickest, creamiest area rug I have ever seen in a living room, I deduce he must not have any pets. The thought of sinking my toes into its softness excites me. I force thoughts of rolling around naked on it with Shaw far, far away, but damn, that takes tremendous effort.

In the ninety seconds I've been here, I know so much more about him. He's clean. Meticulous. Simple and understated. He takes pride in his house but doesn't feel the need to shove his wealth in your face. That makes me like him even more, dammit.

I realize too late he's watching me closely to gauge my reaction. He seems to do that a lot. He's quiet and thoughtful, thinking through exactly what he wants to say before he says it. As if he wants to formulate his words, so he uses the least amount of them possible while still getting his point across.

"What's the verdict?" he asks quietly.

When I sense he really wants to know what I think of his home, I answer honestly. "It's beautiful. You're quite the decorator."

Looking a little embarrassed, he replies, "My sister's doing, I'm afraid. She's an interior designer."

"Ah." I smile, feeling more at ease with every passing second. "Well, you can tell her she did a very good job."

His head bobs slightly. "You can tell her yourself when you meet her."

And just like that, the butterflies are back.

Fooling the general public that we're together won't be that hard. His family, however…that's a deception I knew was part of the deal but one I'm not very comfortable with. It makes me wonder how much they know.

"Oh. Uh, sure."

We stand in awkward silence for a few heartbeats before Shaw clears his throat. "Would you care for a drink?"

I told myself on the way over here I was not having alcohol. Not so much as a drop. It would lower my inhibitions, making me more vulnerable to Shaw's not-so-subtle seduction tactics, yet as I stand here taking in his sexier-than-shit powerhouse thighs and his lean torso, draped in a fitted light green polo, there's only one right answer.

"Sure."

His smile is breathtaking. "What's your poison, Goldilocks?"

You, apparently.

"Uh, I'm not picky. Whatever you have is fine."

"Beer okay?"

I nod.

"Great. Have a seat in the living room. I'll be right back."

"Okay."

I wander into the large, softly lit space, the carpet feeling as soft as I thought it would, and weigh my options. Chair, couch, or loveseat? Another clear choice.

A moment later I'm seated in the overstuffed coffee-colored leather armchair. It seems worn, a piece that gets used frequently. I imagine Shaw here in the evenings while he's working on his laptop or watching the news. The thought that I'm sitting in the same spot he does every night gives me tingles.

"Would you like a frosted glass?" he calls from the kitchen.

"That would be great, thanks."

A couple minutes later, my thoughts are confirmed when he enters the room and his steps falter. I start to rise. "I'm sorry, am I sitting in your chair?"

"No, no. I mean, yes, but...it's okay. Stay."

Nodding for me to resume my seat, I do. He sets my mug on the glass stand beside me. I immediately grab it, taking a drink for something to do. When my gaze flits to his, he's studying me again. This time his expression is strange.

"What?" I chuckle nervously. "Do I have foam on my lip?" I reach up and trail my fingers across my mouth, feeling nothing.

His smile is soft and sincere and sweet. I feel melty. "You look good there."

"Where?" I ask stupidly. He certainly can't mean...

"In my chair. I like it." He adds the last part as an afterthought, almost as if he didn't mean to say it out loud and swear to God, my toes curl as hot desire unfurls inside me at an alarmingly fast pace.

How can six little bland words make me want to stand, strip, and straddle him? With no effort at all, he's effectively made me forget every reason I have for not getting his impressively large cock inside me as soon as humanly possible.

"So, ah...," I start, irritated at the tiny quiver in my voice, "when does this little charade officially start?"

"Three days ago." I cringe at the slight snap I hear.

It's been three days since our meeting. Three days since I

signed the next four months of my life over to him. Tonight was the first time Shaw had a free evening to get together.

I've spent three days wondering what we're doing, when we're doing it, and why. I also realized I have no idea who else is in on this little scam. I'm fine with pretending we've fallen hopelessly in love if that's what he wants, but I don't want to act like an idiot in front of someone who knows we are nothing more than an expensive show.

"Who knows about this arrangement besides Randi?" I ask, resting my glass on my thigh. The cold quickly seeps through my dress.

Shaw sat on the loveseat, which is the closest piece of furniture to me. He now shifts and crosses one leg over the other, which puts his foot within inches of me. Whether by accident or purpose, both of our gazes drop when it brushes against my bare leg. I let my eyes close but suppress a shudder at the bolt of need that zaps straight up between my thighs.

His need is much more evident, unmistakable. I force my eyes to slide back up his body only to catch him staring at my mouth. I feel myself weakening everywhere.

Oh God, stop. Get this under control or you'll end up in his bed tonight.

"Shaw." My squeaky voice seems to jolt him out of his trance, but his lids are heavy, his eyes still molten.

"What?" he asks absently, still staring at my lips. I can't help but lick them and I think I may hear him moan.

I've changed my mind. It isn't going to be hard to stay out of his bed.

It will be impossible.

"I said, does anyone else know about this...arrangement?"

Heated blue eyes flooded with raw desire lift to mine, boring into me. Digging into the depths of me. I want to look away, but the flames I see dancing there hypnotize me. They feast on the oxygen in the room, making it thin as I wait for him to say something. Anything that will break this vortex we're swirling in.

"Yes," he eventually replies in a low, husky voice. I'm not even sure he knows what he's answering at this point.

"Who?" I ask when he goes silent again. "Who knows?"

He draws in a deep breath and shakes his head slightly. The thrall we were in snaps, thank you, baby Jesus. Much longer and my clothes would have been in a pile on the floor. "My business partner."

I spent hours that first night we made our arrangement doing research on Shaw Mercer and found out that he and Noah Wilder own Wildemer & Company, a management consulting firm. It's been wildly successful under the helm of the great, great grandchildren of the original founders. In the past five years, they've almost doubled the value of an already-lucrative business.

I also found that he and Noah are considered quite the fodder for gossip and have both been spotted with multiple women over the years. Noah doesn't seem to be with the same girl twice, but up until recently, Shaw was photographed several times with the same woman I saw shooting daggers my way the night of the political fundraiser.

"Would that be Noah Wilder?" I ask. *My guardian angel.*

He cocks his head along with that lip. Why is his subtle swagger so damn sexy? "I see you've been busy."

I shrug. I want to ask him how someone so sophisticated and connected ended up in Randi's office buying me but I don't. "So, no one in your family knows?"

He brings his drink to his lips. My inner walls tighten when he drags his tongue against his bottom lip to the corner of his mouth, catching a stray drop of beer. I swear he did that on purpose. "About the fact that I'm *paying* you to be my girlfriend?" He laughs sardonically. "No. And it will stay that way. I'd never live it down, and my mother would be very disappointed in me."

A wave of shame washes through me. I don't understand it, and I certainly don't like it. If anyone should feel guilty here, it's Shaw, not me.

"I wasn't planning to say anything," I answer defensively. "I just needed to understand who knows what, that's all. I don't want to look like a fool."

His nod is clipped, close to an apology, even. Then he says, "Tell me about yourself, Summer."

I swallow hard, knowing this is exactly why I came but anxious nonetheless. I need to reveal just enough about myself to appease him and others while safeguarding the true me.

"Well, I'm twenty-six. Never been married. I live with my best friend, Sierra. No pets. I'm not against them—I just don't have time to take care of one. Blue is my favorite color. I run an eight-minute mile, and I'm a pretty mean kickboxer. I love slasher movies, chocolate ice cream, dancing, and fall. I hate plaid, snakes, pizza, and Sunday drivers."

His light laugh draws a smile from me until his words follow. "Sounds like a well-practiced bullet list of superficial bullshit."

I shrug and smirk, annoyance running along my skin. "It may be perfunctory, but it's not bullshit if it's true. We don't need insight into each other's hopes and dreams to pull this off. Just the basics."

The noise he makes in the back of his throat sounds like he doesn't agree, but he doesn't argue.

"Siblings? Parents?"

I school my features, knowing this question would be asked. It hurts like hell anyway. And this is one thing I will be keeping to myself. The pain in my soul does not belong to a man I don't plan to see again after four months. "Just me and my momma."

He looks as though he wants to ask more but lets it drop.

"Do you do anything for a living outside of...*this*?"

Derision. I heard it. My face flushes in embarrassment, but I let the unwelcome emotion fall away. He does not get to judge me. "I have my reasons for what I do, and I won't let you or anyone else make me feel criminal for them."

"What are they?" he asks tartly. He almost seems angry at

my choice of profession, only I wouldn't be sitting here otherwise, helping his ass out of some sort of bind, so how fucking mad should he be?

"That's insight into me you don't need," I reply just as sourly. "But to answer your original question, I do have another job. I narrate audiobooks."

One eyebrow lifts. "Interesting. I listen to a few audiobooks myself occasionally."

Doubtful they're the ones I narrate.

When he decides I'm not going to elaborate, he restarts his twenty questions.

"You're not currently dating anyone, correct?"

"Correct."

"Any exes I need to worry about coming out of the woodwork ready to reclaim you? Because if they're there, it's best to find out now so we can be prepared."

My belly clenches hard at that question. I've dated a few times, of course, but I haven't had a serious relationship since I foolishly left the man I loved behind. So no, there is absolutely no one waiting in the wings to reclaim me.

"No."

"You sure? I sense hesitation."

"No hesitation. Nobody has occupied that space for some time. What about you?" I try to change subjects, tired of talking about myself. It's starting to get too personal. "Do you have any scorned women lurking about that may try to gouge my eyes out?"

His lips turn up wryly. "I'm thirty-six. I have skeletons."

I wonder if he's talking about the brunette beauty, Voodoo Eyes. Another question I want to ask but decide not to. If I don't want him to pry, I can't either. "Will these skeletons throw a bone into your plans?"

His loud barked laugh has me giggling. "Very clever. I don't believe any bones will be thrown, no. Any women I've been with remain firmly buried in the past."

My laughter shudders to a stop as I realize I'll join that

lengthy, scandalous list all too soon. "Hence why I'm here."

"Touché." He tips his glass in my direction before finishing his beer. "Want another?" He looks to my nearly empty glass, and I shake my head. My nerves have calmed, so one is enough.

We spend the next couple of hours making small talk. He tells me about his parents and three siblings. He talks a little about his father's reelection but never admits that's the ruse he hired me for, although I'm becoming more convinced it is. I learn about his love of the water and his dislike for his brother-in-law. I also learn he grew up in Seattle and his great, great grandfather and uncle founded Mercer Island, where his parents still make their home.

Like me, he keeps his facts superficial. When I probe into something he doesn't want to discuss, he changes the subject. But there were two things he couldn't hide: his passion for his company and his intense love for his family. He talked about his niece, Cora, as if she were royalty. Both traits were more endearing than I wanted to admit.

I look at the clock and am surprised to see it's close to nine. I've been here for almost three hours. I've been so at ease, so engrossed in our conversation, it seems like fifteen minutes. *Oh no.* Red flags are popping up like Whack-A-Moles.

"I should go." I untuck my feet, brush down my sundress, and make to stand when he sets his palm on my arm. My heart immediately beats in my throat as my gaze flicks between his intense stare and the place our bodies now spark.

"There was something else I wanted to talk to you about tonight before you leave." When he brings his fresh beer up to his lips, I force myself not to watch his throat work as he swallows.

"Okay," I reply nervously. The hops sitting in my stomach from hours ago churns wildly.

He leans forward, setting his drink on the coffee table before clasping his hands and pinning me with his stare. He's preparing for a fight. I can feel it. "We need to use your real name."

"What?" I squeal. "No. No, that wasn't part of the deal."

"I've been giving it a lot of thought, and I think it's best to be as honest as we can, given the circumstances. The less we have to lie about, the more the press will leave us alone. If they can't find anything about you, *Summer*," he emphasizes my fake name, "they won't rest until they do, and neither of us will like the fallout if they uncover your real profession."

He's right. Of course he's right. And I kick myself that I never thought of this as I was signing my life away for months. He'd mentioned the media, but all I saw were dollar signs.

Still, putting my real name out there in association with Shaw means I'll never be able to come back to La Dolce Vita even if I want to—which I don't—because I will be compromised. Forever associated with Shaw Mercer, my true identity known to the public. I'm starting to understand the gravity of the mistake I've made, money or not.

"Randi will never agree," I state sharply.

"She already has. It puts all of us at less risk that way. Summer ties you back to her. Your real name doesn't."

Christ on a crutch. I'm not sure what I feel most in that moment. Betrayal or panic. Randi knew exactly what she was doing, and the fact that she wasn't completely honest with me up front is devastating, after everything I've done for her. Maybe she was madder at me than she let on.

But panic is quickly snuffing out devastation.

There's a far bigger reason I don't want him knowing my real name. This is just a job, another role, another act. A paycheck, nothing more. Using a stage name not only protects my true identity but it helps keep me grounded firmly in reality. I remember to keep my distance, keep the situation fully in perspective lest I ever forget what it is I'm doing and who I'm doing it for.

Without "Summer," I become vulnerable. I become *me*. This entire charade becomes all too real. The veil of my character is worn, but effective. If I lose that shield, I'm completely defenseless to the drag of his gravitational pull. I've already shown him how he weakens me. I can't let him see any more.

No. I can't hear him whisper Willow in my ear or against my lips. If he uses my real name for the next four months, I will lose myself to him. I will start to believe this insane attraction between us is something that can turn into a future. I can't let the stark reality of this situation morph into girlish fantasy.

No, no, no.

Stall for time. Find another way.

"I need to talk to Randi myself."

His mouth turns down slightly. "Of course. But you know this is the right decision."

It may be. Probably even is, but my mind screams no. "I really need to go."

He looks disappointed but stands when I do. I flinch slightly when he places his hand at the small of my back, feeling it everywhere. Without a word, he walks me to the front door. When I slip into the ballet flats I left on the tile floor, I feel his eyes on me, assessing me.

Reaching for the doorknob, I say, "Goodnight," over my shoulder, petrified to turn around for fear I'll buckle under the power his stare.

Only I don't have a chance to turn it before my back is pressed between the cold beveled glass and his taut body. He palms my face, lifting my chin with his thumbs so I have no choice but to meet his lust-filled gaze.

"Shaw, what are you doing?" I don't recognize my own voice, choked with rising feelings I refuse to acknowledge. His bulk thoroughly surrounds my small frame. It terrifies me that it feels so right. I can hardly think, let alone breathe.

"You can't flinch every time I touch you." Dark eyes run wildly over my face. He's trying to work out my contradicting reactions. It's clear I want him, but he's right. Every time he touches me, it sends a bolt of energy through me. It's electrifying and scary as fuck. I've never felt anything like it before.

"I…I'm not. I don't."

"Yes, you do. If we're going to make this believable, you need to sink into my touch. Crave it with everything in you, not shy away from it."

Oh, fuck. I already do crave it. Too much.

I lick my lips, an automatic nervous reaction. When he runs a thumb over my now moist bottom one, my blood buzzes. I feel drunk on the pure lust swirling around us.

"You are so goddamn beautiful." Low, needy words feather over my face, causing my willpower to backslide, like I'm caught in the middle of a blinding avalanche. "When was the last time you were good and kissed? Painstakingly, completely branded by a man so thoroughly you could still feel the press of his lips and the coiling of his tongue with yours when you went to bed that night?"

"Stop." My demand is a lie on a puff of air.

"There are so many sinful things running through my head right now. So fucking many. But right now, I'm going to settle for giving you a kiss you'll feel right between those clenched thighs of yours."

Oh God.

I try to shake my head, but it's firmly planted between two strong hands. His deep pools simmer with delight as he lowers his face to less than an inch from mine.

"This is part of the dance, Goldilocks."

"Stop calling me that." My reprimand comes out breathy instead of irate as I'd wanted.

"Every couple has pet names for each other. We're a couple now."

"On paper only."

Hot breaths wash over the column of my neck when his mouth travels to my ear. "It's more than just paper, sweetheart. My hands will be on you. Touching you, stroking you, holding you. My lips will graze your ear, your neck, your shoulder, your mouth. *Especially* your mouth. You need to get used to it, because I'll be doing it. A. Lot."

When the softness of his mouth presses to that sensitive indent beneath my ear, I moan, "Shaw."

"Fuck, I love the breathless way you say my name."

"We—God, we can't do this." But my eyes betray me. They're already closed in sweet anticipation as he continues to lightly nibble. Whiskers scratch. Chills erupt. Desire is a kaleidoscope spinning inside me.

"This is exactly what we need to do. We can't have our first kiss in public. It needs to be well practiced before then, kind of like the catalogue of character traits you recited flawlessly earlier."

Before I can call him an ass or voice another protest, he angles my head and melts me with a raspy, "I can't stop thinking about how you'll taste."

Then his mouth is on me, driving all objections away.

His lips are soft and warm but also brim with enough power to let me know he's in charge every second he touches me. It's heady. I like it too much.

Shaw's presence is commanding, absolute. A force to be reckoned with. So, I expect him to claim, own, invade. But he doesn't. He takes his time, imprinting me instead. Slowly branding me as promised, drawing my top lip in between his before doing the same to the bottom.

He repeats the painstakingly slow process over and over, sucking and nipping, applying just the right amount of pressure. It's drugging, sweet, and oh so freaking good. I can't remember ever being kissed like this. By the time I feel the first touch of his tongue on me, demanding entry, I want it so damn bad my lips part automatically, welcoming him inside.

His strokes are light at first, like he's learning me, treasuring me. But they quickly turn deep, urgent. Demanding. I gasp when he bites my lip hard enough to sting before he returns to gorge on me. Groaning, he shifts his weight, pressing his stiff shaft farther into my belly. I throb everywhere.

"Oh God," I whisper. A hot trail blazes along my jaw, down my throat, everywhere his teeth nip and his tongue soothes.

"Jesus, fuck. I want you." His hunger crashes into me as hard as rogue waves, flooding me with voracious need. I almost drown, letting him take me under with him.

"We can't," I choke. My body screams at me, *Why not? Let him take you right here. Right now. It's inevitable anyway.*

"You want me. I can smell it."

So can I. I don't even pretend to deny it.

"It doesn't matter. I'm not going to sleep with you," I pant.

His hands have now joined the party. Their slow climb up my torso attempts to convince me otherwise. My breasts are heavy and aching.

"Oh, Goldilocks, there won't be any sleeping, only fucking. Lots and lots of fucking," he growls as he makes his way to the other side of my neck. I tilt my head.

It's tempting. *He's* tempting. Lots and lots of *only fucking* sounds so incredibly tempting.

"Shaw. Please, stop."

He stills, this time sensing my inner turmoil, but his muscles remain taut, ready to resume where we left off if I just say the word. *Say the word; say the fucking word, bitch,* my girly parts snarl. But I can't. I won't come back from this.

Not pushing me, Shaw gently leans his forehead to mine. We let our breathing calm and appetites settle.

In a gravelly voice, he tells me, "You feel this thing between us just as much as I do. It's not going away. It's going to spread and thicken until it consumes us both, burning so fucking hot and strong it will never be extinguished."

Yes. That's precisely what I'm worried about.

"I need to go," I whisper hoarsely. Before I can't.

Knowing he won't change my mind, he sighs and takes a half step back. I think he'll just let me slip out the door, angry that he couldn't get me naked tonight, but he surprises me by gently cupping my chin and, eyes locked with mine, presses a close-mouthed kiss to my Shaw-swollen lips.

"Goodnight, my beautiful girlfriend." His eyes sparkle.

That stupid label zings through me like a random lightning

bolt. I feel hot and needy and angry that I liked it. His red, sexy, turned-up lips beg me to return to them. "Goodnight," I say before I do.

"Drive carefully." Lust still thickens the voice that follows me all the way to my car. Once I get inside and pull away, I see him watching me from the porch, hands stuffed into his pockets. As he gets smaller and smaller in my rearview mirror, I wonder why the thought of him knowing my real name doesn't scare me half as much as it did just fifteen minutes ago and why I'm now dying to hear how it will sound on *his* breathless lips.

I go to bed that night knowing he accomplished his goal. I unquestionably felt his kiss everywhere, and I swear I still feel his lips pressing to mine as I let sleep claim me.

Shaw

Chapter Eleven

HER SCENT.

Her flavor.

Her curves.

The softness of her lips.

The texture of her skin.

I can't get them out of my head. It's bordering on obsession, this unquenched thirst I have for her. It's built every goddamned day for nearly the past two weeks, ever since I got distracted by Lianna's pathetically sad plea to reconcile and rammed into the back of her.

Ah fuck, I want to ram into the back of her again, but in a much more pleasurable manner this time. For both of us. I want her so fucking bad, my balls have been drawn perpetually tight, and I can't relieve the ache no matter how many times I release the pressure. All I have to do is think of her honeyed skin or her breathy moans and I'm right back where I started. In agony.

She wants me, that much is clear. She's also drawn a line in the sand, which she doesn't want to cross. I understand her reluctance in a weird sort of way. This is a temporary arrangement. A business deal. And we all know you don't fuck (literally) your business partners unless you want to end up fucked over (again, literally) later on down the line.

I don't have a future to offer her. I know this. It's by design, of course, but the reasons remain irrelevant. The only thing available on my menu is pleasure. Immense, intense, unimaginable fucking pleasure.

As shitty of me as it is, I need to find some way to convince her to let down her guard and let me inside, or I will spend four months in absolute misery. Not only did I require her to be celibate during the next long weeks, I required it of myself. Can't very well pull off having a serious girlfriend if I'm caught walking out of a hotel room at two in the morning with a one-night stand. A big part of me is now wishing I'd taken Gina up on her offer last week so I could have at least taken this edge off.

Looking up from my drink, I see the hostess walking my way. It's not until she steps aside and waves her hand that I see *Summer.* My dick twitches.

She is absolutely stunning in her simple black cocktail dress that dips low enough to show ample cleavage without being trashy. She smiles when she sees me, entirely oblivious to the eyes of every man in this room on her right now, which makes her that much more alluring.

I want to know who this woman really is. Not just her name, but how she thinks, what she loves, her sad past.

That screams future, Shaw. Get a goddamn grip.

"You look edible," I whisper, grazing my lips against her cheek.

"Thank you, Drive By." She doesn't flinch when I snake my arm around her waist and pull her close, my mouth purposely lingering against her warm flesh for another couple beats.

Yes, motherfuckers, I'm staking my claim, even if it is only temporary.

I reluctantly loosen my hold and pull out a chair to my right, getting her settled before taking my own seat again.

Tonight is our first official public outing since she was at my home five days ago. Just a simple dinner. But I've made sure it's a well-known, exclusive haunt not too far from city hall.

Our waitress is Johnny-on-the-spot and has her drink order before I can even ask her how her week has been, which surprisingly I really want the answer to.

"How was your week, Goldilocks?" I quirk my lips when her nose crinkles.

"Are you always going to call me that?"

"What?" I feign, holding my full smile in check. I have no idea why I derive so much enjoyment from getting under her skin because that is not who I am at all. That's more Noah's shtick. But I do. Enormously. She is so damn easy to rile, and I love to watch her fire burn. Every poke I make loosens those petrified ashes a bit more so I can fully expose the sleeping volcano underneath.

"You know what. *Goldilocks*?" She looks so fucking cute with her brows raised and an *I'm waiting* look on her face. I want to laugh.

"I already told you, *Goldilocks*, it's my pet name. So, yes, I do plan on calling you that."

"It's stupid," she laments quietly, breaking eye contact as she places the black cloth napkin on her lap and picks up her menu. I don't believe she really thinks that, though I'm not about to argue. I grew up with three women. I learned to pick my battles.

"Maybe if you'd give me your real name, I would use it less."

At that, her brilliant blue eyes snap back to me.

"Did you talk to Ms. Deveraux?" I ask pointedly, holding her glower.

"Yes," she replies after a brief hesitation.

"And?"

"And, what?" She lowers the menu, giving me all her attention.

"And, what did you decide?"

Biting her lip she looks away, breathing deeply. The

waitress interrupts with her glass of red wine but is quickly gone when my stare conveys we need more time. After she takes a sip, her attention returns to me.

"A name is power."

I'm taken aback, confused. "Power? A name is just a name, Goldilocks."

"No." She shakes her head adamantly. "No, it's more than that, Shaw. It's giving up control. It's sharing a piece of yourself that's only yours to give away. It's a connection that ties humans together. It's intimate, even. You curse a name on a roar or whisper it on a breath. You cry it out of unimaginable agony or sheer ecstasy. You use my name and the dynamics between us will shift. This"—she waves her finger back and forth—"becomes personal instead of professional."

She is an amazing creature. Each enlightening word drew me in further. My beautiful sprite holds a chasm of hurt inside that's so full it practically bleeds from her pores, so she tightly clutches the reins of every shred of control she can, no matter how small.

And while her little theory has some merit and may be quite necessary in her job, the problem with applying it to us is that in the short time we've known each other, we've rocketed well past arm's length. This already *is* personal. I know it. She knows it. She just doesn't want to acknowledge it, and I'm not sure why.

Leaning close, I palm her cheek. My thumb moves reflexively in circles across her soft skin. I want to kiss her. I want to fucking inhale her. In a low voice, I tell her, "I know you don't want to believe this, sweetheart, but regardless of whether I know your real name or not, I assure you my feelings for you are entirely unprofessional."

Her eyes flutter shut as I give in to the urge to set my mouth on hers. I move softly, reverently, my gentle exploration confirming she tastes as damn good as I remember from the other night.

"This will be getting very personal between us. It already

has," I whisper against moist lips, forcing myself to pull away when all I want to do is set her on my cock. "You know I'm right."

"I...I don't know what the right answer is." Her soft voice is unsure, and it ignites an angry torch inside me.

"You signed up to do a job. This is too important to fuck up."

And apparently my comment lit a fire inside her, too. When she speaks, her tone is harsh and acerbic. It makes me even fucking harder than I am.

"About that. Maybe if I knew exactly *why* we were doing this, I could make a more informed decision. We are going to be spending a lot of time together after all, and I did sign a nondisclosure agreement. I think you owe me that much, actually. If you leave me on the periphery, I'm more likely to fuck up."

My sigh is heavy. "Can't you just trust me?"

"A river that flows both ways," she replies resolutely.

I stall by taking a sip of my Manhattan. As it is, she's on the right track; can it hurt to be completely truthful with her?

Completely? Yes. I'm doing this for my father, true, but I'm doing it in large part to protect Bluebelle and her sordid past or maybe even her sordid present. But *partially?* That's probably fine.

"All right, well you already know my father is up for mayoral reelection and let's just say his new campaign manager thinks it would be a good idea if I settled down for a while."

She regards me before a slight smile curves her lips. "There's more to the story than that."

"Why would you think that?" I ask, impressed by her insight, although by now I guess I shouldn't be.

"Because, that reasoning is just plain stupid. You taking a girlfriend is not going to get your father reelected, and if his new campaign manager thinks it can and he's convinced your father of that, then not only does his campaign manager need to be fired, your father deserves to lose."

After my shock wears off, I laugh loud enough to draw the attention of the tables surrounding ours, which is tucked in the corner away from listening ears. It's a good place to be seen, but not overheard.

Still chuckling, I say, "You have got to be one of the most perceptive women I've ever met."

Frowning, she cocks her head. "Considering your depth of experience, that tells me a lot about the kind of company you keep."

"Is that so?" I sober, wondering why that prickles more than it should. I've been with a lot of women, yes, but have never been remotely ashamed of how many until just now. Even my family couldn't shame me; they've actually tried on countless occasions. I know this lovely creature beside me wasn't trying to do that intentionally. She was just stating a fact. It makes me pause nonetheless.

Our waitress approaches before she can respond. A few minutes later, she's off with our dinner order, and we fall silent, but our blues don't break from each other.

"So, are you going to tell me your name now?" I press with a slight bite.

"After you finish your story. You know, the real one, not the one that's a well-practiced bullet list of superficial bullshit," she sasses with a self-satisfied smirk.

I blink, eating my own words.

"What's the matter? A little speechless, Shaw?" She puts her elbows on the table and leans into me slightly. "Maybe you don't like a woman who's direct? Maybe you prefer a meek little girl who will bat her eyes, drop to her knees, and submit to you with only the words 'Yes, sir' on her lips instead?"

My weeping cock jumps at her mouthiness. Jesus Christ, I want to dominate and control her. I want to fuck her, brutal and fast and so fucking raw she'll remember well who's in charge here, thinking twice about her sassy-as-hell attitude, even if it makes me rock hard.

With my thumb placed firmly under her chin, I palm her

slender neck and pull her ear to my mouth, rasping, "I swear to the holy man himself, beautiful, if we were anywhere but in a room full of Seattle's finest businessmen and women, you'd be over my knee, your panties would be on the floor, and you'd have my handprints adorning your tight little ass before I fucked you hoarse with my fingers."

My hard dick jerks with her faint moan. I'm so focused on the rapid thrum of her pulse beneath my fingers and the quickening of her breaths—both of which indicate that what I just threatened wasn't actually a threat at all, but a promise she'd like me to fulfill—I forget where we are. I don't hear anyone approaching until it's too late.

"Shaw Mercer, is that you? It is you. How very nice to see you here."

Summer tugs back against my hold, breaking it, but only because it had loosened with our unwelcome interruption. My eyes reluctantly lift to our intruder, and while this scenario should make me happy as this is the very reason I chose this restaurant, all I can think about is how I want to take this woman next to me home and pleasure her until her muscles shake and her brain is mush. I want her submission so much it's practically choking me.

I stand to kiss the city council president on the cheek while strategically holding the napkin over my throbbing, angry erection.

Attempting to clear the lust from my throat, I still rasp, "Emily, nice to see you as well. How are Howard and the kids?"

"They're good, thank you," she lies. I happen to know Howard lost five grand last month, and they were late on their mortgage payment as a result. I also know her eighteen-year-old was busted last weekend, found with enough weed to be charged with intent to distribute. Poor Emily's family is going to shit, and because she's a public figure, that shit is hard to hide. Not impossible, because I've done it, but it's challenging.

Emily's attention now focuses on my lovely date. I smile at the blush still staining her fair cheeks and long to see where else it's spread. "And who do we have here?" she asks with genuine interest.

Emily Smith may be a woman of power in the city of Seattle, but she is also one of the biggest gossipmongers to ever grace public office.

"Uh, this is my girlfriend..." I let it hang like an idiot, not knowing how I should introduce her because she hasn't fucking shared her name with me yet.

But she's already standing, smiling cordially, and extending her hand. "Willow Blackwell. Nice to meet you, Emily."

I swear by all that's sacred, you could have knocked me over with a feather. Until this moment, I've never understood how powerful a name can be. But now I do, because hers just ripped through me like an EF5 twister before settling somewhere around the middle of my chest cavity.

Willow. Music for my soul. And unquestionably perfect for this woman of strength and beauty.

Fuck. What is she doing to me?

"...you meet?"

I was so enraptured with finally learning her true name I've missed half of the conversation between Emily and Willow.

"Oh, Shaw rear-ended me," she bats her eyes and smiles sweetly as she reaches over to twine her fingers with mine. I grip them tightly and paste on a grin of my own. I have no idea why she's straying from the farce we'd worked out earlier this week that we met through a mutual friend.

"Oh my." Emily presses her hand over her heart. "I hope you're okay, dear."

"Oh, I'm fine. Just a bit banged up. My neck is still a little stiff due to the whiplash, but Shaw's magic fingers work out the kinks when I get a spasm. Thank you for your concern, though." Laying a hand lightly on Emily's arm, she adds, "It's very kind of you."

Banged up? Spasms? What the fuck? This is not at all what we'd discussed.

"Well, my goodness, Shaw Mercer, you should learn to drive

more carefully," Emily scolds me, like I'm seventeen again and I accidentally hit the garage door while backing out. So, sue me, I forgot to put it up. Everyone makes mistakes.

"Yes, I should," I mutter, trying to work out how *I* became the bad guy here, when having Willow by my side is supposed to elevate me instead.

"I hope you took care of the damages."

I open my mouth to respond when Willow talks over me. "Well, I shouldn't be saying anything because you and I don't know each other, but he was so worried about my safety in that little Fiat I drive that he refuses to fix it and has ordered me a brand-new Audi. It has a safety rating of ten, and Shaw is a freak about my safety. I never realized just how dangerous that little tin can I drive really is."

The look of pure love and adoration she gives me throws me for a loop, making my heart beat a little faster. She's so damn good she's even fooling me.

"A new car? Oh my. Things must be very serious between you two. I had no idea you were dating anyone, Shaw. Your father hasn't said a word." She sounds skeptical, and I'm trying to shove the whole new car comment to the back of my mind so I can cobble together the pieces of our now shattered story into something believable when Willow answers again.

"We've been keeping it hush-hush, you know. I don't want anything between Shaw and me to upstage the mayor's reelection campaign, which is just gearing up." Again with the lovey eyes. "He's been trying to convince me that we can still keep things under wraps even if he does introduce me to his family, but I've been resisting, so I'm afraid I have to take the blame for the fact the mayor doesn't know about me yet."

Holy.

Shit.

This woman is fucking brilliant.

"Of course, yes, that makes perfect sense," Emily replies, sounding as if she didn't believe it until she just said it out loud.

We're saved from further interrogation when our food

arrives, thank God. I feel like I've been caught flat-footed and am doing a freshman job of recovering.

"Well, Shaw, it was good to catch up. I'll leave you two lovebirds to eat in peace, and don't worry." She leans over, lowering her voice to a scratchy whisper. "I won't say a thing to your father. That's not my place."

"Of course not, Emily. I would greatly appreciate that," I reply, sounding indebted. I believe her. She won't say a word to my father. I happen to know my father can't stand the conniving bitch, but I didn't miss how she didn't say she wouldn't tell everyone else. I guess I'd better plan a family meet and greet sooner rather than later, or I will be on my mother's shit list for the next year.

"What the hell just happened?" I huff after Emily is out of earshot.

"I don't know what you mean," she replies sweetly, picking up her fork.

"You know damn well what I mean, *Willow*." Christ, her name lingers on my taste buds like aged Scotch.

Pausing mid-bite, she slides her liquid eyes to mine. I let my gaze fall to her bare chest, which is slightly flushed now, and if I'm not mistaken, fluttering a bit faster with her quickened breaths. I notice the same dainty silver abstract necklace shaded with a hint of purple sitting right below the hollow of her throat. She's worn it every time I've seen her, and I wonder what its importance is to her. When my eyes finally reconnect with hers, I expect to see desire, but all I see is conflict.

She's playing her role brilliantly while I'm trying to play her.

I'm an asshole. My out-of-control want for her is making me act utterly out of character. I don't chase women. They chase me. It's not ego, it's just fact. Maybe I need to change tactics with her. Ease back and draw her into me instead of pushing her away with my unrelenting pursuit.

Right. New game plan.

Softening my voice, I quirk my lip and say, "So I'm buying you a new car, huh?"

The mood perceptibly shifts when a sheepish smile that reaches her eyes breaks out on her face. God in heaven, my mind is blown every time she does that.

"I got to thinking about what you said the other day, about sticking as close to the truth as possible, and I thought the same thing should apply to how we met. I was going to talk to you about it tonight, but I didn't get a chance and it just popped out. I may have gone a little too far. Sorry."

I chuckle. "No, don't be. You're right, of course. Besides, you'll have a nice little nest egg when this is through to buy your own new car, right?"

I know I've said something wrong when her face falls. "Right," she murmurs.

"Did I say something to upset you?" I look down to find her hand in mine. How it got there, I'm not sure.

"No." She looks away when she answers, and I know she's lying.

"Look at me."

She hesitates.

"Willow." That gets her attention. I'm not sure what I expect when her eyes reach mine, but it's not emptiness. Her façade is securely snapped in place. It pisses me the hell off. I fucked up, sending her back underground, and I have no idea how.

"Hey." I lean toward her so our faces are only inches apart. "I'm sorry for whatever I said to change your mood."

"You didn't say anything I didn't need to hear," she responds mildly.

"Willow," I plead, not even sure what it is I'm begging for. I just want to see that dazzling light back in her eyes when I make her smile.

"It's okay. I'm okay. Really."

Her plastic smile bugs me. When she slides her hand out from under mine and goes back to dinner, I feel the loss of her touch acutely. It confuses me.

We eat in silence until I can't stand it anymore. "So, your neck? Is it really sore?"

I'm treated to another curve of her mouth, relieved it was the right thing to say.

"A little, but no spasms."

"Well, that's a damn shame. I could have rubbed them out for you." I wag my brows, and she giggles. Bingo. "Did you have it looked at by a doctor? I'll pay for any medical expenses you have," I tell her adamantly.

I've been kicking myself that I didn't trade contact information with her the day of the accident. I was so damned focused on my own life, my own inconsequential issues that I acted like a complete bastard.

"No, Shaw. I'm fine, really. It just lasted a couple of days."

"You need to let me fix your car. You pick the body shop, and I'll take care of everything."

"I will. I'm just...I've been really busy with other things. It's drivable. I'll find some time soon."

My mouth turns down, wondering what has her so damn busy she can't take a day or two to get her car repaired. I don't like the fact that she's driving around in a wrecked car because of me. In fact, I don't like that she's driving around in that death trap at all.

"I'm really sorry. About that day. About how I acted."

She sets down her fork. She's barely touched her meal, and I'm sure it's cooled off by now as has mine. "You were distracted. It happens."

"I was a jackass."

"There is that, too." She winks. I laugh. The tension disappears like it never intruded in the first place.

"So...you realize you're going to have to meet my family very soon now."

"Already?" That sends her into a near panic.

"I'm afraid so. You were brilliant with Emily, but that woman invented yayas."

"Yayas?"

"Yeah, that's what my mother calls them. Blabbermouths, chatterboxes, gossipmongers. Emily Smith may be the city council president, but she's best known as the busybody of city hall."

"Oh." Her eyes widen at the realization of what she's just done. "Oh, crap."

"Hey, it's okay." Once again her hand is in mine. It feels so damn good. Too good, in fact. Warning bells should be deafening me with the way this woman makes me feel, but they are strangely absent. "It was bound to happen sooner or later. This is exactly what we need."

"Yeah, okay." She says the words without conviction.

"How did you get here?" I ask quickly, not wanting her temperament to plummet again.

Her smile is thin. "Cab."

"It's settled then. I'm taking you home." I wave down the waitress and ask for the check.

"No, Shaw, you don't have to do that."

"That's the only way a proper date ends."

"But this isn't—"

"Don't even say it," I snap. "This *is* a fucking date, Willow, and I'm not taking no for an answer."

Her fiery gaze burns holes into my skin. It's full of defiance and tenacity. It tugs on my cock something fierce. Her chair scrapes the floor when she stands, and just when I think she's going to leave me sitting here all alone, she gives.

"What the hell. I guess I'm all in now that you know my name. You'll just track me down anyway if I say no."

"You're probably right." I grin, feeling triumphant.

"Probably?"

"Maybe?"

Her supple neck elongates when she leans it back and giggles, causing a chain reaction. Every time her face stretches into a grin, so does mine. Every time her heart races, mine keeps pace. Every time her gaze fills with desire, I want to slide into her and live there.

"You ready?" I hum, my lips skimming her cheek. Christ, how I'd love to feel that hitch in her breath against my root as she holds me deep.

Fuck, what was this new game plan again?

I throw down three one-hundred-dollar bills, which leaves a nice tip for our waitress. With my palm low on Willow's back, I usher us through the throng of tables, politely saying hi to several people along the way, including a reporter for the *Seattle 7-Day*, one of the more alternative newspapers in the area who have a penchant for political gossip. I wouldn't be surprised if there's an article about us on the front page of the next edition.

Once Willow is settled in my Rover, I ask, "Which way?"

"Beacon Hill."

I want to hold her hand, but I don't. Now that we're away from the public eye, there's no reason to. I'm surprised at how much I don't like that. I'm surprised at how upset I got that she didn't want to admit this was a date, although she's right. It's business. I'm surprised at a lot of things, in fact, especially at the thought of what my family will think of her. Why would I even care? In four months' time, I doubt I'll ever set eyes on Willow Blackwell again.

At the thought of that, another surprise hits me in the form of a sharp pang in the middle of my chest.

All too soon, I'm turning onto Court Way and pulling up in front of a two-story condo. Willow's bumblebee Fiat, with its cracked, barely hanging-on bumper, is a beacon, so I know we're in the right place. It's not run down, but it's also not very nice either.

"You live here with your friend?"

"Yeah."

"You sure it's safe?" I push my face closer to the windshield, noticing the trees and bushes are overgrown, giving a perpetrator the perfect hiding place.

"Yes, it's safe. I've lived here for four years without incident."

"Do you have a security system?" I face her.

"You know, I've managed quite well without you my entire life. I think I'll be just fine."

"Have you?" I ask. Now that she's opened that door, I'm stepping through.

"Have I, what?"

"Managed quite well?"

Her face blanks, and we stare in uncomfortable stillness. Not even the air dares move. I see her answer clearly, although she won't voice it. *No. I haven't managed at all.* But it's obvious that while I may have stepped through the door, it doesn't mean she's going to let me stay inside.

The porch light pops on, drawing her attention. I feel the not-so-subtle shove back over the threshold, the glimpse of her vulnerability gone. I almost feel the door stinging my ass when she slams it closed.

"Thanks for a nice dinner. I'll be waiting on pins and needles for your next call," she quips. It's strained, awkward. I can tell she wants to get away.

I'm onto her. I broach a subject she doesn't like, she diverts by running.

"I'll be in touch," I tell her.

What I want to say is: *Come home with me. Let me fuck you until you're sobbing with so much satiation you don't notice your darkness anymore.*

With a tight smile, she pulls the latch, releasing her from my SUV. I let her go without so much as a word or a kiss goodnight. She moves gracefully up the walk, ascends the three stairs on the front porch, and stuffs her key into the lock. The front door swings open, and right when I think she's going to shut it, she turns and flashes a genuine but brief smile before a hated piece of solid wood separates her from my view.

I shift the Rover in reverse and slowly drive away, taking one last lingering look at the condo. It's only then that the biggest, most shocking revelation of the evening rolls through me like a crescendo.

If letting Willow Blackwell walk away from me just now was harder than I imagined, what the hell will it be like in four months' time when I let her walk away from me for good?

Willow

Chapter Twelve

"HELLO?" I CALL INTO THE quiet house, setting my purse and keys on the kitchen table. My gaze roams around the spacious, lifeless room. I don't think anything has changed since the day my father passed away four and a half years ago. In fact, I'm not sure much has changed in the past fourteen since my sister, Violet, died.

I scan the canary walls, noting they could use a fresh coat of paint. My eyes stop on the third cupboard from the left, which still holds a thick, circular dent from where Violet tried killing a mammoth spider with the wrong end of a broom. She got it, but she also was in big trouble when my parents came home and saw the damage she'd done.

I smile when I note the scratches still visible in the middle of the hardwood floor from where Violet and I tried perfecting our runway walk in my mother's high heels. I was five. Violet took the brunt of the punishment that time, too, because she was "older and should have known better."

Violet may have been five years older than me, but she was my best friend. She never treated me like a dumb, annoying little sister. Up until the end, she treated me as an equal. I loved that about her, and I appreciate it all the more now that I'm grown up.

When my attention lands on the dusty KitchenAid mixer, an unexpected wave of sadness washes through me. I miss my sister. I miss my father. I miss our family, the way we used to be. Happy. Oblivious to the tragedies that would befall us.

I run my finger along the shiny, smooth top of the mixer, remembering. Once upon a time, my momma loved baking, and she swore the Jonagold apple made the best apple pie. Every fall we'd take a day trip to Skaggit's to pick bushels of them. Violet and I would eat them until we were sick.

I've seen this appliance week in and week out for years, yet for some reason today, I'm ripped apart by an unwelcome memory.

"What's this?"

"Just open it, Evelyn," my father coaxes. We trade glances. I can tell he's anxious, hoping this will pull his wife out of her depression. I don't agree. Nothing short of raising her favorite daughter from the dead will do that, but I didn't try to talk him out of it either. I've never seen the love of a man for a woman so deep and wide as my father's is for my momma. Even at sixteen, I dream of finding that someday.

"But it's not my birthday."

"It doesn't have to be your birthday for me to buy my lovely wife a gift, does it?"

"I guess not."

"Good." He leans down, placing a chaste kiss on her lips. "Now open it."

She gets a sparkle in her eye as she lifts the bulky box. "It's heavy." When she tries to shake it, I suddenly get excited because she's getting excited, and I can't remember the last time I saw her excited about anything. Maybe my father was right. Maybe this is exactly what she needed.

I lost my momma four years ago, the same night I lost my sister. I want her back. So does my father. I hope this brings her back to us.

The anticipation in the room mounts until I can hardly stand it. My momma slides her thin finger underneath the seam of the wrapping paper, carefully separating the tape that binds the thin sheets together. She always does this with gifts. It takes us forever to get through opening presents on Christmas morning. Violet and I always sat anxiously, trying to shame her into ripping the gift wrap to shreds instead so it could be our turn again. It only made her go slower.

She makes her way meticulously around the rectangle. I'm completely breathless now. I don't think I've taken a full lungful of oxygen in an hour, and I feel slightly dizzy. Finally, when she slowly lowers the paper from the box, time freezes.

Excitement turns to anxiety when she stares blankly at the brand-new KitchenAid mixer in a color that matches her kitchen décor. Silence thickens around us like chunky pea soup, coagulating the longer she remains quiet.

My father clears his throat, which sounds like a tornado bearing down on us. When he speaks, it's as if the sound is being forced through a million shards of glass. "I thought maybe it would make baking easier. My assistant raves about hers."

Without a word, my momma sets the box on the kitchen table and leaves us staring at her back as she walks out of the room. I don't know how long we stand like statues, unable to move, unable to breathe.

"She'll come around," he finally whispers.

I move to his side and wrap my arm around his waist. "Yeah. She'll come around," I agree. We both know it's not true. If she hasn't come around after four years, she's lost to us forever.

To my knowledge, my momma has never used the apple-green mixer my father thoughtfully picked out for her. After she walked away, he pasted on his smile similar to the one I always use and set about unpacking that thing, finding just the right spot on the counter, where it sat untouched. Year after year. If my parents spoke about that gift privately I would never know, but I know it wasn't ever spoken about in front of me again. We all just went about our lives like the thing my momma used to love almost as much as her girls didn't die right along with her eldest child.

The fact that she talks about baking now, incessantly sometimes, boggles my mind. She hasn't baked a thing since I was twelve. Baking was always "girl bonding time" when I was growing up…at least it was before.

That's how I categorize my life.

Before and after Violet.

Before Violet, my mother was engaged, happy, easygoing, loving, teaching.

After Violet, she became withdrawn, short-tempered, anxious, paranoid, depressed.

Before Violet, our house was filled with music and laughter and joy.

After Violet, it was deathly still. The silence was earsplitting.

Before Violet, I admit my prodigy of a sister received most of the attention and that was okay. I also worshipped the ground she walked on. But after Violet? I was all but forgotten by my mother who couldn't move past her death and by my father who had his hands full trying to keep his wife from becoming another statistic. Uncanny that *he* was the one who succumbed to that instead.

I didn't blame my father for focusing on her. In the early years after Violet overdosed, my mother tried killing herself twice until they found the right balance of antidepressants to numb her sufficiently. I didn't blame her for not wanting to live in a world without her beautiful, gifted child. I didn't want to, either. I didn't even blame Violet anymore, although for a long time I did.

At twelve, I didn't get it, but at twenty-six I do. The need to escape from the pressure bearing down on you can sometimes be overwhelming. And while I always envied my sister for her unnatural gift of turning a simple piece of sheet music into something that actually pulsed with life, to her it was a burden she felt saddled with.

"Hey, are you okay?" Millie's voice yanks me by the collar back to the present.

"Yeah, yeah," I stutter, trying to shake ghosts that keep sticking to me no matter how much I try to coat myself in Teflon. "I'm fine. How are you?"

I give my mother's full-time live-in caregiver a hug.

After Violet, we settled into a new routine, and as the years passed by, my mother spent so much time lost in herself we didn't question her forgetfulness or her confusion or the fact that she was nearly a recluse. We'd grown quite used to it, actually. It was the "after Violet" effect, I thought.

I was wrong.

At the young age of fifty-nine, when I was eighteen, my mother was diagnosed with moderate-stage Alzheimer's, a disease that generally affects those in their seventies and eighties. Once we knew what was wrong, it made more sense. Easier in a way to handle, but she progressed quickly to the point it was difficult again.

By the time I graduated college, she'd become a hazard to herself. She started a mini fire in their bedroom upstairs when she forgot she'd plugged in the iron and left it flat on the ironing board. Did over ten thousand dollars' worth of damage. Had my father not come home when he did, she'd probably be dead, the house burned to ashes around her.

I had big dreams when I moved out and went to college. I wanted to move to New York City and land a gig on Broadway. I wanted to make my parents proud. Make Violet proud. I was weeks away from making it a reality. I had an overpriced, run-down studio apartment already picked out. I'd landed a small part in an off-off-Broadway play as an extra. I planned to supplement my nonexistent income with clichéd waitressing. My life was finally beginning.

After the fire, though, I knew I couldn't leave Seattle. My parents needed me. I was all they had. The pressure of his job and caring for his failing wife was taking a toll on my father, and I couldn't leave him to handle it all alone.

But I guess we weren't enough to keep him going, and knowing that just fucking hurts more and more every day.

Millie sets a hand on my shoulder. "Are you sure you're okay, Willow? You look pale."

Swallowing down the melancholy, I croak out, "Of course. Yeah, I'm good. Good."

She scrutinizes me closely. Her eyes give away she knows I'm full of shit, but she's doesn't push. How I ever found this saint of a woman, who cares for my mother like her own blood, I will never know. I feel like my father sent her to both my momma and me from beyond the grave.

Without Millie, I'd have no choice but to put my momma into a nursing home or long-term care facility. I can't possibly care for her myself. I tried that for a few months after my father died. I quickly discovered caring for someone with rapidly advancing Alzheimer's is equivalent to caring for a toddler. I couldn't care for her *and* work, and I had to work to pay both her expenses and mine. So, on my meager salary, I hired a part-time home health provider but two months in found out she was stealing from my momma.

The next person they sent was Millie. When I approached Millie about quitting her home health service and working for me full-time, she was immediately in. She said she felt a special kinship for my momma and me. She's kind of like the mother I lost so many years ago now.

I don't pay her nearly as much as she's worth. Don't get me wrong—she's still expensive. More than I can afford on my day job's salary. After two years, with depleted savings and my options narrowing, the gift of La Dolce Vita fell into my lap.

And with the money Shaw is paying me, I'll be able to easily cover Millie's salary for several years, along with the other expenses it takes to maintain my childhood home. By then I'll have enough of a foothold narrating audiobooks that money will no longer be an issue for me.

"How's Momma?"

"She's napping. It's been a good day, though. A really good day."

"She's lucid?" Those times are further and further between nowadays.

"She's had a few of those moments today. She talked a lot about you, actually."

"Really?" Her conversations tend to lean toward my dead older sister.

"Yes." Millie smiles warmly. "She was telling me about your date for the junior prom."

"Oh my God, she did not," I groan, slapping my forehead with my palm.

Millie's laugh is high and loud and ear scratching, but every time I hear it, it warms me. "Oh yes, she did. She told me all about how Johnny Hankins' mother drove you both because Johnny hadn't passed his driver's license exam yet after three tries. And how she had to drive you to the ER when the wrist corsage made you break out in hives all the way up your arm, and how little Johnny tried to kiss you back in the exam room but ended up with stitches of his own because of a two-inch laceration on his cheek from where you slugged him with the blood pressure cuff."

"I'm pretty sure it wasn't the cuff that did the damage. It was the end of the counter when he fell from the force of the blow. And I didn't tell momma this, but little Johnny actually tried feeling me up, so in my opinion, he got what he deserved."

That makes Millie squeal louder. For just a few minutes, we giggle and forget. It feels good, like when I'm with Shaw. Every time we're together, I'm a little less empty. I hate that he makes me feel the way no one else can and that it will be gone in the blink of an eye.

"Tea?" Millie asks.

"Sure, but don't go to any trouble for me. I know where everything is."

"No trouble, dear. I was just coming to make myself a cup anyway."

After a few minutes of bustling, Millie sets a steaming hot cup of Tazo mint tea between my hands. "Thanks," I mutter before taking a tentative sip. "Everything else going okay around here? Nothing else that needs attention?"

Millie frowns before answering. "No, Willow. Everything is fine. But I really wish you'd reconsider keeping this big old house. You spend unnecessary money heating and cooling it, not to mention the taxes this must cost you."

Millie has never come outright and asked, but I know she wonders how I get enough money to not only pay my expenses but her salary and the upkeep on this house, too. My father did well, and I had enough from his retirement funds to pay off the mortgage, credit card bills, and the like, but there wasn't a lot left over. My parents didn't hurt for money, but they were no millionaires either.

"Millie—"

"Before you tell me I don't understand, I do. I took care of my mother as she went through the exact thing your momma's going through. On sheer principle, I refused to sell her home, the same home she'd shared with my papa for forty-nine years, but at the end, it just didn't matter. She didn't know where she was anyway, and when she died, I had to take a loan just to bury her."

"Millie, I can't. Momma feels comfortable here. This is her home, even if she doesn't remember most of the time."

This was *my* home. Every inch of this place is stuffed with memories. I still see Violet and me lying on the living room floor making a collage of our ideal boyfriend from cut-up magazines or eating raw cookie dough at this very table until our stomachs hurt so much we swore we wouldn't do it again or laying for hours in the tree house out back, her talking about the latest boy she was crushing on.

"What's it like to kiss a boy?" I ask her. We're lying on our backs, watching a spider in the corner of a beam cocoon a fly caught in its web.

"Well, it's wet, and at first his tongue feels weird, but it's...nice."

"You kiss with your tongue?" I ask, flabbergasted. "That sounds disgusting."

Her laugh is musical. "Oh, Willow. You have no idea. But I'll teach you. If you want to know anything, ask me, not momma. She'll freak."

I never got the chance to ask.

My eyes drift over to the staircase that leads up to the second floor, and I see my father's crisp blue eyes beam with pride as I tentatively descended each step at age nine for my first father-daughter dance.

"You're too beautiful for words, my sweet girl," he says when he takes my hands and twirls me so fast my ivory skirt flares wide.

"Thanks, Daddy." I throw my arms around him and hang on to the best man I know.

I easily envision an outline of us seated together on the third step from the bottom, talking through my troubles or my tears at every stage of my life, even in adulthood.

"I think he's going to ask me to marry him, Daddy."

He throws an arm around my shoulders. "You sound scared. Is that what you want?"

"I think so."

He slides a finger under my chin and makes me look at him. "Better do more than think, sugarbug. Better know."

That was "our spot." It was "our thing" that I didn't have with anyone else. Every time I pushed myself from those stairs after one of our talks, I felt lighter. I felt renewed. I felt loved and understood.

There's sorrow and joy and laughter and tears and pieces of each of us in the very fabric of this place. The past hangs in the air in front of me, so real I sometimes think I can reach out and grab it.

Tears well and a sob clogs my throat. I won't let it go. I can't. That feels too much like leaving everyone and everything I loved behind.

"No. I can't possibly sell this house," I whisper.

I would sell myself first.

Shaw

Chapter Thirteen

I KNOCK AND WAIT, ROCKING back and forth on my heels. A minute later, I hear a hushed conversation on the other side. I can't make out a thing until I hear Willow screech, "Goddammit, Sierra Linn Wiseman!"

I'm chuckling when a flustered but breathtaking Willow appears in front of me. I barely get a chance to appreciate her curve-hugging, light blue summer dress before she says quickly, "Hi, let's go." She tries tugging the door closed behind her as she steps through, only her supple body is yanked backward when it's flung open instead.

"Sierra," she growls.

"So," the tall, thin, dark-haired woman now leaning coolly against the jamb starts, ignoring Willow's huff. "Whadya know? Seattle's most sought-after, unattached bachelor is really standing on *moi*'s doorstep. How exciting."

I would say this girl with narrowed eyes and a condescending tone is beautiful, but that doesn't accurately describe her, what with her dozen piercings and bright pink undertones streaking through her dark locks. *Unique* would probably be a better word.

And protective. Very fucking protective.

"And you must be the damned Sierra Linn Wiseman," I answer effortlessly with a slight turn of my lips. I hold out my hand not really expecting she'll take it, but she surprises me.

Her stunning espresso eyes lose most of their venom when they slide to Willow, whom I've now wrapped my arm around and tucked into my side. God, I have surprisingly missed her. This once or twice a week thing is bullshit. I want more time with her. I will make that happen. She's under contract, after all.

"You didn't tell me he had such quick wit," Sierra chides her friend, a genuine smile now making her eyes shine with approval. I suspect getting this woman's endorsement is like rolling a one-ton boulder uphill. It can be done but not without a lot of cunning, strategy, and effort.

"He doesn't," she quips brightly.

I'm chuckling when I turn my head to whisper in her ear, "Punishments are my specialty, Goldilocks. I have a feeling I already know exactly what you'll like."

She tries to laugh, but it sounds choked instead.

"Did you come out here to ogle my date, or did you just want to send us off with a flourish?" When Willow slips her arm around my waist and grabs a handful of my gray button-down, possessiveness surges in my chest. I tighten my hold on her until she squeaks.

With a quick, barefaced scan up and down my body, Sierra's eyes warn when she says, "Nah, clean-cut men with wingback shoes and thousand-dollar jeans aren't really up my alley."

"Sierra," Willow scolds, but she keeps on going while I just grin, amused.

"No, I was just going to tell Mr. Tall, Dark, and Slutty here that if he hurts my best friend who is not only like a sister to me but the best woman I know, I'll personally hunt him down and use his entrails to decorate the corner of Sixth and Pine after I cut off his limbs and his head and stake them on each corner of the state to warn others what happens when you fucking disrespect my friend."

Fuck. Ouch. My dick actually shrunk. I think I believe her. "Wow…that's very…Braveheart."

"Oh my God, we're leaving." Willow breaks for the stairs as Sierra tosses her head back, laughing.

"I like you, Mercer. It'd be a shame to have to follow through."

"I concur," I mutter trying not to shield my withering junk.

"Here, Willow forgot these in her hurry to get you away from me."

I look down at the two bottles of wine she's shoved in my hands. "Thanks, Sierra. I would say it's nice to meet you, but…I was never a big fan of Braveheart. Mel Gibson got the adaptation all wrong."

A howl of laughter follows me all the way to my car, where Willow sits, shooting bloody daggers toward her friend.

"I'm so, so sorry. She's a total loose cannon. Absolutely no one can control her," she stammers the second I'm inside. Her eyes are as wide as saucers, and she's talking so fast I'm only catching about every other word. "She runs her mouth without thinking. She was probably dropped on her head as a child, but she swears she—"

Halfway down the block, I throw the vehicle into park and shut her up…with my mouth.

"Shaw." Her wet lips brush mine. My erection throbs. Jesus, I wish I was taking her back to my place to spend the next eight hours relieving my ache in as many ways as humanly possible instead of taking her to my parents' for dinner. I find myself selfishly not wanting to share her.

"Be quiet, Willow."

Grabbing her by the waist, I help her over the console and onto my lap. Holding her where I want, I kiss her until I feel her muscles relax and she melts into me. Only then do I pull back. But I don't want to. Holy fuck, I want to run my hands up the inside of her naked thighs, plunge my fingers inside her heat, and watch her writhe in ecstasy. If I had time, I would because the way she's panting finally sounds like the sweet breath of submission.

If I touch her now, though, if she would let me, fuck dinner with the family. I would feast on every square inch of her instead. She would be all mine all night long.

Running my palms down her loose strands, I keep her still until her heavy lids open. Her eyes are unfocused and glassy, testing me.

"I'm sorry," she whispers softly.

"What are you sorry for?" My baritone voice slices through the hum of the idling engine.

Please don't say you're sorry for responding to my touch like you want me as fucking much as I want you.

"Sierra. She's...she's—"

As soon as my organs and limbs were being threatened, I knew exactly what was going on. It explained a lot about this scarred creature currently sitting way too close to my dick, actually. "She's ferocious about protecting her friend. Almost as if she's trying to keep old wounds from reopening." The thought that some man hurt her terribly makes my gut twist even though I've been *that* man to so many women. Even though I may be *that man* to her.

Her eyes reflect I've hit the nail straight on. It's there, then gone just as quickly. Jesus, I want to know this woman. I have so many questions, but I resist the urge to push, knowing I'll drive her away.

"We should go." Her voice is soft. I don't think she means it.

"In a minute," I reply, not ready to let her go quite yet. Edging my chin back up, I let my lips linger on her skin. I dart my tongue out so I can catch her flavor.

"Are you nervous?" I ask against the warmth of her throat.

I am. This is not the first time I've introduced a woman to my family, but this is the first time I'm nervous about it. I'm going to chalk it up to the fact that I'm paying Willow to play my girlfriend and our ruse could be found out any minute if we don't play our cards right. That would destroy my mother and anger my father. He wanted me to settle down for a while; he didn't ask me to run out and pay someone to do it.

"Yes." Her "s" stretches into a hiss when I draw down her thin dress strap and begin sucking the swell of her breast. Instead of pushing me away as I expect, her hands weave through my hair, and she holds me close as I lave and tease. Her gasps and moans encourage me, and soon both straps are hanging down her arms, and my tongue is everywhere it can reach.

When her pelvis starts a slow roll against mine, I groan but stop, pressing every inch of her tightly against me. If I don't, I will fuck her right here in my car on the side of the road in front of the three kids playing in their front yard not fifty feet away, scarring them for life. She deserves far more than that.

"They'll love you." A shiver racks her body when my lips brush her ear.

"Yeah, that's what I'm worried about."

She says it with such deadpan it takes a few seconds for her joke to sink in; at least I think it's supposed to be a joke. When I feel her shoulders shake, I know she's laughing. Pretty soon the car is filled with the echoes of her happiness. I can't take my eyes from her. She's exquisite.

"I really like this side of you." I actually really fucking *love* this side of her.

"What side is that?" she asks shyly, her cheeks tingeing light pink.

"The real one you hide under your layers of ash."

Before the last word leaves my mouth, I watch her close off right in front of me, as if the curtains were being drawn after the last act in a play. The happy, carefree woman is dust in the wind.

"Don't do that," I demand, grabbing her face and pulling her close.

"We're going to be late," is her only response. Fight or flee seems to be her regular go-to.

“Willow.” I sigh. “I’m not going to hurt you.”

Her stare pins me to the seat, but her faintly spoken words drive the final nails through my lungs, rendering me speechless. “You won’t mean to.”

She slides back into her seat and adjusts her dress before buckling her seatbelt, leaving me confused.

Fucking women.

I shove the car in drive and steer carefully back onto the street. We spend the rest of the way to Mercer Island in silence.

Shaw

Chapter Fourteen

"ARE YOU READY?" I SHUT the engine off and turn toward her, but not before I note Linc's and Gemma's cars. There's no sign of Bluebelle. My texts and calls to her today have gone unanswered. Frustratingly typical.

It takes a few seconds, but she finally meets my eyes, smiling slightly. "I was born ready." She is resolute, a warrior prepared for battle. I have no doubt by the way she charmed Emily Smith that she'll have my family eating out of the palms her hands within two minutes, tops.

My father called me inside of twenty-four hours after our dinner the other night, so I reiterated to him exactly what Willow had told Emily. I convinced him the timing was some cosmic coincidence, but I could tell he was still skeptical. We're going to have to do one hell of an acting job tonight.

"So...are we going in, or are we going to sit here all night staring at each other, Drive By?" Willow teases. Back to her cheeky self, I see.

I should get out of my vehicle. I should open the door, take her hand, and escort her up to the front door. I need to do one last thing first.

Grabbing her by the nape, I draw her forward until my eyes grip hers and she can't look away. "I'll never be anything less than honest with you."

Her forehead crinkles. "Okay."

My phone buzzes, but I ignore the fucker. I'm not going to let anything ruin this moment.

Breathing deep, I inhale her floral fragrance. I'm so damn hard right now I could jackhammer concrete, and when my voice comes out, it's low and gruff. "God, how I want you, Willow. I'm not sure I've wanted anyone more."

"The unattainable is always the most coveted," she replies without missing a beat. It pisses me off. This is *not* about the rush of finally getting something just out of reach. She is different from any other woman I've met. There is something about her that whispers to me. It sounds suspiciously like *mine*.

That's the second time I've heard that word. I choose to ignore it the same way I did the first.

"No, you're wrong. I *will* have you, my beauty. You and I both know that." She opens her mouth, but I silence her with my finger. "But I truly don't want to hurt you, Willow. I won't lie to you, I won't feed you bullshit lines just to get between your legs, and I won't promise things I have no intention of delivering. You'll always know where you stand with me. There's an expiration date on this, yes, but we're attracted to each other, and there's no harm in two grown, single adults enjoying *life-altering* sex until then." I use her own words with intent. "But please believe me when I tell you it would kill me, *kill* me to hurt you at the end of this. I don't want to do that. If we're both honest with each other about what this is, no one will get hurt."

Her face softens. My cock twitches like mad, and my eyes get heavy when her palm cups my face. It feels so fucking good when she touches me. I can't wait to feel her tight fist pumping me up to the edge of climax before I finish between her tits.

"Sierra scared the shit out of you, didn't she?"

I'm stunned for all of two seconds before I howl with

laughter. She squeals when my hands fall to her sides and squeeze. Pretty soon we're practically wrestling around in my Rover like two teenagers, laughing and batting each other's hands away until we're both gasping for breath.

Then my lips are devouring hers, and she's reciprocating.

Beat for beat.

Stroke for stroke.

Breath for breath.

Her limbs wind around my neck, and her sweet moans linger delicately on my taste buds.

Fuck, I want her.

Lost to where we are, I'm angling her head for better position when I feel a sense of being watched. I pop an eye open, freezing at our audience.

"Please tell me there's nobody there," she rasps against my lax mouth.

"Okay. If that's what you want to hear." I chuckle, giving her one last hard kiss.

Her hands cover her face. "Oh God," comes out muffled.

"Stay there." With a squeeze to her thigh, I grab the bottles of wine and exit, running around to open the door for her. I wave to my grinning family, matching with one of my own before opening Willow's door.

"Come on, baby."

Her wide eyes dart to mine, then to my outstretched hand. I wiggle my fingers until she takes it. When she's safely out of the vehicle, I yank her to me and drop one more kiss on her lips, whispering, "Let's do this."

She smiles up at me. It steals my thoughts. "Let's kill it."

"Let's."

My nerves from earlier evaporate. A couple minutes later, introductions are complete and my mother has commandeered Willow away from me, leading her inside, arm in arm.

Following behind, I fish out my phone, grinning wide when I see a text waiting from Dane.

Project A in the works, sir.

Once inside, Linc and I hold back while everyone else fawns over Willow. It reminds me of the first time we all went to see Nicholas in the hospital after he was born. He was the first grandchild, after all. The shiny new toy that cried and wailed as he was passed around for inspection. Only Willow is not crying and wailing. She's laughing and effortlessly chatting them all up as if she genuinely wants to be here. And they're buying it, because really, what choice do they have? She has this inherent magnetism that draws everyone near her in. She's…captivating.

"So, how did you meet her?" Linc asks me in a low voice.

Neither of us can take our eyes from Willow as my mother shows off her prized glass vase collection from every place she and my father have visited. Some of the pieces are one-of-a-kind and have to be worth a mint. Every once in a while, Willow will look our way and gift me with a small smile that makes her eyes sparkle like a night sky full of stars. I don't know why, but I feel like I'm among a choice few who gets these tiny glimpses of the real her.

I find myself thoroughly enjoying the fluidity of her trim body as she moves around the room. There are very few women who emanate organic seductiveness. Willow is one of them. She's original and wholesome in every way I can see so far. "It was quite by accident," I mumble absently, my eyes tracking her every step.

Or was it divine intervention? my conscience whispers.

I'm not one of those people who believes in fate. I don't believe there's a one-and-only soul that reflects ours walking the face of the Earth. I think meeting one person and falling in love with them is just sheer dumb luck. Staying with them for as long as my parents have been together and still being in love after all that time? Almost a statistical anomaly these days. Animals, by design, were not meant to be monogamous. In fact, there are very few animals that do truly mate for life and homo sapiens are not in that elite category.

But as I stand in my parents' kitchen and watch how naturally Willow interacts with my mother and Gemma, like they've known each other for ages and the passage of time apart means nothing, I have to wonder if I've been wrong about this fate thing the whole time.

How did I happen to run into *her* on the very night my father talked to me about needing my help?

How did Noah happen to bring *her* right to my doorstep when I'd wished she was the one I'd be saddled with for the next few months?

How is it *she* consumes my every thought, and I look forward to spending time with her more than I have anyone else? Ever.

Even though this charade will last but a few months, I find myself wanting to know everything about her. What happened in her past to dim the light inside her? How did she stumble into this questionable line of work? Does she enjoy it? Does she want to go back to it when we're through? Does she want more in life than to adorn the arm of some wealthy man? Why doesn't this ethereal beauty already belong to someone?

"She seems like a good accident," Linc says. Tipping his herbal tea to his mouth, he takes a deep swallow. Lincoln doesn't drink. In fact, he doesn't do drugs, he doesn't smoke, and he doesn't swear. Growing up, he got a load of shit for being a goody-two-shoes brown-noser, but never from us, his siblings. I love my brother. He may be living a hard life, his gender identity on the outskirts of societal acceptance, but he is *the* purest person I've ever met. Pure of heart, pure of soul. Anybody lucky enough to have his love should treasure it like gold, no matter their gender, no matter how they dress.

With difficulty, I tear my eyes from Willow to face my brother. He looks tired. "She is," I confess with surprise candor.

"How long have you known her?"

"Not very long." Yet it seems like a lifetime.

He looks to Willow again and then back to me. "Hmmm."

"Hmmm, what?" I press, standing up a little taller. Is he onto us?

"Nothing. Forget it."

"Don't bullshit me, Linc. Just spit out what you want to say," I growl.

He shrugs. "You're not gonna like it."

Oh. Shit. *He knows.* Thirty minutes in and we're already busted like a cheap McDonald's Happy Meal toy. Gemma has those fucking things littering her house.

"Try me," I grit, getting angrier than I should.

"She's different from the others you've brought home." Like I've brought *soooo* many women home.

"What does that mean?"

"I don't know, exactly." He goes back to studying her. It prickles me. I feel as if he's about to pick her apart like he's done with the few women of mine he's met. If he starts down that path, he and I will be taking this discussion outside. It won't be the first time I've tried settling something with my fists and he with words. I may be the CEO of a Fortune 100 company, but I also used to be a mean street fighter, defending the honor of my sister, Gemma, more than once. "She doesn't seem to feel the need to impress everyone, for one thing."

My fists relax. I chuckle softly. "You're right there. She doesn't have that complex."

"And she seems comfortable in her own skin."

I'm not sure I agree with that assessment, but it just goes to show how good at fooling everyone else Willow Blackwell truly is. "What else?" I prod, curious now that I know he's not about to rip her apart.

"She doesn't fawn all over you. I like that." He laughs when I shove him with my shoulder. "She seems like she'll keep you on your toes."

"Yeah, they're cramping already," I answer sincerely.

Linc has a slight smile when our eyes meet. "There's something magical about her. I have a feeling you'll have to set a lot of traps to catch this one, brother. She may be a little too cagey for Shaw Mercer, businessman extraordinaire and Battleship slayer."

My lungs feel bound, not filling enough to even laugh at his joke about my prowess in both the boardroom and on the game board. "What makes you think I want to catch her? Who says I'm not just passing time like always?"

"Time to eat, boys," my mother calls in the distance.

He clasps my shoulder and squeezes. "It's like I said before. This one is different."

Two hours later, we're backing out of the driveway in moonlit darkness. Willow gives one last wave to my mother, who actually hugged her—*hugged* her—when we left. Turns out I didn't have anything to be worried about. I think by the end of the night, they loved her more than they love me.

My mind reels over how well the evening went. I think every family member caught me alone to tell me specifically how much they like her. In all my years, that has never happened. And outside of Lianna, whom it took a month for my own mother to warm up to, no other woman has ever been accepted with such fondness or open arms.

In fact, when we left, my father specifically told me not to fuck this up. He used those *exact* words. "Do not fuck this up." He rarely swears. I didn't have a chance to ask him if it was because of his election or because he saw the same thing Linc did.

There's something magical about her.

I don't think I could have described Willow any better myself.

I glance over to see she's gazing out the side window, deep in thought. Her left hand rests in her lap, but she's making quick little circles with her thumb and middle finger. I've noticed she does that often, as if she can expend her nervous energy through the pads of her fingers. I don't even think she realizes she's doing it half the time.

Coldplay's "Yellow" is the only thing cutting through the interior. We've not exchanged one word since we left my parents' house. I want to know what she's thinking. Does she like my family? Does she regret doing this? Would she call everything off if given a choice?

The urge to take her in my arms is overpowering. I want to hold her, protect her, *keep* her. I've had my hands all over her tonight, and the absence of her touch is making me restless. Regardless that it's just the two of us, this time I refuse to deny myself what I want. Reaching over, I take her smaller hand in mine. That draws her gaze from the passenger window to our looped fingers and then to me.

"What are you doing over there?" I ask, bringing her knuckles to my lips.

Her eyes bounce back and forth between mine. "I was just thinking," she says somberly.

"Don't worry." I wink. "The first time's always the hardest."

The serious look she had is quickly replaced by amusement. I really like it when I can do that.

"I will have you know that I graduated salutatorian of my senior class."

Why do I cherish every nugget of information from her like they're tiny flecks of gold I'm accumulating?

"You do realize salutatorian is second best, right? That's not really something I'd go around bragging about," I tease.

She rips her hand from mine, but she's laughing. "You're such an ass. No wonder you don't have a girlfriend."

"Ouch." I throw my free hand over my heart. "That physically hurt."

"The truth hurts." She twists in her seat to face me, a dazzling smile on her lips. "So, what about you? What was your class rank?" she challenges. "I realize it may be hard to remember as old as you are. You're probably coming up on, what, your twenty-year class reunion soon, aren't you? The mind is usually the first thing to go. Or the hair."

Oh, Willow.

My eyes slide to hers. When my grin gets wider, she groans and drops her head against the window. "Of course. The only person who can belittle the glory of second best is the first, right?"

"I can't help it I was a born genius."

"You're so full of yourself." There's no bite to her words, only humor, but it makes me harder than fuck. I've been battling a semi the entire night. Once again, I put her hand in mine, and she lets me.

"I have no doubt you'd love it if you were full of me, too." A bold statement that's laced with nothing but raw want. The sharp intake of air she takes swings the energy from light and teasing to thick and pulsing, so I take advantage. "Tell me you're thinking about my cock filling you up you right now."

"Shaw."

She tries to pull away, but I hang tight. "Tell me, Willow," I demand.

Thirty seconds later I'm parked in front of her condo. She still hasn't spoken. I swiftly undo her buckle and try to pull her into my lap, but she resists. She and I both know if her pussy ends up nestled against my pounding cock, it's game over.

Since she won't come to me, I'll go to her. I lean over until she's pressed into her seat with nowhere to go. Grasping her chin between my fingers, I grate thickly, "I want you to tell me that you're thinking about my cock impaling you over and over as much as I am, Willow. I want to hear you say you've fantasized about the ecstasy I will shower over every inch of you if you'd only let me. I want you to tell me you touch yourself in the dead of night wishing my fingers were feathering your clit instead of your own."

"Why are you doing this?" she whispers gutturally before licking her lips. Another damn telltale sign she wants me. This.

"Why are you denying this?" I throw back hotly. Unable to resist, I place a soft kiss at one corner of her mouth, then the other before I rain kisses all over her cheeks and closed eyelids. "Admit you've been thinking of me fucking you just as much as I have," I whisper as I go.

"Yes. God...yes," she murmurs right before I slant my mouth over hers.

"Come home with me," I plead between the kisses I'm drugging us with. I've not once begged a woman to come home with me. She seems to make me do things other women can't.

"No." Her refusal fans cool over my face, making my skin tighten in annoyance.

"Let me come inside then." My free hand finds her bare thigh and crawls up until I'm pushing the hem of her dress up with it. My thumb is almost grazing her honeyed spot when she clamps my wrist, stopping me.

"No."

I tighten my grip on her chin. "Why are you fighting us? You want this just as fucking much as I do."

"We rarely get the things we want," she says woodenly.

That fucking veneer is back. I'm beginning to hate how easily she goes back and forth between open and closed like she's flipping a fucking sign in a window that says: Be Back in 10.

"Who hurt you, Willow?"

She shakes her head. "It doesn't matter."

My heart suddenly aches for her. I realize then that I've never been hurt by another person—I've never *let* myself be hurt by another person—yet it's clear she has, and I have nothing to draw from.

"You're wrong, Willow. You're wrong about so much."

Her eyes dart toward the window so she doesn't have to look at me. She doesn't even fight my hold anymore. I think it's more comforting than she wants to admit. She doesn't want to admit a lot of things. "You're probably right," she says, lowly.

I tug her face until our gazes connect once again. "Let me in," I tell her with conviction.

Her beautiful blue eyes turn glassy as water builds. "I wish I could."

Finally, some fucking honesty. Now we can get somewhere.

"Do you want me to back off? I can honestly say it won't be

easy, but I'll try if that's what you want." I hate those sour words, but the last thing I want to do is hurt this woman whose strength thickly cloaks the fragility of past wounds inflicted by someone or something.

"I don't know what I want."

I let my mouth curl into a gentle smile. "You're wrong again."

I don't let her say another word. Kissing her tenderly, I coax her lips open. Our tongues duel languidly until her breaths pick up and she's making those sultry sounds in the back of her throat that fucking slay me.

I want her. Her pussy, her ass, her mouth. I can picture her now on her hands and knees making those exact noises as she takes every inch of me wherever I desire. I want parts of her she doesn't want to give me. And I want them badly.

But oddly, I want to protect her more. So, for now, I take a half-step back. "You did well tonight," I praise.

"It was easy. Your family is great."

"They are." Letting my lips linger on hers for a few seconds longer, I know if I don't leave right now, I won't be taking no for an answer. With a little effort, I could probably coax her into saying yes, but I don't want her to regret being with me either, so the only thing I can do is, "Goodnight, Goldilocks."

She looks both relieved and disappointed when she responds, "Night, Drive By."

Surprising me, she initiates the kiss this time, but it's fleeting before the door slams and she's hurrying up the walk. I wait until she's safely inside, hoping she turns back like last time. She doesn't.

I go to bed that night with my hand on my dick, coming violently to thoughts of flaxen strands tangled in my fist as I ruthlessly possess her mouth. I picture her bewitching blue eyes sweeping up my body, making sure she's pleasing me with every thrust of my cock. I imagine her swallowing every drop as she hums around my heavy shaft like she can't fucking get enough. I envision her getting herself off so we both fly at the same time.

My body stiffens as I curse my empty release into a darkened room, wishing every bit of what I was conjuring was real. After I'm done, I lay still in a pool of my own cooling sweat and come, the edge barely taken off.

Until I met Willow, I hadn't jacked off to thoughts of a girl since I was seventeen years old. Haven't needed to. I generally have access to all the women I want.

But thoughts of other women don't come remotely close to raising the flag.

That moment is when I know I should be just as worried as Willow. The warning bells that were noticeably absent earlier are now shrieking. Cautioning me to back off. Begging me to call one of many women who would be willing to drive over here and let me use her all night long; but not only does that sound repulsive, it also feels a bit like cheating.

No. I don't want anyone right now but her, so I let all disturbing thoughts blow out of my lust-addled mind. I've taken everything I've wanted my entire life. Willow Blackwell will be no exception. I'm going to fuck her, a lot if I have my way. I'm going to simply enjoy these next long weeks, and then I'm going to let her go, just as planned.

Even as the thought makes my gut sink, I know that's the way it has to be. The only way it can be. I don't know how to do anything else.

Shaw

Chapter Fifteen

"How are you feeling?" I ask lowly against the sleek column of her neck.

"Much better. I think I'm finally on the mend."

Willow came down with a sinus infection the day after she met my parents and spent two days in bed. I wanted to bring her chicken noodle soup and nurse her back to health in the crook of my arm. I wanted to draw her hot baths and wait on her hand and foot. But I didn't. I didn't even mention it, in fact. I kept those unexpectedly tender feelings to myself for too many reasons to count.

"Tell me why we're here again?" she whispers in my direction.

Because for some ungodly reason, I can't get enough of you.

"To be seen, of course." The hard catch in the back of her throat sets my skin on fire. I want to sink my teeth into the soft flesh there and see what other sexy noises I can draw from her.

"This seems like an odd place to be seen." Her voice wobbles. I smile. "Since there's no one here."

"Have you ever been to the Giant Shoe Museum before, Willow?"

Her laugh lights me up like nothing else.

"Can't say that I have. I'm not much of a sideshow person."

"What?" I feign disbelief. "No Seattle native can miss this wicked collection of the world's largest shoes. It's sacrilege if you do."

"Well, I'm glad you've enlightened me, then. I'm not sure how I would have slept another peaceful night knowing there was a pair of two-foot clown slippers I'd been missing out on."

"I'm glad I could help," I quip. Plopping a quarter in the next slot, the curtain spreads to reveal a massive pair of loafers. "My father brought me here when I was eleven."

"Really?" she asks absently, bringing her finger up to the glass protecting this grotesque blob of leather.

"Yeah." I chuckle. "I constantly complained about how big my feet were. At eleven, they were size eleven, and he brought me here to show me that no matter what we think is wrong in our lives, it could always be worse."

I've never told anyone that story. Not even Noah.

I feel her looking at me, though I stare straight ahead. It was such a stupid thing to be upset about, but my shoe size made me clumsy, and I wanted to play basketball more than anything. I wasn't used to not being good at something. My body was disproportioned while it went through puberty. I didn't make the sixth grade team because of it, and I admit, I've never been a gracious loser. I actually came home that day and cried. At eleven, even the most trivial things seem like a mountain you won't be able to climb. Somehow that menial trip to look at ridiculous, oversized shoes made me feel a hundred times better.

"You think your feet are big, Shaw? Be thankful you have feet," my father said as we stared at these exact same shoes.

"He always has a way of putting life into perspective, even something as simplistic as the inches of an appendage."

She snorts at my joke. I turn to look at her, a smile playing on my mouth. Her eyes drop to my feet then draw slowly back up my body. I feel the ghosting of her gaze, like phantom fingertips trekking upward. I swear I feel them circling my cock, tugging playfully before landing back on my face.

"Hmm. It looks like your appendages are perfectly proportioned to me," she says with a cheeky smile.

Metal digs into my dick as it hardens faster than I can blink.

"Oh, my innocent little Goldilocks." Backing her into the closest wall, I push my groin into hers and watch her eyes drift shut on a ragged sigh. My lips only a hair away from hers, we trade oxygen infected with lust. "Looks can be deceiving. Maybe you need to check for yourself."

Reaching between us, I take her hand from the wall behind her and wrap it around my rigid cock, squeezing her fingers with my own.

"God," she whimpers.

Her hand flexes and grips and starts a slow, pulsing rhythm, guided by mine.

I forget where we are when my mouth captures hers in a starving kiss. My free hand wanders to cup her ass, pulling her closer to me, trapping our arms between us. The pressure of both her hips and her palm on my cock pushes me to places I can't go here, out in the open, but fuck do I want to. Lucky for me, the sound of kids squealing makes me ease back before I do something that will get us arrested.

"So, ah…ummm…what's on the agenda after the big shoe reveal?" she asks on a dazed, shaky pant.

"You hungry?"

Her eyes widen. *Oh yes, I knew exactly what I was asking.*

"I could eat something, yes." Her smirk mirrors mine.

Now we're talking.

As I lean back into her, she puts a hand between us and pushes on my chest. "Food. I could eat food," she clarifies with a laugh. She sounds determined, so I let it go. For now. But we're getting closer to changing the degrees of this vertical dance, and we both know it.

"Come on." I grab her hand and lead us out the door and down the street a couple of blocks until we come to a little

French café I like. It's not fancy, but the outdoor seating is spectacular, and it's on the corner of two busy streets. Great place to be seen.

We only have to wait a few minutes before we're seated.

"I remember coming here as a kid every Mother's Day. My mom loves this place. She said it reminds her of summers spent in France with her mother when she was little."

She smiles. "Were you eating Nicoise and smoked salmon carpaccio at the tender age of five then?"

"You would think, right?" I wink, which gets me a light laugh, and in turn, my grin broadens. "No. My undeveloped palate preferred French toast and scrambled eggs. And profiterole, although I had to beg my parents for it every single time because I never finished my meal so I could save room for it."

"I've never eaten here before."

Something swells inside me that I'm showing her things she's never experienced in a city we both call home. "You're in for a treat then."

We chat easily for the next hour, as if we've known each other all our lives instead of just a few weeks. It's nice. Relaxing. Refreshing.

When Kellie, our waitress, comes back around, I order a profiterole, although I'm stuffed.

"Oh, nothing for me," Willow says when Kellie looks to her.

"Bring two forks," I tell her.

"Shaw, no. I can't possibly fit another thing in my mouth."

My brow curves, and I don't bother fighting the grin splitting my lips. A beautiful blush creeps up her chest and face when she realizes what she said. "Oh…that's not what I meant."

"You should choose your words more carefully, Willow. A man may take a statement like that as a challenge."

She leans forward, placing her forearms on the table, crossing one over the other. Her whole face sparkles. "Would this man?"

I match her position, our faces within inches of one another.

I let my finger caress her cheek and my voice drop. "Abso-fucking-lutely."

I'm just leaning in to kiss her when dessert arrives. Damn the luck. Willow watches as I dip my fork through the flaky pastry and thick cream. I bring it to her mouth. Holding her stare as she holds mine, I spoon a forkful toward her; she opens and lets me feed her. It's another intimate moment that makes my blood boil with crazy want for her.

Wrapping those luscious lips around my fork, she closes her lids on a moan. I have to reach down and adjust my pants. They've gotten unbearably tight again. I take my own taste and feed her one more bite before she holds up her hand to stop me.

"What do you think?" I ask, anxious to know.

"It's divine," she replies with a dreamy look on her face. "Thank you."

I reach forward to wipe off a dollop of crème from the corner of her mouth with my thumb. I tap her lips until she opens and lets me slide it in. I actually groan when she closes her mouth and sucks. All I can picture is my cock sunk between her teeth. The way she's looking at me tells me she's thinking the same thing.

"Fuck, Willow."

Reluctantly, I withdraw and lean back when all I want to do is throw her over my shoulder and drag her home with me so I can devour her until dawn. I told myself when I picked her up tonight I would not beg her to come home with me, but my mouth is open to implore her when I hear, "Summer, is that you?"

Willow's face blanks and her head immediately snaps to the street where a tall, lanky man who's spent too much time under the tanning bed stands. Another man who's shorter and stockier but no less interested in her accompanies him. I don't recognize either of them, but my blood is boiling now for an entirely different reason.

She doesn't give me a second glance before standing and

facing our intruders. She shuffles forward a few feet to the wrought iron railing that separates the sidewalk from the restaurant.

"Bill, how are you?" she asks sweetly before holding out her hand. The man named Bill takes it and brushes his lips across her knuckles. I want to thrust my butter knife straight through his beating heart.

"Couldn't be better," our interloper replies in an irritatingly upbeat tenor.

Right before my eyes, Willow transforms into someone else. She's stiff and fake and withdrawn as she talks for a minute or two with these two men who clearly know her through her "job." And not her day one.

When they finally walk away and she sits down, I can hardly contain my unreasonable fury. I knew who she was and what she did before I even agreed to this little charade, yet I can't seem to stop the black hate I feel that other men may have enjoyed her presence as much as I have. And how could they not? I grit my teeth until my molars hurt.

"Old *friends*?" I fully realize I spat that with hostility and loathing. And those fighting words will be the catalyst to make me say a whole host of other shit I will come to regret. My only excuse is that no woman has ever made me feel so damn helpless before. It's an uncomfortably hot place to be. "Cat got your tongue?" I clip when she doesn't answer fast enough.

Willow's cool gaze flickers to the street and back to me. "How did you find me? At Randi's?"

Her attempted misdirection pisses me the fuck off.

"I'm asking the questions here, *Summer*." Her fake name drips with condemnation.

Eyes that sparkled in want and delight just minutes ago turn hard as stone. "Why are you being such a dick? *You* reached out to me, not the other way around."

I should stop right now. Shut my mouth and swallow this irrationality that's clouded my judgment. Only I can't. Steaming jealousy has caused fire to brew, the black smoke too thick to see through. "Because you sure seem to know a lot of men in this city. Job hazard, I suppose."

Christ. The stunned look on her face before it masks over once again shreds me to ribbons. Saying nothing, she rises gracefully from her seat. Grabbing her purse, she starts for the outdoor exit. My temper flares back up at this distance she's always trying to put between us. Things get tough, she takes cover. Well, it's going to stop. This running she's doing is not healthy.

"Where are you going?" I bark, uncaring that we've already drawn an audience from the tables packed around us.

"Home." Her voice is sure and solid. She's such a strong woman, and here I am trying to cut her down like a bastard. But does that stop me? Fuck no. It doesn't.

"I say when you can leave," I practically yell.

She freezes midstep. Her chin goes up, her slim shoulders heave, but she doesn't respond. I stand and close the short distance between us, getting right in her face.

"You can't walk out on me. I own you. For the next three months, you belong to me. You do what I say, when I say, how I say. *That* was the deal you fucking signed." My sharp, muted voice sounds alien to me. Assholes have taken me over.

Her vicious glare gradually morphs into sweet and forgiving and in an instant I know what she's doing. I'm paying her to do it. Hell, I just called her out on it, but to be on the receiving end of it guts me. Absolutely ruins me. Then she opens that bratty mouth I'm drawn to, and the tone she's using may be all sugary, but the words behind them smell vile and taste bitter.

"Wow. Let's get one thing straight, *Mr. Mercer*. You may own my time. You may own how I dress, how I act, what I say, where I go. But to own is to possess. And I am no man's possession. So, no"—in a calculated move meant to fool anyone watching, she leans up and places her mouth close to my ear—"you don't *own* me. You will *never* own me."

Then she kisses me on the cheek and says loud enough to

be overheard, "See you at home, honey," and walks away, leaving me to gape after her like a fish out of water, gasping for breath.

I'm landlocked. Completely out of my element.

No one defies me like that. No one *plays* me like that.

Fierce, barbaric resolve swells inside me until it overtakes me completely.

The fuck I don't own her.

She. Is. All. Mine.

Guess what I want now? More than anything I've ever wanted?

A brand-spanking-new possession.

Willow

Chapter Sixteen

IT'S A BEAUTIFUL DAY. THE sun is bright. The breeze is minimal. The air crisp, like fall is trying to push its way in already, but summer is keeping her out just a bit longer. And I want her to succeed because fall means we'll be closing in on winter before we know it.

And winter means no more Shaw. I'm not sure how I feel about that, but as the days with him whiz by, I know I don't like the disappointment stirring in my gut at that thought.

We are nothing. A job. A sham. And he clearly reminded me of that last night with his cold words at the diner.

I own you.

How fucking dare he? He may be right in many ways, but it was the *way* he said it that pricked my skin like a bed of thorns. It wasn't said with the intense possessiveness of a man who wants a woman to truly belong *with* him. Quite the opposite. I was something to claim. To covet and flaunt until his use for me is over.

It stung, mostly because why should he feel any different? I don't like that I wanted him to.

As if on cue, my phone rings for the fifth time this morning.

I ignore it. To his credit, Shaw's been relentless in his quest to apologize. I'll eventually let him; I just need the hurt to ebb a little first. He's judging me for something he knows absolutely nothing about, and while that's not all his fault because I haven't offered him an explanation, it hurts nonetheless.

This is not a relationship where we trade parts of ourselves that are deeply personal in hopes of injecting them into the other person's life and ultimately their heart. We may be physically attracted to each other, but even I know what we're projecting to the outside world is not real. As much as I'm starting to want it to be.

I flick my left blinker and wait for the cross traffic to pass before turning. Driving through the familiar wrought iron gates, I make my way slowly to my destination. Once I reach it, I shove the gear into "P," kill the engine, and sit quietly, staring out the front windshield at the massive weeping willow whose curved branches seem to shield and protect.

Tears well. They always do.

I'll never forget the first time I saw where my sister would be laid to rest for all eternity. My father stood beside me holding me up because my knees were too weak to do it on my own.

"I bought this plot six months before you were born, Willow."

It was a weird thing to do, I remember thinking at the time. My father was young. He was a long way from dying. But that was my father. Always planning ahead.

"I had intended it for your mother and me when we passed, but now I think maybe I had some sort of strange foresight. I think this is a sign that she'll be okay."

I remember tipping my head back. Looking up into the green underbelly of the giant tree whose lush green leaves seemed to mourn along with us. Even at that young age, I got it. In life, she was my protector. In death, I was hers. I broke down. He had to carry me back to the car and sit with me for an hour before I was calm enough for him to drive us back to the funeral home.

The memory hits me the same every time I pull up to this spot. It's been too long since I've visited. I don't usually let more than a few weeks of time go by, but I've been so caught up in Shaw it's distracting. It's going on two months now. I can't let that happen again.

Letting my gaze fall to the passenger seat, I scoop up the two small bundles I clipped from the backyard of my childhood home. Bringing them to my nose, I breathe deep, inhaling the strong scent of lavender and honeysuckle. I blink hard, letting sorrow burn a path down my cheeks for just a few seconds before I wipe it away.

After a deep breath, I exit the car. Gravel crunches under the soles of my sandals until I reach the muffled quiet of the neatly trimmed grass. Only a few more steps and I stop, kneeling on the lawn that's still slightly damp from the rain earlier this morning. The cold shocks my bare knees but I ignore it.

"Hey, Vi. Hi, Daddy," I whisper, wiping away the remaining moisture on my face with my free hand. I place the flowery branches on each of their graves, which are side by side, and I gather up the dried ones I brought last time, setting them to the side for now.

We're far enough back in the enormous cemetery that all I hear are birds chirping and the subtle sound of air passing through the tiny leaves surrounding me. It's peaceful and quiet.

"I'm sorry I haven't been by in a while. I've been sorta busy." I pluck a few stray long blades of grass from the edge of Violet's intricately carved headstone and throw them aside. I trace the musical notes from the beginning of Metallica's "Fade to Black" etched in the stone, the same as I always do before I sit back on my heels and smile oddly.

Violet played this song all the time. Her own version of it, anyway. My mother hated it whenever she heard it, but my father and I loved the classical spin she put on a heavy metal song. When my mother insisted Violet's marker bear some sort of musical reference, my father and I exchanged glassy-eyed glances and smiled. He told her it was Grieg's Piano Concerto in A Minor. To this day, it's still our secret.

"So, I, ah, met someone," I stutter, wondering why I started with that of all things. Shaw is a blink in time. A memory. Probably a regret and one of my own making. "He rear-ended me," I go on. *He's paying me to be his girlfriend.* "He's kind of an arrogant asshole." *Who I can't stop thinking about one second of the day.* "His name is Shaw Mercer." I pause, trying to think of what to say next. "I…" *shit,* "I like him anyway." *I think maybe I more than like him.*

Damn. Damn. Damn.

How did I let myself get into this position?

"Do you remember when I was ten and had a crush on Tommy Miller?" I was in fifth grade and he was in sixth. He had this longish wavy blond hair that would always fall into his puppy-dog eyes during lunch. He was cute. He knew it and soaked up attention like a sponge. All the girls crushed on him. I wasn't immune. "And do you remember that day I came home from school devastated because I saw Tommy kissing Karyn Vencezzino on the mouth near the girls' bathroom when he told me he liked me just the day before?" I stop and take a breath. "Do you remember what you told me, Daddy? You said, 'It takes a special girl to open a boy's eyes to what's right in front of him, Willow. But when he realizes it, he'll fight to the death for her and only her. Don't settle until you find that man.' Violet just told me to kick him in the balls." I laugh. "But your words were wise." The next week I saw Tommy Miller kissing two other girls who were *not* Karyn Vencezzino.

A car approaches. I wait for it to pass, wondering what my father would say about Shaw Mercer. On principle alone, he wouldn't like him. Had we met under different circumstances, though, had Shaw not been *paying* me to fool everyone around us, I'm still sure my father would tell me to keep on walking. That Shaw's not the fighting kind either, just like Tommy Miller. It makes me sad that he'd be right.

Then another thought hits me about that advice my father gave me and the anger I try to bury burns bright once again.

"Why didn't *you* fight harder, Daddy?" I ask hoarsely. "Why didn't you talk to me? Lean on me? Ask me for help? Why did you just give up on us? Momma and I needed you."

Violet's death was more of a confusing time for me than anything. She made a bad decision that ended with the price of her life, but my father? His was deliberate. For months, I refused to believe it was suicide. It had to have been some sort of accident. My father had *everything* to live for. His career. His wife. Me. But his car was parked in the middle of the bridge, door open, keys and wallet inside. There was no evidence of foul play, of anyone else at the scene. No witnesses, no passersby. Just suffocating pain and a glaring reality I didn't want to believe.

My father took his own life *on purpose.*

He left me and my momma *on purpose.*

That's what hurts the most.

He didn't trust me enough to ask for help. He was proud. A man's man. A protector of both myself and my mother. That's why to this day I struggle with what he did. A big part of me wonders if my father was crippled not only by the loss of his firstborn but also by watching his beloved wife slowly waste away, forgetting him, forgetting their life together. Feeling as helpless as I was to save her. Sometimes I think he was exactly like me, pretending to be fine while he slowly wasted away on the inside.

Guilt licks at me until my skin nearly blisters. *I should have known. I should have done something. Why didn't I see it?*

I could have helped him just like I could have helped Violet. Couldn't I?

Some days I miss my family so much it's tough not to drown in the heartache, but I will admit, the last few weeks it's been a tad easier to breathe, and I don't want to admit why.

Closing my eyes, I concentrate on why I'm here. It's getting harder and harder to remember the little things. The pitch of

Daddy's voice. The dulcet ring of Violet's laughter. The way my father and sister's arms felt around me, hugging, squeezing. You don't realize how you take the small stuff for granted until it's ripped away, leaving a gaping, bleeding hole.

Wrapping my arms around my waist, I let the warm wind blow against my face, pretending they are here, listening. But my mind drifts to places I don't want it to go. I think about what I'm doing with Shaw and why. Try to justify how it's not hurting anyone. I think about the two hundred fifty thousand and how he can afford it. Try to rationalize away that it's for my mother. That if I had another choice, I'd take it. For not the first time, I tell them, "It's hard, but I'm doing the best I can."

I'm sure I hear a faintly whispered *"I know you are."* Or maybe it's just wishful thinking. Regardless, it makes me feel better.

I start updating them about Momma, and several hours later, I finally make my way back to the car, feeling exhausted but lighter. I stayed longer than I intended, but it felt cathartic to be here. I couldn't make myself leave although I should have spent the afternoon recording. I make a mental note to bring Momma out with me next time. Even if she doesn't know why she's here, she usually enjoys the serenity.

Starting the car, I reach into my purse and grab my cell. I have several more missed calls and close to a dozen texts from Shaw. I sigh and decide I'm acting childish. I need to get over whatever this is I'm feeling for him and just do my damn job professionally. I'm done being mad anyway. Mostly.

It would take ten seconds to shoot him a quick text telling him we're all good before the thirty-minute drive home, but I'm afraid that wouldn't be good enough for him. He'd call me immediately, and I'm thirsty and tired and have to use the bathroom. So, I shift the gear to "D" with the intention of calling him when I get home.

When I pull into my driveway, though, I'm surprised to see Shaw's Rover sitting on the side of the road. With him in it. A quick look at my car clock shows it's just shortly after four in the afternoon. Huh. I wonder how long he's been waiting for me.

My stomach starts tumbling with excitement and nerves. I've essentially ignored him all day, and he's come here to track me down. Why? To apologize? Or to make sure I'm going to uphold my end of the bargain? Or maybe it's to fire me.

By the time I open my door to find out, he's already halfway to my car.

"Shouldn't you be at some big important meeting this time of day, Drive By?" I spout with some venom when he reaches me. Guess I was still holding onto the edges of pissiness a bit more than I thought.

"Where the fuck have you been all day?"

Well, guess that answers that. Apologizing isn't at all what's on his mind. Being a fucking asshole is.

My spine straightens like someone just shoved a steel rod up it. "You know, I don't owe you a play-by-play of my entire daily schedule. I've been available every time you've needed me, without question. And wasn't that the 'deal I signed'?" I shoot back sarcastically.

"Except today," he mumbles under his breath.

I start to walk away when he grabs my elbow and gently shifts me back. "You're right. I'm sorry. Can we try this again, please?"

Taking in a lungful of air, I let it go slowly, along with most of my ire. "Do you want to come in?"

"I'd like that. Thanks."

With every step I take toward the front door, I'm overly aware of him behind me, close to me, watching me. I let us inside, knowing we're alone since Sierra's car isn't in the drive. Walking to the kitchen without looking back, I grab a bottle of water from the fridge.

"Do you want something?" I ask, trying to be polite.

"I'm good." His gaze wanders around, and I know he's taking in my meager home. Probably comparing it to his. Our whole condo could fit in his living room and kitchen. "I like your place. It's nice."

"What do you want, Shaw?" I ask, taking a seat at the table so I can put something—anything—between us.

With the length of time he studies me, I start to get anxious. Maybe he's here to end things between us after all. Maybe he's decided he doesn't want to risk being seen with me. Maybe he's decided that I'm not worth the hassle.

Sadly, I'm not sure I could blame him, and a part of me doesn't even want to put up a fight, but then I think of the money I'll lose, and I panic a little.

Clearing his throat, he says, "I'm sorry for last night. It was uncalled for."

I just stare, searching for the right response. He pulls out a wooden chair and sits, leaning back heavily like he's tired. Now that I look closer, he does have bags and circles under his baby blues.

Guess he had about the same kind of night I did.

I look away briefly to gather my thoughts. I want to forgive him, but I need some answers first. "Why did you act like that? You were a jackass. You didn't even let me explain."

He shrugs. "I don't know."

I cock my head and give him the look. You know, the one that says *I know you're full of shit.*

His smile is self-deprecating. "Okay, fine. I didn't like the fact that he was a former client of yours. I didn't like the way he looked at you. I didn't like that either he seemed intimately familiar with you or he wants to be. I didn't like his mouth on your hand. I didn't like his eyes scanning your perfect fucking body. I didn't like the thoughts I could see running through his mind, blaring like a fucking bullhorn. I didn't like any of it."

In other words, a long-winded way to say he was jealous. Hmmm. I have to suppress the happiness that wants to break out on my face like a rash.

"What thoughts were those?"

He leans forward, arms crossed and elbows on the table,

anger crowding out his apology. "That he wanted to fuck you."

I laugh, knowing how untrue that statement is. "Not everyone wants to fuck me."

"You're wrong there, Willow," he says with absolute conviction before easing back. "So very wrong."

"He's not a client," I say quickly, wanting to ease the tension that now hangs as thick as a storm cloud. Shaw sits there, stony, so I continue undaunted. "Bill was the gentleman who shook my hand. I don't know who the other man was. A friend of his, I suppose. Bill works for Randi, and I can assure you he doesn't want to fuck me. His tastes lean in the opposite direction."

He blinks a few times. "Why didn't you just tell me this last night?"

"Because you pissed me off," I retort hotly. "Look, I know you don't approve of what I do, but I don't need your fucking approval. I have my reasons, and I'm tired of you judging me over something you know nothing about."

His entire demeanor softens. "I'm not judging you, Willow. I just..." He drops his head back and stares at the ceiling, breathing deeply. When he rights it again, the warm look in his eyes squashes my irritation. "Come here." He holds out his hand and expects me to obey.

I don't want to, but something compels me forward. I stand and take it; then I'm between his spread legs, his hands kneading my hips. He's staring up at me with a plea in his eyes. "I'm sorry."

I cave like wet sand under the power of the sea. Running my hands through his short hair, I tell him, "You're forgiven."

With a nod and heavy sigh, he pushes back. Rising to his full height, he towers above my short frame, but it surrounds me with a comfort I've sorely missed. "I have to go. I have some things to attend to that I pushed." He sounds as disappointed as I feel.

"Okay," I agree quietly.

At the door, he weaves his hands through my hair and tips

my head to just the right angle so he can lower his mouth to mine and kiss the hell out of me. When he turns to make his way to his car, we're both breathing heavily and my entire body needs doused with ice water to put out the inferno burning inside.

Only when he drives away do I realize I still have no idea how long he waited for me just so he could apologize. Or why I like that thought so much.

Willow

Chapter Seventeen

TAPPING RECORD, I BEGIN. AGAIN.

I open my apartment door expecting Livvy to greet me, but the only thing that does is the scent of vanilla, sultry music, and candlelight. I shut the door, leaving my suitcase by it, and take a few steps inside but freeze at the vision that greets me from the informal dining room.

Fuck. Me. My cock jumps.

A completely nude and blindfolded Livvy is spread out on my table. Her hands are crossed at the wrists and placed gracefully above her head, one slender ankle positioned delicately over the other. Her back is slightly arched, her glossy red lips parted like she's already in the throes of ecstasy, and the shadows from the candles surrounding her dance like entwined lovers over her flushed skin. Two flutes of bubbling champagne sit at the head of the table, waiting to be enjoyed.

I stand there for what seems like an eternity drinking her in. She's so goddamned beautiful I'm struggling to breathe. Every man's fantasy come to life, but she's all mine. She's my everything.

My life.

My breath.

My very fucking sustenance.

My cock has never been so hard.

"Christ, Livvy. You're a goddess," I finally manage to murmur as I walk the length of the table and slowly, deliberately drag a finger lightly from her toes all the way to her fingertips. Her breath hitches, and I watch as goose bumps break out along the path I've taken. I walk around the other side, repeating the same process, this time edging closer to the parts of her I want my hands and mouth on most.

"Fuck it, I give up," I grimace, chucking my headphones onto the desk. I've reread this section of *Forsaking Gray* six times already this morning, scrapping every single recording. Narrating a book from the male point of view can be challenging, but I tend to do my best work in the morning when my vocal cords are still low and scratchy. It's the same time I usually read the very sensual or explicit sex scenes, because my voice is sultrier before it gets completely warmed up. This morning was supposed to kill two birds with one stone, except I think I mutilated them both instead.

Today I could have risen at the ass crack of dawn and it still wouldn't have mattered. I need to *be* these characters when I read them. I immerse myself into their skin, their lives, their highs and lows until I believe I *am* them, but today the only zone I was in was the danger one.

He is all I can think about.

With every word, I pictured myself in this heroine's place and Shaw in the hero's.

I was Livvy. Shaw was Gray.

I was on his table.

I was his sacrifice.

I was *his.*

And I am a fucking idiot. None of that can happen. The sex part, maybe. *Hell, who am I kidding?* There's no *maybe* about it.

I think over the last few days and how my barriers are rapidly collapsing, piece-by-piece. And it isn't his bossy, sexually explicit words that get me. It's his heartfelt ones.

It was his sincere apology for being a dick. It was his jealousy. It was how he was with his family. It's the weight of his gaze that I feel on me when I'm not looking at him. It's his attentiveness, even if it is a guise. It's all that and so much more I don't understand. Underneath his controlling, pushy, sometimes maddening exterior, Shaw is a compassionate, loving man. He loves his family deeply, and if I didn't fully understand why he was doing this before, I do after meeting them.

He's physically attractive, but his benevolence is what actually makes him irresistible. He's the entire package every woman dreams about unwrapping, calling theirs, treasuring for life.

The next time I see Shaw Mercer, there is no way I'll be able to resist him. So, fine, sex will happen, but an unwelcome part of me can't help but yearn for something more. Something beyond physical pleasure. The love that these two fictional characters felt was real and palpable. It jumped off the page and sucked you in. Hell, it even made *me* believe in second chances for the broken.

I want to be someone's life.

I want to be their breath.

I want to be their very fucking sustenance.

But I'm not sure that will ever happen for me.

People can't love you if you don't let them, Willow.

To this day, four years later, my fiancé's words still ring true. I don't deny I'm fucked up. I am. I know it. I fully understand the trials I've endured in my life have left an indelible imprint on me. Closed me off to meaningful relationships full of depth and trust.

I don't push people away, per se, but I also don't invite them inside. And while keeping others on the fringes may seem easy, it's not. Trust me. It's exhausting. I'm not proud of it. But it took me a long time to figure out that I didn't know who I was. I lost myself by being what everyone else needed me to be, and how can you let someone in if you don't know who the hell you are yourself?

I have spent years searching for the real me I left behind. The me I know is in there, waiting patiently to be found underneath the convoluted labyrinth I've created to protect her, and truthfully, I thought she was long gone. I'd accepted I'd never find her, and I was okay with that.

But then I met Shaw Mercer. I hate that when I saw him for the first time, I caught a glimpse of her. The old me. The one who used to be full of fire and hope and vigor for life. I hate, hate, *hate* that when I look into his eyes, I see my light burning inside him. I don't want him to have it. I don't want him to guard it like it's precious and belongs to him.

He's not the right one.

He's using me. I'm using him. He'll hurt me, even if it is unintentional. I may hurt him the same way. I *know* this. Our foundation is nothing but a shifty base of creatively spun deceit. Like tissue paper, it will disintegrate under the slightest pressure because it's weak.

Even knowing all of this, I am foolishly developing feelings for him, yet as much as he wants my body, he's made it very clear there's a No Vacancy sign permanently nailed over his heart. I'm an emotional mess, and he's emotionally unavailable. Moving this...whatever this is...beyond professional is a horrible idea.

Yet...what he said the other night has been echoing endlessly in my head: *"If we're both honest with each other about what this is, no one will get hurt."*

I'm not sure I believe that's true, but is it a choice anymore? I am hopelessly fixated on that damn light he holds like it's going to flicker out before I can figure out how to get it back. I *need* it back. Maybe if I sleep with him I can douse it?

"Lowenbrau, you up?"

I can only laugh when Sierra pounds on my *closed* door. The one I've pinned an "In Session" sign on, hoping it would remind her to leave me alone when I'm trying to work. Guess I'll have to come up with something else.

"It's almost noon," I announce when I open my door. "When have you known me not to be up by lunchtime?"

"You don't have to be a bitch about it."

"Sorry," I mumble. I'm not. "Why are you up anyway? Shouldn't you be sleeping?"

Sierra is one of the hottest DJs in the entire upper Northwest. Definitely the single most successful female in a profession dominated by males. People flock from hundreds of miles around to hear her play at the trendiest club in downtown Seattle. She works odd hours and sleeps even odder ones. Despite living together all these years, I have yet to figure out her schedule.

"Here," she snaps. I look down to see my phone in her hand. It's ringing. "To answer your question, I *would* be sleeping, except this fucking thing won't stop its incessant ringing. Just when I'm drifting off, it starts up again."

"Oh. Sorry." This time I mean it.

Without another word, she heads back to her room and slams the door. My hand vibrates. I gulp when I see it's Shaw.

"Uh, hello?"

"What the fuck, Willow? I've been calling you all goddamn morning," his baritone voice booms.

Jesus, this man knows exactly the right sequence of buttons to push to rile me. "I thought we already went over this. I do have a life. Another job, remember?" I snipe, closing my door before I flop onto my still unmade bed.

"I was getting worried about you." He sounds a smidge less irate than a second ago. "I almost left work to come check on you to make sure you were okay. Again."

Oh.

Well.

Now I feel like a real bitch.

"I'm sorry," I say contritely. "I was recording and I had my headphones on and my door shut. My phone was downstairs charging."

"You're not still mad at me, are you?"

"No," I answer quickly. "I promise."

A long, steady breath comes through the speaker. I can just imagine him pacing around his office stabbing his hands through his hair in frustration. I bet he looks sexy as hell right now.

"I really am sorry. I didn't mean for you to worry." Who knew he *would be* worried? "Why are you calling?"

"Just give me a minute," he breathes.

Is he really *that* upset he couldn't get me?

"Shaw?"

"Yeah."

"Is everything okay?"

A beat passes before he answers. "Fine, yes. It's..." He sighs again. "I'm sorry I acted like a jerk."

"This is becoming a habit," I tease. "Maybe I should have negotiated hazard pay." He laughs, and I feel the energy lighten significantly. "So, what was so earth-shattering you almost called in the National Guard to hunt me down?"

I hear the grin in his voice when he responds. "You're stretching my concern here."

"Am I?" I toss back, amused.

"Yes. It was a mild irritant at most." He's back to the relaxed, teasing Shaw I've quickly grown fond of.

"Irritant? As in someone left just a swallow in the milk carton irritant, or someone just ran into the back of your car irritant?"

His boisterous laugh ripples through me. Tingles explode everywhere.

"I want to see you tonight," he husks.

God, I love it when he sounds needy like that.

"Well, I guess it's your lucky day. I happen to be free. Last minute business dinner?" I add quickly, because surely he doesn't mean he wants to see *me*, me.

My eyes fall to my nightstand, where I notice a faint layer of dust already gathering although I just cleaned two days ago. I absently swipe my finger through it and study the particles gleaming in the light. My gaze goes to the stunning arrangement of flowers delivered yesterday. They're beautiful, but what makes them unique are the red catkin willows sprinkled throughout and the note accompanying it that said:

I wanted to send pussy willows but
I thought that was a little cliché.
~ Drive By

I realize I'm grinning like a besotted teenager when I hear him say, "I'll text you the information this afternoon."

"Can't you just tell me now since you worked so hard to get me?"

"No, Goldilocks, I can't. I wasted so much time trying to reach you that I've neglected my other responsibilities this morning. I'll have to work that much harder to get everything on my schedule done today."

"It won't happen again, sir," I sass, loving how easily we play off one another.

"Fuck, Willow." His tone is about two panty-scorching octaves lower than seconds ago. "Next time you say that, you will be begging me to let you come."

I exhale in a whoosh, my mind immediately picturing being stretched out on his bed; my naked, thrashing body beaded with sweat from the many times he's brought me up to the edge only to leave me hovering in sweet agony.

"I don't beg," I finally manage to push out.

"Mmmm. But if you're gracious enough, I'll make the pain worth it."

There are so many things I hear swelling in his voice right now. Promise. Power. Pure sex. Not one of them is humor, though. He's dead serious.

Holy hell.

"Keep your phone close to you from now on. And answer it when I call."

Omnipotent.

That's the best singular word I have to describe this man. He barks, people act. Too bad for him I'm not afraid of his bite. In fact, I've begun to crave it.

"I'll see what I can do."

"Willow," he says, his voice clearly scolding.

"Don't you have a busy day, Drive By? Best be going so you can find time to text me later."

The muted rumble in the back of his throat sounds wolfish. "I can't wait to school you in the proper way to respect your boss."

I wait for a dark chuckle to follow. It doesn't.

Gulp.

A slow heat magnifies between my clenched thighs.

"I can't wait to learn," I breathe.

Stupid. That's me. I'm goading a lion with only a piece of straw as a weapon. I clearly have no sense of self-preservation.

He clears his throat, but his voice is still husky. Well, huskier than usual. "Don't forget."

I don't think I'll forget a second of this phone call. Not sure which part he wants me to remember, though, I ask, "Forget what?"

"That you asked for it."

Oh. *Shit.* My entire body tightens.

I'm not sure how long it takes me to realize that he's hung up without so much as a good-bye. I toss my cell beside me and blink long, slow blinks. My chest is rising and falling as fast as if I've just finished a five-mile run.

This is it. We're really going to do this. He's worn me down.

It's just sex, Willow, nothing more.

We have a contract, an expiration date. That's it. *Lock everything else down, because if you don't, you could easily get lost in between what is and what could never be.*

I simply can't let that happen.

Willow

Chapter Eighteen

JESUS, I'M NERVOUS.

I look at Shaw's text for about the hundredth time today to be sure I read it right the previous ninety-nine.

Dinner. My house. 7:00 p.m. sharp.

Why would we be having dinner at his house when the whole idea is for us to be seen in public? I see no other cars here, sans a probably expensive silver sports car. It's parked close to the garage and looks like the one I saw outside of Randi's, so it has to be Shaw's. Maybe he had me arrive earlier than everyone else?

Deciding he's not going to call me out on sitting in my car again, I make it halfway to the front door before it swings open. With a lopsided grin and corded arms crossed, Shaw leans casually against the jamb, looking absolutely edible in his faded jeans and an inky-black tee that's stretched across his muscles. Once again, his feet are bare and his hair is damp as if he's freshly showered.

He looks like sex and candy. And sex. Forget the candy. He looks *exactly* like sex.

"Good job, Goldilocks. You cut the time you spent in your car in half. You're making progress."

I ignore his jab, my eyes sweeping over his sinful form before landing on his beautiful face. That sexy smirk grew. "You said we were having dinner."

"We are."

"Then why are you dressed like that?" *Like we're skipping right to the sex part.*

With both hands, he grabs me by the waist and pulls me flush to him. I hate that whenever he touches me I want to purr.

"You don't like what I'm wearing?"

No. I fucking love *it.*

"I…I didn't say that."

"Then you *do* like what I'm wearing." His smug voice falls, and he bobs his eyebrows up and down, making me laugh.

How this sexy godlike man doesn't have women camped outside his house every day throwing themselves on his car like shameless hos is beyond me. I don't follow the gossip rags, and Seattle is admittedly a big city, but I'm surprised I'd never heard of Shaw Mercer until a few weeks ago.

"I didn't say that either."

He swoops down and murmurs before kissing my cheek, "You didn't have to. I see more than you think I do, Ms. Blackwell."

Yeah. That's what I'm worried about.

I deposit my shoes by the door, and he grabs my hand, leading me through his house, straight out the glass sliding doors and onto his monstrous, multilevel deck. We stop at the railing, and I stare in amazement.

"Wow," I breathe, gazing out into the calm, dark blue water. Several boats cut slowly through the glass top, causing lazy ripples to lap across the rocky shore not even a hundred paces away. I envision their passengers, drinks in hand, the wind in their hair and the sun in their eyes. "This is stunning. Truly beautiful."

Shaw leans his forearms on the iron, bending slightly at the waist. His eyes follow mine. "It is. It's not as beautiful as my parents' view, but it's a close second."

I take in his immense, secluded lot lined with tall, grand trees on either side. Right below us is a concrete patio that holds a giant in-ground pool. To the far left are a sunken hot tub and a circle of rust-colored padded chairs surrounding a massive brick fire pit. Plants, flowers, strategically placed shrubs, and boulders round out the backyard oasis.

It's spectacular. I would live outdoors if I owned this house. "Oh, I don't know about that. This is pretty great."

"Thanks," he replies quietly.

"Have you lived here long?"

"Almost four years now."

"It's peaceful. I like it." More than I should.

"It's a good place to hang my hat at night."

I want to look at him, but I keep my eyes on the waters ahead. "Why don't you live on Mercer Island?" This is the third time he's talked with fondness about the island his family founded, so while his home is truly spectacular, I wonder why he doesn't live there.

"At first it was independence. I love my family, but I wanted to get away from my parents when I was younger, so after college, I bought a place of my own. Sold it for a mint and bought this also for a steal when the former owners were foreclosing. My family would love it if I moved back, and maybe someday I will. But I like it here for now."

"I think this place suits you," I tell him.

"Thanks. What about you? You live in Seattle all your life?"

Safe topic. "Born and bred. Grew up in Montlake, went to college at UW. Moved in with Sierra after we graduated." True, though I leave out the part where I moved in with my fiancé for a year before I broke it off and moved back in with Sierra.

"What did you study?"

I slide my eyes to his and smile. "Drama."

His laugh lights my insides up. "Figures. Did you ever put it to use?"

My smile falls. "I use it every day in my job."

"Which one?" I don't mistake the fact that his voice has sharpened.

"Both," I pipe back, unaffected. He may not like what I do—correction, *did*—but I wouldn't be here otherwise.

We fall still as I listen to the soothing sounds of crashing waves. I close my eyes, enjoying the early evening rays warming my face and the peace of being here in this moment. It's the same sense of ease I had last time I was here. I don't know if there's something special about this house or the man in it that makes me feel like I belong here. I don't, but for this one second, I decide not to worry about the whys and let myself just be.

With one of my senses now muted, I'm all too aware of Shaw's slow, even breaths close to my ear. My blood warms, but it has nothing to do with the sun and everything to do with the man who just snaked his arm around my middle. Flutters low in my belly kick into high gear when he turns me toward him and cradles my face.

"Look at me, Willow," he commands in a low-toned whisper.

God, I knew this name thing was going to be the end of me.

I don't know why, but I feel like this moment could change everything between us. Once my eyes connect with his, I'm worried he'll see too much...that I'm teetering on the edge of falling for him and his irresistible charms despite my best efforts. Despite telling myself last night this is only sex.

I am such a liar.

"Why?"

"Open your eyes." Slight pressure against my drawn lids startles me until I register his lips. I have no choice but to obey when he eases away because the sheer need I hear in his voice strips away my defenses. Is he feeling so much as a fraction of what I am right now? Am I alone in these crazy feelings rapidly swelling between us?

We have an expiration date.

Right.

Calling on every single skill I have, I let my gaze focus and join with his. But my effort is pointless. My heart races at the melting pot of emotions I see. They match my own.

Desire.

Confusion.

Affection.

"I don't want you going back to that when we're done."

I want to tell him I can't anyway. That he doesn't get to dictate what I do when we part ways. Instead, I say, "I won't."

His eyes both darken and soften. "What you're doing with me is no act."

"It is. It has to be," I whisper desperately. It simply has to be.

"It's not. I don't want it to be." His strangled confession only confuses me more. The need to protect myself is blinking a bold and blinding red.

"Shaw, we can't muddy what we're doing here."

Time feels suspended as I wait for him to agree. But something ripples through his blue pools that I don't understand, followed by a growly, "What are you doing to me, Willow?"

"I don't know," is the only way I can respond. Only it's a bald-faced lie because it's the exact same thing he's doing to me. A heady combination of wild emotions rushes through me like a raging river, making me dizzy as it takes me under. I'm terrified I'm going to drown in them. In him.

"Whatever it is, I can't seem to stop it," he says before tenderly placing his lips on mine.

Every worry and stray thought is blown away when he slides his hand through my hair and tips my head, increasing the pressure and cadence against my mouth. He's in complete control of me. He takes. I let him. I like it. I want more.

All too soon he pulls away, and I swallow a groan of pent-up sexual frustration.

"If I didn't have plans for dinner, you'd already be naked and writhing under my mouth." His raspy voice showers me in goose bumps.

It's now or never. I either tell him to back off, and I know he will, or I commit. My choice is pretty damn easy what with his intense want for me literally twitching against my stomach and mine drenching my panties. This will change everything, but I can't ignore it any longer.

"I'm not hungry. For food anyway," I say breathlessly.

His lids drop low. He growls as if in pain. "Incredibly tempting, but once I slide between those slim thighs of yours, Willow, it will be a long fucking time before I'll be able to make myself leave. And I'll need the energy. I plan to fuck you until you can't think about anything except begging me to deliver your next orgasm."

Excitement, anticipation, and body-shaking nerves make for a noxious combination in my middle. Knowing that I'm actually going to let this passion between us go from fantasy to reality tonight, I just want to get started before I lose my nerve or change my mind like I did a dozen times on the way over.

"So." I clear my throat, trying again. "So, what are these grand dinner plans then?"

Because all I can think of now is getting it over with so we can move on to the sliding between the thighs part.

Stepping back, he runs a hand down my arm, lacing our fingers. Hungry eyes are locked on me, eating me up. Heat builds between us until I'm sure he's going to change his mind and take me right here, right now, out in the open. I wouldn't object.

Without a word, he leads me back into the house. Stopping in the kitchen, I feel the loss of our connection more than I want to when he lets me go, turns toward the fridge, and tugs one side open.

"I'm grilling."

"Is anyone else coming?"

"Why? Worried about spending the evening alone with me?" he drawls in that cocky baritone brogue of his as he starts to gather several plates of food from the clear shelves.

"No," I lie.

Glancing over his shoulder, he stops what he's doing and says with a straight face and a seriously dark tone that makes my pussy gush, "You should be."

Fucking…fuck.

What have I done? And furthermore, why can't I make myself care?

Shaw

Chapter Nineteen

THREE DAYS.

That's all I lasted before I had to see her again. I was already regretting I said I'd only need her ten hours a week. The truth is…I want more. How much more I haven't figured out yet. All I know for sure is it isn't enough.

So tonight isn't about being seen. It isn't about my father. It isn't about obligation. It's about us. Just us. I want to know more about Willow. I told myself when I drifted off last night this was a bad idea. I repeated it this morning and every time I called. And called. And called her. Only a month in and I'm going off script, but I can't make myself stop.

I *like* her. A fucking lot.

I had to see Willow tonight because I *wanted* to. I was calling her anyway with some bogus reason, but fate dropped a gift, wrapped and all, right into my lap in the form of a *valid* one when Noah popped into my office mid-morning and threw the latest issue of the *Seattle 7-Day* on my already-cluttered desk.

"Vultures," I spit after reading the ridiculous front-page headline:

Has Seattle's very own real-life "Christian Grey" snared another victim?

Christian Grey? Really?

And victim? Jesus, they act as if I have a dozen bodies buried in my backyard because they didn't survive my red room of pain. This reporter is ridiculous.

"Isn't this what you wanted?" Noah retorts. He's confused at my reaction. Join the fucking club.

"Yeah, of course," I mumble. Scanning the brief article, I quickly deduce it's from our first night out. It mentions how we were seen cozily dining at Frenchie's and how we left together. It doesn't mention Willow by name, but I know that's only a matter of time now. I study the picture that accompanies the article. While you can't see Willow's face, as her back is to the camera, you can clearly see mine.

Undiluted, raw desire is reflected in my hooded eyes as I whisper sins in her ear.

It's an intimate moment, and I'm intensely conflicted. I don't want the entire city to be witness to it. Yet this is exactly what we were after. I should be happier than I am. Our first outing brought even better results than I had hoped for, though I find I don't want Willow to be fodder for gossip. I have concrete skin. I could give a flying fuck what the media says about me, but if they start dragging her through the mud simply because she's associated with me, I will bury them.

"Looks like you two are getting on well?" I don't like the laughter I hear in my friend's voice.

"Fuck off, Noah," I snap with heat. Tossing the paper down, I walk to my bay of windows and try to rein in the flailing pieces of confusion whipping around inside me.

"What's going on, Shaw? You're acting weird."

I don't fucking know.

But before I'm forced to come up with another bullshit line, Dane saves me. "Sir, Jack Hancock is on line one. He says it's urgent."

"I'll take it."

When I face Noah, he raises a questioning brow but is wise enough not to say anything before leaving.

I haven't shown Willow the article yet. Not knowing how she'll react, I wanted to wait until after dinner. I know I told her there would be media, but I have a feeling based on the clear want, and more importantly, the *tenderness* I saw on my own face, we will be hounded even more than I anticipated. And while I wanted to strip her down and fuck her where she stood only a half hour ago when she finally submitted, I knew if I did that we would be spending the rest of the night with only our bodies doing the talking.

As much as I'd have been fine forgoing dinner, we need to discuss this. We need to plan and I need to prepare her for what's to come over these next few months.

With a beer in hand, I take turns keeping an eye on the fish and vegetables I'm grilling to watch Willow wander around my grounds, taking everything in. My cock jerks as a gust of wind snags the hem of her pale-yellow dress, and I catch a glimpse of the silky white panties that are holding her pussy captive.

Her head snaps to see if I'm looking. I grin widely. *Yeah, beautiful, I got a glimpse of your heaven.* I expect her to look away, embarrassed, but she doesn't, and we stand still for several moments watching each other. I would have let supper burn, but she's the one who finally breaks the connection by smiling shyly before sashaying toward the lake with her dress now firmly in one hand to prevent another flare.

Fucking hell, that woman embodies the very definition of sex appeal. And the thing about it is, she doesn't even try. *That's* what makes her so damn fascinating. She's confident in herself, but she's also completely unassuming. It's an unbelievably attractive combination you don't find in most beautiful women. She's smart, funny, and sexy as hell. *Everything* about her is sexy. Her voice, her walk, her mind, her lips, her eyes, her tits, that nose ring. I could go on and on and on. She is the entire package of everything I find attractive about a woman wrapped up in about 120 pounds of sheer flawlessness.

I've brought other women to my home. I've cooked for them. I've wined and dined them. I'm not one of those guys who refuses to share his own bed for a night of reckless abandon, but I am particular about who I bring here. One-night stands? No. Women I'm dating? Yes.

Lianna and I spent quite a bit of time here, actually, but I will admit that I always reached the point when I wanted her to leave. In reality, like everyone else, she always seemed like a guest I couldn't wait to usher out the door at the end of the night. Rarely did I let her stay until morning.

But Willow? Totally different. She looks good here in my house. Very fucking good. When I saw her sitting regally in my chair that first night, my breath actually stuck in my lungs. I wouldn't even let Lianna sit there.

Willow, though...she looked like a stately, majestic beauty perched in her rightful throne.

I imagined fucking her in it and fucking her bent over it. I imagined her sitting at my feet while her tongue massaged my cock before taking me deep and blowing my mind. I've imagined so many carnal things that have involved her and that fucking chair. Wait till I get her to my bedroom or to my gym or to my hot tub. I'm afraid I'll never want her to leave.

And that's exactly why I shouldn't have invited her over tonight. It's precisely this feeling of perfection I can't allow to grow out of control, or I'll do the one thing to her I swore I wouldn't. I will hurt her when this ends.

When she told me we couldn't confuse what we're doing, all I could think was the lines are already so fucking blurry I don't know if I can get them back into focus. Then I blurted out something I should have chewed into tiny bits and swallowed instead.

It was true, though. I have no idea what she's doing to me. Being with her is messing with my head. It's making me act like a man I don't recognize. My outburst at La Petite? Driving over to her house to wait two hours for her to get home because she wouldn't answer my calls all day? No...that's not me. That's stalkerish, borderline psychotic even. I don't like it, and I should find a way to stop it. Only I already know I won't.

And while I can admit I want her, I also want her to want me. After I calmed down the other day, I realized I don't want a possession to flaunt. I want whatever is going on between us to be mutual, or she'll feel used. That's the last thing I want her to feel.

I check the fish one more time, seeing it's done. Setting everything on the table outside, I'm getting ready to call for Willow when I see her walking up the stairs.

She freezes as our gazes collide. Something unparalleled passes between us. It twists into place inside, cementing me to her. Or her to me, maybe. I fight the urge to rub my chest at the way my heart just expanded.

Jesus Christ.

This is fucking temporary, Merc. Temp-o-ra-reeeee.

"Dinner's ready," I practically croak.

The fragile moment breaks when her eyes drop. I take a deep breath to clear my head. It marginally works but is all for naught when she stops in front of me and gives me that brilliant smile, sucking me back into her. I'm helpless to fight it, and the kicker is...when she looks at me like this, I don't want to.

I'm fucked.

This is bad.

Bad.

Bad.

Bad.

Willow

Chapter Twenty

"WOW, THAT WAS FAST," I mumble. Shaw mentioned something about the media early on, but I didn't think he was serious. Why would anyone care about the mayor's son and who he dates?

I've read the short, uninformative article twice. I should be worried about what this means for me—I'm going to be exposed to the entire city of Seattle. Pretty soon, everyone will know my name, what kind of car I drive, my schedule. It won't be long before they start digging into my past. My father's suicide and my sister's drug overdose will be consumed by the public as if we're some sort of zoo animals in a glass bubble. I'll have to relive it all over again in black and white and listen to sympathetic platitudes from people everywhere I go.

The thought is gut twisting.

Again, I did not think this decision all the way through.

Right now, I should be in an all-consuming flat-out panic, trying to figure out how I'm going to return the twenty-five percent already sitting in my bank account. But I'm not.

All I can concentrate on is the stark look of want on Shaw's face in this picture. There's something more in his eyes, though, than just lust. Something everyone else will see, too. But is it just an act, or is any of it real?

My gaze lifts, latching onto his. He knows I've seen it, that I've been sitting here dissecting it for the past ten minutes. But he doesn't address it, so neither do I.

"I was thinking maybe I could contact this reporter and see if she wants to interview us." He gauges my reaction, but I'm still processing.

"Why would you do that?" I finally ask. The last thing I want to do is get my name in the press any quicker. The longer they don't know who I am the better.

He pushes off the counter he was leaning against and takes a seat beside me at the table. "Because then *we're* in control. We spin our own story our own way on our own timetable. Trust me, it's far better to control the media than vice versa."

It makes sense, I suppose. "I guess you're right."

"There's no guessing about it. I am right. I've managed the media for years, Willow. This is the right next step. I told you I would protect you, and this is the best way to do that."

I nod. I've had no exposure to this sort of thing, so I have to trust him. "Yes. Yes, okay. If that's what you think is best."

He nods once. "I do."

My eyes fall briefly as he twines my hand with his. Electricity dances on my skin like it does every time we touch. When I raise my eyes, my stomach free-falls at the barefaced yearning I see in the sharp lines of his lightly stubbled face. I start breathing faster.

"Shaw..." My voice cracks along with my willpower.

Tugging me until I stand, he positions me between his spread legs. Placing his hands on either hip, he leans forward and nuzzles my stomach, running his nose in hypnotic, erotic circles from one side to the other. The hot moisture of his breath penetrates the thin fabric as he kisses me through it. I fight hard to keep my head from falling back at the sensations gathering strength inside me like a violent windstorm.

Nudging me closer, he slides his palms to my ass, squeezing each cheek. His hands travel down, down until they hit the bare flesh of my thighs and start their unhurried descent back up.

"I can read your body so well already. The way it reacts when I'm near."

He drags the loose fabric up and over my hips. I gasp and jerk when he places an openmouthed kiss on the flesh right above my panty line. I'm so turned on I can barely get enough air through each slight inhale.

"The pulse in your neck picks up. Your heart pounds fast inside your chest. Your breaths become shallow and choppy, like now."

I swallow my denial. It would be a lie anyway.

Standing, he grips me snug in his desire-filled gaze as I let him completely divest me. I wore no bra, and except for my panties, I'm fully exposed. Vulnerable doesn't begin to describe how I feel.

"You want me to kiss you, don't you, Willow? Slow, deep, so methodical I steal your thoughts until you're only left to feel. You're dying for me to run my tongue down your neck, over your breasts, swirl it around your belly button, not stopping until I dip all the way between those silky folds that are already wet for me."

He's hotter than sin *and* a mind reader. Win, win.

Molten eyes sweep down my now exposed body, singeing me on their descent. My eyelids are heavy with longing, but I fight them open, unable to tear myself away from the erotic way his gaze kisses my skin, leaving prickles behind.

"You are exquisite," he gruffs thickly.

My nipples are painfully erect under his fiery stare. Bringing both hands up, I whimper when he grabs the tingling buds, pinching and twisting them none too gently, sending a flash fire of need to my pulsing, empty core.

He kneads and plucks, and his name fires on a rush of air when he circles one nipple with the wet tip of his tongue. Just when I think I'll explode from sheer frustration, he finally opens his mouth and takes the entire thing inside. His pulls are hard; his bites hurt like hell.

I want his mouth on mine, but I want it exactly where it is, traveling to my other needy breast. I want him to pave his way over my entire body before he fucks me with it until I cry. "Shaw, please."

I knew he'd be like this. Almighty. Potent. Controlling my breaths, my reactions. Working my body like a puppet. Exacting, as though we've already talked in the dead of night about what I crave.

This is precisely why I resisted him and why I won't be able to get enough.

"Please. I need more." I realize I'm already begging, which I said I wouldn't do, but who fucking cares? Pride is just a meaningless five-letter word at this point.

"You have no fucking idea how sweet that sounds." Lips now at my ear, Shaw fills me with wicked words when I want him to fill me with other things instead. His tongue, his fingers, his cock. Anything to ease this interminable ache I've had for weeks. "I know what you need, Willow. You need to fuck my fingers until they're coated in your release. You need to slide onto my cock, slow and steady and let me stretch you until you can't remember what it was like to be without me. Then you need me to fuck you, fast and hard, until your toes curl and I obliterate these crazy thoughts you have that this shouldn't be happening because we both know it has to. Tell me *that's* what you need."

Yes, yes. A thousand times yes.

He is temptation and I am a sinner.

With a murmured *yes,* I surrender myself on his altar of iniquity knowing there will be no angel of mercy that can save me now.

Shaw

Chapter Twenty-One

HER CHOKED SUBMISSION NEARLY HAS me coming in my jeans.

Coalescing need clashes inside me. I want to fuck her violent and dirty and never stop. But I want to take my time exploring every dip and curve with my fingertips and my tongue. I want to kiss her skin with my marks and brand it with my seed. I want to make her come a dozen times before I fuck her until she knows only me.

Digging deep, I draw on my many years of experience, forcing myself to slow down. I *need* to relax, or what I envisioned doing for hours will be over in mere minutes. I'm so close to exploding it's disconcerting.

"Be very sure this is what you want," I rasp against the soft column of her neck before taking a nip. "Once I start, I'm not stopping until I physically can't fuck you anymore." I'm not sure I'll stop even then.

One hand grips the back of her head, angling it for better access to the assault I'm placing down her throat, and the other is already tunneling underneath the line of her panties, pushing them into her crack as I savor the velvety feel of her bare ass for the first time.

My entire body vibrates with such powerful need for this woman I should be shitting bricks about now. I want to tear her completely apart. Rip her open. Own every scrap of who she is. Her breathy pleas and soft moans reduce me to nothing but a crazed Neanderthal.

"I want this," she pants brokenly as I simultaneously drag my teeth down over her collarbone and run a finger between her cheeks until I'm dipping into her wetness.

"Fuck, yes," I groan at how ready she already is for me. Nothing is more ego boosting than knowing you can make a woman drip with want. "I am going to own you tonight, Willow. Every fucking creamy inch of you is mine to do with as I please."

She doesn't answer, but it's probably because I've now dragged a copious amount of moisture to her back hole. I rim the puckered flesh and push in slightly, testing how far she's willing to go.

She doesn't fight it.

She sinks into it.

Damn, can this woman be more perfect?

"Oh yes, sweetheart," I whisper roughly against her lips. "We will get to that, but tonight I'm claiming the sweet pussy I've been jacking off to for weeks now."

"Shaw, please." Sweet desperation already threads her plea. So fucking hot.

"Please, what?" I taunt, sinking my finger into her asshole farther before slowly withdrawing and doing it again. Her body is opening, already undulating in my arms, reaching for more.

"It's not enough."

"I'll give you more than enough, Willow. Trust me on that."

Crashing my mouth to hers, I fuck her with my tongue the way I'm now doing with my finger until I need to catch my breath. I wanted to take her to my bedroom and worship her all night in the softness of my sheets, but by the way she's already clenching around me I'll never make it.

Breaking apart, I force myself to take a step back. She looks dazed like she thinks I've stopped. Only I'm just getting started. Calling on my control, I growl, "If you like those panties, you have five seconds to lose them or they'll end up in the garbage, shredded."

Her gaze darts around the kitchen. "Here?"

"Four."

"Take your clothes off, too."

Her demand is cute.

"Three," I announce sharply when she doesn't move.

Her witchy cobalt eyes turn defiant, wasting several more seconds of her precious time. Just when I'm reaching to rip the flimsy fabric from her hips, she dips her thumbs into the elastic and drags them slowly down her legs, taunting me.

"Jesus, Willow." My breaths come hard and fast when my eyes land on the juices shining on the insides of her thighs. I've barely touched her yet, and she's already gushing. *For me.* My cock is granite fucking hard, and the need to release myself from the sting of my zipper is overpowering. "Spread your legs."

In a carefully thought out move, she takes one of her feet and slides it over a few inches, smug satisfaction written all over her face. "Just so you know, I'm only following your bossy instructions because I want to."

Blatant lie.

The flush on her skin. The rapid movement of her chest. Her dilated pupils. All a dead giveaway that my authority is secretly what she thirsts for.

"You're not following them very well," I pipe back, chuckling lightly.

Though deep inside she wants this, if I expected Willow to be completely pliable in the bedroom, I should have known better. The fire banked inside this extraordinary hellcat burns white-hot, engulfing me entirely. Little does she know my need to make her wholly submit turns me absolutely primitive. Her defiance ignites me like nothing else I've known.

Smirking, I step into her body, wrap an arm around her

waist, and kick her foot over a few more inches. I finger a peaked nipple. She sucks in a sharp breath when I pinch and twist, and her lids slam closed as if I just flipped a switch.

"Your body defies your mouth, Goldilocks," I tell her lowly, dragging my tongue along her jaw. "I think you need to cede control as much as I need to take it from you."

"You're wr—"

I shut off her lies with a searing kiss until every muscle of hers weakens. It's too much to hope her stubborn spirit will follow, but I plan to make each second of her fight worth the surrender she'll give me. "The only thing I want to hear from your mouth right now is 'more, Shaw' or 'don't ever fucking stop, Shaw.' Understand?"

Glazed-over blues blink in slow motion.

I'll take that as a yes.

Releasing her tortured nipple, I let my hand skim down her sexy-as-fuck body until I reach the golden treasure I've been dying to sink my cock into. We're done playing games, and when I thrust two fingers into the tightest, silkiest, wettest pussy I can remember feeling in years, Willow's gasp is a song.

I set a quick pace, mercilessly pumping my fingers through her drenched desire, needing to watch her fall apart in my arms. I wanted to tease, but now I just want to take.

"Shaw, God," she moans. Her hips roll, fucking my fingers the way she needs in order to get off. I love a woman who is unrestrained, taking what she needs, taking what I give her.

"Do you need something, beautiful?"

Yes is but a breath.

"Tell me what you need." Swooping down, I draw one of her rosy peaks into my mouth. Her candied taste is addictive, unlike anything I've had before. I could suck her tits for hours.

"I…need…ahhhh…." She trails off when my thumb circles her hard, little clit, each pass getting firmer, taking her closer. "Please. God. Yes. More." Her one-syllable words are broken and almost inaudible.

When her walls clench around my slick digits, signaling

she's getting close, my heart kicks into high gear. I should withdraw my fingers and taste her whimpers of protest, but I've never anticipated a woman's orgasm more than Willow's. I've never wanted to savor the look of utter euphoria as much before, knowing that *I* put it there.

Needing to soak in the way her entire body reacts to me, I lean back but keep her liquid form steady in my arms. Her eyes are pinched tight and her mouth is open, but I'm only fascinated with the place where our bodies are currently joined.

I watch my wet fingers disappear between her pink folds over and over, working her closer to that place of pure bliss I want her lost in. Her moans escalate, the pace of her hips increases, and her nails dig through the fabric still covering my shoulders.

Her body hums for me. She's immersed herself completely in the moment, and she is magnificent.

"That's it, beautiful. Fuck my fingers just like that."

She mumbles incoherently until her last scream is crystal clear. "Oh God, Shaw. I'm coming."

Fucking hell. When she cries my name as she rides out the wave of ecstasy rolling through her *I* set in motion, I feel the power of it encase the organ beating wildly in my chest. That connection we shared earlier outside before dinner strengthens. I haven't been inside her yet and already I feel more tied to her than any other woman.

I should be worried about what that means, but I'm not.

All I'm worried about right now is how many times I can make her cry it again before we both pass out in utter satiation.

Willow

Chapter Twenty-Two

I'M HIGH.

Weightless.

Floating on a cloud constructed of passion while pure rapture fires through my blood.

The place I've reached is a paradise of indulgent intoxication. Nothing but decadent pleasure dwells here. My visit is brief but unequaled.

Every cell in my body begs me to stay, but suddenly I'm falling, the glorious feeling dimming too fast. Something soft envelops me completely, and I fight coming fully back into reality.

"Willow, you with me, beautiful?"

Shaw.

God. Shaw.

The hoarse need in his voice causes a fresh surge of desire to roll through me. When my eyes flutter open, I dimly note I'm lying on the plush white carpet in the living room, but I don't let myself think beyond that.

I can't take my eyes from the flawless masculine specimen standing above me.

Watching me with hooded eyes.

Wanting me.

Naked.

Stroking his weeping cock. It's as impressive as I thought it felt.

I am in absolute awe.

And a lot of nervous.

Sweeping my eyes up his nakedness, I follow the narrow goodie trail that leads from his dick up to his belly button before it thins out. His abs are cut, his chest is buff and smooth, his arms are thick and corded. He looks like airbrushed, absurd perfection except for the two overlapping puzzle pieces carved into the side of his torso.

"Want me to do that again?"

I'm met with a cocky smirk when I finally rip my eyes away from his tat to meet his gaze. Normally I would fight back at a comment like that, but all the fight left me. I want everything he promised me. And then some.

"Yes."

Stretching my arms above my head, I cross my wrists and ankles and smile when he hisses.

"Fuck. Stay exactly like that, Willow."

The way my body reacts to his authoritarian commands is alarming.

Don't think. Just feel.

With one hand still caressing himself, Shaw brings a foil packet I didn't see in the other to his mouth and tears it open with his teeth. His gaze never parts from mine as he rolls the condom on with practiced moves. I try not to think of how many times he's done this before if he doesn't even need a brief glance.

Kneeling down at my feet, he skims over me from my ankles to my core, letting his thumbs dip between my closed center. My breath hitches and my eyes fall shut when he pries my thighs apart.

"Open your eyes, beautiful," he cajoles.

I'm powerless to deny him.

Strong hands roam all over me as he talks, or should I say orders. "This time I want your eyes on me the whole time I'm making you break apart."

I bring my hands down to touch him, but he presses his warm, naked body to mine and puts them back, wrapping my fingers around the leg of the leather chair I sat in last time I was here. "Stay like this."

His hardness digs into the top of my pubic bone, and there's no way I can stop my body from writhing, trying to get him where I throb. One palm slips underneath my ass, tilting my hips. I think he'll stop me, but he starts moving in time with me. Each roll hits against my clit, and I think I may come again just by this.

"I want to touch you," I whine.

"Willow," he groans in my ear. "If you touch any part of me right now, I'm gonna fucking lose it. Next round. Promise."

"Next round?"

"Oh, yes." He smiles widely. I'm falling so damn hard. "I told you I was fucking you until I physically couldn't anymore. I always keep my promises."

My grin matches his. "You should stop wasting time, then. You're not getting any younger."

His carefree look darkens with one that's nothing short of predatory. It sends shivers down my spine and only heightens my anticipation to be wholly consumed by this magnificent man.

"Oh, my sweet, innocent little Goldilocks. Taunting Papa Bear results in a very ferocious bite."

I'm baiting. He's biting.

Good.

This won't be tender, but that's not what I want. I want rough, hard, dirty. I want him to fuck me so fast it borders on pain.

I *need* it that way, especially from him, to remember what this is and what this isn't.

"I don't mind the sting," I deadpan.

His eyes alight with the dare, I see the second he accepts. On a throaty rumble, he shifts his hips, aligning his cock with my core. I wrap my legs around his waist to help since my hands are tied with my invisible promise.

I'm so ready, even with my vagina's hiatus lately, that it only takes two firm thrusts before he's fully seated himself inside. We both groan at our intimate connection, and Shaw stills as my pussy stretches to accommodate his size. I feel the pulse of his cock with each heartbeat.

"Move," I beg. "Please."

He does, and after only a couple more drives, the burn quickly fades to the most intense pleasure I can remember. I feel like I was made for this man.

"Willow, Christ you feel good." His tone is guttural and reverent. Both sweet and harsh. When he groans "too good" as his lids shut momentarily, I'm lost to the pure ecstasy I see in him that simply cannot be faked.

That's it.

I give.

I'm his.

My body succumbs to him in every way as he braces himself on his forearms, digs his hands in my hair, connects his smoky orbs with mine, and fucks me like a man possessed. Flames lick my insides in the most delicious of ways with every rough withdrawal and violent plunge back in.

He silently demands my surrender.

I soundlessly submit.

He fucks me breathless, boneless, thoughtless.

"Come for me, Willow." His hissed command borders on frantic.

My issue during sex has always been my inability to ask for what I need. That's my issue in most parts of my life, actually. With Shaw, though, I feel safe to be me. To ask for what *I* need.

"Harder. I need harder."

Nostrils flared in surprise, he rises on his haunches, grabs under my knees and tilts my pelvis high, impaling me until he hits the sweet spot that makes me cry out.

"You like that?"

"Yes," I pant. *God, yes.* My walls tighten in small pulses as I hurtle toward the abyss. "Don't stop."

"I'm never fucking stopping, Willow. Never."

I don't want to fall. I want to balance here on this exquisite precipice forever, but seconds later as I tread in Shaw's bottomless depths, I feel an unstoppable current tugging me under, and I begin to sink. I helplessly fracture and drift to the murky bottom this time, shuddering as the heaviness pulls me further and further down into oblivion.

My mind blanks and I just feel.

Pleasure.

Freedom.

Peace.

All too quickly I'm wrenched back to the surface by Shaw's harsh growl. His hips piston so fast, my head now bangs against the chair leg I'd long ago released. His muscles stiffen, his fingers bruise, and his jaw locks as he follows, pumping furiously through his own release. The only time he lets go of my gaze is when he blankets my body and covers my mouth with his, kissing me sweetly. The contrast to the way we just fucked like animals and the way his mouth moves subtly against mine is startling.

"Fucking hell." His hoarse curse mists goose pebbles over my cooling, sweaty skin.

"Yeah," I croak, working to fill my lungs with enough air. Tracing my fingertips down the muscular lines of his back, I smile when he doesn't grumble. I press my palms fully to his heated skin on the ascent back up, reveling in the feel of each line and dip. I'm spent, but I want more of this. Of him.

"I need to catch my breath, beautiful, but then I'm going to eat you before I fuck you bent over this chair."

God almighty, this man has a filthy mouth. And a great imagination.

I arch my neck, exposing my throat to the tongue that's now licking its way up to my ear.

"You're assuming I want that, Drive By."

He never fully deflated, and at that tease, he's already hardening. When he shifts enough to thrust to the end of my womb, I can't hold in my moan. "Oh God," I purr, my hips lifting of their own volition to meet his.

"Yeah. That's what I thought," is his smug reply.

I nearly whimper at the emptiness not only my body but my soul feels when he withdraws, holding the base of the condom so no swimmers leak out. "Be right back, baby," he husks with a brush of his lips to mine.

Before I can get too far into my own head, he's returned with a strip of condoms and a wet cloth, which he hands to me. Flashing me a heartfelt smile, he grabs two throw pillows and a light blanket from the couch and tosses them on the plush carpet beside me before picking up a remote. The fireplace starts with a whoosh when he pushes a few buttons.

Fifteen seconds later, my head is in the crook of his shoulder and he's draped me over him. He covers us; the flames, the wool, and his body heat taking away the chill I now feel.

"You good?" His fingers feather my arm, and I try not to think of how fantastic this is. I didn't take Shaw Mercer for cuddling and pillow talk. I expected to be ushered to the door. Politely, of course.

I nod, the blaze hypnotizing me. "Yes."

"Tired?"

"A little," I admit. "Staring at a roaring fire always lulls me to sleep."

Tugging me tighter, he asks, "And good sex, right?"

"Fishing, Drive By?"

I love his laugh. "Hey, even us sex gods need the occasional validation."

"Sex god?" I tip my head and catch his eyes. When I do, my

sarcastic retort dies a quick death. They're soft and flirty at the same time. *Shit.* So bad. "Okay, I'll throw you a bone."

"So, I *was* good, then?"

I giggle, loving that there's no awkwardness between us. "You're going to make me say it, aren't you?"

"Damn straight, Goldilocks."

Pushing up on my elbow, I lean in close and sober my smile. Running my gaze over his face, I memorize each thin line in his smooth skin, the position of every microscopic fleck of amber in his blue eyes and the sharpness of his high cheekbones. That way I can recall every feature in a few months' time when he's gone. "Better than."

"Life altering, perhaps?" he quips with his sexy signature look, a lopsided smirk and a cocked brow.

Yes, dammit.

"Now who's twisting words?" I reply, a little uneasy.

Life halts. We're wrapped in a bubble, just the two of us. He sees me clearly. Knows I'm lying, even. It's unsettling. The blinds I hide behind are suddenly completely translucent, yet he's gracious enough to give me a pass.

"So." His voice cracks, and he clears his throat. "Did you have a fireplace growing up, or were you a pyromaniac?"

The magnetic pull I always find in his gaze breaks. I'm not sure if I'm grateful or disappointed. My head finds his shoulder again. "Well, after my pyro phase, I stuck to building fires in the fireplace." My father taught me that, I don't add. He taught me so many things. Now there are so many lessons he'll never get to pass on.

"I knew you were trouble the second I laid eyes on you."

"It didn't keep you away."

His finger slides under my chin, and he tips my head back up, giving me no choice but to look upon his gorgeous face once again. "On the contrary, it drew me in."

His sincerity hits me deep.

Now it's my turn to clear my throat. What we're doing right now feels too intimate. Having sex is one thing. It's physical. It's pleasure. It's biological even. I admit I have a hard time keeping emotions separated from the act, especially with Shaw, but I'm trying.

Flirting with your clothes off, though, treads dangerously into *I like you a fucking lot* territory. I was already playing in that minefield before; I didn't need another push. The grenades buried beneath my feet are getting harder and trickier to navigate.

"I got caught playing with matches once when I was six," I confess, trying to shift subjects.

His smile is thin, his face now unreadable. "Oh, so you *were* a little troublemaker?"

I shrug. "I was a rebel, what can I say." Yet I wasn't, and I don't know why I claimed otherwise. Between the two of us, my sister played that role. I toed the line, straight and narrow, always the good little girl.

"Still are, I think."

"No," I say softly, shaking my head. "In fact, I'm pretty damn boring."

He makes a low humming noise in the back of his throat before telling me in a soft voice, "I disagree. I think you're the most intriguing woman I've ever met."

I bite my lip, my chest feeling too full.

His eyes bounce between mine, questioning, penetrating. He studies me so long I start to get antsy. What does he see? What does he *want* to see? What do *I* want him to see? I'm not sure I know anymore.

When he fingers my necklace, I try not to tense. He latches my gaze again. "I like this. You wear it a lot."

"Yes," I answer thickly.

"Is it special?"

"Yes," I manage through a clog of emotion.

I can't look at him anymore, and I definitely don't want him asking more questions I won't answer. I sweep my gaze over his perfectly honed body. I guess being an important executive doesn't keep him from taking care of himself.

"I didn't take you for a tattoo kind of guy." I trace the ink just under his skin, completely aware I'm switching gears. Again. I need to keep this light, but he keeps bringing the heavy.

In an even voice, he replies, "It's my only one."

I briefly flit my gaze to his and prod teasingly, "A night of young rebellion?"

"More like trickery." He smiles thoughtfully. "I was twenty. Noah wanted to get a tattoo and somehow shamed me into getting one, too. I thought the 3-D in this was cool."

I analyze it for a minute. There are two puzzle pieces, gray shading giving them depth. The top piece appears it can be slid into place over the bottom one, which remains empty, but looks as if something is supposed to go in it. A name. A favorite team, maybe. Anything other than blank space. I like it. It's unique, but it feels… "It seems unfinished," I murmur.

"It is. I didn't know what to fill it with."

"For sixteen years, you couldn't come up with something you love enough to complete your tattoo?"

He shrugs. Shaw Mercer doesn't seem like he does anything without meaning or purpose. The fact that he got a relatively meaningless tattoo is surprising.

A yawn catches me off guard, and I throw a hand over my mouth. "Sorry," I mumble through closed fingers.

In a gentle move, he sweeps the back of his hand over my cheek before cupping my nape and pulling me down. His mouth brushes mine on a soft sigh. "Do you want to shut your eyes?" he whispers.

My heart in my throat, I whisper back, "Maybe for a minute," while keeping my eyes shut so he can't see the moisture there at the way his tenderness moved me.

I lie back down and a comfortable sort of quiet blankets us. The only noise in the vast room is our slow breathing, the crackle of gas flames licking the inside of three stone walls, and the one in my head screaming at me to get *The Fuck* out of here.

This feels too good. Too right.

It's too much.

I'm one step closer to hopelessly falling for him. Something I swore I wouldn't do. I have been unknowingly inching my way toward him this entire time, and what seemed like an impossible chasm of space to cover when we first met is now suddenly only a literal breath away.

How did this happen?

I need to leave. Put some distance between us. Get some perspective, but exhaustion trumps my need for protection.

Unable to get my limbs to obey my pleas to get dressed and get the hell out of Dodge before it's too late, I peacefully drift off in Shaw's arms to the rhythmic beat of his heart and the pungent scent of wild sex hanging in the air around us like a fog, knowing clarity won't come like this.

Obscurity is all that's ever found in a fogged mirror.

Shaw

Chapter Twenty-Three

WILLOW'S SCENT CLINGS TO ME as if it's sunk into my very pores. I take it in with every breath. It's intoxicating, even twelve hours later.

I've been racking my brain trying to figure out why my night with her was different from my nights spent with anyone else. Why do I have this unholy connection with her? Why can't I stop thinking about her? Why is her vulnerability endearing? Why did I think fucking her would douse this need burning out of control inside me?

It didn't.

If anything, it threw gasoline on the fucker.

She was right, though she was flippant when she said it. Sex with her *was* life altering.

Now all I can think of is her taste, her sounds, her pussy.

Jesus.

Her pussy.

Snug and hot, it squeezed me like a goddamn vise, molding to me like it was fucking custom made. If I didn't know better, I'd think she was a virgin as tight as she was. I fucked her twice more after I took her the first time. Once over the chair, as promised, after her little nap, and once against the wall leading to my bedroom. I couldn't even make it to my bed before I had to be inside her again. But she didn't seem to mind. She was as delirious for me as I was for her.

With her tucked to my side, we fell asleep right before midnight. Around two, she woke me and said she was going home. I wanted her to stay in my bed, her soft curves pressed against me. I wanted to wake her with my mouth and be buried inside her before breakfast. As much as I loved being inside of her, I enjoyed her in my arms equally. She felt *good* beside me.

I'd had one of the best nights I could remember with a woman, and I didn't want to let her leave, especially in the middle of the night. But when she pointed out spending the night would confuse things between us, how could I argue? She was right, though it didn't lessen the sting. I'm always the one to leave or to delicately show a woman to the door, so this role reversal was a little shocking. I didn't like it.

Now, like some starry-eyed prepubescent teen, I've been checking my phone repeatedly to see if she'll make contact. But why would she? This is a business arrangement that I went and flipped on its side. Changed the rules. Of course she won't reach out to me, even if she wants to, because we are not a couple. We are business partners who just happened to fuck each other's brains out last night. That's all.

Why is that no longer enough?

Why am I craving more? Of everything?

Why is the clock my worst fucking enemy right now, ticking off the minutes we have left together at blinding speed?

I check my phone again.

Nothing, dammit.

"Hey, Shawshank," my little sister's chipper voice calls from behind.

"You're late," I scold, setting my cell on the table when Annabelle takes a seat beside me. Just in case my "girlfriend" calls. *Sap.*

"Jesus, who pissed in your Cheerios?" She throws a bag as

big as a fucking grocery cart onto the floor along with her rain-soaked umbrella.

Switching gears from Willow, I take my sister in, carefully looking her over as I do every time I see her. Searching for the subtle clues that drug addicts think they can hide but can't. Agitation, overexcitement, dilated pupils, shaky hands, weight loss, excessive sniffling.

She's wearing a bouncy pink skirt, black combat boots, and a black Lion King tee that says "I'm Surrounded by Idiots." Other than the fact she has her long hair thrown up in a messy bun and she's donning thick black fashion glasses that make her look younger today, she seems fine.

"I haven't eaten Cheerios since I was seven years old, Bluebelle."

"Ah, that's right. You gave that up in favor of Fiber One, Excel spreadsheets, and pocket protectors for top-brass balls training."

I shake my head at her clueless concept of what it is I do. Before I can reply, the waitress returns and takes our lunch order. She orders a burger and fries, which is a good sign. Now I will make sure she eats it.

She takes a sip of the Mountain Dew I ordered her. She's addicted to that swill. Better that than coke. And by coke I don't mean Pepsi's most hated rival. "So, who's this latest bed warmer of yours Linc was babbling 'bout?" she asks sarcastically after swallowing.

This is the thing I love and hate with equal fervor about my baby sister. She's the same on the outside as she is on the inside, but she has less than zero control of her running mouth.

"Have some fucking respect, Annabelle."

"What?" She doesn't bother to feign contrition.

I'm unfairly angry over her trite comment. Rotating women in and out of my bed is what I do, and I plan to do nothing different with Willow. Why, then, does the truth burn like a hot poker to my side?

Because your little Goldilocks deserves more than that. More than you.

And why are you calling her yours?

"*What?* Well, the *what*, you insolent brat, is that you haven't even met her because you didn't bother to show up to dinner. So you certainly don't get to say a disparaging word about a woman you don't know. She is far more than someone to warm my bed, and you will treat her with nothing less than respect. Understand?"

Her eyes bug in shock. I put up with a lot of shit from my little sister. Her temper tantrums, her wallowing, her lying, her self-destructive behavior. But I will not put up with her saying a goddamn bad word about Willow. Line drawn.

Her blood-red painted lips split. "He was right."

"Who was right? What the fuck are you going on about now?"

"Linc was right. You *like* her, like her. This new," she pauses, choosing her words carefully, "woman."

"Willow. Her name is Willow," I say. More and more I understand what Willow means about the power of a name. Having Annabelle refer to her as just "a woman" is demeaning to Willow. She's not *just* a woman.

"Riiight. Willow. Cool name."

She eyes me carefully, but I give nothing away. I didn't ask Annabelle to lunch to talk about Willow. I'm already confused enough about her without having to justify or define my relationship. I saw things swimming in her eyes last night I know she didn't want me to see. I wonder what was in mine?

I didn't want to process it last night, and I don't want to in the light of day, either.

"So, how's school?"

"Classic deflection. Nice."

I sigh heavily. "I have a meeting in forty-five minutes, Bluebelle. Let's not waste it taking potshots at each other."

"Fine," she replies dryly. "But I want to meet this mystery woman who has you all protective and tied in knots. I don't think I've ever seen blinding stars in your eyes when you've talked about one of your trysts before."

"Annabelle," I growl.

I don't have stars in my eyes. *Do I?*

"Fine, fine." She throws her hands up, narrowly missing the waitress now trying to set our lunch on the table. After popping a few fries in her mouth, she gives me the update I wanted to hear. "It's going good. Organic chem is kicking my ass, but other than that, pretty good."

"Why the hell are you taking organic chem if you're a music major?"

She shrugs a shoulder. "I wanted a challenge. It's an elective."

This is the other thing I may not have mentioned about Bluebelle. She's brilliant. Like off-the-charts genius, so when she says she's struggling in a class, what she really means is she missed a point or two on a test. At twenty-one she already has her degree in secondary education; then she decided she wanted to be a music teacher. All this right in the middle of rehab. This is why I could never work out her drug addiction. She's smarter than that, but I guess even smart people fall victim to its pain-numbing allure.

"And everything else is going fine then?" I prod, watching her response carefully.

She takes a deep breath and blows it out slowly before turning her sharp eyes on me. "Shaw, just ask me what you want to know, and stop beating around the fucking bush. No, I'm not using again. No, I'm not back with Eddie. No, I haven't fallen back in with my old friends. No, I don't want to slit my wrists. Yes, I'm going to counseling. Yes, I still talk to my sponsor daily, sometimes more, and yes, I'm happy. Does that about cover it?"

"Annabelle—"

"Look, I get it. I was a hot mess there for a while. I fucked up. A lot. I put you, Mom and Dad, and everyone through hell. But I'm better now. I swear. I'm not saying every day is easy, and I'm not saying I never think about doing a line because that would be a lie and you'd see through that bullshit. But I have my life back on track. I call Cal when I need him. I'm clean, and I work hard every day to stay that way. Satisfied?"

I nod my head slowly, swallowing hard. This is the first time she's acknowledged the sheer hell she put us all through. It's progress. Reaching over I grab her hand. "I just want what's best for you. I love you, Annabelle. I'd do anything for you." I am doing *everything* for you.

Her demeanor softens. "What's best for you isn't what's best for me, though."

My voice hardens. "I've never pushed any agenda on you, Annabelle. I'm your number one supporter."

"I know you are."

"And so are Mom and Dad," I add. I didn't miss her unspoken words.

She shakes her head. "No, they're not. They expect perfect little children with perfect little lives and perfect little jobs that fit neatly into their perfect little political world. Illusions of perfection are all they care about."

"We're all a light year away from perfection. You're being unfair."

"I'm not, Shaw. You can't see it because you're the son they revolve around. And yes, that's spelled S-O-N, not S-U-N. You're rich, you're successful, and you're half a step away from God status."

I huff. "That's the furthest fucking thing from the truth."

"Believe what you want, but all I ever heard about when I was growing up was Shaw this and Shaw that. You're the golden boy, and the rest of us are a pukey, dingy yellow in comparison. I know Linc always felt ostracized, and Gemma is neutral, I guess. I felt like a nuisance at best and unwanted at worst."

Is that true?

I open my mouth to object, but stop. Annabelle was just three when I graduated from high school and moved out. I was home a lot, but I never lived there again. How can I say what went on in that house, day in and day out, when I wasn't witness to it?

Did my parents make my baby sister feel unworthy, perhaps unintentionally?

"Have you talked to them about this? Linc and Gemma?"

She holds my stare too long, and I can't help the pang of hurt I feel when she answers, "Yes."

Shit. "Is this why..." I swallow hard. "Is this...?" I can't even voice what I'm thinking. Am *I* the reason my baby sister felt the need to act out and numb her pain with drugs? Because she felt like she could never live up to me? Is that why she didn't feel she could talk to *me* about this before now? The thought makes me nauseous.

"Shaw, no." Now she grabs my hand. It's clammy and might be shaking a little. "I made my own decisions. I'm not blaming you or even Mom or Dad. Maybe at the time I did, but I realize now it was my own inadequacies and insecurities that drove me to drugs. It was never you. Please don't think that."

This is the frankest conversation I've ever had with Annabelle. I should be happy that she's finally opened up, but all I feel right now is crushing guilt. I wasn't there when she needed me. I should have been around more when she was growing up. I should have done a better job at making her feel wanted, special, at embracing her uniqueness instead of making her feel like she needed to live up to...*me*. Hell, I'm not even that great. She's fascinating. She's smart and funny and brash and always true to herself. Sometimes *I* envy *her*.

I pull her to me, clinging, uncaring if I'm making a scene. I want to take all her sadness into me and leave her with nothing but happiness and joy and promises of a bright future. "I'm sorry," I whisper hoarsely. My eyes burn, and I'm five seconds away from handing over my man card in a very public place.

"Stop it. You have nothing to be sorry for. If anyone should be sorry, it's me. You're the very best big brother I could have ever asked for, and honestly, Shaw, if not for you, I'm not sure

I'd be sitting here right now, clean and sober. You saved me on more than one occasion. Hell, if not for you and Noah, I'd probably be in jail."

Too true.

"I love you, Bluebelle."

"I love you, too, Shawshank."

"I'd do anything for you."

"I know that."

"I wish you'd try harder with Mom and Dad. Regardless of what happened growing up, I do know they love you. Unconditionally," I tell her softly. I know the time is right to say this. I've learned I have to choose my moments with Annabelle carefully. This is the right one.

"I'll try," she whispers. "Shaw."

"Yeah."

"You can let me go now."

"Oh, sorry."

Just as I release her, my phone rings, and my heart soars—until I look down and see it's our father. Disappointment runs through me that it's not the one person I want to hear from.

I glance at Annabelle. One of our unspoken rules when we get together is no cell phones. I always try to carve out dedicated time just for her.

"It's okay. You can get it."

"You sure?"

She waves to my ringing device before digging into her burger.

"Hey, Dad. What's up?"

"Are you busy tomorrow night, son?"

Yes. I plan to be buried balls deep in Willow. Somehow, someway.

"I don't know. I'll have to check my calendar. I have a Children's Hospital board meeting around the corner; I just can't remember which day this week it is. Why?"

Annabelle slides her gaze my way, clearly wondering what's going on.

"I'm hosting a very informal get-together with a few supporters at my house tomorrow night, and I'd like you there."

I sigh quietly.

"It's short notice. I'll see what I can do."

"That's fair. Oh, and I'd also like you to bring that girl of yours. Willow."

A slow smile spreads on my face. "Yeah. I'm sure we can make that work." Very fucking sure. "I'll just double check our schedules and let you know."

"Perfect. It would make your mother very happy. She's talked nonstop about her since you brought her over."

I sober. Shit. I'm a horrible son. I should have anticipated that my mom would fall in love with Willow. I'm wondering if it's impossible not to.

Having no choice, I push the guilt aside and remember why I'm doing this. For my father. For my baby sister. For my other siblings, to keep their personal shit out of the limelight. I'd sacrifice all that I have, all that I am for them. My mother will be disappointed when Willow and I "break up," but she'll get over it just as she has with every other daughter-in-law hopeful.

"If I have a conflict, I'll try to rearrange so we can be there."

"Thanks, son."

I hang up, excitement bubbling inside. I have a few scheduled events coming up, but not enough, so this is absolutely perfect. Even if we have to spend the evening with a bunch of stuffy politicians and bootlickers, it doesn't matter as long Willow is by my side.

"Something good, I take it?" my little sister asks.

"Yes. Very good," I reply, finally digging into my own meal.

As I devour my greasy fries, I try to ignore the little voice inside my head whispering that my mother may not be the only one falling for this girl.

Willow

Chapter Twenty-Four

I TAKE ONE LAST LOOK at the three circular purple bruises dotted on either thigh before letting my skirt drop, smoothing it to be sure it's wrinkle free. Instead of tonight, I try to focus on them, who put them there, and how damn good it felt to be wanted so fiercely your partner loses all control, marking you as his in the heat of passion.

Even though I'm not.

His, I mean.

He almost had me the other night. I nearly caved and stayed in his warm embrace. I wanted to. Jesus, did I *want* to. But I couldn't. If I stayed cuddled up with him all night like we're really some couple starting a brand-new relationship, I'll fall further into the lie myself. It's one thing to fool everyone else; I can't afford to fool me, too.

Tension twists my stomach again. I don't know why, out of any date we've had so far, this night makes me most nervous. There's an unknown in the air. It's as if I have a sixth sense that something big is going to go down, shifting the path I'm on. Again. I felt it the same the night my sister overdosed. I felt it the same the night my father died.

Maybe it's just seeing Shaw for the first time since we had sex. And that's what it was, I keep telling myself. Sex. Just raunchy, can't-get-enough-of-you, downright-dirty sex. It didn't mean anything. Not a thing.

Except it did.

I wasn't supposed to feel like I did. I wasn't supposed to feel soft and squishy and melted into a pile of goo. I was supposed to feel empowered and reenergized and plain old satisfied. The itch scratched—and scratched well. Instead, I felt...adored.

The urge to call or text or drive to his house and lie naked on the kitchen table, giving myself over to him completely the next day was frightening. It's all I thought about all day, but instead of acting on it, I harnessed it. I threw myself into my narration of *Forsaking Gray* and made great progress.

My gut churns when the doorbell rings. I stand still too long, and it dings again. I imagine Shaw on the other side, impatient. Taking a few deep, calming breaths I check my reflection in the mirror one more time, ignoring the excitement I see staring back.

"Hi," I say evenly when I open the door. *I've missed you* is on my tongue, but I spit it out before it catches sound.

"Hi, yourself," he replies in that baritone voice that's like a warm blanket wrapping around me. I preen under his long perusal, feeling his eyes as they travel the length of me.

"You ready?" I ask, grabbing my purse from the table next to the entrance.

"Not quite."

I take a step back for each he takes forward until he grabs my waist and spins me, pinning me to the inside wall. He digs his hands through my hair once he has me in place. "You look breathtaking, Goldilocks," he growls before slanting his mouth over mine.

Our kiss breathes and pulses and gathers steam until it takes on a life of its own. Desperate need sweeps us up in her maelstrom until I feel raw and stripped and one with him. How can a simple kiss affect me like this?

Because nothing about Shaw Mercer is simple.

"I want to be inside you more than anything right now," he pants, nipping down my jaw harshly. As if he thinks I need proof, he bends his knees, aligning his cock with my core, and nearly makes me weep when he presses forward into my pounding clit.

"I'm not stopping you." I spread my legs apart farther. Fuck it. I'm done pretending I don't want him. I do. Regardless of whether I end up with a broken heart, I want this, and for the next few weeks, I'm going to take it.

"Willow…fuck." I gasp when he drives his hips into me again. "If I hadn't promised my father we'd be there, you'd already be coming around my cock."

"Now you're just teasing." I moan as he keeps up his relentless assault, edging me closer.

"Are you wet for me, Willow?"

"Drenched."

Groaning loudly, he drops his forehead to mine and grips my hips hard, stilling their motion. Ragged breaths drizzle over my face. "We'll stay an hour, tops. Then I'm going to bring you back here, and you're going to let me do whatever I want to this sinful body."

"Okay."

Drawing back, he looks me in the eye. "Okay? Just like that? No snippy comeback?"

I drop my head back to the wall and smile. "I knew it, Drive By. I knew you liked my lip."

He laughs, a mischievous look crawling across his face. "You're right, Goldilocks. I like both glossy sets, actually. Very much." His voice drops. "But I have to admit, I also envision you on your knees, those mouthy lips milking my cock dry, too."

My stomach flips, skin heating when his gaze drops to my mouth and stays. The mood perceptibly shifts from playful to serious.

Cupping one cheek, his body is flush with mine as he leans

slowly into me until only a breath separates our mouths. With every slow exhale, his longing fans my face. My legs wobble when he lightly runs his nose along the side of mine. It's erotic and tender, and oh God, steals a part of me. My lids feel heavy. They weigh a hundred pounds. I give up the fight and let them fall shut just as he says my name, the hoarse whisper sounding like a benediction, reaching my ears only a second before his lips ghost mine.

This time the kiss is sweet, sensual, and drugging. Meaningful. Giving instead of taking. It bursts with promises I want...but know aren't there.

God help me.

I know what this is. I know what's happening.

I'm falling in love with this man despite my best efforts, and I don't know how to stop it.

More importantly, I think it might be too late.

"Willow, dear. So nice to see you again." Adelle Mercer draws me into her bony embrace. She's a slight woman who could stand to eat a few pieces of cheesecake.

"You, too, Mrs. Mercer."

"Adelle, dear. I thought we moved past that last time."

We did, but it's too personal. I'm falling in love with your son and your family, and I'll be but a distant memory by the new year. I manage to smile and say, "Okay, yes."

"You know, Shaw doesn't often bring a woman around more than once," she whispers low.

I believe that to be true. I think about the beautiful brunette and wonder if he brought her here to meet his family.

"Is that so?" I ask.

I turn my head to see Shaw observing us as he did last time I was here. Contemplative is the best way I can think to describe him. Kicking up one corner of his mouth, his smile is easy, slightly cocky and leaves me giddy. *Giddy*, for God's sake.

Like I'm some sort of teenager on a date with the star quarterback.

Shaw held my hand all the way here. Our conversation was light and carefree. Comfortable, not forced. Regardless whether you want it to or not, sex redefines a relationship. I didn't know what to expect when I saw him tonight, but I'm so far off balance right now, if Adelle Mercer wasn't holding my arm in hers as she ushers me inside, I may stumble.

"Can I get you a glass of wine, Willow?" she asks sweetly as we weave our way through her spacious home into the kitchen.

"Yes. White, please, if you have it."

"Of course. Pinot Grigio all right?" The noise escalates the closer we get to the hub of activity.

I smile and nod, and she hurries off to be a good hostess.

All I know about tonight is that it's a party for some of Preston Mercer's political supporters. I know no one in politics or in the mayor's inner circle, but my senses are on high alert nonetheless. The closer we got to Mercer Island on the drive here, the more my stomach twisted.

Maybe my nerves have nothing to do with seeing Shaw at all. Maybe it's the lies we're spinning. Shaw's family is wonderful, and I feel shame at pulling one over on them, pretending we're some happy couple falling in love. The falling in love part is true. At least for me, only there will be no happily ever after for us.

"Willow, glad you could make it."

Preston Mercer hands Shaw a tumbler with a couple fingers of amber liquid and me a half-full stemless wine glass before placing a chaste kiss on my cheek. I laugh when Shaw growls a low warning beside me.

Shaw is the spitting image of his father. The first time I saw him I saw Shaw, only with graying hair around the temples and a few more laugh lines around his mouth.

But looks aren't all Preston passed down to his son. He's just as disarming as Shaw. I would put the mayor in his early sixties, and I liked him immensely the minute I met him. He gives off good vibes and is genuinely sincere. His love for his wife and family is palpable, his passion for this city unmistakable. I think you can tell a lot simply by watching how people interact with each other, more so than their words. And when I watch Preston Mercer, I see strength, confidence, honor, and heart. Much like his son.

He hasn't let success or wealth or power go to his head. He's the real deal, and I can't see how he won't win this upcoming election. He's the people's mayor. Seattle is lucky to have his leadership.

"Thank you for the invitation, Mr. Mayor."

"Oh, shush. It's Preston to you. You keeping my son out of trouble?" His tone is light, but his question is chock-full of meaning.

Forcing a smile, I throw a glance at Shaw before turning back to the mayor. I snake my hand over to Shaw's, twisting our fingers together. "Well, he's a hard one to keep in line, but I'm pretty confident in my abilities."

That earns me a laugh. From Preston. When I look at Shaw, he's not laughing. He's looking at our hands.

Oh. Shaw.

He's so damn baffling.

"Shaw, can I steal Willow for a few minutes? I'd like her to meet some people."

"Sure," he mumbles, dragging his eyes back up to my face. They're blazing and catch me on fire. Before he lets his father parade me around, he tugs me to him using our connected hands. He gently pinches my chin between his thumb and the knuckle of his forefinger, and, without a care that his father—or anyone else—is watching, drops a lingering kiss on my lips.

He tastes of whiskey and banked desire.

"Hurry back, beautiful."

"Okay." I mouth it because I'm stunned and have temporarily lost my voice.

This is not an act. It can't be. It's not on my part anymore. In one breath he tells me this is temporary, yet his eyes say the polar opposite. He feels something for me other than lust. I *know* I'm not making up the look of pure adoration on his face. Our gazes hold momentarily. I wish I knew what he was thinking.

"I won't keep her long," Preston tells his son with amusement before he hauls me away. Shaw gives me a cheeky grin, which I return as I wiggle my fingers at him.

It's a beautiful summer day in Seattle. With the temps hovering around the eighty-degree mark, the party has spilled outside. The entire time I'm led around and introduced to advisors and staff and supporters, I feel Shaw's eyes on me. He subtly moves around so he can keep me in his crosshairs, whether I'm inside or out on the expansive patio. It's a warm feeling I don't think I could grow tired of.

Twenty minutes later when Preston cuts me loose, Shaw is in deep conversation with a man who looks to be about his age. I take the opportunity to wander a little, looking at all the family photos Adelle has lining the walls and shelves. I begin to wonder why I was all that nervous about tonight and decide my sixth sense must be off.

On the grand piano in the corner of the main room, a picture catches my eye of a young, beautiful girl who must be Shaw's sister, Annabelle, whom I haven't met yet. She looks to be about ten in this picture and is playing the piano. It must have been snapped while she was performing because she's wearing a fancy dress and the piano is on some sort of stage. She's thoroughly immersed, lost in the music she's creating.

Though I feel an ache of sadness, I also feel an immediate, unshakable bond.

She reminds me of Violet.

Violet was unnaturally gifted. A musical prodigy. She could write it, play it by ear, and carry a tune. I could sit for hours listening to her practice, never picking out a mistake. But Violet was a perfectionist. Compulsive, like my father. She'd play the same piece over and over and over, and even then she was never completely satisfied. If I close my eyes and concentrate hard enough, I can still hear the smooth notes floating through the house, up the stairs, into my room.

I finger the necklace at my throat, the one that's a combination of us, wondering what my sister would be like if she were alive today. Would she still be tortured, or would she have embraced her God-given gift? Would she be married? Would I be an aunt? Would *two* of us have been enough to save our father?

I'm so engrossed in my memory I don't feel anyone approach.

"You doing okay, beautiful?" Shaw breathes in my ear as he winds his arms around my waist from behind.

I take in a deep gulp of air, blowing it out slowly. "Yes, fine. Why?"

"You seem…I don't know. Lost."

I hate how he sees me so clearly. I hate but need it in the same breath.

Leaning my head back against his shoulder, I let his body heat seep into me, enjoying our stolen moment, focusing on the here and now. I tilt my head up, knowing he's waiting on an answer, and I give one that's true. "You left me wanting you."

"Jesus, Willow. You're going to ruin me," he breathes. "Has it been an hour?" I feel his erection growing at the small of my back. Oh, how I want this man. Somehow, some way, he fills this bottomless cavern I have inside, making the loneliness not so crushing. I'll live in it as long as I can.

"No." I chuckle. "And we're not leaving yet."

"Why?" His attempt to pout looks ridiculous.

"Because it's rude, that's why. And apparently, you need to learn some patience."

"Patience is for nuns and schoolteachers."

"Really? Only nuns and schoolteachers?"

"And maybe daycare providers."

We're both laughing when Preston's deep voice booms, "Shaw, I need you in the kitchen a minute."

Shaw sighs heavily. "Duty calls," he says with resignation.

"Be nice. This is important to your father." He spins me in his arms, and I wind mine around his neck.

"You're an incredible woman, Willow. You know that, right?"

"Why yes. Yes, I do," I sass. He cuts off my giggle with his lips and only breaks free when his father calls his name again. "I want you to come home with me. Spend the night in my bed."

"Shaw..." My teeth find my lip. My heart pounds. This is a bad idea. *Isn't it?*

"Please." His soft plea should kill my protest, but it's his eyes that really do me in.

"Okay," I reply quietly.

His grin is downright boyish and unlike him. With my hand in his and one last peck, Shaw leads me back into the fray.

This is insane. I'm treading on ice so thin it can't possibly hold my weight, but I'm deliriously happy right now. I foolishly tell myself that if I'm careful enough with each step, testing it out before I take the next, I won't fall through.

When we reach the kitchen, Preston is facing us, talking to an impeccably dressed man whose suited back is to us. I met everyone here tonight, and I don't recall seeing him before. He must have just arrived.

"There you two are. Shaw, I'd like you to meet my campaign manager."

The man turns our way, and as his profile comes into focus, time pushes down on me. I hear the squeal of brakes. Feel the g-force of momentum as the second hand grinds to a halt, and I know now my sixth sense was not wrong.

His gaze lands first on Shaw. I see his mouth move, his hand extend, and Shaw firmly shake it. Everything is long, drawn out, clicking along frame by agonizing frame. I feel as if I'm having an out-of-body experience, watching this scene unfold at a snail's pace through someone else's eyes.

This can't be happening.

This can't *be* happening.

This *cannot* be happening.

"And this is Shaw's girlfriend..."

Preston continues talking, but all I hear is *his* sharp intake of air. I feel the moment his gaze lands on me. I see the shock and confusion in his emerald eyes. I may even hear his heart stutter a few beats.

If I weren't stunned to the floor, I would have reacted differently. I would have covered it up. Feigned indifference. Held out my hand and shook his as if the very air between us wasn't woven with history and heartbreak.

But all my acting skills went out the door when I heard him softly whisper my nickname in utter disbelief. "Summer?"

It's the one that stuck after hot summer nights spent on the rocky banks of Lake Union, listening to crickets, waves splashing, drinking cheap wine from a box in plastic cups. Falling slowly in love.

The one I'd purposely used at La Dolce Vita, not to remind myself of him, but to remind myself of all I'd lost for throwing him away like he never mattered, when in retrospect, he was all that did. It reminded me of mistakes not to make again.

I try to swallow through the past now lodged tightly in my throat, but it doesn't budge. I'm hyperaware of both Mercer men's eyes on me, and while all I can think of is how it would be very convenient if the floor opened up and took me whole, I know I won't get that lucky.

So, I stand firm, maybe a little less tall than before, and croak out a hello to a man I once thought was my forever. The one I left sleeping in our bed as I snuck out in the dark of night because I couldn't see past the bleeding agony of grief in my soul.

Hurting him is the one colossal regret that drags me down to this day.

"Hi, Reid."

Shaw

Chapter Twenty-Five

WHAT THE ACTUAL FUCK IS going on?

He's looking at Willow as if she's a fucking hologram flickering in and out of focus.

His face is screwed up in surprise and disbelief.

He called her Summer.

Summer.

The same front she uses at La Dolce Vita.

As.

An.

Escort.

That can't be coincidence.

Is he another "coworker"? Former client? Lover? More?

As everyone stands mute, trying to solve this little riddle, only a clueless fuck would miss the invisible thread of history linking these two. And I think we've already established that I'm not clueless, and I'm certainly not a clueless *fuck*.

When I see him eyeing the necklace she always wears, a pained look flashes lightning fast over his face. I tuck Willow into my side and aim a death glare at the competition across from me, wondering how they know each other. Wondering how *well* they know each other. Wondering who the fuck this guy is or was to her.

The thought that he's tasted her addictive flavor or heard her sighs of pleasure when she's coming undone makes me absolutely feral. Bloodthirsty.

Jealousy and possessiveness seethe black and white-hot through me, leaving dark, sticky, tarry hate in its wake. It's an unfamiliar, unsettling, unwelcome emotion, just like last time. I want to stop it. It has no place between us. This is fleeting. *We* are fleeting.

"You two know each other?" I ask with a distinct bite that tastes foul and hateful.

Reid's—or fuckface as he's now known to me—stunned eyes volley like ping-pong balls between Willow and me, his face contorting even further.

"Uhhhh..."

And clearly, he's not articulate either. How my father ever hired his sorry ass to manage his campaign, I'll never know. But unless he wants a big, fat "L" on Election Day I think it's time he give this guy the boot. Or perhaps a giant shove off Ballard Bridge.

"Yes, we were in theater together a few years ago," Willow answers softly. "It's nice to see you again, Reid."

Theater? Is she telling the truth, or is this just another fucking act, because I gotta be honest...sometimes it's hard to tell with her.

"You, too, Willow," he mumbles. Dumbly. But that's just my humble opinion.

"Will you gentlemen excuse me? I need to visit the ladies'."

"Of course, dear," my father replies.

My hand catches hers before she can sneak away—again, I'm not a clueless fuck—and I pull her back into me. When her eyes drift up to mine, they're blank. Those goddamn shields dropped down like impenetrable steel shutters. Closed for business lit in flashing neon blue.

It guts me.

I need to bring her back to me before she drifts further.

Just like earlier, I don't give a shit who is watching. I ignore the widening of her eyes and let my mouth find hers, kissing her rigid lips until I feel them relax. I admit I want to piss on my territory in front of every male, one in particular right now, but as soon as we make contact, it became about her. Just her. I want her to know she's wanted by me in so many ways.

"You okay?" I whisper only for her ears.

"Yes." She tries to smile, but it falls flat. Then she's gone, and I'm left standing there watching her walk away from me. Running from *him*.

When I pivot back toward this unwelcome interloper, I read my father's face perfectly. *Not here. Not now.* Normally that would be enough but tonight, Fuck. That.

My turf. My woman. My rules.

"So, how do you know Willow again?" I ignore my father's groan.

Yes, I didn't miss how he covered up his error by calling her Willow. So now this situation stinks fouler than Pike's Market before dawn. The thought he knows both sides of her when I fight for every bit of her makes me burn wild.

"As she said, we met at theater."

I take this guy in. About an inch taller than my six-one frame. Maybe a few more pounds on me. Wrinkles starting to show around the eyes and mouth. No gray mixed in his sandy-brown hair. Early thirties, if I had to guess. Fit. Clearly successful if his tailored suit and the way he carries himself is any indication. I don't generally go around judging men's looks on a scale of one to ten because I'm into women, but if I had to rate him, I loathe that he falls toward the higher end.

"Which one?" I challenge his bullshit lie.

His eyes sweep me. Sizing me up, too. Finally, I see a hint of balls. His eyes turn flinty, his lips thin, and if we weren't standing in the presence of his employer right now, he'd probably have taken a step toward me. Hell, I would have already been up in his face.

"Seattle Public."

"What did you do there?"

He debates, deciding on if he'll answer. "We were in a play together."

"Really? A play, you say? And you were...what? Friends? Cast mates? *Love* interests?"

"Jesus, Shaw." My father's voice is tight and carries a warning. I ignore it.

Reid's jaw ticks furiously. He's trying to remain steady. He's as flustered as Willow is, but he can't run. He can't hide. If he so much as moves an inch, I will hunt him down like a fucking rabid dog.

Then a thought hits me, and oh, the irony. *This* guy right here is responsible for me being with Willow in the first place. His brilliant plan for Preston's eldest son to divert the media's attention from the less savory parts of the Mercer family may be backfiring on him a bit.

I breathe deeply and smile, pleased with this outcome.

"How did *you* two meet?" Reid asks pointedly, crossing his arms. A bushy brow cocks in unspoken challenge. My hackles rise. I swear if I had fangs, they would have dropped and been buried in his neck by now.

And I'm not giving him shit. He is a temporary thorn in my side, and I don't owe him a goddamn thing. Whatever I have with Willow is none of his business, regardless of how it came to be.

I throw back the rest of the Scotch I've been nursing, setting the empty glass down on the counter next to me. "You know," I start, pinning him with a glare, "fate is a funny thing. She sets people in our paths when we least expect them but when we need them the most...even if we didn't realize we did at the time."

I've never once in my life believed that to be true. Until now. Until *her*. Regardless of what our future holds, she will be forever embedded in me.

His face is as dark as I imagine mine is. Protectiveness

hemorrhages around him, pooling at his feet. It becomes crystal clear to me that whatever past he shares with Willow, he cared deeply for her. Maybe still does.

I want to bleed him out.

I decide I'm done with whatever this is and leave to find Willow. She's been gone longer than she should, and somehow I doubt she'll return on her own. When he finally speaks, I'm two steps toward the hallway that leads to the bathroom. To *my* woman.

"I couldn't agree more."

That statement is ripe with connotation. My gait falters, but I don't turn. If I do I will drop him where he stands, crowd or not. Election or no.

My father had better keep this fucker far, far away from me, or I'll be creating a bigger scandal than a few unscrupulous threesomes.

Shaw

Chapter Twenty-Six

"WILLOW, OPEN UP, BEAUTIFUL." I rap my knuckles on the door separating her from me. I hear shuffling but don't see the knob turn. I test it. "If you think a flimsy lock is going to keep me from you, Goldilocks, you're dead wrong. I mastered picking every lock in this house by the time I was nine. Now, open up."

I hear her huff a second before the door flies open. I half expect tears. I'm relieved not to see any. I see a myriad of other emotions, though, but right now what's front and center is anger. Directed at me.

"Jesus. Can't a girl get any privacy around here, Drive By?"

"No," I gruff, stepping inside before closing us back in. *And you're no girl. You're* my *girl.* I want to say it, but the words won't come. Christ, how has *this* woman gotten to me, making me think thoughts I've never entertained when no others could?

"You've been gone a long time." I lean against the oak, my hands tucked behind me. I'm afraid if I get any closer to her, I won't be able to control myself. Fucking her in my parents' guest bathroom while a party is going on only feet away is probably considered bad form. I almost don't care. In fact, the thought of *Reid* hearing her scream my name actually sounds quite appealing, making me rethink my restraint.

"I've been gone for less than five minutes," she pipes back.

"That's four minutes too long."

After a heavy sigh, she says, "I was just coming back. The wine didn't sit well."

I study her.

Her eyes. Her demeanor. Her breaths.

Her lies.

"Who is he?"

I swore with every step I took toward this room I would not do this again. That I'd learned my lesson after the other day. I seethe green, but I have no valid reason to. She has a past. I have a past. This is a business deal. *Yes,* my conscience whispers...*a business deal that's suddenly spun on its fucking side.* I may have different feelings for Willow than for anyone else, but that doesn't mean we have a future. It doesn't mean I need to unearth every skeleton she has. I remind myself this is not my business.

Unless he's a threat to what we're doing. Which he very well may be.

Yeah. My irrationality jumps on board that justification train lickety-split and I forge ahead.

"I told you already," she says evenly.

"Was he a client?"

"No," she replies adamantly.

"Another coworker?"

"No."

"Was he your lover?"

"Shaw. Stop."

Fuuuuck.

"Was he more?" I press, deciding I don't care if I shouldn't be jealous. I am.

Did he love her? Did she love him? Does he know things about her I want to know? Does he hold her memories, her dreams, her secrets, her fears, her regrets? Does he know the

Willow who hides behind the shroud? Does he have everything I didn't really know I wanted until this very moment?

She cocks her head, her face unreadable. "I thought we already talked about this."

Nice nonanswer.

"About what? About the fact that my father's campaign manager, the same one who suggested...*this*"—I wave my fingers back and forth between us—"happens to be a long-lost buddy? A scorned lover? That's pretty convenient, don't you think, *Summer*?"

Her eyes harden. Her jaw sharpens. Her body stiffens like a board. The blood in my ears roars so loudly I barely hear her say, "Nothing about this is convenient."

"I'd say."

The quiet that bears down on us is nearly suffocating. By the way her chest heaves, I can tell she's trying hard to hold herself together. I'm having the same problem, but for very different reasons.

She wants to run. I want to chase. I want to pounce, devour, control, own. I want to fuck his memory out of her and lodge myself into his empty spot. The things I want from her should frighten the fuck out of her because they sure as hell frighten the fuck out of me.

Breaking away from my angry stare, she turns toward the mirror, leans her hands on the granite top, and hangs her head in defeat. "I didn't know. I swear," she says with unmistakable pain lacing her tone.

My hostility deflates. I believe her. Another thought crosses my mind. Is this the guy who destroyed her? Is he the one who turned such a vibrant woman full of fire and passion into one who masks her true self for fear of being hurt?

The thought is almost debilitating, raising every protective instinct I have.

I step behind her and cage her in with my much larger frame. One hand on the outside of hers, I let my thumb lightly rub the sensitive flesh of her pinky while I move her long, golden-spun hair off the opposite shoulder. She shivers at my light touch.

"Is he the one?" I ask lowly in her ear.

If he is, I will not rest until I ruin him. He won't even be able to get a job at the county landfill when I'm through.

Her eyes catch mine in the mirror. They beg me to let this go. I wish I could.

"Only my future can unlock my past."

"What does that even mean?" I ask, baffled as all hell.

"It means, Shaw, that I have to draw the line here somewhere. I'll admit that I'm attracted to you, but I'm just doing what you said. Defining what this is and isn't. I see the end. I know it's coming. And as much as I like you, I can't go handing over hurts and secrets and mistakes like they don't mean something to me, because they do. It's another thing you're asking me to give you, to give up, to empower you with. They make me vulnerable and scared. They make me, me. And if I give them to you, then I lose another part of me to you. And don't you see? If I do that, you'll end up with all my pieces, and I'll end up with nothing, broken at the end of this whether you'll mean for me to be or not. I can't go through that."

I'm speechless. I never thought of it in those terms, but apparently, I'm bastard of the year because the only thing I latch onto is *"As much as I like you." Like* you. Not, how much I *want* you. That simple word penetrates a place I didn't know I had. Dozens of women have said the same thing, even professed love, but not one of them shone a fraction of daylight into that unknown abyss like Willow's single, innocent word just did.

"What if I want more than that now?" The question falls from my mouth before I think it all the way through. She's as surprised as I feel.

"Do you?"

Hope. It's all I hear, and it should stop me dead in my tracks. I don't want to lead this incredible woman on, hurting her when I can't commit. Because I never commit. Only I can't make myself take it back.

"I...I don't know, Willow," I admit. *Fuck.* I don't know anything about now, except I hate this place we're in. I spin her and cup her face, trying to make sense of the jumbled thoughts in my head. "I don't want to promise anything, but I also know I don't like this arm's length you hold me at. Don't spill every secret; I'm not asking that. But bend your damn elbow once in a while, because when you do, Willow, when you let your guard down—even a fraction—you are absolutely irresistible. Give me more. I just want...more."

I hate it when a woman cries, but it's never felt like this. Each individual drop of water filling her eyes is a fresh slice to my soul. "How much more?" she asks tentatively.

Everything. I unfairly want all of you. "Whatever you'll give me," I answer softly, wiping away a single trail of moisture.

For long heartbeats, our eyes search each other's. That cloak she covers herself with slips. I see vulnerability. I see into her bruised soul. I see *her.* I want nothing more in this moment than to be back at my house so I can lay her on my bed and devote myself to worshipping her for hours. I want to soothe and reassure her. I want too many things to name.

"Tell me if he hurt you. Please," I plead, swallowing hard. "Please at least tell me that much." I won't let this go until I know how many ribbons I need to shred this asshole into.

I prepare myself for the worst when she shifts her gaze.

"No. I hurt him."

When her barely audible confession hits my ears, I breathe a sigh of relief. But it's brief, at best. I now have confirmation that she did, in fact, have a relationship with this guy, and I don't like it. At. Fucking. All.

I don't like that he's touched her. Whispered her name. Probably made love to her.

And I sure as fuck don't like that he's going to be around for the next several months and I'll have no way to completely skirt around him. There are two fundraisers scheduled between now and Election Day. He's sure to attend, not to mention he will literally be in my father's front pocket until then, practically stroking his dick.

And what if he wants revenge or, God forbid, still has a thing for her?

No. Nope. That won't work for me. I don't care what my father says or what mystical political powers Reid Mergen wields. He's out.

I kiss her hard and fast. "I'll take care of it." I start toward the door when she grabs my arm, stopping me.

"Shaw, don't. Please just leave this alone."

"Willow, he could fuck everything up here. For my father's reelection. For us. Hell, he could go to the papers with this. If that happens, we're all ruined."

"But he won't. He's not like that. You even said it. It was his idea, but I think we've managed to convince everyone our meeting was coincidental. Whatever he thinks he knows, he can't prove a thing." I open my mouth to tell her she has no idea what someone filled with spite or infinite love is capable of, but she talks over me. "I'll talk to him. See what he thinks he knows. Make sure he won't cause waves."

My head starts shaking. "No. I don't want you anywhere near that fucker."

I expect her spine to straighten and fighting words to skewer me from her sometimes-forked tongue. When she steps into me and places her small hands around my cheeks, I'm totally caught off guard.

"Trust me. Please."

"Willow...," I groan. "I do trust you. It's him I don't."

"Please," she whispers right before pressing her lips to mine. I immediately harden, going from zero to sixty in two seconds flat. My overwhelming need for this woman is explosive and insatiable, bordering on fanatical. It's more than desire or passion. It's unfettered neurosis.

And it has nothing—and I mean *nothing*—to do with the

competition outside this room and everything to do with what's been churning inside me.

Angels didn't sing when I met Willow Blackwell. I didn't hear organs or choirs or melodic humming. No. What I heard the instant she opened her clever mouth was the Devil Himself chuckling, whispering almost sympathetically, "Good luck with this one. You're gonna need it."

It wasn't a warning. It was an invitation I couldn't ignore.

She's nothing I wanted, but everything I need.

Snaking one hand in her hair, I forget where we are and grip the strands hard, tilting her to the side so we fit perfectly together. Our tongues duel and our teeth clash in an attempt to win the upper hand. I press her flush to me and let my fingers slip underneath the band of her skirt and thong and down between her cheeks, rimming her tightened rosette, absorbing her gasps and moans. Each declaration of want stacks on the other until I reach my breaking point.

Her hand leaves my face and wanders down my torso. Sliding between us, she wraps it around my throbbing cock. Tightening her fingers, she slides upward in one slow, fluid movement.

And that's the end. I snap. Fuck restraint.

I am going to take her right here, in the bathroom of my childhood home with about thirty-five people twenty feet away. And no one will stop me. I unleash the beast in me that salivates constantly for her, feeling free and alive.

Unzipping her skirt, I let it fall to the floor in a heap. She gasps when I snap the flimsy silk from her hips and throw her thong on the cool tile below. I easily lift her slight frame onto the countertop and watch her desire-drunk pools shimmer, egging me on as I slide her silky fuchsia blouse over her head and drop that on the counter.

She's left in the sexiest black heels that clasp around the ankle and a black, lacy bra that serves her tits high and perfect.

The counter in this bathroom is unusually deep, which I've

never given a shit about until this minute. Bending her knees, I lift them up, setting her feet wide, which opens her up for me and forces her to lean back on her elbows. The back of her head leans flush against the mirror while she watches me pull down the cups of her bra. I step between her legs so I can lean over and suck an already-pointed bud into my watering mouth.

I expected her to deny me, given where we are. What I didn't expect was such sweet surrender. It's almost as if she needs this physical connection between us as much as I do.

"Shaw…" My name is a husky moan when I snag her nipple between my teeth and clamp down. I run my tongue around the furrowed skin that's hard as a diamond and red as a cherry, soothing it before nipping my way around the fullness of her breast.

My gaze floats up to hers as I work my way between the valley of her breasts and down her quivering stomach. "Be quiet, Goldilocks, or the entire house will know what we're up to in here."

"They'll know the second we walk—" She doesn't get the last word out because she's now writhing under my tongue, which I've shoved as deep into her pussy as it will go. I want to take my time with her, but time is not a luxury we have right now. Pretty soon my mother will come looking for us, and while I'd actually like Mergen to know I'm in here fucking Willow, I certainly don't want my parents to.

"Come in my mouth, Willow," I groan. I've never tasted a woman sweeter than Willow. She's like fine Bordeaux, smooth and rich.

"Shaw," she whispers brokenly, her hips surging beneath my tongue. "More."

"Tell me what you need."

Looking down her lean length, soulful eyes bore into me, seeing into me. It has to be one of the most erotically intimate moments I've ever experienced. "Put your fingers inside me. Everywhere."

Jesus Christ.

Okay.

She watches me with heavy eyes as I make sure she's ready so I don't hurt her. With my thumb, I drag her juices down to the crack of her ass and gently push inside the tightest hole imaginable, pressing deeper each time until I have it buried as far as I can. Her breath catches and her eyes slam shut when I thrust two fingers inside her warm pussy, hitch them at just the right angle, and hold.

Slowly opening her lids, she begs on a whisper, "Please make me come." Her plea undoes me.

"This is the one and only time I'll ask you to be quiet."

Then I start moving, her supple body following suit. I watch her mind yield and her body strain. I want to bring her up, balance her on the brink, and keep her there for as long as I can before she tips. Then I want to do it again and again so I can swim in her sweet submission.

But we don't have that kind of time, and this is not the place. Leaning down, I suction her rock-hard clit between my lips. It takes two swirls of my tongue before she's coming around me, squeezing and pulsing and biting her lip to keep her sounds of pleasure inside.

Before she's all the way down, I'm already releasing myself. Grasping her hips, I drag her to the ledge, and, like a savage, drive inside her in one brutal thrust and still.

My eyes roll back in my head, and I groan at the tightness encasing my cock.

"Goddamn, Willow," I grit. "I will never get tired of you."

It takes me several beats to figure out why she feels so fucking amazing. More than the last time I was inside her sweet heat. My hips start thrusting of their own accord, each drag across her thousands of tightly swollen nerve endings feeling better than the last. Then it hits me.

No bubble wrap.

Fuck.

Red light.

"Willow, I...need...shit. I need a condom," I pant. And, shit, I don't have one on me. A new box sits in my glove box, a mighty inconvenient place for them to be about now.

She wraps her lean legs around my hips, the spikes of her heels digging into me like daggers, and locks me in place as I start to reluctantly withdraw. "It's fine. I'm protected. Don't stop."

We share a moment of no return.

I've fucked a woman without a condom before. When I was young and foolish and too drunk to wrap it up. But I have never made a conscious decision to forgo that extra layer of protection, regardless of whatever birth control the woman I am with is on.

It's a flash of indecision that weighs heavy and long and with more importance than my sex-addled brain can comprehend given all the blood has rushed to the place where I'm now joined snugly with her.

But as she watches me with her tempting blue eyes and choppy breaths, my resolve wanes. I want this with her. I feel as if it's another piece she's giving me that she doesn't freely give just anyone. There's no fucking way I'd throw that back.

For several swirling, dizzying seconds, I simply stare at her. With underwires shaping her round breasts, sex-glossed eyes, and her velvety-pink pussy swallowing me whole, even contorted in a tiny space, she is a living goddess.

And she is mine.

All. Fucking. Mine.

It's only then I notice the fingertip-shaped bruises dotting her upper thighs. Pride swells inside when I realize that *my* marks grace her skin.

"You're sure?" I prod, shifting my hips until her eyelids close on a low moan. I won't regret this, but I don't want her to.

"Very."

Knowing we're likely seconds away from being caught, I pull her up and crash my mouth to hers. Her hands wind around my neck, dive into my hair, fuse me to her.

Dragging my length out slowly, I slam back in.

Sharp. Quick. Urgent.

Again. Again.

I fuck her like she's my new religion and I'm her devout worshipper.

All too soon, she's crying softly into my mouth as she milks me dry. I stop my own groan in the back of my throat and pump twice more before fire shoots through my balls and I'm forced to let it out, emptying everything I have into her welcoming temple.

For only the second time in my life, my seed coats the inside of a woman instead of a sleeve of rubber.

And for the first time ever…I want to do it again.

Willow

Chapter Twenty-Seven

THE AIR SEEMS THIN. HARD to drag in.

My stomach feels as though I swallowed a handful of glass that I'm going to vomit any second. I've matted the carpet beneath my feet with my continual pacing.

Sierra insisted she stay. I insisted she leave.

I haven't even told Shaw. He would flip a fucking wig. He didn't like that I needed to meet with Reid, but he understood. All he asked for was a heads-up. Probably so he could sit in his car outside my house counting down the minutes until he thought it appropriate to bust in and start marking the home range. And not that I need Shaw's approval or permission but I should have at least had the courtesy to tell him.

But this is about much more than Shaw's jealousy or Preston Mercer's campaign. This is about Reid and me closing a book that has remained open for far too long.

I met Reid Mergen when I was nineteen years old in my sophomore year of college. I'd just won the lead role in a play called *The Long Way*, about a woman who was on the brink of a breakthrough in her career, but the rest of her life was going to hell in a handbasket. She puts her career on hold and meets a man on her journey to discover her true self. She ends up falling for him and walking away from a life of unlimited professional potential for a chance at true love. Herman changed Summer in ways she never anticipated.

That's what I thought about Reid and me at the time. He was cast as Herman, my—Summer's—love interest. I didn't immediately fall for him; it was more a slow, gradual roll, but he grounded me. He was good for me. Good *to* me. Despite the fact it was hard for me to let him in all the way, he loved me unconditionally anyway, changing me in ways I'm still feeling today. And I repaid him by sneaking out in the middle of the night two weeks before our wedding.

For months after I left him, Reid didn't give up trying to get me back. I refused all his calls. I waited him out when I'd find him lurking outside my condo or workplace. I never talked to him after I left him a note that was nothing but a lie.

Our wedding date came and went, and as time passed, his outreaches became fewer and farther between until I received a text one day that told me he was leaving Seattle. I didn't even have the courtesy to reply.

I hurt him badly, but at the time I was stuck in quicksand, still reeling from the death of my father. I needed space, time to breathe. To find me for maybe the first time ever.

I haven't seen Reid since, until two days ago.

I thought he'd never want to speak to me again. So, when I heard from him yesterday morning suggesting we get together, it was a surprise. I was trying to work up the courage to call him, and he beat me to it. He wanted to meet at a café, but I convinced him to come here. The last thing I need is to be seen in public with Preston Mercer's campaign manager when I'm dating the mayor's son. Talk about fodder for the gossip rags.

The doorbell rings.

Oh God.

I freeze.

It rings again.

I pace.

To say I'm nervous would be the understatement of the century.

Third time. It's a double pump someone does when they know you're home and just not answering.

Fuck. This is hard.

Time to face the music, Willow.

"Coming," I manage to push through my constricted airway.

I stand with the doorknob in my hand and peek through the peephole. Yep, it's him. His stark green eyes stare right at me as if he has x-ray vision and can see through this big block of solid maple. God, he's even more handsome than I remember.

Taking a giant breath, I twist and open. When our eyes meet, tears instantly spring up. I held it together the other night pretty damn well, not breaking down once. In fact, I haven't shed one tear in the last forty-eight hours. But now that the shock has worn off and it's just the two of us, I can't help the rush of emotions engulfing me.

"Hi," I choke out, averting my gaze. I step aside, allowing him to come in.

He enters silently, stopping just a few feet in to look around. After what seems like forever, he says with that deep, spine-tingling lilt of his, "This is a little like déjà vu, huh?"

"Yeah," I agree quietly, remembering all the nights we spent vegged on that exact couch watching sports or a movie. Or…other things. *Jesus, Willow. Stop.* "You, ah, want something to drink?"

I walk past him into the kitchen and open the fridge for something to do. "We have iced tea, Peroni, Bud Light, water. I have a half bottle of white wine, but I think it's been in here for more than a week, otherwise—"

"Summer." The closeness of his voice and that name—fuck, *that name*—shuts me up. I calm my breathing, and when I spin around, he's not even a foot away.

"Please, don't call me that," I can barely whisper. For some reason, I can stomach everyone else calling me that, but not him. It's too…intimate.

"I'm sorry. It's habit. Coffee is fine if you have it." The hurt on his face kills me. I resist the urge to turn away.

"Flavored okay?" I ask, knowing it's not his favorite, but he'll drink it in a pinch. There are so many things I know about him, that I still remember about him. It makes me sad about us and reminds me how little I really know about the other man I'm falling in love with. I don't even know if Shaw likes coffee.

"It's fine. Thank you." I relax a fraction when the corner of his mouth slopes up ever so slightly.

"Sure." I busy myself popping the K-cup into the Keurig. Grabbing a mug from the cupboard I tap my fingers in a fast rhythm, my back to him, waiting for the brew to slowly filter. Trying not to think about how damn good he looks.

His dark hair is trimmed short. A day of growth lays nicely on his jaw. His eyes still sparkle like liquid jade, framed by the longest lashes I've seen on a man. He has a few more lines on his face than I remember, but he's still traffic-stopping beautiful. And he still fills out a pair of jeans better than most anyone I've known. Except maybe Shaw.

God.

Stop.

When the coffee is done, I place a teaspoon of sugar in it and stir before turning to face him once more. I carry it over to the table where he's sitting and set it down. "I hope you still take sugar."

He doesn't take his watchful eyes off me. "I do."

We don't speak. Rubbing my lips together, I twist my hands in front of me until he reaches out and pulls them apart. He hangs on to three fingers of my right hand while the other drops to my side. My gaze falls to where he's touching me. I fight to hold my shit together.

"Willow, you," he pauses and takes a breath, "you look good."

A million butterflies take flight from my stomach to my throat. They stick there. If I open my mouth, maybe they'll fly out.

"Thank you," I whisper.

"How is your mom?"

"Worse," I say, still staring at our joined hands. I don't make a move to pull away and neither does he. A flashback of the first time he told me he loved me almost buckles my knees. He was sitting at this very table, holding my hand just like this to calm my nerves. Just like he's doing now.

"I'm so sorry, Willow."

"Me, too."

His hand slips from mine and I feel…lost. Alone. And sad.

Reid knows everything about me. He knows what I gave up to stay here. He's felt my heartbreak, my loneliness, my joy. He knows more about me than any other person walking this planet, except maybe my own mother, though she doesn't remember most days.

Only for all he knows about me, when I look back I don't think he knew me at all. But that's not his fault, it's because I wouldn't let him. And now there's a chasm of hurt between us that won't ever be forgotten. That makes me incredibly sad. Because *I* put it there.

When I get the nerve to raise my eyes to his, he's staring at me with an indecipherable expression. My teeth sink into my lower lip so hard it hurts. I pivot and grab a Peroni from the fridge, popping the top before taking a seat across from him.

"So…" I leave the open-ended word hovering between us. So…do you hate my guts? What have you been doing for the past four years? Are you happy? With someone? Did you move back permanently, or is this just a temporary stop?

"So," he responds with a slight laugh that makes me smile.

This is one of the things I loved most about Reid. He'd make anyone feel comfortable in an uncomfortable situation. It's a natural gift.

"Do you want to sit in here or go in the living room?"

He looks into the other space then back to me, his face darkening with memories. "I think here is probably best."

"Right," I breathe. "Sorry."

"You feeling better?"

It takes me a minute to put together his question, but I finally do. After Shaw cornered me in the bathroom and fucked me nearly blind, he snuck me out the back way. Once he had me in the car, he ran back inside to tell his dad I wasn't feeling well. I felt like the cowardly lion straight out of the *Wizard of Oz*, but I just couldn't make myself go back into that room with him. Not only did I not want to face Reid for the obvious reasons, the light pink flush on my skin was a dead giveaway. I could *not* do that to him. He doesn't deserve that thrown in his face.

"Ah, yeah. The wine didn't sit well."

His lips purse taking in my fake answer. He doesn't believe it for a minute. The walls awkwardly close in as the tension thickens. I start to pick at the label on my bottle, wondering how you're supposed to apologize for obliterating someone. I'm sorry just doesn't seem good enough, but what else is there?

"Reid, I'm sor—"

"Do you love him?"

My eyes pop up, hooking his. "What? Who?"

"Shaw Mercer. Do you love him?"

Crap. *Can he see it written all over my face?* "Reid…"

"Don't, Willow. Just answer the question. Do you love him?"

"We just started dating. I barely know him." All true, but I purposely left out the falling part. I'm falling, all right, regardless of the fact I barely know the man. I'm on the downside of falling, really, sliding down the damn hill at warp speed with a grove of trees to stop me when I hit the bottom. It will hurt like a bitch at some point.

"That's what I'm worried about."

"What's what you're worried about?" I ask, trying to unravel his riddle.

His face hardens. "That you don't know him."

I bristle, knowing he's absolutely right. But I feel he's alluding to something more than just the fact that he thinks this relationship is a farce. I know it is, but I think right now he only suspects, and I need to convince him it's not. That it's all just coincidental timing. "And you do? Is there something I should know?"

He diverts his eyes briefly before pinning me with a gaze that now flames with…what? Protection? Concern? *Jealousy?*

No. *Why the hell would Reid be jealous?*

This conversation is not going at all as I'd anticipated. I thought we'd rehash the past. I thought there would be tears and pleading on my part, maybe some yelling on his. I'd hoped for closure, for some shaky truce, although I didn't actually expect it.

But I suppose bashing Shaw makes sense. He thinks he's using me and that I don't know it.

"How did you meet?" he asks pointedly, crossing his arms.

"It was an accident," I reply smoothly.

"An accident?" He sounds like he doesn't believe me, but so what? This part of the story I can tell without one ounce of guilt.

"Yes. He rear-ended me at a stoplight a few weeks ago." When his eyes widen, I add, "Like I said, it was an accident. Did you see my bumper when you drove up?"

He nods, his jaw clamping. "And you two…what? Just clicked while exchanging driver's licenses?"

I almost want to laugh. Click wouldn't be the verb I'd use. Clash, maybe.

"Yes. He called me a few days later for a date." Also true. Sort of.

"And why isn't your car fixed yet?"

"I've been busy." I huff. Actually, I finally took it in yesterday for an estimate. Over $2,500 for a hunk of pressed plastic, along with an estimated three days in the shop. Highway robbery at its finest. I walked out with my middle finger in the air and some not-so-ladylike words on my lips. "What difference does it make if my car is fixed yet or not, Reid? Ask me what you really want to know."

Taking a sip of his vanilla bean coffee, he watches me over the rim of his cup. I see the wheels spinning behind his jeweled eyes. He's carefully selecting the words he thinks will have the least potential to tick me off. He was a quick learner when we were together.

"I just think it's pretty convenient timing, that's all."

I draw on all my skills to fake genuine confusion. We've managed to convince everyone else we're a real couple so far, and while convincing Reid may be a bit more of a stretch, I've no doubt I can do it.

"Convenient timing? I have no idea what that means, Reid. It was pretty inconvenient to be rear-ended, actually, but it led to meeting Shaw, so I can't say I'm all that upset about it."

The pause is excruciating until he says, "It means…nothing." His breath is long. "I'm sorry. I shouldn't have said anything."

"Okay."

"Will you tell me one more thing and then I'll let it go? I promise."

I let a corner of my mouth turn. "Okay, shoot."

"Does he treat you well?"

Oh, Reid.

The fact that he even asked that question tells me everything I need to know. Although I do not deserve it, he still cares about me. It makes me strangely ache.

"Yes, he does," I answer softly. Also truthfully.

His mouth thins out, and he bobs his head up and down a few times before silence reigns once again. It's stilted and awkward, and I hate it. We used to be able to sit for hours in comfortable quiet, neither of us feeling the need to fill it with pointless chatter.

"I don't want him to hurt you, Willow. I'm worried he will."

Me, too.

"I thought we were done talking about him," I reply with no heat.

"I guess I'm not." He lifts and drops a shoulder, his tone unapologetic.

That earns him a laugh, which makes him smile.

His eyes soften. "I've missed you, Willow. So fucking much." His sincerity floors me, the emotion I feel from him bowling me over. It would have knocked me on my ass if I weren't already sitting.

He missed me.

Missed me.

After what I did to him, he missed me. You could never have convinced me the man I ruined would say those words to me. Never. But then again, Reid has always been in a league of his own.

I swallow hard, my chest aching something fierce.

"I've missed you, too, Reid." There's so much I want to ask him, so much I want to say, confess, apologize for. "Can I ask you something without you thinking I'm being selfish?"

A smile tugs his full lips. "You never asked permission to talk before, why start now?"

I laugh briefly. "Yeah, well…it's one of the things you loved about me."

The tone of the whole room shifts at my stupid word choice.

Fuck.

I'm an idiot.

Reid looks down at the cup he's now shifting back and forth between his hands, lost in the sloshing liquid. The thread we've been balancing on since the second he rang the doorbell seems to have unraveled. "I loved a lot of things about you, Willow Blackwell," he says on a pained breath, but then he raises his eyes to mine, and the love I see madly swirling stops my breath cold. "Still do."

Holy shit.

He still loves me? After everything I did to him, to us? How is that possible?

"Reid…." Tears blur my vision as I let my gaze drop, unable to watch him watch my reaction. I can't let him see what I'm feeling because I don't even know myself. "How could you?

After what I did? How could you possibly feel anything toward me besides contempt? I'm sorry," I tell him on a choking sob, water now splashing in tiny puddles onto the pressed wood table I'm staring at. "I'm so very sorry, Reid. I'm sorry." I keep muttering the same damn thing under my breath like a scratched record that someone won't take the needle from.

I hear the chair scrape, and I think maybe he's headed toward the door, but when his hands wrap around my biceps and he pulls me up and into his arms, I cry uncontrollably into his chest, soaking his shirt.

Then I'm in his arms and he's carrying me to the couch. Sitting me down first, he takes a seat beside me, hands me a few tissues, and throws an arm around my shoulder, tucking me close.

He holds me tight and steady. He strokes my hair and whispers in my ear, gifting me forgiveness I most certainly did not earn and will have a hard time accepting.

I lose track of time, but pretty soon I'm spent, my entire body a bowl of liquid, unset Jell-O. I sag against him, enjoying the press of his body against mine again a little too much.

When I'm finally quiet, he slides a finger under my chin and tilts my head toward his. His eyes search my face. I don't know what he's looking for, but I suddenly wish I could hide. "You're a mess."

My laugh comes out as a sob. "You know I always ugly cry."

"Oh, Willow." He sighs heavily. "Even with a blotchy face, red eyes, and a runny nose, you are still the most breathtaking woman I have ever met."

"Reid," I push breathlessly when I can finally get my vocal cords to vibrate. *How am I supposed to respond?*

"I didn't realize how big of a hole I'd been walking around with for the past four years until I saw you again."

"I—"

"No, please, let me finish in case I don't get another chance."

I nod, and he drops his finger. I still hold his eyes, desperately wanting to be anywhere else but here. I'm nowhere near ready for this.

"You gutted me."

The jagged shards of agony in his voice stab me a million times over. It hurts so fucking much. The water that stopped flows again.

"I—"

"Shhh," he says gently. He cups my cheek, placing a thumb on my lips, but doesn't remove it when I stop. Instead, he focuses on that one spot where he's now hypnotically rubbing it back and forth. The friction heats my body more than it should. "I died a thousand deaths when I woke up and you were gone. But after I got over the hurt and the anger, I understood."

His eyes track back to mine. The reverence in them makes me feel weak all over.

"I'm not even sure I do," I tell him quietly. And now that I'm looking into his forlorn eyes for the first time in four years, I mean it.

"You were grieving."

"I should have stayed." I mean that, too.

He looks sad. "I wish you would have."

"I'm sorry, Reid." My voice is scratchy. I wad up the used tissue in my hand.

"You're forgiven."

His gaze drops. The silver that lies below the hollow of my throat heats under his inspection. Shivers run the length of my spine when he drops my hand to lightly run a finger over it. I don't realize how fast I'm breathing until he looks back up.

"You still wear it," he whispers almost brokenly.

"Yes." I saw the pain on his face when he spotted it on me the other night.

"Why?"

Because it's the most precious and thoughtful gift anyone

has ever given me. Because when I wear it I feel like I carry her everywhere. "So I don't forget."

He strokes my cheek. "Some things are unforgettable."

I can't help but melt into him a little although I shouldn't. All my pent-up emotions rush to my mouth and spill. "I thought you'd forgotten me."

Bright eyes soften like silk. "I would have to be dead to forget you, Willow." His voice is warm yet serious. "And even then, it would be impossible."

He presses his forehead to mine. We both close our eyes and breathe each other in, remembering, wishing perhaps. The moment is ripe with poignancy and something else I don't want to name.

When he hooks a finger beneath my jaw and lifts my face, I know exactly what's coming. My lips tingle in anticipation. I loved this man once upon a time. I slept in his bed. We made plans. I was weeks away from pledging my life to his.

But I can't. Not now. Everything is different.

"Don't, Reid. Please." I tug against his hold. He lets me go. I'm torn in two between wanting it to happen and knowing if I do, I will betray Shaw. Even if what we have is a farce, I'm falling in love with him, and contract or not, I wouldn't feel right kissing another man.

"Okay," he breathes with resignation. "Okay. I, ah, I should go."

"Yeah, okay."

We both shift and awkwardly make our way to the door. He opens it and stands there, staring out into the street. "I want to see you again, Willow."

"I don't know if that's a good idea, Reid." I remember how volatile Shaw acted about Reid the other night. And with my confusing feelings...

He turns to face me. "Why?"

"Because I'm dating Shaw," I reply quietly.

"And he forbids you from having friends?" he asks angrily.

"You're more than a friend, Reid, and we both know that."

He smiles sadly, cutting me once more. "No. We were, as in past tense. So…yeah. I'll call you, and fuck him. He doesn't need to know. And even if he finds out, I don't give two shits. I'm happy to take him on."

Before I can respond, he's pressing his lips to my forehead. Then he's walking at a clipped pace to a dark red Prius. I stand on the porch, watching him back out and drive away.

I'm a wound-up steel ball of conflict. Knowing I'll see Reid again brings me a little peace but anxiety at the same time. And guilt. A whole heap of that, too, because I know Shaw won't like it. But on the other hand, why should I care about what he wants? We are not a true couple.

But you would be if he wanted that.

He'll let you walk away.

Maybe he won't. Maybe he really does want more.

I stare at the empty street, conflicted…until the sun starts to set.

My entire being hurts. My skin. My soul. My heart. That hurts a lot.

Shaw had a board meeting tonight. He insisted he come over around nine thirty when it's over. I agreed but decide I can't see him. I'm too wrung out, and I'm not up to any explanations about why.

I text him that I have a migraine. I take a hot bath, throw on pajamas, and head to bed early, hoping he doesn't decide to come over anyway. That sounds like something he'd do. He takes what he wants. I'll admit that's one of the things I find most appealing about him.

Just when I'm dozing off, he texts back.

***Shaw**: Anything I can do?*
***Me**: No. I just need sleep.*
***Shaw:** In my bed sounds as good a place as any.*

Yeah, I knew it. He's still peeved I insisted he bring me home after the debacle at the mayor's house when I had agreed to spend the night with him. But I was a goddamn mess. I needed time to process what in the hell having my ex-fiancé back in the picture meant for me. For us. If anything.

Me: *I'm tucked in already.*

His delay is a little longer this time. I start to get a little worried he'll pound down my door any second or maybe just not respond. Then, finally...

Shaw: *We have an interview with the reporter tomorrow.*

Wow. That was fast.

Me: *What time?*
Shaw: *5:00 pm*
Me: *Oh. Okay.*
Shaw: *You sure I can't swing by? Rub your head...or...other body parts? I heard once that sex cures all that ails.*

I laugh out loud into the quiet and consider taking him up on his offer. It's scary how much I want him here. How much this doesn't feel like pretend anymore. In the end, though, I need some time alone to decompress and regroup. Tonight was harder than I imagined, and having him here to make me feel better feels too...addictive.

Me: *It's a hard offer to pass up.*
Shaw: *Yet here you are...passing it and its mystical powers up.*

That makes me smile. So damn big my face now hurts. I settle on my back, not wanting this banter back and forth to end.

***Me**: I'll let you make it up to me.*
***Shaw**: I'll hold you to that. Call you tomorrow. Make sure you answer.*
***Me:** Sir, yes, sir. Nite, Drive By.*
***Shaw:** Groan. I like that way too much. Night, my sweet little Goldilocks.*

The brief exchange lifts my spirits incredibly. I end up drifting off with a grin on my face but mass confusion still twisting my heart.

Shaw

Chapter Twenty-Eight

"LISTEN TO THIS SHIT," NOAH announces, waltzing into my office without even a courtesy knock. Where the fuck is Dane?

"Rude, much? I could have been in the middle of an important call."

Instead I'm standing in front of the window, lost in the middle of my own fucking head, which seems a bad place to be right now. I have an investor meeting in three days I'm nowhere near prepared for, next year's corporate fiscal budget to approve, an agenda to review for our two-day executive planning session next week, plus a dozen calls to return. I can't afford to waste a single second of my overpacked day daydreaming about a blond, blue-eyed slip of a woman who won't leave the space between my ears. Yet, that's all I've done.

"But you're not, so stop your whiny bitching."

"I want to fucking throttle you sometimes, you know that?"

"Ah, I feel the love, brother."

I finally spin on my heels to see Noah working furiously on his phone. "Well, what's so goddamn important you had to barge in here unannounced?"

Yes, I'm in a pissy mood, and I'm taking it out on my friend, but he lets it roll off him like he's been double dipped in waterproofing. It takes a lot to rile Noah. For that, I'm glad because my temper can be on a short fuse, especially these days.

I'm not sure why I'm on edge, but I suspect it has everything to do with the jealousy still creeping like lava through my blood. On the way back to Willow's place the other night, she convinced me—*begged* me—to let her talk to that bastard, Reid Mergen.

Alone.

I reluctantly agreed, knowing she was right. If I spent even sixty seconds alone with that fucker, he'd be sporting a collar of bruises around his neck from where I'd try to squeeze the life from him. My fingers have itched to call my father and demand he fire this asshole, but Willow convinced me she'd take care of it, and I have to trust that she will.

Another thing I've never done. Trust a woman like this. She'll probably never understand how hard this is for me to sit back taking no action when every cell in my body screams at me to fix this. To protect *her*.

"Listen."

Noah's voice cuts through my brooding. He punches a couple buttons on his cell before setting it on the edge of my desk. A very sultry, very familiar voice starts playing through his speaker.

"I want to touch you...everywhere. Taste you all over. Devour you and consume you. And trust that this is merely a weak form of expression compared to what I'm feeling." His eyes shut briefly. When he opens them again, I witness the restrained hunger in their depths. "But I'll only ever do as you ask. This is trust between us. When you say stop, I'll stop. When you demand more, I'll exert myself until you're satisfied." His face is so close to mine, I just have to inch forward...one little inch...to taste him. "Now those are the clear safe words between us. So tell me to taste you and not to stop until you're coming in my mouth."

"What the fuck?" I go instantly stone-cold hard and take a seat to cover it up. God knows I don't need any more shit from Noah.

"That's your girl if I'm not mistaken." The grin on his face is bursting with self-satisfaction when he sits down across from me.

"What is that?"

"It's an audiobook."

"An audiobook? Of what?"

"Well, this one's called"—he fiddles with the app before answering gleefully—"*With Visions of Red* by Trisha Wolfe. It's an erotic thriller." Crossing his legs, he gets comfortable. "Pretty fucking hot, isn't it?"

I knew Willow recorded audiobooks, but *Fuck. Me*. I should have asked more questions. Romance? Erotica? I make a mental note to buy this one and listen to the whole damn thing. In fact, I make a mental note to find every audiobook she's ever recorded and buy them all. I don't even care about the stories. I just want to listen to her siren's voice, that's how pathetic I've become.

I swallow hard and breathe. "Yeah." I lift my eyes to his. "How did you get this?"

Suddenly that murky vat of possessiveness I've been steeping in gets hotter and deeper and very fucking uncomfortable.

First "Bill," then Mergen, and now Noah?

Why does this slice my skin apart?

Is it because *Noah* was listening to the woman I've temporarily claimed as mine, or because any other jackass who downloads audiobooks can listen to her seductive voice, too?

Or is it something else?

"Fucking Maris. I need to fire her. Caught her listening to this at her desk, and when I unplugged her headphones from her computer, I heard Willow's voice. It's pretty distinctive. How are things going with the 'girlfriend' by the way?"

He air quotes girlfriend, which pisses me off. I can't focus on that, though, because the clouds edging my vision thicken. "And how is it you two met again? You never did say." My swirling drum of envy is staining my skin. It's not an attractive color on me.

His smile falters, but he recovers quickly. "Really? I thought we covered that already."

"We didn't. You're avoiding the question just like you did the last three times I've asked."

"No. I'm pretty sure I told you we met at—"

A commotion outside my office, followed by loud voices, one of them a familiar female, cuts off what he was going to say. Suddenly my door flies open, and standing there in all her glory is the very woman I can't seem to shake.

And she. Is. Pissed.

But she is still so goddamn beautiful, my heart stutters. I feel her presence surround me completely. She's not a breath of fresh air—she's a fucking wind of change. I feel the transformation she's brought to my life in every molecule, every blood cell. She's bold, unique, challenging. I've been convincing myself she's just a growing obsession that will pass, but I don't think that's true. She's something bigger than me.

"I told you, miss, you'll have to wait until he's free," Dane practically squeals. His eyes plead with me to do something, but I only smile.

"Oh, he'll see me, *Dane*." Her sugary words drip poison. She may be talking to my assistant, but there's no mistaking the razor-sharp murderous tips are directed at me.

"Don't interrupt until I tell you," I instruct Dane. After a few tentative glances toward Willow, he nods, backs out, and closes the door softly behind him.

Blue to blue, our gazes hold fast until a noise to her left alerts Willow we're not alone. When she shifts to Noah, her fire immediately dampens. A genuine smile brightens her stormy face.

"Noah? Hi." She says it so sweetly I feel like a seven-year-old who's overdosed on Halloween candy.

"Well, hey there, dollface." In less than two seconds she's in his arms and hers are willingly folded around him. All I can do is gawk.

"I see you're still covering this up." She plucks at his dress shirt like maybe it will magically melt away under her fingertips.

"Well, I can remedy that if you like," he banters lowly. She laughs. So does he. He drops his voice, asking, "You making better decisions these days?"

Sobering quickly, her eyes shift nervously to me then back to him. She nods.

"Good to hear." Dipping down, Noah kisses her on the cheek like they're long-lost fucking loves, and I watch, dumbfounded.

Ready.

To.

Blow.

My mind is racing. Making up all kinds of shit that I don't like. Outside I am perfectly still, but inside I am a raging fucking firestorm of hatred. And it's all aimed at my best friend of thirty-six years, whom I could easily choke the very life from and not feel one iota of remorse.

"I'm sorry, am I interrupting?" she asks him. *Him*.

"And if you were?" I interject sharply, tired of the two of them making lovey-dovey eyes and acting as if it wasn't *my* office they both barged into without invitation.

"No sugar, you're not interrupting a thing." Noah shoots me a puzzled look before turning his attentions back to *my* woman. "So…this asshole here treating you right?" He thumbs my way with one hand. "Because if he's not…"

The innuendo he leaves hanging snakes my way slowly, like an oil spill. It pools at my feet until I fear I'm sinking into its inky-black void. When his other hand slides down her back as if it belongs there, it takes every ounce of will I possess not to lay him flat on my carpeted floor. Or stab him in the carotid with my Hermès pen.

Willow's eyes slip to mine, and for a just a split second, I see undisguised affection before the fire of her wrath burns it to ash. I know exactly why she's here. I expected it, even, albeit sooner in the day.

"I need a moment with said asshole, if you don't mind."

Noah winces. "Uh oh. That's my cue if I ever heard one. Nice to see you again, sweet thing. Good luck." He throws the last part over his shoulder, but I'm not sure if he was talking to Willow or to me.

When Noah's gone, I take deep breaths until I marginally calm. Slowly I stride across the floor until all distance between us is gone. She watches me with a little trepidation, and I see the bravado she walked in with waning. It's as if she can see the tendrils of possessiveness rising from my skin, stretching for her, wrapping around her so many times she knows she won't ever break free.

I reach for her, and she takes a step back.

Oh.

Fuck.

No.

Faster than she can run, I whip my arm out and curl it around her waist.

"Stop," she whispers. Her hand covers my mouth on its descent to hers. I wrap my fingers around her wrist and drag it to her side, holding fast.

"Shaw...no." Her voice is shaky. She sounds as nervous as she should feel about now. I am the hunter. She is prey.

I'm crazed.

Bestial.

A savage on the rampage to show his woman she belongs to him. Only him.

Mark.

Claim.

Ravage.

These primal words loop through my head, the frantic mantra garbling together until all I hear is...

Mine.

I've known this woman barely more than a month, yet she has me unhinged like nothing else. My craving for her is illogical and unprecedented. But instead of fighting to get it under control, I continue to let it sweep me away.

She didn't make it far inside my office, and it takes me no time to back her up to the wall, pinning her hands behind her back.

"Don't tell me no again," I rumble with reined-in fury.

Eating her rebuttal, I crush my mouth to hers. Sweeping my tongue inside, I twist it with hers, taking everything I want. I remind her with a bruising force that, for now, she's mine and no other man's.

She responds instantaneously, her mouth reaching for mine when I pull back to look into her eyes, making sure this is okay.

Fuck. I only see hazy capitulation. I blink a few times to make sure I'm not making up her submission because it's something I want, something I desperately need from her. But I'm not. It's still there, flickering soft and sweet. It calms my raging jealousy.

"For the love of God, Willow, you're going to destroy me."

I think maybe you already have.

"The car," she croaks on a ragged breath.

She's referring to the sleek black custom Audi A6 I had delivered to her house this morning. I had that train wreck of a Fiat towed away. One can only hope it's being used for scrap metal already. I knew she would protest, her pride keeping her from accepting my gift, which is why I had that piece of shit hauled away. She'll have no choice but to keep the Audi if she wants to get around in anything other than public transportation.

"I don't want to talk about the fucking car," I growl. I don't want to talk about anything other than how fast I can push my greedy cock inside of her welcoming heat.

"But I can't—"

I clamp her lips together with my fingers. "Not. Now."

Gaze bolted with hers, I reach over, lock my office door, and punch a button on the wall that starts the descent of the automatic blinds before leading her by the elbow across the room to my desk.

She watches me carefully, her heaving chest tinged the delicious shade of want. Her shallow breaths whisper softly, but the language is dirty, raw. The words sinful. It takes true control not to rip the goddamn dress she's wearing smack down the middle, conquering her like a medieval warrior who's returned from battle, amped up on adrenaline.

My voice is thick and rough when I speak. "I want to devour you, Willow. Eat you. Drink you. Gorge myself on you. Expunge every other fucking man from all parts of you."

Her eyes close and open again in slow motion.

Once her blurry gaze is fastened on me again, I step fully into her. Brushing my chest to hers, I lay a finger gently on her temple and lower my voice to barely audible. "I want only me in here." I tap.

Her breaths quicken, and that sexy pink darkens. It's intoxicating, fueling my insatiable need for more. Feathering down her cheek, I trace her lips until they tremble. "And here." Leaning in, I press my mouth perfectly to hers, sucking her lower lip when I ease back.

She fights the droop of her eyelids as I skim her collarbone, teasing past the swell of her breast. When I pause over her heart, her muscles tense, and I watch those shutters close. Guess the idea of owning this piece of her is off the board.

Fine, I'll move on. For now. But instinctively I know I'm circling back for that.

Never looking away, I take my time skirting over the flat of her stomach, the curve of her hip, the strength of her toned thigh. I watch her liquefy further and faster the lower my hands slide. She moans my name loudly, grabbing hard to my biceps. Probably because two fingers are now buried deep in her snug, dripping heat. She's primed and panting and already writhing against my palm, lost to me once again.

"And I unequivocally want to erase every fucking man from

this sweet spot, Willow. This," I pump fast, working her up quickly until I feel her walls flutter with her impending orgasm. Then...I stop. Her eyes fly to mine as a whimper of protest leaves her throat. "This belongs to me."

Sweet Lord have mercy. When her pussy clamps down on me as I say that, I struggle to back away. I fight the temptation to drop in front of her, spread her thighs, and defile her until the sun goes down.

But I need her to concede. *Need* it. Her strength is my weakness. So, taking a step back, I lean against my credenza. I slowly lick the fingers I just sank inside her, fighting the urge to strip her myself when she curses low.

I leisurely scan her body, commanding, "Lose the dress."

A slim brow curves in a show of expected defiance, yet when she speaks, her voice is high and breathy and wanting—a dead giveaway this turns her on. I wonder if she realizes she's closed off in every other aspect but so easy to read in this one?

"Do you always have to be the person in charge?"

I cross my arms. "That's rhetorical, I assume."

She laughs, only it's short-lived when she sees I'm serious. Licking her lips, she looks at the door briefly, deciding how to proceed. My forehead creases when I widen my eyes, just daring her to defy me.

Do it, I silently challenge. *Push me. Deny me. Unleash the beast salivating for you with nothing but your impudence.*

"I don't need an excuse to redden that creamy ass, but holy fuck, do I want one."

Her pouty lips fall open in the perfect shape to fit my straining dick. I swallow my need to push her onto her knees and have her take me to the back of her throat until neither of us can think, but only because I want to bottom out inside the hot, enveloping warmth of that sweet cunt even more.

"Is that so?"

I smirk, waiting patiently. Goddamn, I'm hard.

Moments click off as we both fight for power, though she's not fighting that hard. In fact, she's folding quicker than a losing poker hand. But it doesn't matter. The smallest taste of her insolence has enslaved me. It's a push and pull that's addictive, and she's my own personal brand of contraband. I understand Annabelle's plight so much better at this precise moment. This high Willow's giving me is unique and nothing short of habit-forming.

The moment she gives, I sense it. Her demeanor changes, becoming more playful.

Face bright with mirth, she reaches behind, and my cock jolts at the sound of metal teeth being separated. When the maroon shift slips off her body, I audibly gasp at the vision before me in tiny candy-apple lingerie.

"Fuck, Willow. Are you trying to kill me?"

The silk hugging her tits showcases her high, perky, barely covered nipples. In fact, I see hints of areola peeking out the tops. And the panties? *Jesus H. Christ.* The panties have bows that tie at the sides. In one swift move, they'll be laying on the floor next to her clothes.

"I take it you like?"

I force my eyes away from her sinful body back to her gorgeous face. A corner of her mouth is kicked up in sass. I simply stare. Could I ever tire of her? I'm not sure it's possible. "I more than like."

The shy smile she gives me is temporarily blinding. But the impairment lasts only seconds before I remember I have a half-naked Willow standing in front of me, waiting on her next command. And *half* naked just won't do.

"As fantastic as that bra makes your tits look, I want it gone."

Surprisingly, she obeys. She silently reaches between her mounds and flicks her fingers. With a simple pop and straightening of her arms, the sexy garment slides down and joins the growing pile at her feet.

I look to the only remaining piece of clothing—if one could call them that—and gruffly command, "Take them off, Willow. Slow. Sexy. Make me crave you so fucking much I can hardly breathe."

"You sound a little breathless already," she pushes cheekily.

I can't help the tug I feel at the edge of my mouth. "Panties. Now."

"You seem to have a thing for me undressing for you."

I grin broadly, owning it.

She bites her lip. I groan. Regardless of what comes out of her mouth, she can't hide how her body reacts to my dominion. She loves it. Needs it even, I've decided. Which works just fine for me.

Pushing myself up, I step into her. Cupping her cheek, I look deeply into bewitching seas of blue that have undoubtedly trapped hundreds of men in their depths. "Do you want to know why?"

In my hold, she nods, her lips now parted.

"The answer is quite simple. I want to know that you're giving yourself to me, Willow. *Me*. That you're thinking of *my* breath grazing your neck when you tug the zipper open. That it's *my* mouth sucking your straining nipples when you unwrap them for me. I want you fully aware that it's *my* cock that will be sliding between those quivering thighs when you step out of your silk and lace." I let my lips fall to her ear, brushing the rim with each syllable. "Because, Willow, I want you handing me the reins of control. Willingly, graciously, no reservations, trusting that I won't take anything you're not offering."

Her peaked nipples brush my starched shirt with each quick rise and fall of her chest. I wonder if it's as arousing to her as it is to me.

"Oh," she expels on a strained breath.

I chuckle lightly, easing back to the table behind me. I drop my gaze quickly to her little bows as I loosen my tie. "Now, where were we?"

With a straight face, that little minx does exactly as I ask.

And it is *the* sexiest fucking thing I have ever seen. Hands down.

Twisting one knee in front of the other, the move presses the juncture of her thighs together. Eyes meshed to mine she grasps the end of one ribbon between her thumb and forefinger and pulls away from her body. The bow unravels, but because of the way she's now standing, gravity can't catch the fabric fully.

She shifts positions so the opposite hip faces me, the opposite knee bends. This time when she parts the silky lengths, the triangle covering her bareness falls away. Smooth red ribbons hang down her pale thighs, past her knees. She could easily open her legs and let the piece fall.

But she doesn't.

Oh no. My vixen taunts. Performs. Gives me a show, but she's really doing as I asked—giving herself to me with no reservations.

Reaching down, she grabs the scrap and closes her eyes on a rush of air when, inch by agonizing inch, she eases the fabric through her pussy lips.

Fuck.

That. Is. Hot.

By the time she's done and the clearly damp panties flutter from her fingers, she's breathing so fast I know she's close to orgasm again.

"Oh, you bad, bad girl," I whisper hoarsely while jerking my tie from the collar of my dress shirt. I rip the first two buttons savagely apart, my need to completely possess her overtaking me once again.

Her throat works to swallow. To her credit, she remains steady.

"Turn around."

"Shaw."

Gripping her shoulders, I spin her myself and guide her forward until her thighs hit wood.

"Do you need to come that bad, Willow? That you can't wait for me?" I rasp in her ear, watching goose bumps travel the length of her arm. Air pushes brokenly from her lungs, but she doesn't answer.

Running my palms down her arms, I grip her wrists and bring them to the small of her back, shackling them together.

With my free hand between her shoulder blades, I gently push her torso forward until she's bent at the waist, bare breasts pressed to my cold desk.

My eyes travel the line of her spine, over the arch of her back to the curve of that perky ass just waiting for my hand. She looks so fucking good. I want to spread her thighs and memorize every succulent inch of her. Every time I sit in my chair from now on, I'll have a hard-on thinking of her glistening pussy spread for me, ready for me.

"Higher." I give her right cheek a hard smack. She squeals but that arch in her back gets more pronounced, causing her hips to shift up several inches. I focus on the blood that's rushing to the surface in the shape of my palm. Mother of God, that looks good. "Good girl."

Taking the thin silk tie still clutched in my hand, I ease it between her spread ass cheeks and slowly drag it upward. Even that slight touch has her flinching, wanting more.

"Shaw, please."

"Please, what?" I lay down a slap on her left side, relishing in both her low moans and the mirrored handprint now developing. I've wanted to mark her in this most primal of ways since the second I saw those long, lush legs snake out from her Fiat at the crash site.

Because I can, I place two more quick blows before kicking her legs farther apart. Once again, I drag the tie between her drenched folds, only this time I hold both ends taut and press the thinnest edge of it straight into her center, right over her clit. She mumbles my name, but it's just a broken mess of syllables barely strung together.

I lean over her, still fully clothed, pressing my lips to the sleek column of her neck. "You are incredibly gorgeous right now, do you know that?"

She doesn't answer. She pants. She wiggles. Begs me for everything with just the gracefulness of her body currently under my command.

Dropping the ruined tie beside me, I stand and slide my

hands over her ass, her hips, the backs of her thighs. Wasting no more time, I wind around front and dip a finger through her slit, easily pushing inside.

"Oh, Willow. Jesus fucking Christ you're wet."

Her hips begin to rock, brushing the erection now nestled in her ass with every swivel. With the other hand, I grip her hard, making her stop on a gasp.

"Did I do this, or did you with your naughty little trick?"

My fingers flex when she stays silent.

"You," she answers quietly.

"Do you want to take care of it, my little imp, or do you want me to?" She intentionally clamps her walls around that single finger, and I want to both throttle her and ram inside her, making her cry for me either way.

"You." Her reply is wispy, thin. Needy.

I lick my way up her spine, biting along her shoulder, leaving my marks behind. Bending the digit buried in her, I press against her front wall until I feel the tiny smooth patch I'm seeking. When she exhales hard and bucks, I know I've hit the magic spot.

Drawing my finger slowly out, I add a second and press back in, rubbing against that place that's making her meld with the dark wood.

"And if I asked you to? If I asked you to sit on the edge of this desk, face the window, spread your legs wide, and get yourself off for me while I watch, Willow, would you?"

"Shit," she breathes. My fingers drip with how much that thought excites her. Jesus. She's incredible. I let her get close then stop.

"Would you?" With a quick slap to her outer thigh, she yelps with the answer I'm looking for.

"Yes, yes I would."

"Oh, how I want that," I groan raggedly. I want to watch how she brings pleasure to herself while it's my eyes she's looking into. I want her at my feet, sucking me. I want her riding my cock, head thrown back in ecstasy. I want dirty and depraved, sweet and romantic. I want it all. I won't let her go until I have it.

For a third and fourth time, I'm merciless. I bring her close, leaving her hanging on to nothing but a pained sob. She's covered in a slick sweat of exertion, at her breaking point, and my dick is about to riot if he isn't plunged inside of her within the next thirty seconds.

Guess playtime is over.

Pulling away, I quickly undo the buttons on my shirt and shrug it off my shoulders. I throw it to the floor, uncaring about wrinkles. I have three others hanging in the closet. I let my dress pants fall to my knees but don't step out of them.

Then I snap up the black tie I'd discarded earlier, now coated in her arousal on one side. I bring it to my nose and inhale deeply, enjoying the musky smell of how I affect her before I wrap it several times around the wrists she's obediently kept crossed, quickly tying it off. The contrast between the black binding her hands and her fair, pale skin is mesmerizing.

Stepping back, I grab a stolen moment to admire her. High, smooth bottom. Trembling fingers. Nude heels that shape her lean calves. Golden hair spills to the side opposite the way she's facing with closed eyes and short breaths parting her lips.

I'm enthralled by her. Humbled, actually. A woman has to put total trust in you to allow herself to be this vulnerable.

She's bound. Willing. Wanton. Completely open and bared and so fucking turned on, her desire slicks her inner flesh.

It's all for me.

For *me*.

Quickly handling my briefs, I forgo everything else I wanted to do, my sole goal to bury myself to the hilt. Make her moan. Make her come harder than she ever has. I don't want her to ever forget this. Or me.

The second I grip her again she relaxes, molding to me like hot wax in my hands. And when I sink inside, slowly driving root deep on a long low groan, I wholly fall into this woman. I'm spellbound, totally and absolutely.

It's intense and all-consuming to indulge in Willow Blackwell like this.

I slide out. Inch back in.

"Faster," she pleads, trying—failing—to push back into me.

Slow. Methodical. *I* control it.

"Shaw, please."

I hold her still.

Out.

In.

First shallow. Repeat.

Then deep. So goddamn deep, I lose my mind.

"More. I need more."

She's in exquisite pain. Pain heightens pleasure.

More pain.

More pleasure.

More, period.

I draw out and slam back in so rough my desk shifts. "Like this, beautiful?"

Her fingers curl, nails scratching my stomach. "Yes," she chants as I do it again and again until I'm sweating and her walls tighten. *Fuuuuck.* They clamp so hard I'm gonna blow already.

I still and breathe long and even, buried so fucking far I feel the comfort of home. "Willow, my God, you are heaven," I groan. Fucking heaven. And hell. The undivided reach in between.

Time is meaningless, space nonexistent.

My head drops back.

I'm reeling.

Falling.

Falling so goddamn hard for her.

I want this to last. I never want to leave the warmth and pleasure of her, but my body has other plans. My climax gathers steam, tightening my balls more with every deliberate, torturous drag against her swollen center.

Her body trembles, both inside and out, and with a featherlight touch over her clit, she's gone. Clenching, writhing, back arching beneath me until I can't hold back anymore. Stars explode in my vision as I empty myself into her, biting my lip to keep from roaring in absolute fucking ecstasy.

Breathing fast, I fall over her.

Sweaty.

Replete.

Wrecked.

She's ruined me.

And when the first husky words out of her mouth, after I've just fucked us both boneless are, "the car," I know I'll never be the same.

This beautiful, stubborn golden sprite will be my downfall.

Willow

Chapter Twenty-Nine

I SWALLOW THE THICK BILE threatening to escape my stomach, but it's too late. The rancid taste already lingers on my tongue. Reaching into my purse, I retrieve a cinnamon Altoids and pop it. Closing my eyes, I drag the warm summer air into my lungs, let it reinvigorate my blood, and push it back out. Slow and intentional. I concentrate on only the breaths I'm taking versus the interrogation—er, interview—I'm about to undergo.

While I'm trying hard to erase my mind, my cell dings. I ignore it. It dings again. And again.

And yet again.

Really?

Fuck it. It doesn't matter. My Zen is so damn far away, I may as well haul ass to China to get it back.

I pluck the phone from the gray leather dashboard of my brand-new car, which I will *not* be keeping, although it's the most beautiful car I've ever owned, and see the rapid-fire texts from my friend, Jo.

Girls night tomorrow 9:00 pm
LD kickoff at Skyfall

No is not an option
Text ltr with deets

Shit. It *is* Labor Day this weekend. Skyfall, where Sierra works, has the biggest, badass three-day-long party to celebrate the last few unofficial days of summer, called Emfest—named after the Emerald City, of course.

They have Emerald Sky martinis and key lime beer, oddly good. The waitresses wear tiny, chartreuse skirts and nothing else but ornate body paint in varying designs. A dozen live bands will rock the three-story club throughout the weekend, but Sierra kicks it off on Thursday night with a dance party that can rival the likes of the hottest downtown Manhattan club. A line forms by noon, and the club doesn't even open until five.

Jo and I, along with a couple of her friends, never miss it. We get passes to the third-floor VIP lounge where they have their own separate dance floor where it isn't *quite* as crowded. We usually get a hotel room at the Alexis—Jo's treat—so we can continue the party in the penthouse, where a band or two hosts a get-together. With her contacts, Jo always manages to finagle us an invitation.

Thursday is tomorrow night, but I haven't given it a second thought, and neither Sierra nor Jo has mentioned it before now. Even if they had, I'd probably have still forgotten.

All I can think about is Shaw. I'm obsessed with him. Seeing him, talking to him, touching him. The last few weeks have absolutely blurred by and with another sharp twist in my belly, I realize I'm seven weeks closer to this business arrangement with Shaw being over. In fact, since it's now early September, that means the election is only eight weeks away. I know this arrangement goes through Election Day, but I wonder how long afterward he'll keep me around before he cuts me loose, staging the fake breakup to our fake relationship.

On the other hand, things shifted the night of the mayor's dinner party and again this afternoon when I showed up at his office unannounced. I felt it in the air, sharp as a bullwhip. He seemed absolutely feral over the playful attention Noah was giving me, even though he really should be far more jealous of Reid.

A man who doesn't care about you doesn't go all Hulk over other men paying attention to you, does he? A man who's going to cut you loose in a few short weeks doesn't hover over your heart, telling you with a simple look he wants you to hand it over...does he?

I want more.

Today's possessive display was unquestionably consistent with that statement from the other night, but...how much *more* does he actually want? How much more am I capable of giving?

I don't know, but there's one thing I do. And this isn't wishful thinking; this is fact. Shaw Mercer commanded my body and my mind today like he knew exactly what I needed.

I was his playground. His toy.

He directed. I readily obeyed.

I climbed.

I teetered.

I slid.

I spun.

I flew.

I hovered high in the tower until I crashed to the soft sand below, his arms cushioning my fall.

I loved every last second of the sensual ride he put me through. It's a ride I want to go on again and again. My body temp rises just remembering the feel of silk over my wrists and the dirty words he left in my ear.

No one has ever talked to me the way he does. So direct, so aware of what turns me on before I know myself. I never thought I'd like being wholly possessed by a man, but with that authoritative presence Shaw has about him, he had me today. Hook, line, and sinker. I was his willing plaything.

He's not the only one who wants more.

"Daydreaming, Goldilocks?" Shaw's smug voice floats through the open window, startling me.

"Uh...." I turn to my left to see Shaw's handsome face framed by my window. His smile is sensual, and I know he's remembering this afternoon just as I am. I could lie, but why bother? "Yes."

My lips tingle when his gaze drops briefly to them. "About me, I hope."

"Another fishing expedition, Drive By?" I hedge. Smug bastard.

"What can I say? I need a lot of validation." With every inch he moves forward, I retreat until my head pushes against the headrest. "Now...admit you were remembering how thoroughly I fucked you earlier and how your pussy is still feeling me inside."

I shrug one shoulder and try not to smile through my breathless reply. "I'll admit no such thing."

Laughing, he steps back, opens the door, and holds out his hand for me to take. I realize my cell is still in my hand, and I haven't replied to Jo. I send her a quick one-letter reply: *K*. Throwing my phone in my purse before rolling up my windows, I take Shaw's hand and let him help me from the car.

Once I'm outside, he gently closes my door then backs me up against it. His body is flush with mine. When he weaves his hands through my loose hair, my blood sparks with desire.

Lowering his lips to a hair from mine, he husks, "If you weren't daydreaming about this afternoon, I demand a do-over to make sure you can think of nothing but how much you enjoy being tied up and at my mercy."

I was. I do. Christ, my entire body still buzzes.

"A do-over?" I internally cringe at how excited I sound.

A self-satisfied grin splits his lips a second before they're on mine, kissing me mindless right out in the open. "Oh, yes. A do-over is definitely in order." His rough promise trickles over my now puffy mouth, making me wish we could get to that do-over now instead of the interview we're about to give for the *Seattle 7-Day*.

With a quick peck, he asks, "Should we go in?"

I nod. "Okay."

"You nervous?" He takes my hand in his. It's probably clammy.

"A little," I reply.

When I look up, the smile he gives me relaxes me even more. His strength and calm pour through me. "It will be fine, baby."

Although that sweet endearment sends shivers up my spine, I find I weirdly prefer when he calls me Goldilocks instead. It's unique, and I'd like to believe it's only mine.

"Come on." He tugs on my arm, pulling me forward.

I parked on the street across from the five-story, red brick building with a crude sign in the second-story window that says: Seattle 7-Day. We wait for traffic to pass before we dart across the street, down the block, and into the building. Since it's only one flight up, we take the stairs instead of the elevator, my clicking heels echoing in the stairwell.

At the top, Shaw opens the glass door for me, speaking to the receptionist when he steps to my side. His arm slides around my waist and his lips find my temple—as though we are a true couple. I grin involuntarily, feeling ridiculously giddy.

"You smell like me," he whispers in my ear.

Oh. My. God.

Heat blooms on my face. I went to Shaw's office early this afternoon. By the time I left, not only had we not resolved the car issue, but I was late for my momma's doctor's appointment because an afternoon delight wasn't in today's tight schedule. It turned out her doctor was running an hour late, and when we were finished, I didn't have time to go home and shower, or else I would have been late for this.

"Shaw," I scold on a muted choke.

"I really love the way I smell on you, Willow. I could get used to it."

When he says things like that, butterflies bump against the walls of my stomach, and I foolishly fall further into what could be instead of what is. I pull back to see both warmth and lust fill his eyes. I'm sinking so fucking fast into Shaw Mercer that only a sliver of daylight remains before I'm completely under.

"Shaw Mercer, nice to see you," a gruff, feminine voice calls from behind me. Shaw's eyes stay connected with mine for a few moments longer before he looks over my head and straightens.

"Carrie." He nods politely and twists me in his arms until I'm facing a petite brunette standing barely above the five-foot mark. At first glance, you wouldn't describe her as beautiful, but the more I look at her, the more I see it. Behind her thick black glasses are arresting chocolate eyes. Heavy, black hair hangs in a straight bob around her oval face, but she has one side pushed back behind her ears. A smattering of light freckles dots her tiny pale nose, and her face is makeup free except for a light gloss on her thin lips.

She looks unassuming and meek, only I will soon find out she is anything but.

Shaw

Chapter Thirty

I KNOW CARRIE REYNOLDS FROM high school, though I haven't seen her for several years now. She was two years my junior. Her parents own five very successful restaurants in the Seattle area, so her parents hobnobbed with mine, and they both continually tried to push us together. When I was a junior, I gave in to my mother's pressure and took her on a date. One. It was a disaster. The entire time she talked my ear off about the guy she was obsessing over, Will Hankley, a friend of mine. Will had had the same girlfriend since the seventh grade, and Carrie wanted my assistance in plotting the relationship's untimely demise. I refused. She was pissed. Will and Kate have been happily married for fourteen years.

So, when I saw her name underneath the article about Willow and me, I cringed. I hadn't seen her at the restaurant that night; I'd seen a colleague of hers, but Carrie must have been sitting at his table. I tried to pull strings with Kayla, the editor-in-chief, to assign a different reporter, but that got me nowhere. There's also no love lost between us, either. Sometimes your bad decisions come back to haunt you and this would be one of those times. Although in fairness to me, she wasn't the EIC when we slept together.

That being said, I laid the ground rules solidly before I walked through the door today. I will not be ambushed or undermined. This interview is a coup for Carrie. She's green, having only been a reporter now for fifteen months or so. It's her second career after a second failed marriage. I'm just hoping twenty years has erased the torch she wanted to burn me with, but one can never know with women.

After we spend twenty minutes in front of the camera posing for our cover picture, we sit at a small round table in a glass-bubbled conference room. "So, how did you two meet?" Carrie asks innocently enough after she clicks on her recording device.

Willow and I talked about this after we both came back into our bodies from the best fuck I've ever had in my life. *It was more than a fuck, you asshole. It was...hell...it was transcendent.* She wanted to argue about my gift. I thought our time was best spent preparing for this afternoon's interview instead. It was mutually agreed I would take the lead; she'll add color commentary.

Tightening my hold on Willow's hand, which is planted on my lap, I launch into the story of our accident. I even throw in the new Audi she's driving in hopes that once it's in print, she'll have no choice but to keep it.

Carrie is cordial, nice even, and half an hour goes by uneventfully as we answer question after question. It's a light, easy atmosphere, and I find every answer out of my mouth is truthful instead of some story I'm trying to weave for the press or my father.

Just when I think we've wrapped up with the list of preapproved questions I'd authorized earlier, Carrie says, "I have a couple more questions for Willow, if you don't mind?"

Unease settles in my gut, and my stare hardens. Carrie ignores me, turning to Willow, who grips my hand harder.

"Of course," Willow says congenially.

Carrie drops her eyes, flipping through a few pages of her notebook. Willow and I exchange glances, and I see the nerves that were there earlier flare up again.

"Willow, your father was Charles Blackwell, correct?"

Was?

Willow's entire body goes rigid.

"Yes," she roughly responds after wetting her lips.

Carrie's voice turns sympathetic when she continues. "I'm sorry for your loss."

"Thank you," Willow mumbles almost incoherently.

"And didn't your father work in research and development at Aurora Pharmaceuticals?"

Willow nods slowly.

Oh fuck.

Oh. *Fuck.*

Her father worked—as in past tense—at Aurora Pharmaceuticals? In R&D? My mind races, trying to piece this together, but it's not that hard once I really think about it.

CJ Blackwell. The brilliant researcher who invented a potential cure for Alzheimer's. The same one who committed suicide, falling to his death from Schultz Bridge. It was not only a tragic loss for the scientific community, it almost crippled Aurora Pharmaceuticals. I remember it well for so many reasons, not the least of which I had my own bullshit issues with Annabelle to deal with that very night.

CJ Blackwell is *Charles* Blackwell.

CJ Blackwell is Willow Blackwell's dead father.

Un-fucking-believable.

Why did I not put this together before now?

Then Carrie turns to me. "And isn't Aurora Pharmaceuticals one of your clients, Shaw?"

My jaw ticks. Willow tugs her hand from mine, her brows creasing in confusion. Carrie's devious eyes bounce back and forth between us, glee sparkling in them.

Well, fuck her. Fuck *this.*

"What's your question, Carrie?" I spit, rage welling inside

me. I reach over and take Willow's hand back, holding tight. It's shaking.

"No question, really. People just eat up a love story with a great twist, and yours definitely has one."

"That's hardly a twist. That's pure coincidence," I snarl. Holding fast to Willow, I stand, pulling her with me. She's visibly upset, her entire body wracking with shakes.

We get within a foot of the door when Carrie adds, "Maybe, maybe not. But the fact that her father was solely responsible for the initial discovery of the drug that's going to make Aurora Pharmaceuticals, along with Wildemer, billions when you help them launch their IPO early next year is."

And my bad. I didn't give an inexperienced reporter nearly enough credit.

Leaving Willow by the door, I stalk toward Carrie who is now holding her little notebook to her chest like that will help protect her against me. As fucking if. I tower over her by a good foot and let my size and breadth intimidate her as I easily enter her personal bubble.

"You print this, you're through," I grit. "You'll be done here. You'll never get another job in journalism again, and you'll be forced to find a third husband who will support your pitiful ass."

She bristles, and her red face turns to steel. "It's public information, Shaw. I'm not printing anything that's slanderous or untrue."

She's right. CJ's—*Charles's*—death is public information. Aurora Pharmaceuticals' initial public offering is public information. The fact they are a Wildemer client is public information. But the media has a way of taking an innocent set of coincidences and twisting them into something that's nefarious and reeks of scandal.

"Let me tell you how this is going to go. You're going to print the story we just gave you. It's going to be glowing and happy, and you're going to stick to the script. Not one mention or innuendo about Willow's father or his death or Aurora, or the next call I'll be making is to the president of Lock Media."

Her face pales.

"Yeah, that's right, sweetheart." I lower my voice. "Lock Media, the same group that owns the *7-Day*. John and I were frat brothers in college. I went to his wedding. I'm the fucking godfather to his baby girl. So, I assure you, John's loyalty to me runs far deeper than this piss-poor excuse of a newspaper. You print that garbage, I make a call, and this place is shut down within twenty-four hours. You'll be solely responsible for forty people standing in the unemployment line, yourself included. Now, you have to ask yourself, is getting one over on Shaw Mercer after twenty years really worth the pain and suffering that will rain down on you?"

She stands there, mute.

"Is it?" I prod, demanding an answer.

"No," she mutters.

"Good. Glad we understand each other. You e-mail the article to Dane before it's printed. It doesn't see the light of day without my approval, or I make that call."

I spin on my heels without waiting for a reply. It's a demand anyway, not a fucking question. In just a few steps, I have Willow's tear-streaked face in my hands.

"You okay?" I whisper, my thumbs brushing the moisture away.

She nods. More tears spill. She's not okay. I want to kill Carrie for upsetting her. Fucking bitch.

"Someone else will connect the dots, Shaw. And they'll print it. You're only delaying the inevitable," Carrie says softly behind me.

Another tally in the win column for Carrie, but I have more influence over the other media in town than I do this shitty little paper, which is why I needed to get them in my pocket. Now all I've managed to do is delay a fucking war.

"One more thing, Carrie," I snarl after I secure Willow to my side. "This newspaper breathes anything with mine or Willow's name associated with it without my prior authorization, you can pack your bags. Just give me an excuse to shut your doors permanently."

With that, I guide Willow through the maze of low-cut cubicles, out the front door, and to the elevator. Once the doors shut, I wrap my arms around her, holding her tight. I feel her shake with each sob. My heart hurts for her, and I wish I could take away every ounce of pain.

Once the doors open, I walk us to a bench that's pushed against the wall, pulling her into my lap. She buries her head in my shoulder and cries.

"Willow, baby." Jesus, she's killing me. Why is it that every woman's tears before made me cringe in annoyance, but hers slice my heart like a blunt knife? I physically hurt simply because she's hurting. That's a new one.

"Shhh," I soothe. I run my hand methodically from the top of her scalp to the tips of her hair. Over and over until she calms. Until I can take a breath again without the pain of her agony stabbing me.

Easing a finger under her chin, I tip her tearstained blotchy face up. My God, she is breathtaking, and I can't resist kissing her softly, tasting salt and despair.

"I didn't know," I tell her quietly.

"How could you have?" she answers in a broken voice.

I could have. I *should* have, though I never knew CJ Blackwell by anything other than CJ. And I didn't know him personally, though I met him when Jack Hancock interviewed our firm several years ago now. Although he was a brilliant man, he was also charismatic and genuine.

"I met him once. Your father."

Those incredible blue eyes widen. "You did?"

"Yes. At a business meeting. He seemed like a good man."

Her glassy eyes well again. I can tell she's barely holding herself together, the pain of losing her father still an open, bleeding wound.

"He was," she whispers.

I'm at a loss for words, unfamiliar with how to handle such

an emotionally intimate moment. "I'm sorry, Willow. It was tragic." Those welling tears overflow, creating a waterfall of pain flowing down her face. "Willow, fuck, you're killing me. Please don't cry. How can I help?"

She bites her lower lip, and I wipe away the drops rolling down her face.

"Would you really do that? Get the newspaper shut down? For me?"

Oh, Willow. I think I'd do anything for you. I'd burn this place to the fucking ground if that's what you wanted.

I chuckle, shaking my head. "I would if I could."

Her brows dip. "But you said you know the owner?"

I let a slow smile spread across my face. "Technically, yes." I see a hint of a smile on her lips and breathe a sigh of relief.

"Technically?"

"Met him at a party once last year," I confess on a laugh. "He and his wife had just had a baby girl. Elana, if I remember right."

"So, you're *not* frat brothers or godfather to his daughter?"

Grinning, I tuck a stray hair behind her ear. "'Fraid not. Although it would be very convenient right about now."

"Wow. I believed every word you said."

And that was the point. Lies told with authority and conviction suddenly take on a life of their own, becoming truth when even those who know otherwise start to believe and defend them.

"So did she."

I watch in awe as the sadness melts away, replaced by the most mind-blowing smile I've ever seen on her. It lights up her entire being and does something funny to my heart. She leans in and places her soft lips on mine, moving her body closer when she winds a hand in my hair. I grow hard beneath her as she takes her time as if she's making love to my mouth.

"Thank you," she says quietly.

"For what?" I breathe fast, wanting her mouth back on mine.

"For protecting me like you said you would."

There are so many responses I could give, that I want to give, but the one that plays on my lips is a lie. *"I'll always protect you."* I don't know if that's true. I don't know if I can protect her from the media, who love to sink their bloody teeth into a good story and rip it apart. I don't know if I can protect her from *me*. I cup her cheek and settle for, "I'd like to hear about him sometime. When you're ready."

Her eyes latch onto mine and don't let go. "I'd like that, too."

Time hangs.

Of all the interactions I've had with Willow over these past several weeks, this seemingly inconsequential one is the most profound, the most impactful. It sinks far and deep, and I know, no matter what, it will stay with me forever.

Because this? This moment changes everything.

The door she keeps firmly sealed cracks open just a hair. And I felt a piece of her slide into me permanently.

Shaw

Chapter Thirty-One

"I'M GETTING TOO OLD FOR this scene," Noah grumbles loudly beside me.

So am I, especially since this place is jammed with barely legals, but Willow is here somewhere, and I couldn't make myself stay away. I haven't come to Emfest for years. I should be anywhere but here. Willow has a life of her own, friends of her own, interests of her own that don't include me. But I want them to, and that small voice that tells me this will be over soon keeps being drowned out by the bigger part that just doesn't give a fuck.

I want her. Jesus, do I want her. More and more and more every goddamn day. And this is more than sex. Far more. I want her laugh, her smiles, her trust, her everything. I'm walking a tightrope of emotional suicide, and let's face it—I'll fall. I've not once made it across that fucker, but the ground has never seemed so far away before. Why should what I have with Willow be any different?

Because you've never had anyone like her waiting on the other side.

"You're full of shit, Noah," I finally say when I watch his

eyes rake down a practically nude waitress as she passes by. She has on the tiniest skirt known to man, and her small, perky tits are painted with what appears to be a series of thick, interwoven, gold-tipped, green chains that cover her nipples and areolas but leave the sides of her breasts bared completely. It looks as though she has a heavy necklace on, but it's body paint. It's brilliant and sexy as hell, and whoever is responsible for the art this year has outdone themselves.

But I find I'm barely giving these beautiful women more than a passing glance. I mean, I am a guy after all, so if I say I'm *not* looking, you'd be well within your right to call bullshit. But before, I would have sought them out. Maybe even picked one I wanted to end the night with. Now I'm not.

Tonight, all I care about is locating my woman in this writhing mass of bodies...to watch her from afar. I have a feeling she'd be very unhappy with me that I'm here. Good thing we're tucked into a corner where we're hard to see but have a great view of the entire room.

"Find her yet?" Noah asks with a shit-ass grin on his face that I ignore.

"Find who?" I reply calmly.

He laughs. "You think I don't know why we're here, Merc?"

"No idea what you mean," I feign. I take a sip of my Clix on the rocks and scan the room again. I figured Willow would be in the VIP section, what with her roommate working here, but I haven't seen hide nor hair of her. Maybe she changed her mind and stayed home instead. God, I hope so. I don't want every guy in the place trying to pick her up.

After the debacle at the *7-Day* yesterday, we walked the few blocks over to Pier 57, got two tacos from a food truck, and ate them on the Great Wheel as we gazed out into the harbor.

We talked the entire twenty-minute ride around in the sky.

I wanted her to tell me about her father. She didn't, but she did tell me about growing up with Sierra. Her friendship with Sierra sounds a lot like mine with Noah. I reciprocated and talked about what it was like growing up and running a business with my best friend.

It was the most real night we've shared so far. It felt like an actual date for just us and no one else. I asked her to come home with me again. To stay the night. Jesus, I can't believe how much I wanted to wake up with her in my arms this morning. Only, she politely refused, saying she didn't think it was a good idea.

And once again, I found it pissed me off, because I want much more than she's giving me. She holds herself in reserve. I'm beginning to wonder if it's from everyone or just me? I want to believe it has everything to do with that fucking contract. I feel like it's a wall between us but one I'm still reluctant to tear down. I lay in bed alone last night wondering why the hell I wasn't just ripping it up.

Do I want to give myself an out? Make sure if I end up hurting her I can make myself feel better by pointing to the rule book?

"You never said how things are going with her."

I pin my friend of thirty-six years with a stare. "And you never said how you met her."

"Back to that, are we?"

"Back to that."

I don't hear him sigh as much as I see it. "Why is it so important, Shaw?"

"I don't know, Noah," I growl. *Maybe because I need to know how slowly to gut you.* "Maybe because you're evading. You two seemed pretty chummy in my office the other day."

Memories fill his fleeting smile. Hate fills my mind.

"You'd better tell me how you know her." And so help me God, if I find out he's fucked her, I will kill him. Dead. On this very fucking spot.

"Little territorial for a fake girlfriend, aren't you?" He grins cockily. It drops only briefly but then gets as big as ever when I reach across the table and grab him by the collar, dragging him toward me.

"Tell. Me. Now."

He laughs. "Jesus, I met her at Harrington's fundraiser. Relax, Merc." He grabs my fingers and pries them off his shirt, sitting back down. "It was entirely innocent. I haven't touched your fake girlfriend."

I want to tell him to stop calling her that. And then I want to know what she was doing at my father's competitor's fundraiser, but that's a question for Willow, not Noah. Remembering what he was supposed to be doing that night, I say, "But you want to."

"You're kidding, right? What guy with a functioning dick wouldn't want her? Jesus, she could make a ten-year-old pop his first fucking woody. I mean, just look at the way those leather pants kiss her every curve." His eyes flit over my shoulder, and I follow, thinking he's fucking with me. I've never seen Willow in anything but a dress.

But he wasn't. There she is, standing at a table in the corner across the room that has a reserved sign on it. Her profile is to me, and she's hugging and greeting several other women who were already there.

"Holy shit," I breathe.

My mouth dries. My pants grow uncomfortably tight as I let my eyes fall down her deliciously sinful form. In addition to painted-on black leathers, she's wearing those same black heels that wrap around her ankles and a sleeveless, deep-green halter top that fits her torso snug but flares slightly at the bottom. I can't see the front, but if it dips and shows off her fantastic rack, we are out of here.

"Jesus Christ, she is sexy," I hear Noah say a little too excitedly.

I can't find it within myself to be mad at him for saying that. She is. She doesn't even try, and she's the sexiest fucking woman in this entire place. On the planet, maybe.

"Did you know she's CJ Blackwell's daughter?" I tell him absently, my eyes still trained on my sexpot "girlfriend."

"You're shitting me," he replies incredulously.

"I am not."

He's quiet, and when I finally manage to tear my gaze away from Willow, I see his lips are turned down and his brows are scrunched in concentration. "Huh," he finally says.

"Huh, what?"

He shakes his head, clasping his fingers around his glass. "Nah. It's nothing."

"It's something. Spit it out."

He shifts in his seat and takes a swallow of his cocktail. "It's just...the night I met her, she said something I didn't understand. But now it makes more sense."

"What?" I prod. Jealousy seethes below the surface, but I have to put that away. At least with him. Had Noah not met Willow and hooked us up, I'm quite sure I'd be suffering in perpetuity with Lianna by now.

I steal another glance at Willow, wanting to simply stare at her all night long. As expected, my dick swells. But something right in the center of my chest swells, too. I tip my tumbler to my lips, letting the chilled vodka slide down my throat as I force myself to look to Noah once again.

"She said something like, 'Sometimes life doesn't afford us choices.' I told her she needed to keep better company. She was there with Paul Graber." He snarls that slimy bastard's name, and I bristle for many reasons, not the least of which is the fact that fucker was anywhere near her.

Once a big supporter of my father, Graber has apparently jumped camps to the man he thinks will approve his petition to tear down the historic Ellsworth Storey cottages so he can build hotels he claims are luxury. They're nothing but a front for high-end brothels.

"You think this is why she was working for your friend? Because of her father's death?" When Willow came to my house that first night, she mentioned it was just her and her mother. Did her father leave her mother destitute?

Noah's mouth curls at my use of the word friend, but he doesn't bother to deny it. "She didn't say, but money would be the obvious assumption."

I'd already gathered that. Willow doesn't seem the type to hang off the arms of rich men simply because she gets a thrill from it. Then another thought hits me.

Surely her father had some type of profit sharing or stock ownership incentive or options that would pay out to his estate when the IPO launched or when the drug was FDA approved? Hell, I'd be surprised if Charles Blackwell didn't have a patent on the drug itself.

Does Willow know this? Does her mother? We talked about the IPO a bit the other night, which she was surprisingly unaware of, but due to confidentiality reasons, I wasn't able to share anything about the clinical trials, and that killed me. I wanted to brag about her father, about how his legacy will live on through his work. How he'll be a household name in just a matter of months. Even if it is none of my business, it's something I plan to delve into further with Jack Hancock because I have a feeling Willow knows none of this.

"Obviously. Do you happen to know anything about Willow's mother?"

"You act like we're friends or something, Shaw. I know very little about her. I talked to her for five minutes at a party. Why don't you just ask her what you want to know?"

I sigh heavily, wishing it were that easy. "She's very private."

"Well, this is just temporary, right?" he says matter-of-factly. "I mean, you don't expect her to lay out her entire life to you when you won't be around by Christmas, do you?"

I don't respond because the thought of letting her go causes a giant pit not only in my stomach but a weird twisting in the middle of my chest. Yet that's exactly what I expect. What I want.

I take a sip of my cocktail, signaling for another round when the waitress catches my eye. Then I sit back to watch Willow.

I watch her smile.

Laugh.

Gab.

She's carefree.

Happy and relaxed.

She looks young and more beautiful than I've ever seen.

It's obvious these women know her well and she's let them into her life, not keeping them on the sidelines like she does with me.

I've been comfortable on the periphery of relationships my entire life. My family and Noah notwithstanding, I never had a deep ache to get fully invested in someone else. I'm not emotionally barren or have something inside that's missing; it's just not been a priority or a craving.

But with her, it's turning into an incessant longing, and I'm not sure how much longer I can ignore it. I'm finding I like it less and less to be on the outside looking in, especially when she easily shuts me out like turning off a light switch.

When I told her I didn't want her to spill all her secrets, I lied, because I do.

When I told her I didn't know how much more I wanted, that was also a lie, because I want it all. Every piece. Every inch. Everything. It's unfair and selfish, but I want it anyway. But that also means I need to reciprocate. Can I do that?

"She's something else, isn't she?" Noah says. It's rhetorical, but I answer anyway.

"Yes," I murmur, not sure if he heard. I turn to Noah, and he's watching me thoughtfully. "Why did you pick her?"

He looks toward Willow, lingering a moment, then back to me. "There's just something about her."

There's no one like her.

"Yeah," I reply, my mouth curving. "That seems to be the consensus."

Noah hesitates a few moments before saying, "Honestly, I

thought maybe she'd give you a run for your money, Merc, and I'd pay top dollar to watch that unfold."

My curved mouth turns into a full smile. "And what do you think now?"

He chuckles and takes a long swig of his beer. "I'm enjoying the show. Immensely."

I'd like to tell him he doesn't see shit, but Noah Wilder knows me better than anyone on Earth. I say nothing.

My attention drifts back to Willow. She's taken a seat that faces me, but since it's relatively dark where we sit, she doesn't spot me. A waitress brings of tray of cocktails to their table. She hands Willow a martini glass with clear liquid and sets a round of shot glasses on the table that brim with brown liquor. All four of the other women grab them up. A striking, graceful African-American woman picks up two and hands one to Willow. Willow shakes her head, but the peer pressure is clear from here. After a roll of her eyes, she accepts. They clink their glasses in the air and down the alcohol. Willow wrinkles her nose slightly before she throws her head back and laughs.

It makes me warm to see her happy.

Noah and I sit in this very spot for the next two hours, chatting a little, but mostly just watching the goings-on in the club. It's still relatively early for a party night. Not even eleven. Unlike most of the young people in here, I actually have to work tomorrow. I have an early morning meeting, but I don't care. As long as Willow is here, I'm staying.

I keep my eye solely on her while every once in a while, Noah will drag my attention away to point out a potential hookup for the night. He's been gone and back a couple of times now, while I've stayed right here. Watching Willow.

This is what we used to do when we trolled in our younger years. We'd scope, we'd rank our options. We'd feel them out, see how pliable they were, how far they'd go. Then we'd invite one back to a hotel room we'd secured for the night and fuck her until we all passed out. Now we don't have to troll because they come to us. Just like the buxom brunette walking our way right now.

"What do you think of her?" Noah asks lowly. She's the third who's stopped by our table tonight.

She's smoking hot, no doubt. Nice face, come-hither smile, killer body. "I think she's barely weaned from the bottle," I reply on a laugh.

"Just the way I like them, bro. Easier to corrupt." He winks and turns his attention back to the gazelle now standing in front of us. And that's exactly what she is. An innocent who's entered the lion's den without even knowing it. If this were two months ago, Noah and I would have worked together in tandem to pervert her in as many ways as possible before tomorrow morning. Now I find I have absolutely no interest, although she seems very willing already.

"Hi," she says shyly, her eyes trained on Noah. Red-tipped fingernails graze the tabletop back and forth as she stands there nervously in her skimpy red dress.

"Hi, doll," Noah replies with his signature boy-next-door grin. Funny. He's anything but. He nods at her to take a seat and asks her what she wants to drink. For the next few minutes, we chat politely. We find out Sadie just graduated college last spring and works as a paralegal at a premier Seattle law firm while she's figuring out her next step, which she thinks is law school. It's not long before Noah's leaning close, whispering in her ear while his hand skims her bared thigh. When her eyelids get droopy with lust, I know he's reached his target.

Not waiting until he starts fingering her, which will be any second, I turn back to find Willow again except she's not at her table. In fact, none of the women are. Their drinks still sit there, unattended, and I see a pack of cigarettes in the center so I know they haven't left.

Noah and I are at a high top, and the floor in our section is slightly raised, giving me a good view of the entire VIP floor. Within seconds, I spot her group on the dance floor, and I don't even try to tear my eyes away from the effortless way her body glides to a song I don't recognize, but Willow does.

She's liquid, languid, graceful. With eyes shut and arms above her head, she mouths words about x's and o's while her hips swing back and forth fluidly like she was made for dancing. Or fucking.

My hard-on is painful, throbbing. There's no way I'll be able to go home tonight without easing this ache inside her first. No way in hell.

I should leave her alone. I should get up, walk to my car right now, and jack off at home to thoughts of the way those damn pants hug her perfect ass and leave nothing about her pussy to the imagination. I should visualize peeling them from her body before I claim her fast and rough, and come violently to thoughts of making her mine.

Before I know what's happening, I find myself drifting toward her. Sweaty bodies part on either side as if everyone can feel the ten thousand volts of energy buzzing around me. Just before I reach her, a guy with lust in his eyes slinks up behind her, grabs her hips, and spins her around to face him.

And as I get closer, I realize it's not just *any* guy.

It's Reid fucking Mergen.

I practically knock over the rest of the people in my way in my quest to get to Willow. "Get. Fucking. Lost," I growl with teeth bared, pulling Willow from his arms into mine.

"I think we should let Willow decide what she wants," he jeers, fisting his hands at his sides like he's ready for battle.

Bring it on, motherfucker. I am more than ready.

He tries to reach for her until I grip his wrist painfully. "She is mine."

"Jesus, you act like she's cattle or something, you self-righteous prick." He takes a step closer, and Willow wedges her way between us, pushing us apart with her tiny arms.

"Reid, please. Just go."

His jaw ticks back and forth, and I think for a second he'll plow right through her to get to me, but when his spiteful eyes drop, meeting hers, they soften. It fucking guts me that he looks at her that way. He reaches for her again, but thinks better of it, dropping his hand to his side. Nodding reluctantly, and with one last hateful glance my way, he spins on his heels to leave us alone.

Willow's small hands touch my face, turning me toward her. I think she's going to be angry, but she's not. Her flushed, sweaty face bears a mask of confusion. "What are you doing here?"

"What is *he* doing here?" I spit, hardly able to contain my rage that his hands were on her.

"I have no idea. I didn't even know he was."

Her voice begs me to believe her. I do. Jesus, if I hadn't been here, I'm absolutely certain that fucker would have made a play for her. At least now it's clear what he's after. *Her.* My eyes drift across the room looking for him again.

"Hey." She grabs the waist of my jeans and tugs me into her. "Don't worry about him."

She keeps moving her head to catch my eyes until I pay attention to her and only her. Then she smiles, and it's bright and brilliant and warm. It reaches her eyes and is just for me. I blow out a slow breath, releasing this murderous feeling eating me up.

I refocus on her and try to let the hatred I feel dissolve. It's not too hard when she runs her hands up and down my chest and looks at me with her doe eyes. The erection that abated a minute ago is raging back.

Out of the corner of my eye, I see her friends still dancing, but watching us with interest as the song changes to a sultry one by Tove Lo.

"Willow," I groan.

I drop my lips to her forehead and run my hands slowly up her torso. Raising her arms with me as I go, I clasp them around my neck. With a knee wedged between her thighs and my hand at the small of her back, I bend slightly and begin to sway us to the music.

"What are you doing?" she asks breathlessly.

I'm stiff as a rod.

Aching.

My cock pulses against her stomach. I know she feels it. I want her so fucking much, and I want so much from her it's fucking with me.

"I think that's obvious, my sexy minx. I'm dancing."

Her head swivels, but I don't let her get far. She's mine now, and I want all her attention on me. Not her ex. Not her friends. Not the people around us.

Never losing my rhythm, I slide a hand in her hair and lower my mouth to within an inch of hers. "God, I've wanted to kiss you for hours. You're so damn sexy out here."

She bats her eyes a couple of times processing the fact that I've been here, watching her. "What are you waiting for then, Drive By?"

I push the last two taunting words back in with my tongue, kissing her hard and deep. Palming a leather-covered ass cheek, I push my hardness farther into her, needing relief. She gasps into my mouth. I swallow it, relish in the rich and heady taste of her desire. My scalp stings from her grip, and I realize the hand on her ass has now slid up her back, underneath her blouse.

Her lips leave mine, trailing to my ear. She nibbles the lobe, breathing heavy while her nails score down my back. My face is buried in her neck, sucking on the sensitive skin that meets her shoulder. The place that drives her wild.

"How wet are you, Willow?" I rasp in her ear loud enough to be heard over the music.

"It's a river down there," she rasps back, chest heaving.

Christ. I want her this very minute, but I'm also thoroughly enjoying her curves pressed against me as we dance, so while her movements and breaths are getting more frantic, I slow mine down.

I want to make her mind buzz and her blood thrum with need.

I want to make her beg.

And yes, I want to make Reid fucking Mergen seethe with envy that *I* will be the one buried inside of Willow tonight and every night to come. Whatever chance he had with her, it's over. He won't get another if I have anything to say about it.

Anchoring her hips, I direct her seductive sway, making sure her pubic bone hits against my unyielding cock with every twist of our bodies. I scatter kisses along her jaw, down her throat until she moans long and loud. I whisper filthy words in her ear that make her breath catch. I forget where we are, getting lost in her, my plan backfiring completely. I'm the one buzzing and thrumming. It's not until the beat of the next song reverberates through me that I remember we're in the middle of a dance floor surrounded by hundreds of other people, but my mission is complete anyway.

She eases back, eyes bouncing between mine. "I want that do-over," she announces roughly. "Now." She grabs my hand and tries pulling me off the floor, but I yank her back to me.

Face between my palms, I tell her, "You're spending the night tonight. No excuses." I don't want her to go home like she's just a passing moment. She's not, and I'm tired of her pretending she is. I'm not sure what we are yet, but we are more than either of us intended.

I watch the war her mind wages like a movie, the questions coming in rapid-fire.

No or yes?

Defend or surrender?

Play it safe or take a risk?

My entire body sags in relief when she answers so soft I strain to hear, "Okay."

Finally. One fucking barrier down.

And after tonight? After seeing another man's hands on her? After I hold her naked body against me for hours on end?

Game over. I intend to tear down every single one that remains standing because I can finally admit that I want more than her time or her body or for her to help me keep the press out of my family life so my father can win his election.

I can finally admit I want her heart.

And I want to keep it, even if I'm not yet sure I won't break it.

Willow

Chapter Thirty-Two

MY STOMACH CARTWHEELS AS I slide the key card inside the door. Shaw's exhales tickle the back of my neck with each feathered kiss, and I have to try again, keeping my eyes open this time. He chuckles lightly, knowing exactly how he's affecting me. The light turns green, and I shove the handle down, letting us inside.

As predicted, Jo secured us all hotel rooms in the Alexis, along with an invitation to party with Errow, one of the premier bands rocking Emfest this year. I was actually looking forward to spending the evening with my friends. Gossiping, drinking, dancing, and laughing. Things I don't do enough of anymore.

But the second Shaw's arms came around me, that disappeared. All I wanted to do was get him naked and lick him from head to toe. He looks so fucking sexy in his dark-wash jeans and slim-fit charcoal button-down that my mouth actually watered.

I should be mad he showed up on my evening out with my friends, but I'm so far from mad I'm scared. I knew I felt him there. My skin tingled from the moment I stepped foot onto the VIP level. I felt his presence. I felt watched, protected. Desired.

Once we're over the threshold, steel bands wrap around from behind, pressing me into a solid masculine body. I hear the soft click of the door closing before his husky statement trickles over me. "I want to fuck you, Willow. So goddamn good and hard you never forget me."

You're utterly unforgettable. Those words balance on my tongue before I let them tumble away, afraid to voice them, afraid to scare him away.

"I want you," I whisper instead. My head swims and my blood buzzes with the alcohol I drank. That, and sheer, raw need. I want Shaw, but on my terms tonight.

I don't know if it's the buzz or the ticking clock that gets louder every day, but tonight I want to be the one in charge. I want to unravel the coiled power he holds tightly to. I want to bring the measured, dictating Shaw Mercer to his everlovin' knees. I want to fuck him so hard *he* never forgets *me*, my memory haunting him when I'm gone.

Leaning my head back on his shoulder, I slide a hand between us to cup his rigid cock. My grip is firm, my strokes are sure, and I know I have him when his guttural voice grates, "I love your hands on my cock, Willow."

Spinning in his arms, I pull his head down and kiss him with every feeling inside me. It's desperate need and wild hunger I've never had for another human being. His hands grip my waist as he leads us back into the spacious suite. I know exactly where he's headed, but I don't want to go there.

This is my night.

My show.

My stage.

I pull my mouth from his and dig my heels into the carpet to stop us. Shaw looks down at me with undisguised lust in his hooded eyes. The way his chest rises and falls quickly makes my womanly pride swell.

With a slight smile, my hands reach for his shirt buttons. I undo the small discs with quick efficiency, and the raw groan that leaves his throat when I suck a flat, manly nipple into my mouth makes me moan. I make my way to the other side, repeating the action.

"Fuck, Willow." His sexy growl gasses my fire.

His jeans are next, and I have the button and zipper open before I fall to my knees and pull his thick length from black boxer briefs. He's steel encased in velvet. Smooth and hard and so thick my fingers barely touch. Gazing up the taut, flat plane of his torso, I ask, "And how would you like my mouth on your cock?"

His answer is to grab a fistful of my hair in one hand, his cock in the other. Stroking himself a few times first, he taps my mouth with the mushroom head, and I can't stop my tongue from darting out to lick the droplets of pre-come coating the tip, drawing a low curse from him.

"Open up."

His throaty command is primal, stirring the submissive part I didn't know I had in me to obey. I do, letting him think he's controlling this. But he's not. I am. He will do everything I want and won't even realize it.

And I want this.

When he slides inside my mouth, I moan around him. God, I'd do this every day of the year. He tastes like sweet musk and virile man. He tastes like mine.

I flatten my tongue as I take him deep. When I ease back, I hollow my cheeks and suck hard. I grasp the base and squeeze, letting my fingers tickle his balls before twisting my hand as it follows my mouth back up.

"Holy Christ." He tugs on my hair until my eyes sweep up to catch his. They're burning. Crazed. "Again. Just like that."

Smiling around my mouthful, I swirl my tongue around the underside and play with him until he's panting before I take him to the back of my throat again and repeat.

"So good, Willow. Jesus, don't stop."

I don't, until all the signs of climax appear.

His eyes drop.

His head falls.

His grip tightens.

His breaths pick up.

His thighs tense, his cock swells, and he starts pulsing before thrusting faster, rougher, need dissolving control. More saltiness coats my tongue. I want nothing more than to finish this, finish him until he roars and his knees weaken, but I have other things in mind before I take him over.

The next time I come up, I let his dick fall out with a loud pop. Shocked, he loosens his grip on my hair, and I take the opportunity to jump to my feet and walk backward before he can grab me again.

"Get back here," he rumbles, stalking after me.

I hold my hand out before he gets too close. "Stop."

"Willow, what the fuck? Get your mouth back on my cock and finish what you started."

He sounds desperate, needy.

Uncontrolled.

Finally. Mr. Cool is melting under the pressure.

He takes another step until his heaving bare chest pushes against my palm. My eyes travel over his perfectly honed body. Tanned flesh, taut muscles, a smattering of hair in just the right places. Jesus, the man is sin walking. Lucifer's angel.

"I want to do something for you," I breathe, almost losing my nerve.

"I want you to do something for me, too." His voice holds little amusement. He's really peeved. "I want you on your knees sucking my cock bone dry."

"God, Shaw." My eyes close briefly, his wicked words nearly luring me down before I shove him back. I nod to the chair behind him. "Sit down. You'll like this. I promise."

His eyes darken and his jaw clenches. For a split second, I don't think he's going to. I think he's going to grab me, push me back to the floor, and shove his angry, bobbing cock back inside my mouth. But with a heavy sigh, he takes a few steps backward and eases into the overstuffed armchair, pinning me with a quiet stare.

Jesus, he looks good. With his chest bare, legs spread wide, and cock standing at attention from the denim still encasing his hips, he looks like some sort of hedonistic king in his throne.

Taking a few steps back, I never look away as I begin to slowly drag down the zipper on the side of my blouse. I've never stripped as much for a man as I have for Shaw, but it's something he loves, and I want to please him.

I loosen the ties on the halter and shimmy the cloth over my head, letting it fall whisper soft to the ground. I want to drag this out. That was my plan. Strip and tease, but the second I free my swollen, aching breasts from my strapless bra, Shaw palms his cock and starts leisurely stroking it. The sight is so damn erotic I throb everywhere. I want to straddle him, sink, and ride until I forget who I am.

"Don't stop now, Goldilocks," he prods with a smirk when my fingers hesitate.

Eyes sweeping up, I know my smile is sultry when his lips thin and his gaze turns positively ravenous. Unzipping my pants, I turn and bend, peeling them down my lean legs with purpose. I want to keep my heels on, but I can't slip my pants over them, so I quickly unbuckle and remove them, hyperaware the entire time that the only thing separating my soaked pussy from Shaw's view is a one-inch-wide scrap of lavender silk.

"I could stare at this vision every day until I'm dead and never tire of it," he rasps thickly.

God, when he says things like that...

I remove my thong and straighten, peeking playfully over my shoulder before turning around. Shaw's face is pinched tight, and he's fisting his cock faster than a minute ago. I smile, knowing I'm about to blow his mind.

Bending my knees, I sit on the edge of the square coffee table and spread my legs wide. We didn't turn the overhead light on, but the moonlight shining through the opened balcony blinds spins the perfect sensual ambiance, rays of bright blue acting like my very own spotlight. There's no way he can miss how much I want him.

"Jesus, fuck, Willow," he grunts when I palm one breast and tweak the hardened nub on the tip, gasping at the slight pain I inflicted on myself. Running a finger through my slit, I drag the wetness up to my throbbing clit and round it slowly before plunging two fingers inside.

"Tell me how you taste," he demands, voice full of gravel.

Tasting my own desire isn't something I've done before, except on the lips of a man, but I already know what the answer's going to be before I suck the thick fluid from my two middle fingers. "I still taste like you."

His dark eyes fall shut on a harsh sound. When they open again, he's absolutely wild. The lines of his face are sharp, wolfish. Every muscle is coiled and ready. He wants to fuck me so bad right now I can taste it.

The upper hand is mine.

My hand slinks back down my stomach and slides through my wetness once again. I circle the highly sensitive bundle of nerves lightly at first, increasing the pressure with each rotation. "You do this to me, Shaw," I whisper on an honest breath. "You make me wet, ache, want things."

You. A future. Happiness.

I left every inhibition I had outside the hotel room door and couldn't care less that I feel my juices coat the table beneath me, making it slick.

He leans his head against the cushion, his lids drooping so he can keep watch on my gyrating fingers and hips as his own keep time with mine. The fingers of his other hand fondle his sack and the harsh, ragged breaths leaving his lungs echo mine.

"You make me feel beautiful and desired."

"You are. So damn beautiful and so fucking wet."

"For you," I pant, nearing the goal line. "Only you."

"You're close."

So are you. His hips thrust violently with every jerky sweep of his closed fist. He's losing it.

"Yes," I agree raggedly.

"Come, Willow. I want to watch it, watch you let go wishing my fingers were on that honeyed cunt right now instead of your own."

I was wrong.

I never had the power. Shaw always did, because at his hoarse, raunchy command, I do his bidding, my body helpless to stop its surrender. He held the reins, and I held his stormy eyes until I couldn't anymore. Until the tidal wave of pleasure my fingers created but that he owned swept me away and I lost myself murmuring his name, ecstasy cleaving and crashing inside me like whitecaps.

"That's it, beautiful," he urges quietly.

Letting my head drop back, I come.

Hard.

Brutally.

Beautifully.

My muscles shudder uncontrollably as the addiction that is Shaw Mercer ravages its way through my body, obliterating everyone before him.

I have no idea how long it takes before I'm aware neither of us has moved. When I can right my head back up on my shoulders, there he sits. My powerful, handsome, hedonistic king. Thick, erect cock still in his hand and pure awe on his face.

"I've never witnessed anything more beautiful than that, Willow. Thank you."

If I wasn't liquid before, those reverent words totally melted me. I didn't think I was going to be able to move until smugness tilts his lips and he bosses, "Get on my cock. Right now. Your next orgasm belongs to me."

"That one belonged to you, Drive By," I declare with my own satisfied smile. I close my legs and glow when his starving gaze follows.

Grin widening, he curls his index finger, motioning me over.

I could play coy, hard to get, use a few more smart retorts to rile him up, but why? The game is finished. He's the leader and I'm the follower.

And I'm okay with that.

Standing on wobbly legs, I make my way to him, my blood hot and my wet fingers tingling. While I was in my postorgasmic coma, he must have shucked his jeans and shirt because he's gloriously naked. When I reach him, I silently climb onto his lap as he rests his hands on my hips. I hover above eight inches of solid length, anticipating his next instruction.

He knows.

"You're so fucking perfect, Willow." Palming my nape, he pulls me down for a whispering kiss against my mouth. "Sit down."

Holy shit, I love how this man talks to me.

Coating him with the remnants of my orgasm first, I line him up and sink, inch by inch until he's fully seated. I whimper at the exquisite fullness.

"Ride me. Don't hurry. I want to feel every ridge of that scorching pussy when you lift up and down." With one hand securing the back of my neck and one on my hip, he's the maestro. He directs. I move. The Earth shifts.

The Earth shifts.

I thought that was a bullshit line made up by Hollywood or romance authors. But with Shaw's intense eyes locked hot on mine, I feel something significant transform in the atmosphere, once again changing our relationship somehow.

"Willow," he whispers softly. "You are mine."

My hands cup his face, and I lean my forehead to his, shutting my eyes so he can't see the water or uncertainty now filling them.

"You're mine," he rasps again on lazy thrusts and tender kisses. "I want you to be mine."

"But the contract...," I choke. That fucking contract hangs

over our heads like a storm cloud, and it clearly says I am *not* his after the next few weeks pass.

"Fuck the contract. *Fuck* the contract," he repeats again with more force, his body reacting the same way as his temperament. His drives are no longer lazy and languid; they punctuate his point with savagery. His kisses are no longer delicate and soft; they're rough and scorching. His touch is no longer gentle; it's harsh and bruising.

And moments later, when we tumble headfirst into the blinding vortex of bliss together, his sweet lyrics convince me I could be his and there's a possible future together, regardless of how we started.

When I willingly fall asleep wound around him that night, after another round of wicked and dirty sex against the shower wall, the darkness of dreams isn't the only thing that pulls me under. That last sliver of light I had been focusing on fades into nothingness, and I know, without a shadow of doubt, that I am his.

I did what I swore I wouldn't do.

I went and fell head over heels in love with Shaw Mercer, a man who I also know, without a shadow of doubt, will shatter my heart beyond all repair.

Willow

Chapter Thirty-Three

LOVE.

Four simple letters, one single syllable.

Seemingly straightforward in its definition, but it's far from that. It's complex and confusing. It's contradictory, paradoxical if you stop to really think about it.

On one hand, so much warmth and happiness fills you, you're sure your skin will split and sunbeams will pour out. Your heart is full, your life right. There's a comfortable peace that surrounds you that you don't realize is there until it's shattered into a million pieces, lying in the dirt around you.

On the other hand, though, is sheer, raw terror at losing the one thing in the world you can't fathom existing without. The thought of not seeing that person's face or hearing their voice is simply incomprehensible until you're faced with the stark reality the one you love is gone for good, and the only place you'll see them again is in faded memories and sad dreams.

Whether it's a parent, a child, a sibling, a friend, or the love of your life, we all love, we all fear, we all eventually lose someone. I think I'm particularly sensitive to this conflict because I've lived it. Many times before.

So, if loving someone—anyone—eventually leads to heartbreak, loss, and mourning, why do we do it? Why do we continue to let people into our lives, our hearts? Steal our very soul out from under us before we realize a vital piece of us is forever missing?

Simple.

No matter how hard we deny it or push it away, love is inevitable. We fall in eyes wide open, the pain of loss well worth the beauty of everlasting memories, no matter how fleeting they are.

That's where I'm at right now.

Memory building.

Memorizing.

Stealing pockets of time, stacking moment upon moment as fast as I can so I can pull them out later when Shaw is gone.

The masculine scent of his skin that lingers with each inhale.

The slow, even cadence of his breath in sleep.

The feel of his muscular thigh pinned underneath my leg.

The weight of his arm banding me tight.

The rightness of my head nestled in the crook of his shoulder.

The way my lips lightly graze his chest, tiny hairs tickling me.

I will remember them all with crispness and clarity. I won't let them fade. It's the only reason I gave in to spending the night in his arms. I selfishly wanted my memorial pillars to be high and wide and so damn dense I'll never see over or around or through them. I'll see *only* them because I already know I'll never love another man like I do him.

I fell in eyes wide open, all right. I watched it unfold right before me, helpless to stop it. He's my once-in-a-lifetime, and without a doubt, everything that's happened to me was another brick in the road that led me to him. It was destiny, I'm sure. I've been wondering a lot lately if my father's death, in particular, hasn't paved my way to him.

I would be married to Reid by now, if not for that. I wouldn't have been working for Randi, if not for that. I would have never met Noah, if not for that. Is my father still watching over me from beyond, directing me where I need to go in life?

"What are you thinking about so hard, beautiful?" Shaw's thick voice, gravelly with the remnants of sleep, startles me, and I twitch.

"Nothing," I lie.

I feel the hand that was just crawling up and down my arm slide into my hair. With a tug, I'm now looking into his questioning ocean blues. "Do you know that whenever you're nervous about something you worry your fingers together?"

I'm totally taken aback. Yes, I knew that. It's an unconscious habit I picked up at nine when my momma put some nasty stuff on my fingers so I'd stop biting my nails to the nubs. But the fact Shaw recognized it is...wow. "Yes."

His gaze travels over my face, and I see concern creep in. "Do you regret spending the night with me?"

"No," I answer with no hesitation. None whatsoever.

"Then what is it?" he asks, sweeping the back of his hand lightly over my cheek. "What's got you wearing down the pads of your fingers so far you're rubbing your fingerprints off?"

"I...I don't know exactly." But that's not at all truthful, and I face another defining moment of indecision. Let him in, or keep him on the fringes. I take a deep, shaky breath. "I'm just not sure what this is."

His eyebrows pinch together. "What what is?"

"Us."

A half smile plays on his lips. "I think other people call this a relationship."

We've never talked about it directly, but there've been enough innuendos by Shaw and his family to know he's not been serious about a woman. Ever. So why me? "I didn't think you did relationships."

He sobers, withdrawing a little. "I'm not sure I do, Willow, but I…I want to try. I'm trying to be as honest as possible here."

I prop myself up on my elbow and look down at his handsome face, thick with untrimmed scruff. His dark hair lays against the bleached, white pillowcase, and his eyes sparkle in the morning sun streaming around the cracks in the curtain. He's relaxed and serene and even more appealing when he freshly wakes. I take another mental snapshot for my growing portfolio.

"Why now? Why me?"

I have to admit, in part I wonder if it's because of Reid. He's become extremely possessive since Reid showed up, and last night I thought they were going to come to blows over me right in the middle of the dance floor. The thought Shaw wants me simply so another man can't have me feels worse than if he didn't want me at all.

His shoulder moves up, then back down. "I don't know. Do I have to have a reason?"

"Yes, Drive By." I laugh. "You do."

"What do you want to hear?" he asks almost absently as his eyes follow the finger he feathers down my neck, over my shoulder, and down my bare arm. Chills, followed by a rush of heat, race after his touch.

"The truth," I tell him on a hush.

"The truth." He repeats the low words as if they're almost foreign to him before speaking again in a slow, measured voice. "Well, the truth is…" He follows the same trail all the way back up, grasping my chin between his finger and thumb, holding me spellbound. Keeping me breathless. "You captivate me like no one else has before, Willow, and what I feel for you is…new for me."

Is this his way of saying he's falling for me? When I swallow, it hurts because a whole heap of emotion sits in the middle of my chest. It threatens to close off my airway.

"Is that honest enough?" he asks, his smile wry.

I want to ask about the contract and if he still means what he said last night. I want to ask if he's falling in love with me, but I don't want to shatter the moment, making him say something he's clearly not ready to. So I nod, feeling tingly everywhere.

"Good. Now, lay back down before I lose all control and fuck you until you pass out from exhaustion."

My eyes travel down the length of him, stopping when I reach the tent that's now pitched in the center of his body. "That doesn't sound so bad," I whisper.

His genuine smile takes my breath away. Again.

"I agree, but if you don't mind, I'd like to talk first, because after I'm done fucking you, you'll be too tired to form sentences; and if you're not, I'll have to try again."

With a huff, I plop back down. Okay, so he pulls me down, because I was reaching for his tent pole. With one arm pinned between the bed and his side, and Shaw holding my free hand firmly against his chest lest it wanders, I ask, "Don't you have work today or something?"

"No. I, uh...I took the day off," he says a little sheepishly.

I tilt my head upward. "You took the day off? When? Can the CEO of a major corporation just take the day off on a whim?"

"It's my company. I can do whatever the fuck I want. Besides, there was nothing earth-shattering, so I pushed my meetings to next week. E-mailed Dean last night before I slipped into bed."

He's trying to downplay this as not a big deal, but it so is. I know he works hard, twelve to fourteen hours a day, including weekends. Taking an unexpected day off *means* something. Why does that make me feel all fluttery?

"For me?" I ask, hoping he says yes.

"Yes, Willow." He taps my nose playfully. "For you. I knew once I had your gorgeous limbs wrapped around me, I wouldn't be able to make myself leave you naked and alone in this bed this morning. I was right." He husks the last part.

I beam. There's no other way to put it. The smile on my face feels a mile wide and an ocean deep. It makes him laugh. He looks five years younger when he's relaxed and lets himself go.

I'm so fucking in love with this man I want to shout it to the world. I want to whisper it against his lips. But I don't. I swallow it down and think on his words, *what I feel for you is...new for me*. I decide I'll take it. I know it was sincere and a little hard for him to admit—that has to mean something. All of this *has* to mean something. Right?

"You look happy," he says thoughtfully.

"I am."

"I'm glad. I like to see you happy, Willow. More than you know."

I'm smiling so damn hard the muscles in my face hurt, but then Shaw asks me a question that deflates me like an accordion and brings the reality of my life hailing down around me. The hits sting the same every time.

"Why do you work for Randi?" I stiffen and try to pull away, but he holds me fast. "Willow, I'm not judging. I'm just curious. You're a beautiful, smart, talented woman with a lot going for her, and I'm wondering what about life brought you to La Dolce Vita. I get the distinct feeling it's not something you aspired to when you were young."

I blink a few times before I gently extricate myself from him. He reaches for me, but I'm not running again. I just can't have this conversation while he's touching me. I don't plan on telling him the whole story; I'm not sure I can, but for some reason, I want him to know I didn't have a choice, and I didn't take the decision to work for Randi lightly.

I lean against the headboard with a sigh, dragging the sheet up over my breasts. My entire body feels chilled, and it shakes with a shiver.

"I'm sorry," Shaw says, twining his fingers with mine, bringing them to his lips. "You don't have to tell me if you don't want to."

He pushes himself into a seated position, leaning next to me. We sit silently for an eternity.

"No. It's okay. I want to." But I fall quiet again. The

unpressured time Shaw gives me to talk about my parents is a quiet blessing.

"My mother has Alzheimer's."

He stiffens beside me before slowly sitting up to face me. He looks positively shocked, but we're both thinking the exact same thing.

"Your father..."

I nod. The words are hard to come, even harder to push out. "Yes, I know what my father was working on when he died." Which is all the more reason I carry around guilt like a two-ton weight I can't shake.

My father discovered a biotech drug that could possibly stop Alzheimer's in its tracks if given early enough in the disease's onset. Ironically, it was too late for my mother, but to know he was responsible for finding a possible cure for a devastating disease that impacts so many, saving them and their families the suffering my family has endured, fills me with unending pride. That he chose to take his brilliance away from not only the world but his family is a hard pill to swallow.

"I don't understand. Didn't your parents have money? Life insurance? Stock? Retirement?"

"My father was the sole breadwinner, and regardless of what people think, scientists don't work for the money; they do it for the passion. He made a decent living and had some savings, but I had their house and bills to pay off, and it's expensive to take care of my mother. My momma needs full-time care, and I ran through most everything after the first year. I just can't manage on my other salary. And as far as life insurance goes,"—I pause to blow out a long breath—"the policy is void when one takes his own life."

For an eternity, we're quiet, before his voice breaks with sincerity. "I'm sorry, Willow."

I shake my head and look away. "Don't be. It's my fault." The last part slips out before I can stop it.

A palm slips around my cheek, and he turns me toward him so I can't look away. Sympathy and annoyance are written all over him. It's the same look everyone gives you when you say how you feel responsible for the suicide of a loved one. But unless you've been through it yourself, you have absolutely no idea how you'll feel. What signs did I miss? Did they say anything I should have paid more attention to? Why didn't they just talk to me? Why didn't they love me enough to stay?

"How is it your fault, Willow? He..."

Yeah. It's hard to speak the word out loud. It is for me, too. Overdose is just as hard and has all the same feelings attached to it as suicide does.

"He was stressed. With work, with my mother. I should have seen the signs earlier. I should have..." I try my damnedest to hold my voice steady. I don't.

"No. Stop. Just stop," he practically barks. His eyes widen and turn firm. "This is not on you, Willow. Your father's *actions* are not on you."

This is the same speech Reid gave me for six months after my father died. Verbatim. It doesn't lessen the guilt any more now than it did then.

"You don't understand."

Suddenly I feel completely unworthy of anything remotely good. Just like I did with Reid.

Happiness.

Peace.

Love.

Him.

I pull from his hold and move to get off the bed, intent on gathering my things and taking a cab home, when I'm being pressed into the soft mattress and covered by almost two hundred pounds of angry man.

"Don't," he growls.

"Don't what?" I keep my eyes closed, terrified to see what he must think of me.

"Don't shut me out. I fucking hate it when you do that."

My scalp stings where he grabs a fistful of hair at the crown of my head in one hand. My cheeks pinch together between the fingers of his other. "Eyes on me, Willow."

I want to beg him to leave me alone, but I need him so damn much I ache everywhere. And it's not a physical need. It's entirely emotional. For once in my life, I want to let someone else lighten my load. I *need* to let someone carry me for a change instead of me carrying them. I just don't know how.

My lids flutter open, and my heart races at what I see.

Unadulterated determination.

"Yeah, that's it, Goldilocks. Come back to me."

"Shaw." I push against his chest, panic setting in. I'm raw and vulnerable. Close to a breakdown. It's utterly terrifying to drop that wall all the way. My skin feels tight. I can't breathe.

The fingers around my face tighten, stopping just short of pain. "I'm not letting you go, so just stop with whatever shit is running through that head of yours."

"Why?" I choke out. "I'm damaged goods. Can't you see that? I'm too much work. You have no idea what you're getting yourself into."

He shakes his head as if I'm the stupidest girl in the world. "You don't get it, do you? Because, Willow, you are the only woman I have ever met worth fighting for, that's why. The only one."

It takes a special girl to open a boy's eyes to what's right in front of him, Willow. But when he realizes it, he'll fight to the death for her and only her. Don't settle until you find that man.

He turns into just a blob as my vision blurs with emotion.

"You with me now, beautiful?" he asks in a softening voice.

I nod, twin tears rolling down into my ears.

He's hard and tender in the same breath when he says, "You deserve happiness, Willow. Let me do that for you. Let me take away your sadness and replace it with joy."

I'm not sure I can accept it. *That's* the real issue. "Why?" I still don't get it. He could have any woman he wants, yet he's chosen one with a jungle of shit to wade through.

"Because you are worth fighting for," he repeats again.

Shaw shoves his knee between my legs, opening them wide. "And I will tell you that as many times as I have to until you believe me."

Before I know what's happening, he's slipping inside on a muted groan. I'm wet and ready for him. I'm *always* ready for him when he's near me. My body reacts involuntarily, hips rolling with each lazy thrust.

With the hand in my hair anchoring me, the other wanders, reverently worshipping me in small, tiny strokes like I'm porcelain and will break if he squeezes too hard. Slanting his mouth over mine, he lavishes me with sweet affection before whispering, "How long has it been since someone has taken care of you instead of the other way around?"

I choke in a sob. *Since I was twelve.*

"Too fucking long I would guess. That ends now. With me. Let me take care of you. I *want* to take care of you."

He's so adamant it nearly breaks me. "I don't know how." My voice is haunted. Like my soul.

His pacing steady, he frames my face and gazes at me with flat-out devotion. "I want in, Willow. I'm not stopping until you let me worship you and take care of you like you deserve. Until you let me show you how much you mean to me. How worthy you are of everything good. How you're worth fighting for."

His movements are calculated, his kisses are tender, and his quiet words of worth wrench tear after tear from deep inside. It's cathartic, leaving the smallest pockets of room for happiness to fill them up instead of sadness and self-loathing. By the time he skillfully makes us peak at the same time, I start to believe him.

And when he rasps on a broken breath, "You are extraordinary, Willow. Extraordinary just the way you are," into the column of my neck, I let myself weep.

God, this man.

Shaw Mercer dominates his world with commanding force, but with one soft breath, he just ruled my heart.

Banding my arms around him tightly I hang on for dear life.

I hang on to what I've unexpectedly found with him, praying what we have is real and will be able to stand the tests that undoubtedly lie ahead of us.

Because in any relationship, there are always tests, and I know we haven't even begun to take ours yet.

Shaw

Chapter Thirty-Four

I HAVE A DOZEN TO-DOS on my calendar this Monday morning that shouldn't wait, but they have to because my first and only priority is Willow.

She's strong in so many ways yet so fragile I think she may shatter into pieces with one wrong word. She has a tremendous amount of responsibility on her plate yet shoulders it with grace and elegance and not one ounce of resentment. She does what she needs to do to survive, and I respect the hell out of that, regardless of if I hate it.

Somehow, I convinced her to spend the entire weekend with me until last night, when she insisted she sleep at home. I didn't want to let her go. I wanted her dreams to run wild with me so I could hear my name mumbled in her sleep. I wanted to watch the sun play in her hair and run my tongue down her spine in the morning before reaching her wet center. And I wanted her to wake up moaning for me when I slipped my fingers between those ready thighs like I have every other morning for the past three days.

And oddly, I wanted to come home tonight to her sitting in my chair, a smile on her face and nothing else. I want to cook for her, cuddle with her, buy her anything her heart desires, travel the world with her.

I want things I never thought I'd want.

A future.

I had the most incredible three days with a woman ever. Willow opened up about a lot, letting me in slowly. I treasured every single morsel she gave me, desperate for more. We talked about her business, her passions, her goals, her dreams. I learned how she put her Broadway plans on hold to be close to her mom and how when she was little she actually wanted to be a ballerina instead of an actor. She even took me to see her mother—albeit at my insistence.

It was a sad thing to witness. Someone you love so much who doesn't recognize you. She kept calling Willow Violet, and no matter how much gentle prodding I did, Willow would only say she was confused. But I know there's more to the story she's not telling me because pain doesn't lie. And I saw it in spades in the tightening of her muscles at every mention of Violet's name.

But if I've learned anything about Willow over the past few weeks, it's that she has to give up these pieces she holds dear in her own time. And I'll wait for them, even if it takes years for her to give them all to me. That's why instead of pressing her more, I brought her back to my place and crowded out every ounce of pain with pleasure. So much goddamn pleasure she passed out on me with a satisfied sigh.

Another reason I didn't want her to go back to her place. It seems when we spend too much time apart, she drifts away from me, and I have to work that much harder the next time to just get us back to where we were before.

I unconsciously rub the twinge I feel sitting heavy in my chest. I can't believe how much this tiny but grandiose woman has come to mean to me in such a short period of time.

Is it love?

I don't know. How the fuck would I? I've never been in love before, but if it's the kind of feeling that makes it hard to breath, impossible to concentrate, and constricts your chest with pain at the thought of not having her in your life…well, then, maybe. But I'm not ready to label it yet. I'm scared as fuck, truth be told. We are two peas, that. All I know is it's something a helluva a lot deeper than infatuation or lust. I already miss her, and it's been less than twelve hours since I last saw her.

Regardless of what I call this thing between us, I meant what I told her the other night. I want to take care of her. I want to unburden her heart and her life, but I know that will take time.

What I know won't take time is helping her financially. She'll be pissed, just like the car, but fuck it. I'll happily deal with the blowback because there's no way I can let this go. She deserves to at least have that burden eliminated, so my second stop this morning is to visit Jack Hancock to discuss what provisions may have been in Charles Blackwell's employment agreement that aren't being honored. There's no way a man with his intellect and worth wouldn't have some sort of significant patent or project-based bonus due him. Even death does not erase their financial obligation to his family.

But my first stop this morning is with a man I'd sooner send packing to the Antarctica with nothing but swimming trunks and flip-flops than have a conversation with. Trust me, if I could figure out a way to get him on the next cargo plane out of here, I would. I can't have him getting in the way of what I'm building with Willow, and I've no doubt he's going to try.

The bell above the paned door jingles when I open it, drawing the attention of a very young woman sitting behind a low counter. She looks like a college student.

"Can I help you?" she asks cheerfully, setting down the pen that was in her hand so she can give me her full attention.

"Yes. I'm here to see Reid Mergen."

Her face falls slightly. "Do you have an appointment, Mr…?"

I lean my forearm on the white Formica ledge that's seen better days and deliver my killer smile. She obviously doesn't know who I am. "No, but I have a checkbook. I assume that's enough?"

"Oh, yes. Of course. Your money's always good here." She laughs. I smile, caring about nothing but getting to Mergen. "I'll just buzz him that he has a guest."

She reaches for the phone, and I place my hand gently on top of hers. When her head rises, the look she gives me is one I've seen a hundred times over. She would do anything I asked of her right now, including sucking my cock in the open office space if I walked around the padded wall separating us and unzipped.

"I'm an old friend, and if it's all the same to you, I'd like to surprise him. So if you could just point me in the direction of his office, I'd be most grateful." When I wink it's like yanking on a fishing line, my hook embedded deep.

"Ah, yes. That's...that's so s—sweet," she stutters. "It's, ah, down the, ah, hall to the left. Last, ah, office on the right."

"Thanks." I give her another wink for the road and weave my way quickly through the cubicles toward the opposite end. I note the last office door is closed, but I couldn't give a flying fuck. My hand is turning the knob before I think better of it and quickly glance through the glass slice on the left to ensure my father isn't in there.

When I see Mergen reading the fucking newspaper, I go ahead and let myself in, uninvited. The look on his face when he tears himself away from a riveting article is priceless.

"Well look what the wet cat dragged in," he drawls mockingly.

I shut the door behind me and make myself at home by taking a seat across his incredibly neat desk. It's so neat, I wonder if he's actually doing any work for my father, or if he's here just to weasel Willow out from under me.

"Busy getting my father reelected?" I ask nicely. Well, I suppose "nice" is open to interpretation.

"Is that why you're here? To make sure I'm doing my job?"

"Are you? My father's ahead by only eight points in the

latest poll, so I'm wondering just how good at your job you really are. I thought you were supposed to be some fucking political miracle worker."

"I'll get your father reelected if I can keep his loose cannon children in line."

"You'd better watch what you say about my family, motherfucker. You know nothing about us."

His smug face irritates the shit out of me. "I know more than you think. Now, why are you really here?"

One corner of my mouth turns up in a snarl. "I want you to stay away from Willow."

Asshole leans back and laces his hands, resting them on his stomach. "And I'm supposed to care what you want?"

"I don't give endless fucks what you care about, as long as it isn't her."

He laughs. It's bitter and grates on my last raw nerve. When his eyes drop to the newspaper on his desk, mine follow. With a smile, I realize it's the *7-Day*, opened to the article on page two I approved yesterday. The picture they selected is perfect if I do say so myself, and it clearly shows two people who mean more to each other than a passing fling. When I saw it yesterday, it struck a chord with me. And when I brought it home—*home*—to Willow, she threw herself into my arms before dropping to her knees to suck me off. Jesus, I'm growing hard just thinking about it.

"You put on a good show, I'll give you that," fuckface says.

"That's no show." I nod to the article. "That's the real deal."

His smile is more of a toothy jeer. "You're telling me you're in love with Willow? After just a few weeks of knowing each other?"

I think I could be.

I know *I could be.*

It's more than "could be." It is. Fuck labels. I'll own it.

"You know, my parents got married thirty-one days after they met. Not one of their friends or family was supportive. Said they didn't know each other well enough. Would end up divorced after just a few months. You've met my parents. What do you think of their relationship after forty-one years of marriage?"

Not one person could dispute the love Adelle and Preston Mercer have for each other. They both place each other on pedestals so high their noses should bleed.

"You didn't answer my question."

"It's not worth answering. It's none of your fucking business what Willow and I have."

Campaign twat grabs a cheap Bic pen and starts twirling it fancily through his fingers while eyeing me. "I know about you, you know."

"Oh? Enlighten me." I throw an ankle over a knee and settle in. I don't give a shit what he thinks he knows, what he's heard, what dirt he has on me. None of it matters because none of it will ever come close to touching Willow.

"Tell me, does she know about your philandering threesomes with the boy wonder? You and your left nut, Noah Wilder, aka *Wildman*? At what point in the dating ritual do you begin to share?"

I always loved Marvel comics when I was a kid. I desperately wanted a superpower and prayed about it regularly when I went to bed at night. Back then, I wished I could fly at the speed of sound. But now? Now I wish it was spontaneous combustion, because this fucker's ashes would already be dusting my Brioni David loafers.

"You're toeing a very fine line. I don't know what my father sees in you, but I assure you, I have far more pull with him than you do, and I'd say since you aren't doing a stellar job at blowing away the competition, I could easily have you replaced with one phone call. On a plane out of here by noon."

"You and I both know this was my idea. The press. The girlfriend. The diversion from the fucked-up lives you and your siblings have in common. I wonder what Willow would think if she knew she was being used?"

I keep my face neutral. At least this allayed one of my

worries. He doesn't know Willow knows, and he doesn't know about her "job." That's good. Very good. And I, of course, knew he knew about Noah, but I'll deal with that if it comes up. I don't plan on sharing Willow. Ever.

"You're grasping at dust motes here."

"Am I?"

"I slammed into the back of her car. That wasn't orchestrated."

"I wouldn't put anything past you. I know how much you love your father, how you'd do anything for him, for your family. But I also know Willow. Very, very"—I want to plant my fist in his face for the way he unnecessarily drags out those fucking adjectives—"well. And I think she'd eventually forgive you for it if *she's* in love with *you*."

Jesus that sounds selfishly good.

"But?"

The reptilian smile he gives me should have been my first clue he's more of a snake in the grass than I ever imagined possible. "But...I don't think she could possibly see past your little sister's role in her father's death, do you?"

Faster than I can think, I'm out of my chair and over the desk in his face, his throat twisted in my hands. "What the fuck are you playing at, you son of a bitch? My sister had nothing to do with Willow's father's death. He committed suicide, you sick fuck."

When he talks, it's strained because I'm cutting off his air supply, but what he says chills me to the bone. "Am I playing, Shaw?" he sneers. "You picked up your sister that night from the police station. Miraculously got her off on coke possession charges. Wasn't she soaked to the bone? Distraught? What bullshit story did your drug addict sister feed you that you bought with the gullibility of a five-year-old?"

"You're lying," I seethe. My entire body is vibrating with dark hate as my mind spins with the force of a tornado. My breaths are coming fast, and my hands squeeze him tighter, trying to choke the very life from his rancid soul.

"I can see the doubt in your eyes, thinking through that night, trying to remember the details," he chokes, now clawing at my hands.

"And how would you know any of this?"

He keeps his face stone-cold neutral, not giving anything up. I squeeze harder. He's not twenty seconds from taking his last breath, and Jesus fucking Christ, I want to watch it leave his body. Suck in the life force slowly draining from him. Instead, I release him with such energy his rolling chair flies back and slams into the wall behind him. I hope the fucker got whiplash. His hands fly to his throat, and he massages the damage I've done.

I don't have to see my face to know rage is written with a blood-red pen all over it. I don't sit. I don't move a fraction of an inch as we stare each other down. I purposely keep that night's events in the back of my mind, not wanting to put any credence into what he's saying. It's lies. Every fucking word.

"You think a man with a rising career who discovered the drug of the century would take his own life? No, that's not how it happened," he croaks.

"And how the fuck would you know that? I think *you're* the one who has something to hide here if you have those kinds of details. Does Willow know you know this?"

Confidence.

It's floating plain as day in his eyes. He really believes this horseshit he's spouting.

What the *fuck* is going on here? And how is he connected to it?

"I'm not hiding anything, but doubt is a fucked-up thing. Once it's planted, it sprouts and roots start winding around every inflection, every unspoken word, every shift of the eye, until it grows and grows and takes on a life of its own, suffocating fragile trust in a new relationship. You've probably already learned Willow's not terribly forthcoming or trusting. Are *you* willing to take that chance, Shaw?"

Leaning on his desk, I get right back in his face. My knuckles turn white with the pressure I'm putting on them in order to keep them locked into the wood instead of laced around his neck.

"You listen good, because I'm only going to say this one time. You don't know what the hell you're talking about, you lying piece of shit. And if you plant these lies in Willow's head, I will fucking end you, you hear me? You'll end up homeless and penniless on the streets. I'll make sure even homeless shelters turn your sorry ass away."

Easing toward the door, I turn back around and say with a steady breath I didn't know I possessed at that moment, "I know you're still in love with her, and honestly, I can understand why. She is...life changing. But she's mine now, and I assure you, I will do anything—any-fucking-thing—to keep her. So, whatever bullshit plans you think you've conjured up to win her back won't work. I don't lose. Ever. And I will never give her up."

"Yes, you will. Just like you've done with every other woman who's passed through your revolving bedroom door. And I'm the one who will be here for her when you throw her away. I'm the one who will pick up the pieces, and I'm the one she'll marry. The one she was always meant to marry."

"You fucking stay away from her," I spit with venomous hatred.

Then I turn my back on him, but as I walk out, those seeds of doubt that he planted have already sprung. They're already trying to find purchase, erode trust, tear relationships and lives apart.

And by the time I walk past the receptionist at the front, who's trying to get my attention, which I ignore, I'm terrified. My heart is beating faster than a racehorse, and I've broken out in a cold sweat all over. When I hold out my hand, it's unsteady, tiny tremors of fear racking my usual calm.

I have finally stumbled across the one thing I thought I never wanted, and although I told Mergen she was mine, she's not. Not really. Not completely. Not now. Maybe now not ever.

Especially if...

Fuck.

Fucking fuckety fuck.

Fuck!

Could my baby sister *really* be responsible for Willow's father's death?

As much as I want to think otherwise, it's not out of the realm of possibility. She was arrested close to that bridge. She was a fucking mess that night. Distraught, haunted, hysterical. Utterly broken.

And I've always wondered why such an intelligent man would take his own life when he had everything to live for, especially after meeting Willow's mother who clearly needed him.

My insides are bleeding. Clawing at me to find the truth.

But what happens then?

What if Annabelle *was* responsible? What would I do?

Is there a statute of limitations on something like that?

She could be charged with fleeing the scene of a crime. Fuck, she could be charged with involuntary manslaughter.

She could go to jail.

I'd lose her. Possibly forever.

Everything I've done in my entire life was to protect my family. If Willow wasn't in the picture right now, I would leave no stone unturned to protect Annabelle from this, too. I'd bury anyone who tried to hurt her.

But I'd also bury anyone who tries to hurt Willow.

I just found her. I don't want to lose her.

I *can't* lose her.

I *won't* fucking lose her.

But then I could lose Annabelle.

Jesus Christ.

Mergen is playing the two women I love most in the world against each other. Suddenly, I'm faced with an impossible, lose-lose situation. Could I really be forced to choose between my sister and the woman there's no question I'm in love with?

No.

No...I'm not going to let that happen.

Reid Mergen is playing a dangerous game. And he's the one who will end up with third-degree burns. He's fucking with the wrong man, and I'm going to put a stop to it right now before it gets out of control. Then I'm going to get his ass fired and shipped out of Seattle on the first bus tomorrow.

First thing's first, though. As I walk down the street to my car, I slide my phone from my pocket and dial, relieved she answered.

"Hey, what's up Shawshank?"

"Bluebelle, where are you?"

"Studying. Why?"

"Do you have time to meet?"

"What? Now? Won't you lose a few mil if you're away from the office during the middle of the day?"

"Annabelle," I growl.

"Jesus, fine. I have an hour."

"I'll be at your place in twenty minutes."

"No, I'm at the campus library."

"Fuck," I mutter. It will take me an extra ten minutes to find parking. "Fine. Stay put."

"Shaw?" she asks just as I'm ready to hang up.

"Yeah?" My voice cracks.

"Everything okay? You sound upset."

"Everything's fine, Bluebelle. See you in a few."

Everything is not fucking fine. But it will be.

It *has* to be.

I have found my breath.

My heartbeat.

The other half of me I didn't know was missing.

Every new good memory will be wrapped up with her, by her. Every laugh delivered because of her. Every peaceful dream will be because she's in my arms, buried in my soul.

Weeks ago, this started out with me just wanting to get into

Willow's bed, but all along I've known it's been more. This was supposed to be temporary. A means to an end. Only now it's so much more. There is no end in sight. When I look just around the corner or all the way down the road, she's there. She's all I see. All I want.

And I won't accept any other outcome than a future with the only woman I've found who has shown me how very lost I've truly been all these years without her.

To be continued in

Found Underneath

coming May, 2017

Other works by K. L. Kreig:

Standalone: Black Swan Affair

"OMG what did I just read? This book... WOW!! It's been years since I read a book straight through. Yes, seven hours I was glued to the pages of this book. A yo-yo of emotions that left me breathless with every scene. *Black Swan Affair* is a must read!!" ~ **Nashoda Rose, NYT and USA Today Bestselling Author**

"I was rapt from the first page, consumed by its every word, and I still cannot stop thinking about it. This rare gem of a story is a top recommendation from me." ~ **Natasha is a Book Junkie**

The Colloway Brothers series:

Forsaking Gray
Undeniably Asher
Luke's Absolution
Destination Connelly

"This series is absolutely amazing. Brilliant. Intense. Passionate. Suspenseful. K. L. Kreig really brought her all when she introduced us to the Colloway brothers." ~ ***Renee Entress's Blog***

"The Colloway brothers are some of the most swoon-worthy, panty-soaking, endearingly flawed men in contemporary romance today. They are full of grit, intelligence, and sex appeal that will leave you breathless and begging for more." ~ ***Rachel Caid, Author of the Finding Home series***

The Regent Vampire Lords series:

Surrendering
Belonging
Reawakening
Evading

"If you like J. R. Ward, Sherrilyn Kenyon, or Kresley Cole, you'll love K. L. Kreig. This series just got even better! Books like these are the reason we, the reviewer, should be able to give six stars!" ~ ***L. A. Wild, Author, Chance The Darkness***

"This author has done it again. I was captivated and transported into the story right from the first chapter. A truly fantastic vampire book with romance, suspense, twists and turns, keeping you on the edge of your seat all the way through." ~ ***Hooked on Books Forever Bookblog***

My musical inspiration for writing Lost In Between:

"Let Me Be Myself" by 3 Doors Down
"Wide Awake" by Katy Perry
"Fallen Angel" by Three Days Grace
"Talking Body" by Tove Lo
"Nearly Forgot My Broken Heart" by Chris Cornell
"Hymn for The Missing" by Red
"Crash Into Me" by Dave Matthews Band
"Wildest Dreams" by Taylor Swift
"If Only For Now" by Pop Evil
"Ex's & Oh's" by Elle King
"Jenny" by Nothing More
"So Far Lost" by Thousand Foot Crutch
"I'll Follow You" by Shinedown
"If You Only Knew" by Shinedown
"Everybody Hurts" by REM

Babbles...

To caveat, I wrote this last minute and it's unedited, so forgive my misuse of commas or missing words.

Unless you've written a book before you can't possibly understand that many times the characters drive you versus you driving the characters. It sounds ridiculous but it's true. You start out with grand plans, a whole plot and flow, conversations in mind and a solid, plausible ending. But then they take you over entirely and hijack your story, the bastards. And no matter how hard you try, you cannot get them back on the rails. They've gone rogue and you have no choice but to follow if you want to finish your damn book.

I had a vision for the way *Lost In Between* was going to go and, well, this wasn't it! My characters started fighting me. For real! Events happened even *I* never saw coming.

That being said, I am incredibly happy with how this story will end in *Found Underneath,* and I think you will be, too. Once I accepted where the characters took me, I was completely onboard and understood it could be no other way. I am in love with Shaw and Willow, but Noah and Sierra are something special. I never expected to love them as much as I did, but I often do that. Fall in love with my side characters, too.

Look for the shocking conclusion of Shaw and Willow's story in Found Underneath, due out in May 2017 (I feel like Chris Harrison from the Bachelor saying that). Make sure you're signed up for my newsletter for specific release date announcements, crazy fun and monthly giveaways. https://goo.gl/MxHvHg

As always, thanks to **Nikki Busch**, my editor, for smoothing my manuscript and making me look good. Special thanks to my friend and collaborator, **LL (Lauren) Collins** for reading this last minute when I was in a panic and providing me your honest feedback. I absolutely adore you and know we were meant to meet and be besties for life. **Heather Roberts**: girl I wouldn't be where I am without you. #truth. You talk me into crazy new things and off the ledge when I'm ready to jump. You are my Master of Quan, lady. Last but never least, thanks always to my **husband** who loves everything I do. *Everything*. You're my biggest fan and I love that about you.

A big shout out to Trisha Wolfe, who let me use part of *With Visions of Red* in the book. If you're wondering what the other two excerpts are, they're mine. Chapter 1 starts out with the Prologue from *Black Swan Affair* and Chapter 17 referenced *Forsaking Gray*, book 1 in my Colloway Brothers series. Both of these are available now! And let me tell you, Trisha's *With Visions of Red* is incredible and it's FREE! Don't miss out on that here!

Friends, family, bloggers, authors, betas, pimpers, Kreig's babes, and most importantly MY READERS: if you supported me in any way, shape, or form, you know who you are and you know I thank you from the bottom of my heart. I am nothing but sincerely, eternally grateful for your belief in me. Every message and each e-mail I get from someone who wanted to personally reach out to me and praise me for how my work touched them in some way is *truly* a surreal feeling and *that's* why I do this. Because you all encourage me. For that, I thank you.

For the love of God...help an author out! LEAVE A REVIEW wherever you purchased this book. Even one or two sentences or simply rating the book is helpful for other readers. Reviews are critical to getting a book exposure in this vast sea of great reads.